Dear Reader:

I was looking for a book to sweep me off my feet. For something sexy, funny, dark, nerdy, and mysterious. Maybe a bit old-fashioned. A little strange. As I drove home from the bookstore, I kept sneaking glances at the moody thriller and the period romance sitting shotgun. And I kept wishing that the two novels were *one* book.

Rain dripped through the cracks in my A-frame bedroom as I curled up to read. I dozed off beside the Patricia Highsmith mystery and the Jane Austen novel, dreaming about the storms at my grandparents' house in Eastport, Maine. The salty, mossy scent of a place frozen in time. In my dream I started composing a story—the novel I hadn't been able to find at the bookstore. Then I woke up and struggled to get it all down.

Set in my grandparents' dilapidated Cape Cod–style house in the '60s, this story follows Billie through the woods and windswept islands of my childhood. *Etiquette for Lovers and Killers* is a novel like a tall, dark, nerdy stranger. A partner in crime for all the girls who couldn't decide between the pulpy thriller or the rom-com in the bookstore. Because honestly, why can't we have both?

Anna

# ETIQUETTE
## FOR
# LOVERS
## AND
# KILLERS

ANNA FITZGERALD HEALY

FLEET

FLEET

First published in the United States in 2025 by Putnam,
an imprint of Penguin Random House LLC
First published in Great Britain in 2025 by Fleet

1 3 5 7 9 10 8 6 4 2

Copyright © by Anna Fitzgerald Healy

The moral right of the author has been asserted.

*All characters and events in this publication, other than those
clearly in the public domain, are fictitious and any resemblance
to real persons, living or dead, is purely coincidental.*

All rights reserved.
Penguin Random House values and supports copyright. Copyright fuels creativity, encourages diverse voices, promotes free speech, and creates a vibrant culture. Thank you for buying an authorized edition of this book and for complying with copyright laws by not reproducing, scanning, or distributing any part of it in any form without permission. You are supporting writers and allowing Penguin Random House to continue to publish books for every reader. Please note that no part of this book may be used or reproduced in any manner for the purpose of training artificial intelligence technologies or systems.

Map by Anna Fitzgerald Healy

Excerpt(s) from AMY VANDERBILT'S COMPLETE BOOK OF ETIQUETTE:
A GUIDE TO GRACIOUS LIVING by Amy Vanderbilt, copyright © 1952, 1954 by Amy Vanderbilt, copyright renewed 1980, 1982 by Curtis B. Kellar & Lincoln G. Clark. Used by permission of Doubleday, an imprint of the Knopf Doubleday Publishing Group, a division of Penguin Random House LLC. All rights reserved.

A CIP catalogue record for this book
is available from the British Library.

Hardback ISBN 978-0-349-12734-7
Trade paperback ISBN 978-0-349-12735-4

Printed and bound in Great Britain by Clays Ltd, Elcograf S.p.A

Papers used by Fleet are from well-managed forests
and other responsible sources.

Fleet
An imprint of
Little, Brown Book Group
Carmelite House
50 Victoria Embankment
London EC4Y 0DZ

The authorised representative
in the EEA is
Hachette Ireland
8 Castlecourt Centre
Dublin 15, D15 XTP3, Ireland
(email: info@hbgi.ie)

An Hachette UK Company
www.hachette.co.uk

www.littlebrown.co.uk

To my friends, conspirators, and
perennial bad influences

*Now nothing remains for me but to assure you in the most animated language of the violence of my affection.*

–Jane Austen, *Pride and Prejudice*

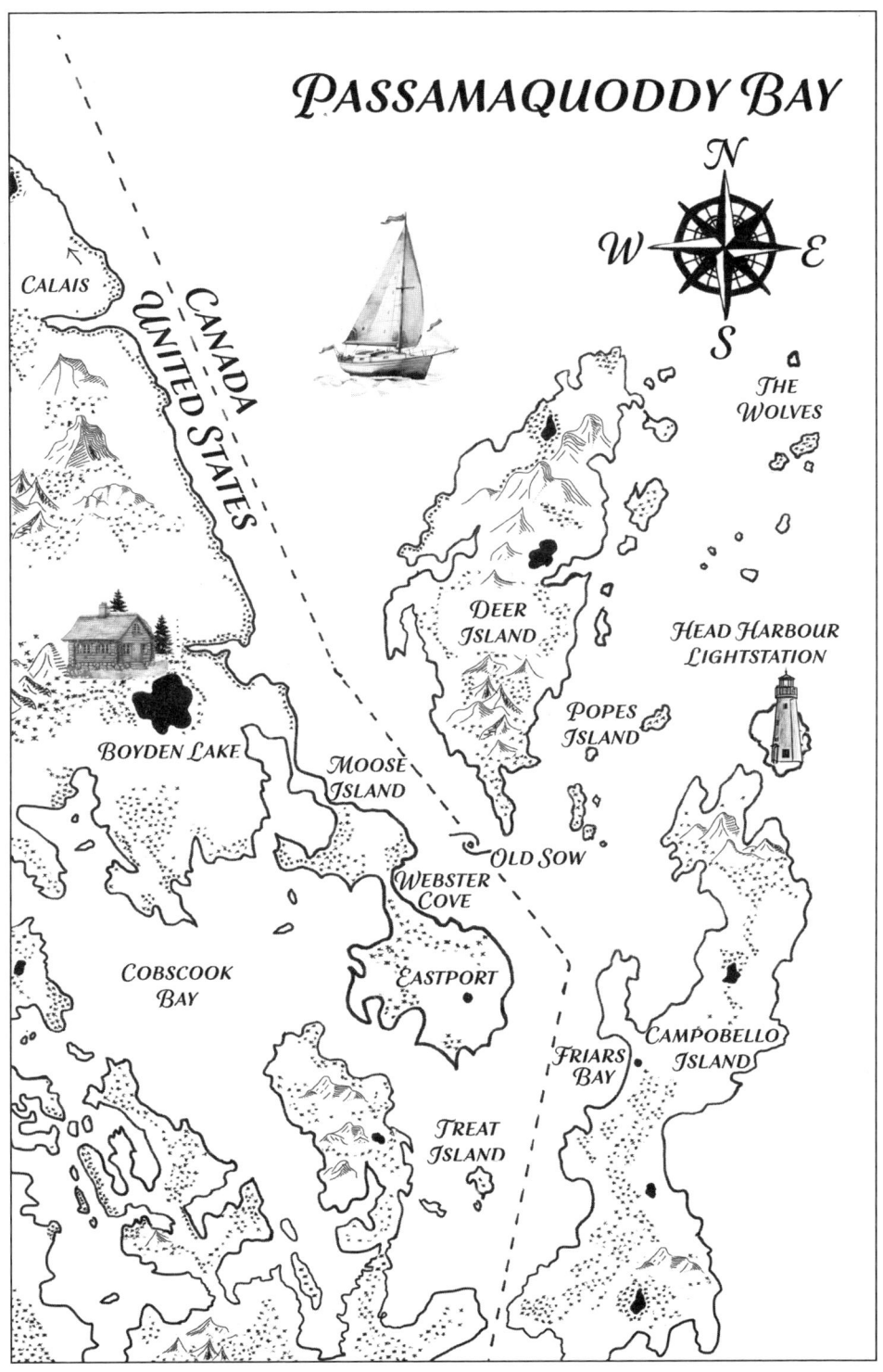

# ETIQUETTE
## FOR
# LOVERS
## AND
# KILLERS

## PROLOGUE

# PRIVATE PURSUITS

*Whispering is rude. Whispering and giggling at the same time have no place in polite society.*

The fire has burned down to a single flame, flitting across a bed of ash. Shadows dance over the ceiling. They twine around each other and then dart away, like lovers with commitment issues. "Will you tell me something?" he asks. His voice is deep and conspiratorial as he traces the lines of her ribs with his fingertip. Her long red hair pools across the pillow.

"Anything," she whispers. "But I can't promise to tell the truth."

"Gertrude, just put me out of my misery. Tell me who else you're sleeping with."

"Everyone." She giggles. Her laughter seeps into the velvet drapes and the brocade cushions, dampened by the room's oppressive elegance. That's the thing about old money—it hides things. It takes each ugly truth, salacious lie, brutal kiss, and tepid embrace, then swallows them whole. "Now my turn. A guilty secret, please. What's the worst thing you've ever done, or ever *wanted* to do?" she asks as she studies the naked jealousy on her companion's face.

"Kill you," he says, then grabs her wrists and presses them back against the headboard.

"I love it when you talk dirty to me. But why?"

"Because it sounds like fun," he replies, running his lips across her neck.

"Darling, I don't think you know what that word means." Her laughter rings out again—and this time, not even the woven tapestries, the high ceilings, or the crown molding can stifle it.

## CHAPTER ONE

# INTRODUCTIONS

*When a man is introduced to a lady, he does not offer his hand unless she makes the move first. A casual, "How do you do?" is sufficient. A spontaneous, "It's so nice to meet you," is fine–but never obligatory.*

I make a left onto Sea Street, walking past the library, the drugstore, and my grandfather's dilapidated boat repair shop. The dry cleaner waves to me as she walks door-to-door with a basket of freshly pressed linens, each tablecloth with the owner's initials embroidered in the corner. She opens the door to Muriel Grant's house and leaves her laundry in the front hallway. We don't lock doors here.

We don't have crime in Eastport, Maine. Well, not really.

And we don't have secrets, either. At least, none that we can keep.

The milk truck from Long Lost Farms rolls up beside me,

Leo Mills chewing a piece of straw at the helm. I see him note the stop sign, grin, and then barrel forward unchecked.

Oh, and traffic laws here are less of a rule and more of a casual suggestion.

I continue down Water Street, past the row of crumbling redbrick buildings and the bronze mermaid sculpture with her corroded seashell brassiere. Eastport is the most easterly town in the United States, one last outpost of New England kitsch, gazing longingly across the water at Canada. In the 1700s it was the Wild East, a frontier town of traders and explorers. In the 1800s it was the smuggling epicenter of New England. In 1900 it was a commercial hub for canned fish, and in 1964 it is (essentially) purgatory. The sardine factories have all closed and our dwindling human population is outnumbered by seagulls ten to one.

The bell chimes as I breeze into Primp and Ribbon Alterations. Mrs. Pridmore watches from behind the cash register, the ruffles on her blouse fluttering in silent indignation. In a shocking turn of events, I'm five minutes late.

"I'm so sorry," I wince, but it's hardly an award-winning performance. Then I hang up my purse and set to work. I watch the hours tangle up together from my perch behind the pink Singer Featherweight. Nine thirty is the faded indigo of Ben Jordan's torn overalls. Ten o'clock is the pearly white of Lydia Peyton's First Communion dress. Ten thirty is the unfortunate green lace on Annie Porter's sweet sixteen dress. (I don't have the heart to tell her that it makes her look like an overstuffed peacock.) And at eleven Florence Pelletier swings by to make my life a living hell. This is the third fitting for her black cocktail dress this week. As she swishes sixteen layers of crinoline in my face, I imagine how I would murder her.

"Should the skirt be bigger?" She purses her lips as she sways her hips from side to side, analyzing the orbit and trajectory of her petticoats. Eastport is a decade behind the fashion world, so the slim lines and dropped waists of the 1960s haven't hit us yet; our silhouettes are still trapped in 1950. "I want to make a splash this weekend at Webster Cottage."

"The summer people are having a party?" I ask as I pin up her hem, my voice unnaturally bright as my lips twist into a poor imitation of a smile. "Florence, you'll knock them dead."

Mrs. Pridmore evaluates my acting skills from behind the cash register. As Florence struts outside, Mrs. Pridmore turns to me. "Couldn't you just pretend to care?"

"I'm trying," I reply honestly. Nothing is harder for me than small talk.

"Try harder. Service with a smile, Billie!" she says with an eerie, vacant grin.

At noon Mrs. Pridmore retreats to the stockroom for her daily sandwich / soap opera ritual, and I make my rounds. My first stop is the library. I look both ways as I slip a mangled copy of *A Spy in the House of Love* through the book drop, then retreat before anyone can charge me for it. My second stop is Fernald's Pharmacy, where I beeline for the hair aisle.

"Has it already been six weeks?" Bobby Fernald asks as he rings me up for the box of Blushing Violet hair dye that my grandmother requests like clockwork.

"Already?" I laugh, because it feels like an eternity.

Next up is the post office. My saddle shoes squeak across the linoleum floor as I open up my PO box to find two envelopes lurking inside.

As a little girl, I dreamed about working in a museum. I fantasized about long marble hallways filled with dusty rays of light, and flirting with archaeologists while they assembled dinosaur skeletons. I imagined sweater-vests falling to the floor while stone tablets were pushed aside in the antiquities archives, and heavy petting in the decorative arts gallery. With these scholarly pursuits in mind, I enrolled in a course on cultural linguistics. I planned to land a position translating archaic texts, marry the dreamy archaeologist, and live out my days in nerdy splendor. But it turns out that dead languages aren't exactly a hot commodity. And now they're just killing me, as I'm slowly but surely rejected by every museum in the country.

I frown at the first envelope, from the Triton Classics Archives, addressed to *Miss Wilhelmina McCadie*. Anything bearing my legal name is trouble, because whoever sent it knows nothing about me. I skim through a passive-aggressive rejection letter, crumple it up, and toss it in the trash. Then I direct my glare at the second envelope.

It's thin. Rejection-letter thin. And it doesn't even have my name on the front, just my PO box number. The two stamps on the front are unusual but don't spare the envelope from my ire. There is no reason to open it if I already know what's inside. My hand hovers over the bin.

"Billie!" Mr. Townsend pokes his head out of the mail room as I hastily stash the letter in my purse. I'd hate to offend the postman by throwing out unopened mail in front of him (is that a federal offense?). "A guava for you." He beams, his white hair glinting in the fluorescent lights. Mr. Townsend regularly gifts me exotic produce. I think it's because he sees how sad I am whenever I check my mail, so this guava is a sticky consolation prize. I thank him, then continue on my way.

The flower market is bursting with peonies, and Mingo's Bakery is overflowing with students coated in cookie crumbs. I hurry past the row of cannons from the War of 1812 then squeeze past Leo Mills as he clutches a milk crate against his starched white chest. An army of housewives watches my progression from the big bay windows in the Salon by the Sea as they sharpen their talons and coif their beehives, in preparation for their nightly battle with a pot roast. The briny sea air sweeps in around me as I approach the pier, but I hardly notice because to me, it just smells like home. A desultory catcall comes from the navy ship that has pulled in to refuel as I climb down to the breakwater and totter across the large granite boulders.

I eat my guava, gazing out at Passamaquoddy Bay. Lobster boats haul up traps and seals bask in the shallows as I dangle my feet off the edge of a sun-warmed rock. The fruit is tangy on my lips and sticky on my fingers. I wipe my hands on my skirt, then reach into my purse.

The envelope is eggshell white, made of fine cotton paper. No return address, just my PO box number scrawled neatly across the front. On the back is a wax seal that crinkles as I break it.

*My dearest Gertrude,*

*What is it about human nature that compels us to destroy perfection? Perfect: your lips. Perfect: your delicate hands. Perfect: your red hair gleaming in the sun. All my life, I've* dreamed of meeting someone just like you—elegant to a fault, steadfast in demeanor, and foxy as all hell.

Our weekend in Bermuda is the closest I'll ever come to heaven. Do you remember when the power went out and you lit our suite with candles? The lines of your body in the flickering lights will be engraved in my memory for as long as I live. We walked down to the beach and made love in the sea. The water glowed in the moonlight, but it paled in comparison to you.

By this point, you probably know that I had you followed. I must apologize—hiring a private eye was rather childish of me. When he called to tell me that you were meeting with your ex, I became incensed. I thought the world had shattered around me. Then I drowned my sorrows in gin and ruined everything. You saw the lipstick on my lapel. You know that I strayed.

What despair to learn that you were only meeting him to return his ring! I've lost the only ~~thing~~ person in my life who matters. Darling, my world is empty without you. I would do anything to make it right. If you could find it in your heart to forgive me, you would make me the happiest man alive. But if you can't, I'm not sure if the world is big enough for both of us. I might do something wretched.

Passionately yours,
Edgar

My jaw drops as I study the precise cursive handwriting. What is the word for confused delight? Is there such a word?

Because I've never felt more enthralled or bewildered than I do at this moment. Who is Gertrude? And who is Edgar? And *how* did this wind up in my PO box? Thank God I didn't throw it out!

Waves sweep in against the breakwater as questions swirl around me. And, it's an odd response, but tears prickle at the corners of my eyelids. Because part of me has always hoped that something strange like this would happen. This letter is steamy, tasteless, and I'm hooked. The couple is straight out of the novels I devour every night. As I slide the pages back inside the envelope, something small falls into my lap. I peer down at it. Nestled in the folds of my pleated skirt is a rose-gold engagement ring. The princess-cut diamond sends prisms of light across my sweater set. I squint. Could this be a boredom-induced hallucination?

"Well, hello there," calls a pleasant voice.

My smile falters as I take in the young man perched on a boulder a few feet away. "Oh no," I murmur as I stash the letter and ring in my purse. He's one of the summer people, who I try to avoid at all costs. They're awful snobs with more money than manners, who sweep in with the June lilacs, then wilt away in the August heat. Golden figures I sometimes glimpse on the periphery—speeding down the road in a flashy car, dashing into the supermarket to buy a watermelon and a bottle of vermouth, or at the helm of a sailboat, causing traffic jams in the harbor.

"Can I help you?" I ask curtly, hoping he'll go away.

He is Brooks Brothers handsome with ironic arched eyebrows and a lazy smile. His sandy hair is flecked with the barest hint of silver that glints in the sun. It's lightly tousled, which gives an impression of carelessness to his otherwise faultless appearance. A small mole beneath his left eye hints at an artistic temperament. He's tall-ish (although, to be fair, everyone is tall compared to me) with high, almost architectural cheekbones. His mottled gray eyes regard me with amusement.

"Why haven't we ever spoken before?" he asks with an accent like trust funds and rowing teams. And it's true, we've locked eyes on multiple occasions, but neither of us bothered to bridge the gap of social hierarchy to speak. That's not a skill they teach in row club.

"Because life is too short to talk to attractive strangers?" I reply with a shrug. "What if you turned out to be an awful bore? It's much better to live with the fantasy of what might have been."

"So I'm already boring you? That escalated quickly."

"You were wittier in my imagination," I offer briskly, surprised by how easily the words slip off my tongue. By how *not* stuttering and *not* shy they are. Some of the boldness from that letter must be rubbing off on me.

"My apologies, Miss . . ." The intruder looks at me expectantly.

"Wilhelmina. I mean, Billie," I correct myself. I start to offer my hand, but then realize it's still sticky with fruit juice.

"And I'm Avery," he replies with a wry grin. He doesn't add his last name, because he doesn't have to. The gleaming copper *W* on the gate to Webster Cottage might as well be printed across his tan slacks, or engraved on the face of his brown leather watch.

"Oh no." My eyes widen as they take in his watch. "What time is it?"

"Five past," he replies with a slight smirk, as if he knows what's coming next.

"Perfect. I'm late for work."

"How scandalous of you." His eyes glint with amusement. "What if I walk you back?"

"Oh, please don't. I would absolutely abhor it," I parry, then pause to see if I've offended him. Sarcasm isn't Eastport's native language, so it's best to tread lightly.

But he just plays along. "I'm glad that I've made an ideal first impression."

As we climb back to the pier, I consider my own first impressions. They say to watch out for the quiet ones, with good reason. Because my shyness hides a sense of humor a little too caustic for my cheery hometown. So I keep my mouth shut and my cynicism to myself. But I've spent years dreaming about meeting other people who have nothing nice to say, either.

We receive nods, smiles, and several raised eyebrows as we walk back to town. But everyone is looking at Avery, not at me. I'm old news, while Avery is a walking gossip column, shrouded in the glitz and high utility bills of the upper class. Leo Mills strolls past as we turn onto Water Street. His empty milk crate dangles from his left hand as he tips his starched white cap to us. Marsha Crimp pauses outside the bank, pushing down her sunglasses to lock eyes with me, then mouthing, *Jealous*.

"Where do you work?" Avery pretends not to notice her.

"Hell. I mean, the dress shop," I murmur as Primp and Ribbon Alterations rears its frilly head in the distance. As we approach the dreaded pink awning, I drag my feet. A part of me hopes that we never reach the end of the block.

The smell of wet paint drifts out of the hardware store as Avery pauses on the sidewalk. "So on a scale of one to watching-paint-dry, how dull would you rate our conversation?" he asks.

I regard him with wide eyes. "Am I *not* watching paint dry?"

"What a pity. Perhaps you could tutor me in some of the finer points of conversation?"

"I doubt you could afford me. I went to school for linguistics, so I'm terribly overpriced," I say, then motion to the shop, as Mrs. Pridmore taps her watch through the window. "This is me."

"Well, today has been an unexpected pleasure, Billie. Perhaps I'll bore you again sometime," Avery replies. He nods, then walks away, leaving me to slip into the cool recesses of the dress shop. I sit down behind my Singer Featherweight with such a curious, fluttery feeling in my chest. My palms are dewy, but it must just be from the summer heat. As I begin sewing, my heart skips a beat, but I'm sure it's just vibrations from the sewing machine.

At 6 p.m., I switch off my sewing machine and tie off my seams. I weave through the tide of activity, skirting a throng of housewives congregating by the butcher's shop, a crowd of fishermen drinking outside the Thirsty Whale, and a group of slow-moving tourists. It's June, and the vacation season has just started with all its buttery, lobster-obsessed aplomb.

I swing by Swann's Market, where Iris Swann raises one overplucked eyebrow as she rings me up for a bottle of Blue Nun wine. I open my mouth, perhaps to explain my wine consumption or to lie and say that it's for my grandmother, then close it again. As Iris checks me out, I try to imagine what she must see. A pale girl, maybe a little too skinny, with mousy hair and a naive yellow cardigan. A button nose, underwhelming cheekbones, and lips that have never been properly kissed. I bite those lips as I shrug off my feelings of inadequacy.

But there's one thing about me that Iris Swann doesn't see, and that's the letter in my purse. So I hold my head high, ask her to add the wine to our charge account, and walk out with the barest hint of a strut. For the first time in my life, I have a secret.

---

The sunset is the color of the apple blossoms drifting down Key Street, carpeting the redbrick sidewalk and lining the steps to my grandparents' house. The rhododendrons rustle as I hurry through the side door, into a kitchen like a giant can of Campbell's chicken noodle soup. It's wholesome, nostalgic, and the same murky yellow.

A baseball game plays on the black-and-white television, and the smell of mayonnaise and fish pervades the room. "There's a tuna casserole on the hot plate for you," my grandfather informs me, but I'm already pattering upstairs. The house sighs and groans around me, a dusty family heirloom a century past its prime. *Home*[a] is a funny word, don't you think? It's

---

[a] **Home (n.): 1.** *one's place of residence.* **2.** *the social unit formed by a family.* Derived from the Old English *ham* and the proto-Germanic *haimaz*, *home* can be traced back to the proto-Indo-European root *tkei*, "to settle, relax, to dwell." (Proto-Indo-European [PIE] is a language spoken some 6,000 years ago. Its úse straddled Europe and Asia, drawing upon common roots in Latin,

meant to describe a space that you own, but so often, it is the place that owns you.

"Billie, come in here," calls my grandmother.

"After my studies," I reply. I don't have any studies. It's early June, and I graduated from college four years ago, but Grace doesn't argue. She might not know what year it is.

I shut the door to my bedroom and turn on my record player. The Beatles keep time with my thoughts, churning and skipping. I frown at the peeling floral wallpaper, bleached to a dull beige. It's the same color as my rumpled linen sheets, whitewashed bookcase, and the paperbacks inside it that have all faded in the sun. Just about the only things in my room that aren't inoffensive and off-white are the words inside of them. Words bursting with color and passion. Words that add a dash of intrigue to my pink rotary phone. A blush of lust to the crocheted doily underneath it. A stain of espionage to my ivory Smith Corona typewriter.

The heroines in these books are my friends, conspirators, and perennial bad influences—offering invaluable lessons in romance and bad behavior. I wanted to be just like them when I grew up. But as the years pass, my social calendar remains empty and my skin untouched—and I'm starting to realize that some dreams *don't* come true. That I'm not going to just wake up some morning as an ingenue in a Brontë romance, because Eastport is about as far from *Wuthering Heights* as you can get.

But tonight everything is different.

---

Sanskrit, and Persian. I studied PIE in school. It's my own personal love language.)

"Hold Me Tight" spins on my record player as I reach for the corkscrew in my sock drawer. The soothing *glug* of cheap wine into the hobnail glass from my night carafe. The acoustic guitar trills as I sip wine and study the letter. I trace Edgar's signature in my diary, then slip on Gertrude's ring. *It fits!*

I lie back in bed and lift my hand up to the light. The diamond is gaudy and rose gold is dated, but ... it kind of suits me. It's just as silly and indulgent as the novels in my bookcase. Another sip as I make doe eyes at the ring, watching how it catches the light as "I Want to Hold Your Hand" croons through the speakers.

Rain seeps down the windowpane to drip across the rotten floorboard. I wake up to a light drizzle and a wet pillow, shaking off yet another dream about my parents. Charles and Laura McCadie died in a car accident two years ago, and I've been having Dalí-esque nightmares about them ever since. Blurry images of loss that linger with me long after I've brushed my teeth, washed my face, and chided my subconscious for not having better taste.

I open the window and blink away the dreamscape. These tacky nightmares are a problem. They're probably why I still live with my grandparents and certainly why I can't get a real job. Because my parents' death halted my development in some essential way, and now I'm stuck. Unwilling to move forward but unable to step back. I breathe in the musky spring rain as I try to calm myself, then cough on the slightly less ethereal scent of bacon.

I poke my head into Grace's bedroom, where Lucille Ball and Desi Arnaz are sparring on the television screen. Ball is dressed as a fruit basket, Arnaz is wearing a suit, and my grandmother appears to be disguised as a rosebush, draped in a floral dressing gown on a peony bedspread. Her skin is as pale as tissue paper, and her hair is done. Strangely, it's always done, although she never leaves the house. In her heyday, Grace McCadie was the "celebutante" of Eastport, Maine: a small-town beauty so revered that she flirted with celebrity. But as her skin began to wrinkle and her hair to gray, she started devoting more and more time to "putting on her face." When my father died, Grace retired to her bedroom and never left. She primps and paints, hiding her sadness for her son under layers of Peaches N' Cream face powder. "Did you get my—"

"Special delivery." I toss the Blushing Violet hair dye on her bed, then follow the greasy aroma into the kitchen. Victor is seated in a vinyl captain's chair. His hair is as white as Cream of Wheat, and an absent smile rests perpetually on his lips. A handheld CB radio chirps blithely beside him, scanning the channels for police traffic. My grandfather isn't a cop, he just loves to pry.

"How was work yesterday?" he asks. "Todd Kinney said he saw you talkin' with—"

"Far out." I steal a piece of bacon, then leave before he can give me the third degree.

My bag is heavy with books and a beach towel, and I'm wearing a swimsuit under my dress. I have today off work, and I'd like to spend it pretending that I *don't* live in a Betty Crocker commercial. So I stash my things in my wicker bike basket and make my escape. Tall stems of seagrass rustle across the sand dunes as the drizzle begins to clear off. I bike past the train station, the mustard mill, and the boatyard. I slow down to gawk at Webster Cottage, where a traffic jam is underway. The florist and dry cleaner exchange heated words from their trucks, while gardeners trim hedges as though their lives depend on it.

*The New York Times* recently profiled Eastport as "an island playground off the coast of Maine." In the summertime, this "gem in the never-crowded little world of Passamaquoddy Bay" plays host to tourists in motorhomes and the international elite. Down East Maine represents one of the broadest wealth disparities in the nation, with fishermen squatting in trailers and Vanderbilts languishing in mansions. On Moose Island, we have the Websters (the owners of a shipping empire, although I've always liked to imagine them as dictionary tycoons). On nearby Campobello, the Ashcrofts' compound gleams in the bashful sunlight, then on the opposite side of the island is the Roosevelts' country estate. Farther down the coast, the Rockefellers, Pulitzers, and Fords all have summer homes in Bar Harbor, where Evalyn McLean notoriously walked her poodle down Main Street with the Hope Diamond dangling from its collar. Maine is a veritable who's who of American dynasties, with people whose names are followed by Roman numerals, who have probably never operated a broom and dustpan before. The haves and the have-yachts.

Webster Cottage has better ratings than the top radio drama, and we all tune in, year after year. Watching with bated breath as the baker loads up his van with layer cakes for their garden parties, and knitting our brows in consternation at articles like: "Shut Down: Websters Say 'No' to White Shutters," in the local paper (the *Quoddy Current* brings the phrase "investigative reporting" to new lows). After years of spying on them, actually *meeting* one of the Websters yesterday was like running into James Dean. But a sort of sad, unassuming James Dean—a gentleman without a cause.

As I cruise over the bridge to the mainland, the clouds burn off. The sun makes its blushing debut as I turn down the road to Boyden Lake. The lake is surrounded by log cabins—in Maine we call them "camps." My parents had one when I was growing up. Now they're gone, but I continue to come here in their memory. And trespass.

I pass several occupied cabins before I find a likely suspect, with a rowboat collecting dead leaves in the driveway and a tangle of weeds in the yard. Juniper berries burst beneath my feet and Queen Anne's lace brushes against my shins as I sneak across the lawn to sunbathe on the dock.

I spread my striped towel across the sun-bleached planks and lay out as dapples of light filter through the white spruce tree overhead. *Komorebi* is the Japanese word for that. The silence is punctuated by the drumbeat of a woodpecker and the aria of a chickadee. As I leaf through my battered copy of *Northanger Abbey*, I look up some Regency-era slang in my etymology book. Words like *tittupy*, "bouncing all around," and *coxcomb*, "a dandy who is in love with himself." I envy the main character, with her endless whirlwind of parties, beaus, and emotional roller coasters. Then I set down the gothic romance and double my jealousy.

*My dearest Gertrude,*

I blink at the love letter. I wish that someone would do that to *me*. Memorize the lines of *my* body in the steam. Make love to *me* in the glittering water. But that would require actually going out and meeting someone, which sounds like an awful lot of effort.

*Darling, my world is empty without you.*

Who is Gertrude? Clearly someone adept at flirting. Someone who drives men so wild with desire that they lose their ability to properly operate a stamp and an address. I imagine her little black book of lovers and indiscretions, then walk over to the cool dark water and dive in.

---

Friday is one of the longest days of the year, made even more interminable by an endless stack of alterations. Mrs. Pridmore plays a single Nat King Cole record on repeat in a jazzy kind of torture. Florence swings by to pick up her new frock. She has an air of Cinderella post–fairy godmother, with a breathless smile and blond hair rolled up in curlers, and meanwhile, I've gone full scullery maid. Safety pins are stuck in my hem, a seamstress tape is looped around my neck, and my hair is tossed up in a bird's nest.

"Bunny, I heard that you threw yourself at one of the Websters," she purrs as she sits down on my desk, smooshing the pleated skirt I'm taking in. "Watch yourself. Those boys are the big leagues, and you failed out of Little League."

"Florence, I don't think that Little League *is* something you can fail out of–"

"Shush." She holds up one pale pink finger as "Those Lazy,

Hazy, Crazy Days of Summer" builds to a crescendo. "I *know* what I'm talking about." Then she turns and squeaks out of the shop in her Keds, a garment bag swishing from her shoulder.

Mrs. Pridmore leaves to run errands, and I turn off the record player. *Northanger Abbey* joins me in my silent revolt. When the front door jingles open, I look up from my book to discover Avery standing in the entrance.

"Got you." He grins.

"Can I interest you in a cocktail dress?" I ask.

"I'm not interested in dresses, but I *am* interested in cocktails. I was rather hoping to offer you one this evening." Avery strides across the hardwood floor to place a card beside my pincushion. The invitation is pearly white, embossed with lobsters and champagne flutes. The background holds a faint watermark with the Webster family crest.

> You are cordially invited to
> A SUMMER SOLSTICE PARTY
> at Webster Cottage
> on June 19th, 1964.
> Join us for surf and turf,
> where the land meets the sea.

"What a pity, I'm supposed to have drinks at a *different* mansion this evening."

"Whose mansion?" Avery demands. "Tell me their address. I'll burn it down."

"Please don't," I reply, eyes wide. "Arson is a very serious crime."

But he just smiles. "Until tonight." He nods, then strides away.

## ETIQUETTE FOR LOVERS AND KILLERS

*Should I go?* I walk over to the clothing rack to browse through our array of last-decade cocktail gowns. I've always dreamed about attending an exclusive affair. My *grande soirée* fantasy is a personal favorite, involving a poofy ball gown, minuscule hors d'oeuvres, and a steamy make-out session with a prince in the powder room.

When I was little, my mother served me etiquette[b] lessons with dinner each night, giving me unrealistic expectations of cummerbunds and twelve-piece place settings. "Politeness opens doors, Billie. And I want your world wide open." But so far, knowing the difference between a fruit fork and an oyster fork hasn't opened *quite* as many doors as I'd hoped. My mother would tell me to buy the shimmery blue dress I can't afford. And to go to the party. And to charm the pants off everyone.

But I'm not her and I never will be. And imagining a swanky party and attending one are entirely different activities. I'm a faux pas waiting to happen. I should spend the evening curled up with my *Merriam-Webster Dictionary*, not making small talk at Avery Webster's estate. Impressive as I'm sure the Websters' guest list is, I doubt there's any royalty on it. And what's the point of attending a soirée if there aren't any princes to flirt with in the bathroom?

---

[b] **Etiquette (n.):** According to Amy Vanderbilt, "This rather daunting word describes a system of rules that regulate social behavior. The word literally means 'ticket' or 'card,' and refers to the ancient custom of a monarch setting ceremonial rules and regulations to be observed by members of his court. This antiquated term stems from the Old French *estiquette*, 'a little note.'" So you could say that etiquette is a love letter to civilized behavior.

## CHAPTER TWO

# THE SEMIFORMAL GARDEN PARTY

*The requisites are as follows, though the necessity for perfection increases in proportion to the formality of the occasion: guests who are congenial; a perfectly prepared menu; faultlessly laundered linen; brilliantly polished silver; expert dining-room servants; a cordial host; a hostess of tact, sympathy, poise; and perfect manners.*

There is an expectant stillness tonight in Passamaquoddy Bay. A hush among the crickets and sandpipers, as if they're audience members waiting for the curtains to open. The trill of a clarinet and the croon of a trumpet. The percussion of laughter and tinkling crystal. My heart is racing. The show is about to start.

Dusk creeps in as I park Victor's Buick opposite the gates to Webster Cottage. I shut the door, then smooth my hair for the umpteenth time. My shyness fought against my curiosity all afternoon, but curiosity finally won. So I bought a dress, curled my hair, and stole my grandfather's car. I've promised myself that I'll only stay for an hour. I'll drink some champagne, gawk at the house, and leave before I break anything irreplaceable.

My white kitten heels sound anxious—skittering across the road, tapping down the cobblestones, faltering before a topiary dog, and slowing to a halt as the redbrick mansion comes into view. Webster Cottage[a] is a "hut" in the Georgian Revival style, with gold-leaf gables and a carved slate roof. According to local gossip, the château has fourteen bedrooms, a glass solarium, a library for books, a library for maps, and a Swarovski-crystal chandelier. A Garage Mahal houses their inventory of roadsters, a gazebo graces the front yard, and an *allée* of Italian cypress sways at the far end of the property. The *allée* was imported at great expense by Avery's grandfather and is Victor's favorite detail about Webster Cottage. "Ayuh, Billie. It's classy 'cause it's French," my grandfather has told me, unprompted, on one too many occasions.

A navy blue carpet leads between two fluted marble columns to an oversize door with flowery scrollwork. Two men in boat shoes and beige linen stand guard, one on either side, watching with bland superiority. My foot hovers over the front step, half expecting alarm bells to sound and the door to slam shut.

Sure, I went to a good school, but no one cares about that. I'm "accomplished," but accomplishments went out of style decades ago. We live in the same town, but proximity has no bearing when you live worlds apart.

---

[a] **Cottage (n.):** *a simple house often located nearby a lake or beach.* This word derives from the Old French *cote,* "humble home," which was borrowed from the Old Norse *kot,* "hut."

With a feeling of recklessness, I take that first step. I track a fine film of dust across the front steps, receiving a bored nod from one doorman and a blank stare from the other. "Can I help you?" he asks. He sees it. He knows that I don't belong.

But one glance at my invitation, and I'm duly admitted into a glossy foyer. A white marble table supports a silver pedestal vase with an elegant tumble of dogwood, heather, snapdragons, and magnolia blossoms. A sweeping double staircase curls protectively around the centerpiece, the stairs meeting at the mezzanine, then continuing their graceful waltz to the roof. A tiered empire chandelier hangs down through the center, with thousands of crystal prisms glinting in the light. The spiral staircase looks like the double helix of a DNA molecule, which is fitting, because this kind of wealth runs in the blood.

There are no smudges in Webster Cottage—this isn't the sort of place where people touch things. Despite the June warmth, a chill permeates the interior. The place reeks of old money, sterile and expensive as the lobby of an overpriced department store. As I take it all in, I repress an irrational wave of empathy for Avery. What is it like to grow up in a place where nothing is warm or soft?

A middle-aged man approaches. From his gray pompadour to the fleur-de-lis on the pocket of his sports coat, everything about him exudes education and class. The butler(?) nods as he extends a frothy orange cocktail on a petite serving platter. "May I present the house cocktail," he says with great dignity. "The Temperance Punch."

I choke on a mouthful of sherbet, limoncello, gin, and 7UP.

"This doesn't taste very temperate," I protest, but find myself taking a second sip against my better judgment.

He nods. "I believe that is the point."

A black-and-white marble hallway leads to a solarium overflowing with hothouse flowers. The smell of butter and clams draws me through a pair of French doors overlooking the gardens. Chefs in floppy white hats attend to steaming lobster pots, and maids flutter about like black-and-white butterflies. A tiered Jell-O loaf jiggles faintly in the breeze. Waiters meander through the gardens with platters of deviled crab cakes, anchovy puffs, lobster crostinis, and cheese balls coated in pretzels and cranberries. I sip my punch as I take it all in.

And I'm not dazzled by the chandeliers hanging from the boughs of an old oak tree. Or the tower of champagne coupes stacked like a glass house of cards. Or the scent of lilacs that permeates the grounds. I inhale deeply. This far north, lilacs only bloom for two weeks each spring. I wonder if the party was timed to coincide with them, or if it was a happy accident. Then an old man climbs up a ladder to pour a stream of bubbles across the champagne glasses, and I grin. *Obviously*, the timing was intentional. Nothing here is left to chance.

"Bunny!" Florence barrels toward me, the satin folds of her Grace Kelly evening gown flapping anxiously around her. Her cheeks are as red as her wine, and her blond hair is starting to frizz. "You're trespassing!" She glances around anxiously, as if someone might throw her out by association.

"I'm not trespassing, I was invited," I correct her as I trade my empty cordial glass for a champagne coupe. The old man winks at me.

"Billie, don't lie—I know you snuck in. My father had to pull *strings* to get us on the guest list," Florence hisses as she links arms with me, steering me toward a cluster of petticoats at the edge of the dance floor. The local seafood-heiress debutantes gather around us like so many sardines in a can—sticky, smelling slightly of sea air and drugstore perfume. Muriel comments on the fog while Marsha pretends at concern, and Wendy Liu studies her reflection in her wineglass. If wallflowering is an art, then these four have brought it to a new low. After a moment of pleasantries, the small-town beauties turn to fix me with identical blank stares. Waiting.

I open my mouth. Am I supposed to entertain them now? *Florence, you're a vision. Wendy, that saxophonist has his eye on you! Muriel, your beehive is the bee's knees. Marsha, give me the skinny: Are you reducing?* I *should* try to be nice and normal like them.

But honestly? I would rather die.

I've grown up listening to their sock-hop hopes and Tupperware-party dreams, but my aspirations don't fit in a casserole dish. I want big things. Cultivated things. Whispered *tête-à-têtes* with sommeliers. Rendezvous with beatniks in dimly lit art galleries. There's so much life that I long to experience. So many fancy rabbit holes I'm aching to climb down. But I don't want to make the gals uncomfortable, so I keep it to myself. Nodding and smiling, while hoping (desperately!) to meet somebody else with champagne secrets, too.

I guess that's why I spend so much time with my books, because those characters aren't afraid to shock or offend. They don't apologize for their differences; they celebrate them. They always know what to say and how to say it. They make me long for a life with better character development and more satisfying dialogue, because what I'm getting from these retired homecoming queens just doesn't cut it.

Oh right, I'm not breathing.

I suck in a labored eighty-year-old-smoker breath, as the four girls exchange an amused glance. Together, we suffer through one last awkward pause, then I say, "What a delight!" with a glassy smile and hurry away from the evening's inaugural faux pas.

A drowsy mist seeps in across the gardens as I follow a path lined with wild beach roses down to the dock. Half a dozen boats are tied up, swaying lazily in the surf. Gazing out at the water, I see the shifting veil of condensation across Passamaquoddy Bay. This foggy evening is straight out of an Impressionist painting. From far away, everything is clear, but from up close, it's just a swish of oil across a canvas.

"I must apologize for the lousy party." I turn to find Avery standing under a copper onion lamp mounted to a dock post. The honeyed light washes over his beige slacks and light gray blazer and gleams off the pilsner glass in his hand.

"Ah! The most boring guy in town." I fake a yawn.

And just like that, I'm myself again.

"I'm glad my reputation precedes me." Avery brushes the hair out of his face. "Can I bore you with a boat tour?"

"If you must," I reply with a complacent shrug.

He leads me over to a long mahogany speedboat, then hoists

himself up onto the prow and offers to hold my things. I slip off my heels and scramble up after him. "This is a Hacker-Craft Sportabout," he explains, handing me my glass as I walk barefoot across the cool, lacquered deck. "It's an American-made mahogany sport-fishing boat. It's actually rather similar to the one that Hemingway has in–"

"Sorry, I need to go home and shampoo my hair," I interrupt, sitting down on a cushioned leather bench at the back.

He laughs. "Is your aversion to speedboats or Nobel Prize–winning writers?"

"It's actually to young men talking about them," I reply over a lingering sip of champagne. I feel like Avery wants to dazzle me with his boat, which is redundant, seeing as my capacity for wonder was already exceeded several minutes ago. The waves sigh softly around us as I size up my companion. And I have to wonder, what is a dreamboat like him doing here? Shouldn't Avery be chatting up the Princess of Luxembourg or a *Vanity Fair* model? "Why are you paying me so much attention?" I ask. "Is it because I'm a novelty? Because I'm a townie?"

"You *are* a novelty, but not because you're from here. Honestly, I can't stand that clique of local girls. They're all so–" Avery pauses to search for the right word, and I resist the urge to supply it for him (vapid? judgmental? silly?). "Sad," he finally says, "and small."

"They're just products of their environment. This is a sad little world."

"No, it's not. It's as big or small as you want it to be," he murmurs as the boat rocks in the gentle surf. "It's all just a matter of your perspective." I'm certainly not dazzled by the mist seeping around us. Or Avery's fancy boat. Or his seaside philosophy. Or his slightly parted, pale pink lips, which are so close to mine. I'm dazzled by him least of all.

At least, that's what I tell myself, as I recross my legs and pretend at composure. "I'm disappointed in you, Avery. You promised me burning mansions, but so far, I haven't set fire to a single one."

"Oh, that's after the champagne toast," he replies, then nods up at the cottage. "What about that house? We could start by burning that one down."

I consider the sprawling estate. "It *is* a bit of an eyesore."

He drops his voice. "Isn't it atrocious?"

"You hate your house!" I choke on a mouthful of bubbles.

He locks eyes with me. They're fascinating eyes—gray-flecked hazel, like lamplight flickering through the fog. Against my better judgment, I feel my breath catch a tiny bit.

"Our secret," he says, then looks down at his watch as a shadow passes across his face. "Come on, we should go back and waste our lives at this stupid party."

"Do we have to? Can't we stay here instead?" I protest.

"I'm afraid my dance card is rather full for the evening," Avery says as he hops down to the dock. He reaches up to take my things but doesn't offer to help me down or take my hand, and I feel irrationally disappointed.

As we return to the party, the jazz band launches into a dreamy rendition of "Moon River." Avery offers a slight bow, then deserts me. I bite my lip and survey the scene. Should I join the wallflowers preening at the edge of the dance floor? Or play lady-in-waiting to the only other familiar face in the crowd, Mrs. Doris Cobb? A less than enticing prospect, as Eastport's rich widow has always terrified me with her Prohibition-era black gowns and habitual glass of iced tea. The widow doesn't drink and she doesn't smile, either. Or maybe I could try my luck on the social ladder and see how high I get before tumbling down? To be honest, I doubt that I have the requisite social skills or the necessary upper body strength.

Then I hear it. The medley of *thank you, pardon me,* and *oh, this old thing!* across the Websters' lawn. The chorus of social niceties draws me into the semiformal garden party. Manners are social camouflage that helps us blend in. A set of rules that I learned as a little girl, then promptly forgot. But I could probably fake it. After all, it's just etiquette.

Exhibit A: One Avery Webster, strolling through the party with the widow on his arm. Even icy Mrs. Cobb warms at his attentions. The matron sneezes, and he extends his handkerchief. *Swoon.* Then he catches my eye and raises a single eyebrow. *Double swoon.* I feel like we're in league, both bored by manners and mundane conversations. But he hides it with careless humility. He's so polite that it's practically a joke, but no one is laughing.

I follow his lead, nodding and smiling my heart out. I compliment an old man on his cummerbund as I make my way to the bar. "A glass of lambrusco, please," I ask the bartender with a demure smile. Another thing about manners: Refinement is an art of subtlety. Because nothing is more bourgeois than overdoing it.

Exhibit B: The couple striding toward me are a walking illustration that money and class don't always go hand in hand.

## ETIQUETTE FOR LOVERS AND KILLERS

They're too attractive for their own good, and they're overdressed. His chestnut hair is slicked back to one side, accentuating his Burt Reynolds mustache. He cuts a rakish figure in a poorly considered burgundy suit with a bow tie hanging open at the collar. But he disappears beside her.

Her red hair shines in the lamplight, styled in a flipped Hollywood bob that frames her face and tumbles down to her shoulders in graceful coils. Her fuchsia dress has a fitted balconet top that cinches and lifts in ways that defy gravity. The vibrant color accentuates her skin—casually sun-kissed and rosy around the edges. Her perfume drifts across the bar, overpowering the lilacs. She smells like coffee, vanilla, and jasmine—sweet, smoky, and intoxicating.

"Two bourbons, neat," she says in a husky voice. The candlelight puddles around her, flickering off the diamond on her finger as she signals the bartender. My eyes widen at her engagement ring. It has a rose-gold shank and a princess-cut diamond; it's virtually identical to the ring I received earlier that week.

"Gertrude, let's run away together," Mr. Mustache says, and I almost spill my sparkling wine. "We could keep cruising up the coast. Just you, me, and my thirty-eight-footer." Mr. Mustache plays with her hair while he strokes her arm. His touch looks stifling. "Let's elope."

I pretend to watch the jazz band while I study them over the rim of my glass. *Pretty*[b] is too delicate a word to describe

---

[b] **Pretty (adj.):** *attractive in a delicate way.* This chameleon of a word has completely transformed over time, stemming from the proto-Germanic *pratt*, "trick, lie," which led to the Old English *praettig*, "cunning, skillful." In

Gertrude—her beauty is abrasive. Her face is shockingly symmetrical, her eyelashes bafflingly long, and her hourglass figure impractical in design. Her sex appeal is sweet and slightly sticky—I feel it clinging to me as I snag a mini-quiche from a passing tray of appetizers.

She's chic, with glossy red nails filed into flawless oval tips. She's impulsive, knocking back one whiskey, then winking at the bartender as he pours her a refill. She doesn't have to ask, because he's hanging on her every word, too. She's fast on her feet, effortlessly sidestepping the proposed elopement as she informs Mr. Mustache (*Is he* Edgar? *Is* this *the couple from the letter?!*) that she's already challenged someone named Skip to a sailing race.

"Baby bear, I'm just *pining* for Campobello. It's *right here,* and Skip will be ever so cross if we don't swing by. Of course, I'm just *dying* to elope, but it would be so nice if it were at the Plaza, and I was wearing a ball gown, and everyone I've *ever met* was invited."

Her fiancé's mustache twitches as he withdraws his hand. "You called Skip?" he asks, a vein bulging down the center of his forehead. Her chestnut eyes widen in response and Gertrude starts to reach out, but then stops herself with a scornful giggle. She turns away, traipsing across the lawn in her vertiginous heels, chiffon billowing around her. Mr. Mustache heaves a sigh, then trails dutifully behind her.

My eyes follow Gertrude across the lawn. She slows as she

---

the fourteenth century *pretty* was used in an ironic sense for someone "good-looking in a diminutive way," but eventually, it lost the irony, and "beautiful in a slight way" became its chief meaning.

passes Mrs. Cobb, her pout hardening into a sneer. "I thought that you brought me to a party, *not* a nursing home," she stage-whispers to Mr. Mustache, then looks back at the widow and mouths, *Old cow*. I hide my scandalized grin behind my cocktail napkin as Gertrude tosses her hair and struts away.

A gasp ripples through the crowd as Gertrude almost trips, then digs her fingers into Mr. Mustache's arm. All eyes are on her, and she meets them with unconcealed pleasure, as the party swirls around her like the layers of her slightly sheer skirt. She's the leading lady, and we're all supporting roles. And me? I'm just an extra being paid minimum wage. The camera pans right over me.

The quartet plays a jazzy rendition of "Be My Baby" by the Ronettes, as the saxophone peels off in a volley of high notes. The trumpet croons out the melody while the dance floor swells with party guests. Marsha, Wendy, and Muriel swivel their hips and do the twist, while a young man spins Florence across the dance floor, crinoline whirling around her. A passing waiter bobs his head in time with the melody, while the old man in the cummerbund shuffles his feet in a triple step. They've all done this before. Maybe hundreds of times. But everyone seems oddly invested in the moment. As the guests groove in time with the beat, and waves lap against the shore, there's a feeling that anything could happen tonight. And the band seems to feel it, too.

The wall of French doors is open to the night, beckoning me inside. I drift through them with the mist, then stop short in the marble hallway. Gertrude is pressed up against the wall, with a tall blond man leaning into her. This is *not* Mr. Mustache. He runs his lips over her neck and fingers a hint of red lace peeking out over her bustier top. Her leg is slightly raised, wrapped tightly against his calf.

Unruly stubble runs down his bull-like neck, disappearing in a tangle of chest hair. He has strapping shoulders, dark circles under his eyes, and his biceps strain through his wrinkled shirt sleeves. He looks like a jock who got lost in a liquor store on his way to football practice, and now the only touchdowns he scores are in the back seat of his car. He locks eyes with me as he runs his hand down Gertrude's skirt to clench her upper thigh. The top four buttons of his shirt are undone, which pairs nicely with the cologne wafting across the hallway. He smells like pine trees, patchouli, and rubbing alcohol—like a lumberjack at a strip club. He might be attractive if you couldn't smell, see, or hear. But unfortunately, I can, and all of my senses cry out in revulsion.

"Do you want to join us?" He chuckles. "There's more than enough of me to go around."

Gertrude's throaty laughter cuts through the silence as her garnet earrings catch the light. "Claude, you bad boy, don't scare her. Run along, love. He would eat you alive." Then she yelps as he presses her back against the striped pearl wallpaper.

Her eyes follow me as I hurry down the checkerboard hallway into the bathroom. As I lock the door behind myself, I note a metallic taste in my mouth. What is that? Is it jealousy? Longing? But why? Is it because Gertrude is so alive? So unapologetically herself? Or is it because she makes me feel so small in comparison?

## ETIQUETTE FOR LOVERS AND KILLERS

I powder my cheeks in the mercury glass mirror. My hair, which my grandfather once kindly described as "the color of toast left just a second too long," is swept up in an untidy French twist. My mother's pearls gleam on my earlobes. My dress is the cool gray blue of longing, paired with a matching clutch. I thought that I looked elegant, but now my sweetheart neckline strikes me as naive, and the satin sleeves seem silly and superfluous. The pencil skirt constricts my legs. I'm flushed from champagne and decreased airflow. I close my compact and frown. I should go home soon. This has all been too much.

Shouting greets me as I open the door. "Ungrateful hussy." "Silly little bitch." "Using me for every cent I've got." I pause in the entrance of the solarium, where Mr. Mustache and Gertrude look poised to rip each other's throats out. A row of rattan pendant lights trembles above them.

"Skip was *happy* to hear from me," Gertrude seethes between drags of a menthol cigarette. "Darling, you were such a lovely toy, but now you're breaking *all* the rules." Gertrude totters over to a side table and reaches for an ashtray, swaying slightly as she picks it up. Ash drips off her cigarette as she weighs the heavy crystal ashtray in her hand and sizes up her opponent. "Remember? Jealousy is only sexy if it's a secret."

I choke on a laugh. *What kind of rule is that?* They turn in unison, him with outrage and her with wicked amusement. Another half laugh as I hurry across the parquet floor, then step outside. *What a display! I'm obsessed!*

The party swells, then deflates around me. The Jell-O loaf is melting, and the champagne tower loses its bubbles. Ties are loosened and inhibitions cast aside. Florence flirts with the bass player while the tall, smelly jock berates a bartender. Even widow Cobb lets her hair down, sneezing and swaying rhythmically across the dance floor with her iced tea. Then she sways a little further, and a hush falls over the crowd.

But Avery is already there to catch her. I'd almost forgotten about him, he's such a calm, collected presence in the midst of this insanity. With the help of a few other men from the party, he carries the prone woman inside. Then the band picks back up and dancing resumes.

I walk down to the dock and take a deep breath, watching Avery's speedboat rocking gently in the surf, the name *Poppy* on the prow. I grin. What an old-fashioned gentleman he is to name his boat after a wildflower. I linger awkwardly, with no reason to stay but a reluctance to go. A waiter offers me a lobster-filled croissant, and I eat it too quickly. My eyelids are drooping, and my fingers are greasy with butter as I walk inside to wash my hands.

I stop short in the entrance of a lavishly appointed parlor. Corinthian columns open onto a room with absinthe-green wallpaper, an emerald couch, and a mint carpet. Gertrude is splayed out across the center of it like a swathe of holly in a bed of ivy. Her red hair cascades over the silk rug, and her fuchsia dress is tangled around her thighs. One pink satin stiletto has slipped down to dangle from her toes. It's such an intimate pose, as if she were lying in bed waiting for a lover. An expression of surprise is painted across her features. Her eyebrows are raised, and her lips form a perfect O. Bruises line her neck like a tiered choker. A piece of paper pokes out of the pocket of her skirt, with a few dark red spots splattered across it.

My eyes flicker to a tear in her dress and a gash in her chest. Tissue and bone are visible through the sliced edge of fabric. Blood seeps out, staining her bodice and dripping down her side to puddle beneath her. Gertrude's blood is a deeper red than her hair, and it seems to dye the room crimson as well. There is no sign of a struggle. No overturned chairs or slashed curtains. Her nails aren't even chipped.

I take in Gertrude's red hair and redder blood, then stagger into the bathroom and throw up. I vomit lobster and lambrusco into the toilet, then set down my clutch and drink from the tap. My features look murky and dull–less animated than Gertrude's. As I study my stunned reflection, the enormity of the situation hits: this is an etiquette nightmare.

What is the polite reaction when one discovers a corpse at a social function? If I make a fuss, I'll ruin the party and offend the hosts. But if I *don't* do anything, then I'm the girl who found a body and didn't bother to inform anyone. A bumbling idiot. A morally deficient human being. A possible suspect.

Should I make sure that Gertrude is really dead? She certainly *seemed* dead, but perhaps it's rude to make assumptions about that sort of thing? Should I bring her to a maid's attention? *Excuse me, but I just found a redhead bleeding out across your priceless carpet. You better hurry and get some hydrogen peroxide before that stain sets!*

I stumble out of the bathroom and straight into one of the staff. I yelp and back away, gazing at the doorman with guilty eyes. He has a reserved smile and a small scar on his left cheek. My hand trembles as I point to the parlor, then rush away.

I want to run and hide, but that would only draw attention

to myself, so instead I walk sedately through the French doors, to the gardens. I clench the buffet table with both hands and pretend at composure, willing the stained silk rug and Gertrude's startled pout from my mind. Then I look up in surprise as the widow reemerges, supporting herself on Avery's arm.

"Just a fainting spell," she confides bravely. "The young man is a treasure."

A scream issues from deep within the house, and all eyes turn toward the sound. The chef puts down his spatula. "Did you hear—" He's cut short by a second, longer scream. A maid rushes out the French doors and pauses on the top step. She has olive skin, and her sable hair is wound up under a flimsy lace mob cap. She screams a third time, then her chin crumples as she points inside. I suppress an irrational stab of jealousy; now *that* is how it's done.

A distinguished-looking man in a seersucker suit (Avery's father?) strides up the steps to thank everyone for coming and wish them a *bonne nuit*. Two men come to stand guard outside the French doors as the quartet plays a farewell march. Someone left a corsage on the buffet table, and I pick it to bits while a pair of maids escort the guests out through the gardens back to their cars. There is an air of theatricality to the proceedings, as if the entire thing were rehearsed.

A waiter shoos me off in the direction of the receding party guests, and I follow unwillingly, leaving a trail of carnation petals in my wake. My kitten heels falter on the cobblestone driveway. The front door is slightly ajar, with soft amber light leaking through it, drawing me inside.

*I should leave.* I should depart with the other party guests and do as I'm told. I should go home, brush my teeth, put on pajamas, and pretend that this evening never happened.

But I'm already walking in the opposite direction. The navy blue carpet isn't spotless anymore, it's speckled with dust and dirt as I stride across it and poke my head inside.

"Billie!"

Avery is sitting on the stairs with a beer, the arms of his gray sports coat rolled up. After a moment of hesitation, I climb up to join him. We watch a police car arrive, and two policemen come dashing out. I take a sip of his beer. The pilsner glass is still cold.

"Did that really just happen?" I ask. Tonight has been surreal, to say the least. Fantasy and fiction are entwining so tightly that it's hard to distinguish between them. *Goya* is the Urdu word for that.

Avery gives me a funny look. "Yes, of course. Why do you ask?"

Admitting that I've lost my mind might not increase my desirability, so I change the subject. "This might sound unkind, but I think that Gertrude was looking for trouble. I saw her cheating on her fiancé tonight."

Avery laughs. "That's hardly front-page news."

A handful of policemen are canvassing the area. Some I grew up with, while others are more recent transplants. Officer Luke Blackwood was in my grade at high school. He waves at me while he wraps the columns with caution tape. Chief Deputy Gordon Abbott, our resident doughnut-toting police chief, trudges past, spraying sweat across the marble floor. The strobing flash of someone taking crime scene photos issues from the parlor as shouting echoes through the mansion. I hold my breath as Mr. Mustache is escorted outside in handcuffs. He thrashes in the policemen's grip, his mustache twitching irritably. As they push him through the door, Avery and I reach for his beer simultaneously. A jolt of electricity races up my arm as our fingers collide. I look up at him in surprise, and he looks back with embarrassment.

"Do you think that anyone is a suspect?" I ask, unable to stop myself.

Avery raises one sarcastic eyebrow. "Billie, *everyone* will be a suspect."

I burst out laughing as a passing policeman looks at me sharply. "Even me?"

"No, probably not you," he replies thoughtfully as he takes another sip of his beer.

"Should I talk to the police? Or–"

"My father will give them the guest list. They said they would interview everyone once they sorted themselves out," Avery explains as Chief Deputy Abbott trips on the front step, then drops a roll of caution tape and groans as it unspools across the marble floor. "But that might take a minute."

A vision in peach silk slinks up the stairs. She's a woman of an uncertain age, frozen in time somewhere between thirty-five and sixty. She looks at Avery as she dots her eyes with a hankie, then her hand hovers over his head. Is she about to ruffle his hair? But instead, she drops her handkerchief. *Oh right, people don't touch things here. Including each other.*

The man in seersucker follows closely behind. "Quinn, were you raised in a barn?" He shakes the handkerchief after the receding waif, then turns to Avery. His salt-and-pepper eyebrows knit together. "What are you doing right now, son?"

"Squandering the family fortune?" Avery offers with a shrug.

"Why aren't you on the phone with *every single person* we keep on retainer? Get my lawyer on the phone *right now*, or get another family." Mr. Webster glowers at Avery, then continues up the stairs.

"Well, he was pleasant," I say when he's out of earshot.

"Just another day in paradise," Avery shakes his head, then glances over at me. His eyes widen as he checks his watch. "Billie, what are you still doing here? It's so late!"

I bite my lip. "I'm 'the Last Guest to Leave.' There's an entire section devoted to it in Amy Vanderbilt's *Complete Book of Etiquette*."

His eyes light up. "By far the worst faux pas of the evening. Do you live in town? Would you accept a ride?"

My breath catches. "Why—yes! Absolutely."

Avery nods distractedly, then calls downstairs. "Hayes, could you drive this young lady home? I think she lives somewhere over there—" He gestures vaguely to the east.

"You aren't going to drive me?" I try to contain my disappointment as Hayes appears in the foyer. He's the man with the pompadour who served the punch earlier.

"I think that fleeing the scene is generally discouraged." Avery chuckles.

Hayes ushers me outside to the carport, then opens the door to a blue Mercedes. I sit down in the back, gazing glumly out the dark window.

As the butler drives me home, I consider the problem of Gertrude. Because she is *definitely* a problem. Is it strange that I received a love letter for her earlier this week? *Yes.* After seeing her, though, I feel like some part of me has been writing her love letters for years. I picture her, standing there among the orchids with her menthol cigarette, about to hurl an ashtray at her fiancé.

And I feel myself getting whisked away by the mystery of it all. Who was she beneath the fuchsia facade? And how did she seamlessly insert herself into every facet of the evening? Was she a villain, a victim, or both? Gertrude was everything that I'm not. She's the sort of heroine who people write books about. Lovely, brilliant, and insane. I want to know everything I can about her.

But I guess I'll have to start by finding out who killed her.

## CHAPTER THREE

# CONDUCT IN THE STREET

*A lady's deportment is never so at the mercy of critics, as when she is in the street. Her dress, carriage, and walk will all be exposed to notice and every unladylike action will be marked.*

"If you were at a party and someone died, what would you do?" I nestle into the gossip bench with the phone pressed to my ear. The phone nook is an ideal place for whispered scandals, with a chaise longue upholstered in crushed yellow velvet, the scuffed cedar staircase curling protectively around it. The chaise is a battered hand-me-down with rosewood grapevines curving along its arches to form a base for the phone and my teacup.

"Is that a hypothetical question?" I can practically hear Debbie grinning.

"No," I respond guiltily. It's 10 a.m., and I'm officially procrastinating. I'm still wearing pajamas, twining the cord lazily around my fingers, while Victor's Buick languishes a mile and a half away. "But I haven't killed anyone. Promise."

"Not yet, man-eater."

"Sadly, you are misinformed. I'm neither a trollop[a] nor a cannibal."

"*Ooh*, love a trollop," Debbie replies. One of the main reasons we're friends is because Debbie loves old words as much as I do. She stood out from the other girls at the Ashburn Linguistics Institute, most of whom had little interest beyond acquiring their MRS. degree. Debbie majored in library science while I studied cultural linguistics, but we both minored in smuggling wine into the dorms. Since graduation, Debbie has gone on to work at some of the most prestigious libraries in the country, while I've refined my technique at patching denim overalls. But for some reason, she doesn't think I'm a loser. She has more faith in me than I do. Our relationship is a lot like this chaise longue: comfortable, well-worn, and designed for hot gossip.

"But there *is* a guy." I drop my voice so my grandparents won't hear.

"A real one?" Debbie clarifies. She sounds more shocked by this than by the murder.

"I *think* he's real," I reply, although I'm starting to doubt it myself. Avery is an anomaly, checking all four of the boxes of desirability. "He seems to have a brain, manners, a sense of hu-

---

[a] **Trollop (n.):** *an immoral or promiscuous woman* (often used facetiously). Some linguists claim that this dated insult stems from the Middle English *trollen*, "to stroll, to roll about," while others argue that it derives from the Old Norse *troll*, "witch, gremlin, wizard." But why is it either/or? Why can't we have both?

44

mor, and he isn't completely hideous." I twirl the phone cord around my finger as I consider the New England dreamboat. I'm a cliché in polka-dot pajamas: just one more girl who took the fairy tales a little too seriously and held out for a prince who doesn't exist. Now at twenty-six, I feel like the punch line to a trite joke. But the local male population can hardly tempt me. I'm fairly certain that some of the fish in the bay have higher IQs than our bachelors. They aren't what I'm looking for, and I'm not what they want, either. They take me out for drive-in movies and root beer floats, but I always find myself longing for the moment when I can return home to my books. To get in bed with male leads who actually compel me.

"And he's real, most importantly," Debbie repeats. "So will you investigate this murder?"

"That's what I'm trying to decide." I study the phone as I weigh my options. "Should I solve a crime or paint my nails? I'm just so swamped right now doing nothing."

"The first rule of detective work is the trench coat," she informs me. Debbie normally works at MIT's Hayden Library in Boston, but she's on loan to a research facility for the summer and seems a trifle starved for excitement. "You need a stylish jacket that will make you look street-smart and intimidating."

"Go on, I'm taking notes."

"The second rule is the dingy office. I'm envisioning a run-down brick building with broken Venetian blinds and a thick layer of grime coating every surface. Maybe a stack of unwashed coffee mugs and a few empty whiskey bottles? You also need to develop a taste for the stronger stuff–Riesling isn't gonna cut it. A few skeletons in your closet would be nice.

Maybe you have a secret criminal past? Or a rare illness? Or you deserted the army? I know, you're a gambling addict and suffer from random blackouts but—"

"Debbie." I blink away tears of laughter as the antique springs squeak beneath me. "I was asking for advice on how to investigate a *crime*, not on how to play the lead in a film noir."

"Is there a difference?" She hangs up for dramatic effect, then calls back a moment later.


Alfred Hitchcock would have serious qualms about my casting as the hard-boiled detective. My yellow beach cruiser is highly conspicuous, and my bleary smile seems unlikely to inspire fear in the heart of a killer. I bike out to retrieve my grandfather's Buick and stash the bike in the trunk, then walk over to the gate. My eyes narrow as I consider the mansion beyond it.

Webster Cottage is sleeping. The curtains are drawn, the doors are shut tight, and the gardens are deserted. I rest my hands on the iron bars, marveling at how cold they are.

As I drive home, images from the party replay themselves in my head. The champagne house of cards. Gertrude's scarlet nails clutching the crystal ashtray. That brute in the hallway with chest hair peeking out of his shirt. The mist sparkling on the bow of Avery's speedboat. Florence spinning across the dance floor. Gertrude's blood spilling artistically across the mint-green rug. Her fiancé's used-car-salesman mustache. Is *he* the one who wrote to me? What are the chances of receiving a love letter and an engagement ring for a stranger, only to see her murdered the next day?

## ETIQUETTE FOR LOVERS AND KILLERS

I pull up at my grandparents' house and hide the car keys in Victor's jacket pocket, then retreat to my bedroom. But *Northanger Abbey* has nothing on Webster Cottage. I burrow into my sheets as I study the sketch of Jane Austen on the back cover. Mysterious, detail-oriented, and jaded to a fault, now *she* would have made a great detective. Austen's books all follow the same formula: flirtation, rumors, and a romantic setback. Next comes the half-hearted investigation, which invariably leads to being handed the truth on a silver platter along with a proposal. If Austen were investigating a murder, where would she start?

I get up and plug in my curling iron. *Obviously*, she would follow the trail of gossip. There is a bit of truth hidden at the bottom of every rumor, and some batting eyelashes and a few murmured *Why, I never*'s are generally how Austen's characters uncover it. So I stash her book in my purse, dab on some blush, and do the same.

My first stop is the biggest busybody in town, my grandfather. I find him hunched over the kitchen table with his CB radio, a newspaper, and a cup of Folgers. "Car Mike Bravo seventy-two, are you receiving?" beeps the police channel on his handheld radio. "Don't mention the red ball if you swing by the ten-forty-two club. Chief deputy's orders. Over."

"Darn it, where is my codebook?" Victor grumbles to himself as he shuffles into the hallway in his worn leather slippers.

The receiver vibrates again. "Car Mike Bravo, do you copy?" The leather case is creased and worn from my grandfather's fingers. I glance at the *Bangor Daily News*, but there's no mention of Gertrude—just an article about a box full of puppies found on the interstate, titled "Gone to the Dogs." I step back when Victor returns with a pamphlet clasped in his age-spotted hands.

"Victor, did you hear anything unusual on the radio last night?" I ask as he flips through the spiral-bound booklet. In an effort to maintain some degree of autonomy, I call my grandparents by their first names, preferring to think of them as "roommates" rather than my keepers. But they aren't thrilled with the distinction.

"No," he replies too quickly, furrowing his snowshoe hare eyebrows at me. "Actually, there was one car theft. A 1955 Buick sedan was stolen right out of an old man's driveway. This town is going to hell in a—"

"Sorry, I needed a ride."

His bushy eyebrows ruffle in annoyance. "That's a code ten-thirty-seven, Billie. You best watch yourself." Victor hates it when I take his car. He resumes flipping through the police booklet, while I survey the counter for something to snack on.

"Were there any other codes last night?" I ask, munching halfheartedly on a saltine.

"A ten-forty-nine." Victor frowns at his pamphlet. His eyes are bloodshot behind his thick glasses, and his crow's-feet are more pronounced than usual. He wears a slightly sheepish expression. "I don't know who called it in. None of my business." My grandfather gazes dolefully at his coffee. "They probably called the operator, then she would'a transferred it to the police.... Maybe it was a joke." He glances at me without interest. "Where were you last night, Billie?"

"Across the Canadian border, selling stolen Buicks," I call as the door swings shut behind me.

The second stop on the trail of gossip is behind the Venetian blinds quivering in the second-story window of one of the brick buildings downtown. I climb up a carpet runner encrusted with decades of salt, slush, and mud, then step inside the *Quoddy Current* News Bureau.

With rolls of gray newsprint, battered fans, and an impressive inventory of broken typewriters, this is where headlines go to die. Debbie would approve of the *Quoddy Current*'s dented coffee machine and leaning tower of unwashed mugs. The antique printing press coated in dust would also gain her stamp of approval. But I doubt she would care for Thomas Cahill, the editor, or Diane Bean, his one reporter, neither of whom would pass a Hollywood screen test. They're both rumpled and drab, with complexions as faded and gray as their newsprint.

"May I help you?" Ms. Bean looks down her aquiline nose at me. For a reporter, she isn't very observant. We've walked past each other hundreds (maybe thousands) of times, but she doesn't even know my name.

I lean against a cluttered desk, resting my hand beside a stack of business cards embossed with the newspaper's lobsterboat masthead. "If it isn't too much of a bother—" I try to find a delicate way of putting it.

"Spit it out, Billie. We haven't got all day," Mr. Cahill reprimands me.

"I was just wondering if you have any leads on last night's big... to-do?" *Murder* sounds so aggressive.

Cahill and Bean both frown. "'To-do!'" the female reporter exclaims. "Why don't you just go 'to-do' yourself right out of here?"

"So you *don't* have any leads. On the situation?" I ask as they exchange blank stares. Then I suppress a smile. *They don't have a clue what I'm talking about!*

"Are you trying to pitch us a story?" Mr. Cahill smirks.

"Shoo." Ms. Bean makes a batting gesture with her hand, as if I were a stray cat. "Get out of here, or I'll call your mother."

I suppress a disdainful smile of my own. Because if Diane Bean were any kind of reporter, she would know that my mother was dead. And because she isn't very observant, she doesn't notice when I grab a handful of her business cards and stash them in my purse in silent revolt. Feeling slightly vindicated by the petty theft, I turn and march down the crusty stairs.

My third stop is the Tide & Tackle Diner. Situated directly opposite the police station, the greasy restaurant is ideal for a stakeout. A thick porcelain coffee mug warms my hands and a slice of toast leaves crumbs on my lipstick as I watch the station house.

A waitress in yesterday's mascara and a stained apron mans the phone. "We got blueberry, strawberry-rhubarb, lemon meringue, Nantucket cranberry—"

The door to the police station bursts open, ejecting one portly police officer and one sleazy mustache. I perk up immediately. Gertrude's fiancé stumbles down the front steps with Chief Deputy Gordon Abbott in tow. The burgundy blazer that looked so dapper last night is creased and stained. Mr. Mustache clutches a paper bag in his right hand, shaking it belligerently at the police officer.

The waitress's voice goes up an octave. "Are you crazy? I can't hold *all* of the pies for you!" I turn, distracted from the legal drama by the crisis in here, as the shopgirl leans protectively over her bakery case. "I know you want them but . . . *sir*, a lot of people want pie. I can't hold *all* of them just *in* . . . Well, you didn't last time . . . Yeah, I understand that you're coming on a boat."

I grin. It's one of the more obnoxious things that the summer people do. They sail into town to buy out entire bakeries and lobster shacks, then lug the spoils back to their boats, looting and pillaging like preppy Vikings. I wonder if the pie-needing cohort is associated with the scandal in some way? All the summer people are connected. They move in their circle, just as we move in ours.

I choke down the dregs of my coffee as those two circles collide outside. Mr. Mustache hurls himself at Chief Deputy Abbott on the sidewalk. "This case has 'wrongful arrest' written all over it," he seethes as I slip outside. "I was drunk when you questioned me! You took advantage—" He lifts up his brown paper bag again and shakes it pathetically at Chief Deputy Abbott, then wheels off down the sidewalk.

The sun glints off the shop windows on Water Street as I tail Gertrude's grieving fiancé. He runs into an old clammer with a plastic bucket and rubber wader boots, then yelps and stumbles down the sidewalk. I've never followed anyone before, and I hope that I'm doing it right, keeping an eye on Mr. Mustache but trying not to stare. I have a feeling—sort of like reverse déjà vu—that this tailing will be the first time of many.

Clearly I'm a natural at stalking, because I stumble straight into a cop.

"Sorry, Luke. Some things never change," I murmur as I

disentangle myself from the strapping young policeman. Suddenly, all the gossip I've been so wrapped up in strikes me as rather passé. Because who gives a damn about summer people versus locals, rich versus poor, when we're all just tourists compared to Luke.

Passamaquoddy Bay is the ancestral homeland of the Passamaquoddy Tribe. The People of the Dawn have been here since, quite literally, the dawn of time. The changing seasons, fashions, and industries washing across this archipelago since baguette-toting French explorers first stumbled across it in 1604 take up mere seconds in the island's lifespan.

Luke's face is as sharply defined as the rugged granite coastline, hewn by glaciers when his forefathers arrived here eons ago. They say that still waters run deep, which is clearly the case with Luke. Concern flickers in the depths of his rich brown eyes. What is hiding at the bottom of them? And what anchors Luke? What holds him here?

"I think that the sidewalk should be the one apologizing, not you," he murmurs, pointing to the cracked pavement beneath our feet. Luke was one of the students bussed into school from the Pleasant Point Reservation each day. He was always kind to me, I guess because we were both outsiders in our own way. I kept to myself because I didn't fit the mold. And Luke kept to himself because he fit an entirely different one.

"It's a death trap. This sidewalk is out for blood," I concur, which earns me a sharp glance from the young cop. *Right. Maybe I shouldn't joke about death traps to a young man who just cleaned up a murder scene.*

"I think we're all a bit thrown off today," Luke replies, settling himself. "Billie, I don't mean to pry, but I saw you there last night, after—"

"After the hothead with the mustache got taken in?" I glance down the sidewalk. *Mr. Mustache is getting away!*

Luke straightens his creased shirt and smooths down his inky hair. He must have been up all night, too. "Yeah, Teddy has one hell of a mustache."

"Teddy?" I turn back in surprise. *Gertrude's fiancé is named Teddy?*

"Teddy Brixton is a summer resident of Bucks Harbor," Luke explains. "We took him in because—"

"His mustache is a crime against humanity?" I counter, and Luke coughs awkwardly. *Shoot. My sense of humor isn't doing me any favors right now.*

Luke flexes his hand unconsciously, drawing my eyes toward the calluses on his palms. "Teddy was in a relationship with the deceased. They were seen in a dispute before she— anyway, he got pretty sloppy, so we threw him in the drunk tank to cool off and consider what he'd done."

"But what *had* he done?" I resume walking in the direction that Teddy disappeared off to.

"With this sort of crime, it's often the significant other." Luke drops his voice as he falls into step beside me.

*You don't say.* I struggle to contain my eye roll. "But if he's your top suspect, then why did you release him?"

"The deputy flipped over a chair, then Teddy started screaming about malpractice lawsuits so . . ." Luke quiets, realizing that he's said too much. "Billie, watch out for that family. And cool it with all the questions. We've got this." He pats my shoulder, then asks where I'm headed, and walks me to a park overlooking the harbor. "Take care of yourself," he says with one last worried glance as I settle onto a bench and pull *Northanger Abbey* out of my purse. As Luke walks away, I lean forward, eyes fixed on the bar across the street.

The fourth stop on the trail of gossip is Eastport's one bar: the Thirsty Whale. I might have lost Teddy, but if *I* had a hangover, a mustache, and a dead girlfriend, *I* would head to a bar. And the Thirsty Whale is his only option.

I watch the tide of inebriated fishermen pushing through the swinging saloon doors, then blink up at the clouds overhead. They also look like they're struggling through a champagne hangover. I note the man sitting on a bench at the back of the park in a khaki jacket and a fedora. Now *he* looks like a proper detective. Then I glance back at the bar and stifle an exclamation.

Mr. Mustache has stumbled outside to lean against the whitewashed wall, the Thirsty Whale sign swaying above him. He wipes his eyes with the back of one hand, then raises a beer to his lips. Both his velvet jacket and his paper bag are missing, but his bow tie hangs open at the collar of his shirt.

I gather my courage and amble across the street. "Is everything okay?" I ask.

"You hussy," Teddy growls. His eyes are hooded and dim, fixed behind me.

I'm shocked by his language but try to control myself and keep him talking. "Did you write me a letter?" I ask. I feel like the letter and Gertrude's death are intimately connected, so if I figure one out, the other will also become clear.

"You and your letters. Always scheming. Always fooling

around behind my back." Mr. Mustache seems to be confusing me with someone else. As he draws up to me, I wrinkle my nose. He smells like whiskey, sweat, and something else. What is that? Is it fear? Anguish? Humiliation? His breath is sticky and hot against my neck as he digs his greasy fingers into the small of my back. I flinch and swat his hand away. "I want to hurt you as badly as you hurt me. I want to watch you beg for mercy." He hiccups, then throws his beer against the ground. I yelp as the bottle shatters around us.

"Teddy bear, stop scaring the nice lady," an amused voice calls out behind us. I step back, careful to avoid the broken glass, as a young man in a captain's hat walks up. He has red hair, patchy red stubble, is of medium build, and wears a striped blue shirt. A young man shuffles behind him, clutching a stack of five pastry boxes against his chest.

"My hat goes off to you, sir." The man in the captain's hat slaps Teddy across the shoulders, then tips his cap. "That bitch *died,* you got *arrested,* and now you're getting *loaded* at the Thirsty Whale. I am *honored* to be your friend."

"Skip," Mr. Mustache says hollowly. "I didn't do it."

I step to the side, retreating around the corner of the building. So *this* is the famous Skip, who Gertrude and Teddy were all heated up about! I've never seen Skip before, but I know who he is. *Everyone* does. Skip Ashcroft's palatial summer home on Campobello is a veritable breeding ground for state senators and Wall Street CEOs. He's the next best thing to American royalty (although, in classic confused-American fashion, his home is actually on the *Canadian* side of the border).

"Come on, buddy, let's get you home. I got us some pie to

celebrate." Skip nods toward the anxious young man struggling under the mountain of pastry boxes from the Tide & Tackle.

"Celebrate?" Teddy's mustache twitches.

"It's not every day that someone gets murdered. Attention must be paid." Skip erupts in a fresh volley of laughter as he places the captain's hat on Teddy's head.

"Are we taking the ferry?" Mr. Mustache looks around himself in confusion.

"Don't insult me. I took the cruiser," Skip calls as he begins walking to the pier. The assistant grits his teeth, then scurries after him with the pies.

Perhaps it's adrenaline, unease, or my mild hangover, but I have the strangest sensation as I walk home. It's as if I'm being followed. Goose bumps prickle across my skin, but I tell myself that it's only nerves. I didn't get enough sleep last night, and now I'm jumping at shadows. No one is watching me. I'm just exhausted.

But I know it's just in my head, so I don't turn around.

"Harlem Shuffle" plays on the radio alarm clock. I blink at it wearily. It's 10 p.m. and I'm half sitting / half sleeping against the headboard. My head feels wobbly and loose, as if it might fall off. Fatigue drags at my limbs as I reach for the box on my nightstand and hit the button to silence it. I'm exhausted, but I can't rest. I keep thinking about how Victor said *I don't know who called it in.* What if there was a way to find out?

I reach for my pale pink rotary phone and dial *1*. My eyes are tiny slits, unwilling to open, as I make the fifth stop on the trail of gossip: the operator.

ETIQUETTE FOR LOVERS AND KILLERS

"Bell Atlantic of Eastern Maine!" announces a squeaky voice on the other end. She sounds altogether too chipper to be talking to someone like me. "How may I direct your call?"

"Were you working the switchboard last night?"[b] I ask through a yawn.

"I beg your pardon?" She sounds confused. People call the operator all day long, but no one ever really *talks* to the women working the phone lines, they always just ask to be redirected.

"Were you working the switchboard last night?" There can't be *that* many operators working the graveyard shift in Down East Maine, and I bet they work the same hours each day.

"I ... why ... no."

"Goodbye, then," I say and hang up. Another yawn, as I dial *1* a second time.

"Bell Atlantic of Eastern Maine. How may I direct your call?" asks an old woman. She sounds frail and worn, like my fraying phone cord.

"Were you working the Eastern Maine switchboard last night?" I ask.

"Go to hell!" The operator hangs up in a huff.

I grin, then dial *1* a third time. "Hi, were you working this shift last night?"

"Yes," the operator replies warily.

---

[b] **Night (n.):** *the period from dusk to dawn without sunlight.* Derived from the PIE root *newkt, night* is a mystery in five letters. In over twenty languages it breaks down to a combination of *n* plus the number eight. In English: *n* + *eight* = *night*. In Spanish: *n* + *oche* = *noche*. In Portuguese: *n* + *oite* = *noite*. In French: *n* + *huit* = *nuit*. Anomalies like this drew me to study language in the first place. I like to imagine myself as something of a word detective, solving the mysteries of language one definition at a time.

"This might be an odd question . . . but did you get any strange calls?"

The operator hesitates, and my eyes open a little wider. "What is this about?" she replies after a long moment. This operator has a thick Maine accent and sounds slightly gruff, as if she's recovering from a cold. There is curiosity in her congested voice.

"It would have been at about this time last night? Someone asking to be transferred to the police station?" My voice ticks up at the end of each sentence, betraying my nervousness. "Do you remember anything unusual?"

"Maybe. But why should I tell you?"

*Why should she tell me?* I squint at the phone. *Because I'm nosy and bored? Because Gertrude deserves justice, and I doubt that Chief Deputy Abbott has what it takes to give it to her? Because life is short, and we should make it as interesting as possible?* "I can't go into too many details, but something happened last night to a . . . charming young woman. And I'd like to help. I thought you might have some useful information, but if you don't, my apologies for bothering you." It's not a good explanation, but hopefully it's enough.

Silence echoes through the receiver, while the operator weighs her professional discretion against her natural inclination to gossip. "All right, but you can't tell *anyone* I told you this." Luckily, gossip wins.

"My lips are sealed," I assure her.

"Last night 'round ten fifteen I got a call. They were upset. Talkin' real fast. Askin' for–"

"Was it a man or woman?"

"Female. Fancy accent," the operator replies after a moment of thought. She sucks in a breath and coughs. "Maybe from Europe?"

*Was that a housekeeper? The mother?* "What stood out about the call?"

"First she said it was an emergency and asked to be transferred to the hospital. But then she changed her mind and asked for the police. There was a lotta noise in the background. Then she apologized and asked me to hold on, which is weird, because *no one ever* apologizes to me." The woman huffs, then drops her voice. "Then she whispered, 'She's dead. She's finally dead.'"

"'Finally'!" I clamp a hand over my mouth so I don't wake up my grandparents.

The operator's laughter is as congested as her voice. "Thought it was an odd choice of words, myself. Normally, when we get an emergency, they want to speak to the cops right away. But this was different. I keep thinkin' about her voice. Spooked me real good."

"And then—" I nudge her for more details.

"Then I heard this guy in the background. He said, 'Please wait.' He sounded stuck-up, too. Then the girl hung up, and I never did get to transfer it." The operator coughs again. "So what happened? Did someone really die? I thought it coulda been a prank call."

"Someone was murdered last night."

A gasp across the switchboard. "And you're a private detective, investigating it?"

I swallow a laugh. "Exactly."

## CHAPTER FOUR

# MAID SERVICE

*The parlor maid takes up her mistress's morning cup of tea and assists her in dressing, sewing, and attends to her beauty regimen. She does the housemaid's work, sweeping, cleaning, dusting china, and attending to the flowers. She cleans the silver and the lamps, then gets up the fine linen. She does pantry work and opens the door to callers in the morning and the afternoon.*

Elizabeth Taylor is on the tip of everyone's tongue. Her flower crown and yellow empire-waist wedding dress are all anyone can talk about. I swing by the Salon by the Sea for a trim and some rumors at the shampoo station, but no one mentions Temperance Punch or bloodstains on silk. The beauticians just gush about Hollywood's leading lady over the gentle buzz of the hairdryer, unaware of all the gossip much closer to home.

A finger is pressed to the lips of the local law enforcement, and I wonder who it belongs to. As the days pass, the hush deepens. Are the police unwilling or *unable* to release details of the scandal? I don't mention it to anyone but Debbie, because it isn't my story to tell. Not yet.

Elizabeth Taylor goes on her honeymoon—first to Boston and then on to Puerto Vallarta. I imagine her sipping a margarita while yellow-chevroned parakeets and Blue Morpho butterflies flit through the orchids and ferns on her balcony. I go nature watching as well, gazing at the humpback whales on migration in the bay and the monarchs (who also just got their passports stamped in Mexico) wafting through the pale June sunlight. I walk downtown, keeping my eyes peeled for the black-and-white butterflies that sometimes flutter out of the great houses. "The help" know all the dirt, and which carpet has grime swept under it. I'm desperate to speak with one of the Websters' employees and find out who made that call.

Marsha's mother swings by with a bolt of plaid fabric and an order for four curtains. I use pleater tape on the heavy cotton, folding the edge up under each loop, then pinning it to the top of the hem. As I sew her ugly plaid panels, I keep one eye trained on the window. Butterfly hunting.

My sewing machine screeches when one flutters past.

Mrs. Pridmore is out to lunch, so there is no one to stop me from disentangling myself from Mrs. Crimp's poor taste and rushing into the stockroom. I grab a pageboy hat and a blazer, checking to see if any tags are sticking out. Then I lock the door and hurry after her. The maid is halfway down the block by the time I catch up with her. A nervous sweat glistens under my stolen cap as I take a note out of my purse (*my grandmother's shopping list*, I notice with amusement), then drop it on the sidewalk.

"Excuse me, miss?"

Heavy mesh shopping bags drag down her shoulders as the young woman turns, displaying the traditional black-and-white uniform of a lady's maid. She's striking, with a slender frame and a cloud of raven hair gleaming in the midday sunshine. Her angular cheekbones and defined jaw contrast sharply with the rose-petal shape of her eyes. A doily of a hat is pinned to her head. As our eyes meet, my jaw drops. She's the maid who screamed so nicely at the end of the Websters' party!

"Me?" she asks. Her accent is as difficult to place as her facial features.

"Did you drop this?" I pick up the scrap from the ground.

"Oh lord, I probably did." She inclines her head toward the shopping bag on her right, with butcher paper sticking out of the top. "Could you drop it in here, please?"

"Of course." I tuck the list of beauty products in her bag, then square my shoulders. "Forgive me if I'm completely off base here, but . . . do you work at Webster Cottage?"

The widening of her pupils is response enough.

"I write for the Lifestyle section of our local paper, and I would *love* to ask you a few questions." I assume an expression of mild curiosity.

"The newspaper!" the maid repeats in surprise.

"Yes! And I'm just desperate for cleaning tips," I say with a bland laugh. "I won't mention your name or your employer's." Obviously, there is no Lifestyle section of the *Quoddy Current* newspaper, and even if there were, I doubt the Websters would allow their employees to contribute to it. But this is the best I could come up with.

The maid considers me for a long moment, fiddling with her apron, then raising one brazen eyebrow. "Why not?" she replies with a daring grin. "I've always wanted to be famous. Can you call me 'the Dutch Maid'? Everyone always talks about French maids or English maids, but Holland trains some very fine lady's maids as well."

I lead the Dutch maid over to a picnic table overlooking the harbor, then motion for her to sit down. It's a calm day. The sky is bright and unblemished by clouds as the waves roll in lazy ripples. As the maid unburdens herself of her heavy shopping bags, I dig through my purse for my slim leather diary and a business card. "Thank you for speaking with me. I'm Diane Bean of the *Quoddy Current* newspaper," I introduce myself with a thin smile as I offer her the card. "And you are–"

"Lieske." The young woman doesn't offer a last name.

"So nice to meet you! Lieske, let's get down to the dirt, shall we? I'm curious about what the average day looks like at Webster Cottage. What is your secret for keeping a house spick-and-span? I'm sure you could clean circles around the rest of us."

The young woman's lips can't seem to move fast enough as she rattles off a list of chores that seems overambitious at best and like indentured servitude at worst. She does quite a bit of sewing and cooking in addition to catering to Mrs. Webster's every whim. As Lieske talks, I nod encouragingly, making animated doodles in my notebook. After five minutes of dusting, darning, and carpet-beating advice, I interject: "We're all curious about how the other half lives. Could you tell me something surprising that you've seen while assisting such a prominent family?"

Her smile drops. "I can't say."

"I don't want to get you in trouble, but I would love a better understanding of life at Webster Cottage. My readers are awfully intrigued by the inner—"

"Something happened last weekend," Lieske blurts out, then covers her mouth.

"Was it good or bad?" I try to look unbiased, yet vaguely supportive.

"Both." She cocks her head to one side, carefully selecting her words. "There was this woman . . . a favorite of the family. She's from Connecticut so she was always popping by the Rhode Island house. She was awfully rude to me—and very messy! She had *no respect* for tidiness or personal boundaries. I don't know if she did it on purpose or if she's just naturally a slob, but every time she came over, there was a *lot* of extra work for me, cleaning up after her."

"Navigating the big personalities in such a great house must be challenging."

"You can say that again," the maid says with a resigned laugh. "She was just as bad as he is."

"Who is 'he'?"

Lieske starts to answer, then thinks better of it. She taps her trim pink nails against the picnic table as she bites her lip. "I actually feel a little guilty." She drops her voice and fiddles with the lace fringe on her apron. "Because I cursed her."

My jaw drops. "I beg your pardon?" *Surely, she didn't say that she—*

"I prayed that something bad would happen to her, and then it did!" The young woman picks at paint flaking off the edge of the picnic table. "Do you think I'm to blame?"

I study my diary to hide my dismay. Black magic wasn't *exactly* the direction I was anticipating from this interview. "What happened? It's hard to offer an opinion when I don't know the—"

"They were necking!" she blurts out.

My eyebrows shoot up. "Necking!" I repeat.

Lieske swallows a scandalized giggle. "Yeah. The woman I didn't like—she was fooling around in the parlor. I cleaned up afterwards, and I found one of her earrings under the couch cushions, which had *clearly* been sat on. *All* of the pillows needed to be plumped. Then I found a garter under the sofa—I didn't know that people still wore things like that!" Her cheeks turn a deeper shade of olive. "It was hot pink."

"What did you do with the garter?"

"I threw it out." Her voice is demure, but her blush tells a different story.

"Is this the first time that something bad happened at the cottage?"

Lieske reaches for her apron, then stills her hands with a concerted effort. "This can't go in the newspaper, but—"

"I'm sticking to lemons, dish soap, and white vinegar for the article, but now you've piqued my curiosity and I just want to make sure that *you* are okay," I say with a sincerity that surprises me. "This conversation won't leave the picnic table."

"Well... Claude has a temper." The maid sighs, massaging one wrist.

"Is Claude the father? Is he violent with the staff?"

"No, he's one of the sons." She bites her lip. "He's never touched any of the employees. Just his brother."

"Claude beats his brother up?" It's growing increasingly difficult to maintain my composure.

"He doesn't know how to control himself." She shakes her head, and I get the sense that this Claude is a prevailing source of frustration in her life.

"Did you tell the police?" I ask, then immediately regret it. As usual, my mouth is getting me in trouble.

"I tried to, but they were all too busy." Lucky for me, she doesn't notice.

"Jerks," I murmur. She looks up sharply as I snap my journal shut. It's time to wrap this up before I blow my cover completely. "Thank you for speaking with me today, Lieske. My readers will be absolutely thrilled to learn your tips for removing—"

"Don't use my name. Just 'the Dutch Maid,'" she pleads with her rose-petal eyes.

"I never reveal my sources. By the way, very neat that you're from Holland. I've always wanted to go."

"I'm half Dutch," she replies mysteriously. "The employees are from all over. We even had a valet from Malaysia, but he just left. The Websters keep an international staffing list."

*I bet they do.* "And now you're from here."

"Only until tomorrow. They're sending us back to the primary residence in Rhode Island," she says, then picks up her shopping bags, staggering under the weight of them as she resumes her trek.

Back at Primp and Ribbon, I put away my disguise, then return to my sewing machine. As I resume pleating curtains, I run through the conversation, then pause. That's funny—I didn't blurt out anything awkward or get tongue-tied once. I guess it's because I was busy pretending to be someone else.

I mull over Lieske's confessions as I brush my teeth that night. The phone rings, and I spit out my toothpaste, then pad over to my bedroom to answer it. "Hello?" I murmur, but there is only static on the other end.

I'm gargling when the ringing resumes. "This isn't funny," I tell the rotary phone, my breath minty with Listerine.

"Gertrude," says an unfamiliar voice on the other end. "My world is empty without you."

I catch my breath, then glance accusingly at the love letter on my nightstand. "Is your name Edgar?" I drop my voice as I pour myself a glass of water from the night carafe.

"In the flesh," Edgar replies sarcastically. "Gertrude, punish me! Maul me! Do your worst, my darling, just don't cast me off like this," he exclaims, and I almost drop my glass.

"I'm sorry, but you have the wrong number. I am *not* your Gertrude," I tell the phone as I take a sip of water, trying to rinse the unpleasant taste out of my mouth. "You don't know me."

Laughter mixes with static. "Darling, I know everything about you. For instance, I know that you lied to a young woman today. And I know that you're in danger."

And this time, I *do* drop my glass. It shatters across the whitewashed floor, followed by the B-flat of the dial tone.

"Did anyone catch your eye at the party?" Florence asks the next day.

I stifle a yawn as I sift through the stack of skirts that she brought in to be hemmed. The creepy caller shocked me into insomnia last night, and now Florence is adding insult to injury.

"Maybe the younger Webster?" she continues, trying on a pillbox hat.

"Maybe," I reply as I flip her tweed skirt inside out, then line up my ruler beside it.

"He is a *specimen* of handsome. Talks real fancy-like."

"He does seem capable of completing a sentence." I begin pinning the hem. "Apparently, he has an elder brother—"

"Football star. Beefcake.[a] Ripples and muscles, *oh my*," Florence simpers as she hops onto the upholstered fitting platform. She looks over her shoulder, admiring the shape of her calves in the trifold dressing mirror.

"There was also a man with a mustache," I murmur through another yawn. "Was he—"

"Teddy Brixton. Less of a specimen, but I've kissed him," Florence informs me with a devious giggle. "On the cheek. I met

---

[a] **Beefcake (n.):** *an attractive man with well-developed muscles.* This 1940s slang was inspired by *cheesecake*, a colloquial term for "sporty women with well-toned legs." Not to be outdone, the hunks of the era adopted a matching superlative, composed of *beef*, which stemmed from the Latin *bovem*, "ox, bull," and *cake*, borrowed from the Old High German *kuoho*, "a sweet pastry."

Teddy at a beach bonfire on Campobello a while ago. He hangs out with that whole Ashcroft clan." She pauses expectantly.

"Oh, Florence, that's very impressive."

Her reflection beams back at me. "It's nothing. I've just always moved in these high-end circles. The thing about rich people"—she lowers her voice confidentially—"is that they're just like us. They just want a bit of a laugh. A bit of a flirt. *I* know how to talk to them. That's why I'm always on the guest list." Florence doesn't mention her father's boatyard, which I suspect is the real reason behind her overflowing social calendar. Pelletier Yachts repairs all the expensive boats in the area, so the summer people try to keep Mr. Pelletier in their good graces. Boatbuilding is big money in Down East Maine. Not Brixton or Webster money, but Florence is still a cut above the rest of us. "Teddy and I had a moment once. I think he has a crush on me."

"But didn't he bring a date to the party? The one with—"

"The fabulous dress! Yes, I saw her!" Florence gushes. "Maybe I'll call him. I'm sure the Brixtons are in the phone book." She flounces over to inspect the skirt I've been working on, then wags her finger at me. "One inch shorter. Don't be such a square, Billie. Miniskirts only," she says. I reach for my seam ripper.

Florence's visit leaves me with four vital pieces of information.

1. That she's seriously delusional.
2. She has no idea that Teddy's girlfriend is dead.
3. What my next step should be in the investigation.
4. That I need to invest in some shorter skirts.

On June 27, the doorbell ends another fitful night of sleep. Sunlight streams past my curtains as the buzzer pulls me out of bed and over to the window. My grandfather's Buick is gone, so I'll have to answer it. I steal a quick glance in the mirror as I slip on a robe and tie back my hair. I look bad, but there's not much I can do about that in thirty seconds, so I square my shoulders and head downstairs.

Chief Deputy Gordon Abbott is standing on the front step, picking something out of his teeth. The policeman has the face and demeanor of a geriatric bulldog. "May I help you, sir?"

"Billie, a pleasure!" he wheezes as he lumbers into our living room.

I try to stop him, but he barrels past me. Use of the sitting room is highly discouraged. It's less a living space and more a showpiece, a prime example of all-American frump. Complete with a wood-veneer television / record player, a peacock fireplace screen, and novelty plates ornamenting the walls, the living room is my grandmother's pride and joy. A delicate film of dust carpets the interior. I'm pretty sure if you look up *dowdy* in the dictionary, it shows our quilted olive couch wrapped in plastic, like a giant green Twinkie.

Chief Deputy Abbott tracks mud across the carpet as he lowers himself into my grandfather's chartreuse La-Z-Boy recliner. "Do you remember seeing me at the party?" he asks. Abbott's thick Maine accent is a cross between a Southern drawl and a Scottish brogue and is virtually incomprehensible to outsiders. It clips his consonants and slurs his vowels beyond all recognition. For instance, he pronounces the word *party* like *potty*.

"Yes, at Webster Cottage." The couch squeaks as I sit down on it.

"You were the only guest allowed inside at the end of the night." The deputy grunts as he settles into the corduroy eyesore.

"Allowed inside!" I fume. "No one *invited* me in. You say that as if I were in cahoots–"

Chief Deputy Abbott raises a single finger as he puts his boots up on the footrest. "As I was sayin', you were seen *inside* the house at the end of the night. Now, you might *think* that something happened, but I'm here to tell you that it didn't. You're a smart girl. You understand this is a *sensitive* situation. We don't want word gettin' out or reputations gettin' damaged."

*Did the chief deputy just threaten my reputation?* "You're telling me not to mention what I saw?" I clarify, running a hand over my hasty ponytail.

"I'm *askin'* you not to imp-p-pede in my investigation." As Abbott trips and trembles over his words, a thin veil of sweat forms on his upper lip.

"So there *is* an investigation?"

"We don't want this turning into a witch hunt," Chief Deputy Abbott murmurs, and I narrow my eyes at him. That's a funny choice of words, considering the conversation about black magic I had earlier this week. "Our force is small and stretched thin at the moment. We have certain ways of doin' things 'round here, and I'm under a lot of pressure from–" He stops short.

"From the Websters?" I venture.

"From *unnamed* parties. So don't go blabbin' all over town. Don't go tamperin' with the other witnesses. Don't meddle." Abbott taps his fist against the armrest for emphasis with each word.

I blink at the chief deputy in confusion. How does he know that I've been asking about the murder? Did Lieske report on me? Then my jaw drops when I remember Luke warning me to keep my distance. *He told his boss! He sold me out!* My fingers itch to go through the phone book and give Luke Blackwood a piece of my mind.

"So if you think you seen somethin', keep it to yourself. I'm tellin' you this as a man of the law."

"But whose law?" I try to look intimidating, despite the pillow marks on my face.

"Huh?" The police chief's face scrunches up in rolls when he frowns, and his pink cheeks deepen to an irritated mauve. Sweat splatters across the chartreuse corduroy as he rises to his feet.

"Whose law are you upholding?" I rephrase my question. "It can't be President Lyndon Johnson's, because I'm pretty sure that he would *care* if someone were murdered."

But Chief Deputy Abbott doesn't reply. He walks back to the front door, raising a single finger. "I'm warnin' you, Billie. *Stop askin' questions.*"

"Sweet pea. Come up here," calls my grandmother.

Five minutes later, I'm sitting on the gossip bench with the phone book clenched between my knees, my fingers poised to dial the Blackwoods' number. "Now isn't a good time."

## ETIQUETTE FOR LOVERS AND KILLERS

"Honey bunch, I need you *now*." Grace's voice is steely under the sweetness. My hand leaves a smudge in the phone book as I reluctantly set it down, then climb upstairs. I find Grace sitting up in bed with the sound off on her television. An index card covered in purple ink rests on her wicker breakfast tray. "Won't you be a dear and fetch me these things?" She presses the card into my hands; I frown at her list.

- *Crème de menthe*
- *Ladyfingers*
- *Cosmopolitan, July issue*
- *Custard-flavored baby food*
- *White crème de cacao*
- *Hershey's strawberry syrup*
- *Beer shampoo*
- *Knee rouge*

"Grace, I'm kind of busy right now." This is one of the (many) problems associated with living with grandparents. They think I'm their personal errand girl. It's Saturday, and I'd like to spend it lying around, not on some senior-citizen scavenger hunt.

"Yes, I'm busy, too. Busy imagining how bothered your grandfather would be if he knew about the conversation I just overheard," Grace says as she turns up the volume on *Guiding Light*. "But I suppose that my silence *could* be bought."

## CHAPTER FIVE

# CLOTHES FOR YACHTING

*Your costume depends on the size of the boat. A sweater, a bandana, or a beret, are advisable even if you start out on a hot day in relative calm.*

I pick up a jar of "knee rouge" and catch myself glancing warily over my shoulder. As I wheel my cart into the baby food aisle, I wish I'd worn a disguise, because I don't want anyone seeing me with "beer shampoo" in my cart. I heave a sigh of relief when I reach the checkout counter, but *that's* when I'm finally spotted.

"Billie!" Avery approaches holding an achingly normal shopping basket containing a six-pack of beer and a watermelon. Carelessly bronzed by the summer sun, he's Ivy League casual today in a worn blue T-shirt and crisp jeans. His hair is carefully disheveled.

"No." My heart sinks as I throw a jar of bikini wax back into my cart.

"Yes." He smiles. "You're perfect."

"For what?" I step between him and my cart to block the incriminating evidence.

"For this afternoon. What are you up to today, besides"—he looks past me at Grace's contraband—"shampooing your hair with beer and making grasshopper cocktails?"

"I'm not—"

"Don't deny it. You have all the ingredients in your cart," he says, indicating the dusty bottle of crème de cacao. "What do you say? Want to get in some trouble?"

"Oh, I started that hours ago." I grin sheepishly as Priscilla Lyons begins ringing me up.

"It's settled then. Meet me at two p.m. at that boat you find so off-putting."

"Gosh, I didn't mean to insult your boat." My face turns an even deeper pink than my grandmother's strawberry syrup. *God, why was I so rude?* "It's more Hemingway that I don't care for. His writing is so ... masculine. It's *so* embarrassing, because who doesn't like Hemingway?" I'm officially blabbering. Priscilla regards me with pity as she rings me up for the Gerber custard baby food.

"Don't worry," Avery says with a furtive grin. "Your secret is safe with me."

"I'm afraid there are a number of them."

"Yes, I'm beginning to get that impression." He nods toward the counter as Priscilla picks up the jar of knee rouge.

I'm still spiraling over my encounter with the police as I return to the crime scene later that day. Based on Chief Deputy

Abbott's profuse sweating (*hyperhidrosis*), he was under immense strain. He wouldn't be my *top* choice to head up a murder investigation.

My bicycle tires whine as I coast down the cobblestones to Webster Cottage. My eyes narrow, scanning the grounds. But the lawn is empty and the driveway is, too, with just one green Porsche parked out front. The parents seem to have left, taking their Dutch maid with them.

Foxglove rustles around my skirt and delphinium brush against my shins. The chandelier hung from the oak tree sends sequins of light across my faded blue sundress as I hurry past rows of wild beach roses. Passamaquoddy Bay extends before me—a deep indigo dotted with white sailboats. It's a hot day, and the cool ocean air is a welcome relief as I join Avery on the dock.

"Perfect timing." Beads of sweat lightly moisten his temples as he carries a small red cooler over to the mahogany speedboat. "I hope you're up for an adventure."

"And I hope that you're not overselling it," I quip as I reach into my bag. I wasn't sure what to bring for a boating excursion, so I grabbed a sweater and a snack. "For you." I extend a blue-and-white packet.

Avery's eyes narrow at the bag of Chips Ahoy![a] "What is that?"

---

[a] **Ahoy (exclamation):** *an interjection used to hail another ship on the water.* Derived from the Middle English cry *Hoy!*, this nautical term was primarily used while sailing. Like *aloha*, *ahoy* is multipurpose and can be used for "hello," "goodbye," or as a warning.

"Are you familiar with cookies? Or are they too lowbrow for you?"

"I've never seen a baked good before in my life." He chuckles as he places the packet on the cooler, then lifts my bag into the boat. The tightly corded muscles in his forearms subtly flex as he unties the Sportabout from the rubber guards on the dock. He neatly coils up, then motions for me to scramble into the hull.

"My mother told me never to show up to someone's house empty-handed," I explain. "But she didn't specify what to bring for a boat, so I figured, Chips Ahoy! It's nautical, right? Although I'm not sure why."

"One of the great mysteries of our time," he replies as he flips the ignition and steers us away from the dock with careless precision.

Water splashes against the gunwale as Moose Island recedes behind us. Sunlight glints off the windshield as a seagull cries overhead. The salty wind ruffles my hair and rustles the pleats on my hemline. I'm elated to be out on the water. Then I catch Avery watching me with slightly parted lips and inscrutable gray eyes, and my happiness twists into something less cheery, but infinitely more appealing. I open the packet of Chips Ahoy! to distract myself. "An important question for you: Chips or cookies?" I ask, as a droplet of sweat traces the arch of his collarbone. I study the cookies intently.

"What about chips *in* cookies?" he counters, reaching for one of the cookies.

"Not an option." I hold the packet out of his reach.

"Cookies," he replies with a grin as we cut through a school of menhaden, spangling the waves with flecks of silver. We cruise into the Western Passage, a turbulent stretch of water running between Maine and Canada that extends across the imaginary country line. He angles the boat to the right, and the slight shift brings me closer to him. The incessant beat of the ocean speeds up around us, as if it's also on a first date.

"And to your left, you'll see Old Sow. Undoubtedly the *worst* name for a whirlpool in history." Avery affects the voice of a tour guide as the whitecaps grow around us, and I wobble over to the port side of the boat to study it.

"It *is* rather garish, isn't it?" I call over the churning waves as spume shoots up to spangle the air. Old Sow is the largest whirlpool in the western hemisphere, so named for the piglike noises that it makes when spinning. The bathtub-drain aesthetic is caused by forty billion cubic feet of water flooding into the bay at high tide, which collides with the rivers and streams that also empty into the ocean. When these opposing currents meet over a trench bisected by an underwater mountain, they create an eerie circle of water that dips beneath the ocean's surface, then spirals down to the ocean floor. Dozens of boats have flirted with disaster and lost here over the years. But that doesn't stop the local male population from coming back for more. Because there's nothing quite so macho as getting shipwrecked for absolutely no reason.

"Frightfully overdone." Avery shakes his head and gives the whirlpool a wide berth.

Something glints in my peripheral vision, and I narrow my eyes at Webster Cottage on the distant shore. I hadn't realized that the estate was located directly across from the whirlpool.

What does that say about the Websters: that they built a mansion with a front-row view of a natural disaster? We turn to the right, passing the grim little column of the Deer Island Point Lighthouse as a hush settles between us. "A fun conversation or a comfortable silence?" I ask, offering him a cookie.

"Comfortable silence," Avery replies, as he eats it thoughtfully.

"That's a lie." I frown. "You're not an introvert. You were so gregarious at the party."

"A sad truth. But please don't tell anyone; I would hate to ruin my reputation," he confides as he steers us past Cherry Island. The island is cute, much like Avery's embarrassment at this moment.

"So let's be unfashionable together," I murmur, crunching on another cookie. "We could have our own private club of outcasts."

"That sounds too trendy for me," he replies as he turns the mahogany wheel. As *Poppy* cuts through the waves, it finally dawns on me: *That* is why Avery wanted to show me his boat the other night. Where I have my books, he has this dumb boat. They're both just tricks to keep us from feeling lonely.

Passamaquoddy Bay is home to over two hundred islands. Some are tiny tufts of grass rising above the waves, while others are craggy monoliths. Eastport is on Moose Island, which vaguely resembles a giant pair of antlers. Farther out are Bliss Island, Treat Island, Popes Island, Hospital Island, and the Wolves, a cluster of desolate rocks scattered along the entrance to Passamaquoddy Bay. The islands grow progressively more rugged the farther they drift from shore. Avery motions toward a sandstone cliff shaped like a giant stick of cotton candy. It looks half eaten and diaphanous, as if a single wave might send it crashing down.

My father used to take me sailing and point out these islands, much as Avery is doing now. Recently, I've shied away from those memories, because they became too painful. But being out here on the water today, laughing and eating awful cookies while the sun beats down, those memories aren't quite so awful. Because my grief has softened. It isn't a whirlpool anymore, but more like the salt air–faint but pervasive. And it doesn't stifle me because I've learned how to breathe.

We approach a sheltered cove lined with wind-worn cliffs and a tall red lighthouse perched high atop the bluffs. The Head Harbour Lightstation is one of the oldest lighthouses on the East Coast. Hazy sunlight glints off the giant lantern to dazzle my eyes. Avery sets the engine in neutral and drops anchor. The chain jangles loudly as it unspools through the windlass, then Avery pushes down the chain stopper to secure the line to the bow cleat. He unstraps a kayak from the back of the boat while I try not to stare at the casual definition of his triceps. Instead, I grab a couple of beers from the cooler and put them in a canvas tote. He takes the bag and motions toward the kayak. "I hope you're not scared of the water."

"Wouldn't that be hilarious?" I reply as I climb down the ladder and lower myself into the kayak. As I hold on to the ladder, Avery passes me a paddle, then climbs in after me.

We paddle to a beach carpeted in smooth, round pebbles.

**ETIQUETTE FOR LOVERS AND KILLERS**

Avery opens a beer (*Rheingold Extra Dry,* I note with amusement, the most pretentious beer available), and we pass it back and forth as the afternoon puddles around us. It melts over his skin, coating him in an even deeper shade of bronze. The air is sweet and salty–jammy with sun-ripened blueberries and briny with seaweed, gently rustling through the saplings and wildflowers that cling to the sheer cliffs. We lounge across a sun-soaked ledge and point up at the clouds. One looks like a rabbit and the other a martini. It's hard to imagine being happier than I am at this moment. I'm on actual cloud nine.[b]

"I'd seen you in Eastport a few times, but I could never work up the courage to talk to you," Avery confides, his eyes fixed on the fluffy cumulus clouds high above us.

"Because I'm so intimidating?" I turn on my side to gaze at him.

"Because you looked so content on your own. I didn't want to take that from you."

"Well, I'm glad that you did. Because this has been a very welcome distraction, and ... a nice date." I glance at him shyly, then lie back against the warm granite, training my eyes on the flimsy tufts overhead. The first strokes of pink and purple are starting to drip across the pale blue canvas of sky.

"Billie, no one said this was a date," Avery corrects me with amusement.

---

[b] **Cloud nine (n.):** *a state of bliss.* The first edition of the *International Cloud Atlas* (p. 1896) documented ten types of clouds. *Cumulonimbus* was the ninth kind, you know, those lovely, fluffy white clouds, way up high. Most clouds hang about 3.75 miles over the earth, but *cumulonimbus* rises over 6 miles into the atmosphere. *Cumulonimbus* clouds are rare, which makes sense, because you can't be on *cloud nine* all the time, or it wouldn't be very special anymore.

"Wait, it isn't a date?" I sit up, frowning in confusion.

"It's mostly an apology," he murmurs, pushing the hair out of his face. "To be frank, I'm mortified about the party the other night—"

"Avery, I don't blame you for what happened!"

"You saw a lot of bad behavior. Unspeakable lack of decorum. Even *my father* was rude to you on the stairs. We're normally polite people. Actually civilized on occasion. And I'm just . . . I'm deeply ashamed by what you saw," he says, shaking his head.

I reach for my beer and absently pick at the label. "Did you know the woman at the party?" I've been trying not to fixate on Gertrude this afternoon, but now Avery has mentioned the party, so she's back with a vengeance.

"I mostly knew of her. She was a bit larger than life."

"She was *such* a leading lady," I murmur, and he chokes on his beer.

"She would have loved to hear you say that."

"Do you know her fiancé as well? The one with the Mark Twain mustache?"

Avery snorts, and a shadow passes across his eyes. "Teddy, that son of a bitch."

I frown at my Rheingold Extra Dry as I try to organize my thoughts. *So I know of three men claiming a relationship with Gertrude. My primary suspects:*

- *Teddy, with his nasal voice, silly bow tie, and twitching mustache.*

- *Edgar, who sent me the letter that sparked all this. His gravelly voice recently disrupted my beauty sleep, but I've never actually met him.*
- *And the big blond brute from the hallway. Name unknown.*

She certainly had *wildly* diverse taste in men.

"It was no secret that Gertrude was cheating on him," Avery continues, setting down his beer. "And Teddy just turned a blind eye. What a spineless fool."

"Do you think he's capable of killing someone?" I reach for Avery's beer and begin picking off his label, too.

"Teddy could barely order a drink on his own, let alone cover up a murder," Avery says with a shrug. "He's as complacent as a lapdog, but I suppose that even poodles go rabid." He pauses as I succeed in peeling off his label and toss it on the rocks. "Darling, please don't litter. I hate a mess." He scoops it up.

"A little mess might be good for you," I reply, taking in Avery's crisp T-shirt, jeans, and the languid swoop of his sandy hair. Carelessly neat, his one imperfection is the fine dusting of salt clinging to the blond hairs on his forearms after our afternoon on the water.

But he doesn't respond, just shields his eyes and gazes out toward the west, where the sun hangs low over the horizon. "We should head back soon. It's time."

"Time to trespass and climb to the top of the lighthouse?" I ask, hoping to delay the inevitable. I'm not ready to return to my grandparents just yet. I'd prefer to keep living in this daydream a bit longer.

His laughter is so deep that I feel my skin prickle in response. "No, although I must say that your interest in criminal activity is—"

"Concerning?"

"I was going to say 'charming.' Will you think I'm an awful bore if we stay down here?"

I gape at Avery as the waves splash against the pebble beach. "Wait, you wanted to come all this way and *not* climb the lighthouse? Why bother going to a party if you're going to stop at the door?"

"Okay, but if we go to jail, *you're* paying the legal fees," Avery admonishes, rising to his feet. As I follow him up the eighty stone steps hewn into the cliff face, a blaze of orange and gold ignites the glass dome at the top of the lighthouse. "Can we really go up there? What if we get in trouble?" He frowns at the ladder fixed to the side of the octagonal crimson tower.

"Why do you love rules so much?" I counter, my left foot already on the first rung. "Avery, the first rule of dating is that a little danger increases your sex appeal," I say with a flippant hair toss, channeling Gertrude as I pull myself up the ladder. The wind whips around me, tugging at my clothing as I reach the narrow platform at the top.

Passamaquoddy Bay is iridescent, like a mud puddle swirled with gasoline. The sunset glistens off the waves as a wall of fog sweeps in from the north. The view is breathtaking, and the wind even more so. It whips around me and yanks at my dress as a gust threatens to hurl me off the edge.

"The breeze is fierce, isn't it?" Avery says as he joins me at the top.

"It's a little too much for me," I call over the rising wind as we stand there together at the top of the Head Harbour Lightstation. Avery is so close that I can feel his body heat curling against mine. The wind whips my hair around, and a few locks boldly stroke his cheeks. He reaches up to brush them away, then pauses to study me. Do his eyes light up, or is that just the sunset's reflection?

"I love how it has messed you up," he murmurs softly.

"But I thought that you hated a mess," I reply, my heart in my throat.

"I lied," he admits, then leans in. And for a moment, I forget about being pummeled by gale-force winds. Forget about Gertrude, the police, and the diamond ring. For a moment, his expression drowns everything else out. Then Avery puts a hand out protectively over the edge of the parapet. "Billie, you are ruining my lighthouse experience. Please be careful."

I lean back against the glass dome as the blood hammers in my ears. Here I am, thinking that we're having a romantic moment, and he's just concerned that I'm a safety hazard! A gut-wrenching boom sounds off behind us, giving voice to my internal dismay as the foghorn chases away any last fleeting whisper of chemistry. Like the honk of a colossal tuba, it's both a warning and an advertisement for the treacherous underwater terrain in Passamaquoddy Bay. My eardrums quake as the high-decibel noise broadcasts from the top of the lighthouse. I glance up at the wall of windows and mirrors, then out at the distant fogbank. This light is going to turn on any second. We should probably save going deaf *and* blind for date number two.

*Oh right, but this* isn't *a date.*

"Let's get out of here." Avery motions toward the ladder. "Ladies first."

Maybe I *have* gone deaf, because I can't hear anything as I climb down from the lighthouse. Or as I rush down the steps. Or as I clamber across the pebble beach. My eardrums finally start working as I climb up the ladder into the speedboat, and Avery directs me to turn on the ignition. He pulls in the kayak and reels in the anchor.

The lighthouse turns on as we hurry away from the cove. The fog nips at the stern, hovering at the edge of our navigation lights. Avery keeps his eyes trained on the growing waves as we race through the gathering twilight and the beam from the lighthouse recedes behind us.

Webster Cottage glitters under a veil of mist, with the light from the mansion reflecting back toward itself. I steer *Poppy* up to the dock while Avery throws down the rubber fenders on the starboard side. I switch off the ignition as he ties us to the mooring cleats. I'm feeling rather pleased with myself. I've never driven a speedboat before.

We make our way through the gardens up to the carport. A new car is parked out front, this one a flashy red Aston Martin. I approach the hunter-green Porsche that I noted earlier, which has the words *1600-SUPER* printed on the back. That seems like a misnomer, seeing as the convertible isn't so much "super," as it is sexy as hell. Avery grabs my beach cruiser and wheels it over to the Porsche. "But what about your upholstery?" I protest. "What about–"

"You're not biking home in the dark." Avery waves away my objections as he lifts up the hood of his car. "That would be very unchivalrous of me."

"Someone stole your engine." I peer past him into the empty recess at the front.

He laughs as he grabs a blanket, then shuts the hood. "The engine is in the back. Things are different in Germany." He lays the blanket across the soft-top canvas hood, then picks up my bike and lowers it into the space between the front seat and the retractable roof, which fits my bike like a glove. Then he opens the passenger-side door and gestures for me to climb in. Sliding onto the seat, I study the cream interior. Everything is supple or lacquered to within an inch of its life. Even the wooden steering wheel is wrapped in soft tan leather. There are wooden accents throughout and a gold Porsche logo on the dashboard.

The front door of the house opens, and a dark shadow leans across the entrance, backlit by the brilliant foyer. "You can't escape from me that easy," calls the silhouette.[c]

---

[c] **Silhouette (n.):** *a dark outline of a shape against a lighter background.* Black-and-white portraits called *silhouettes* became wildly popular in France during the 1750s. For unknown reasons, this design craze was nicknamed for the minister of finance at the time, Étienne de *Silhouette*. His surname stemmed from the Basque *Zulueta*. *Zulo* means "gaping hole," and *eta* means "abundance," so *Zulueta* literally translates to "an abundance of nothing."

Avery grits his teeth, then turns with a smile. "Claude, you made it."

As the figure approaches, I suck in a sharp breath. *It's the brute from the hallway! The man who was kissing Gertrude!* The newcomer is at least five inches taller than Avery, with a shock of blond hair and a fresh scar on his temple. He still reeks of cologne and he still has a swathe of chest hair, so at least he's a reliable villain. There is something of the Big Bad Wolf in his demeanor. I wonder which piglet I would be in this scenario: the one who built her house out of straw, sticks, or bricks?

"There's my girl." Claude raises one eyebrow as he takes a lingering sip from his rocks glass. And it's his eyebrow, more than anything else, that stops me cold. I look toward my driver and consider his arched blond eyebrows. They're the same. This is Avery's brother, the one Lieske warned me about.

"You know each other?" Avery's expression of ironic disinterest looks slightly more strained than usual.

"In the biblical sense," the other man replies with a lecherous smirk.

"He just made a crude joke at the party. It's nothing." I narrow my eyes at him.

"What's your name, sugar?" Claude asks as he leans against my door.

"That's Billie," Avery says. I'm amused by the possessive tone in his voice.

"Well, 'Billie,'" Claude says, "you must return to entertain me some evening."

Avery flicks on the lights and revs his Porsche. "I'll catch up with you when I'm done playing chauffeur," he calls to his brother, then edges the convertible along the wraparound driveway. Moose Island is already sleeping, with just a few lit houses surrounded by empty shoreline and dense fog.

"Why don't you like your brother?" I ask as he turns left onto Route 190 and begins driving back to town. He switches on the heat, and it puffs out of the vents as the cool night air eddies around us. The contrast of hot air against the chill night sky is exhilarating. This is the first time I've ridden in a convertible—a milestone I hadn't realized I was missing until this moment.

"I would keep my distance from him if I were you," Avery replies without inflection.

"And what about you?" I ask curiously.

"I keep as much distance from him as possible," he responds briskly, switching on the car's 8-track player. A cheerful voice emerges from the single speaker, accompanied by upbeat percussion and the trill of a saxophone.

"What is this?" I ask as we pass Pelletier Yachts with its graveyard of unfinished boats.

"'Sunny' by Bobby Hebb," Avery replies, his face briefly illuminated by the glare of oncoming headlights. The lyrics of the song are as perky as the title, but the chorus has an underlying melancholy, much like my driver. The Porsche seems a little pensive as well, lingering along the island's curves as fog drifts past us in breathy tufts.

"Why do you come to Maine?" I ask as the piano and guitar strings flirt across the stereo.

"I like the peace and quiet. And the ocean. It's a nice place to think." He glances at me with a hint of something deep, solemn, and almost sad glinting in the depths of his pewter eyes.

"And what about your brother? What brings him to Eastport? Oops, turn here."

Avery grins as he almost—but doesn't quite—pass my house. "One can only imagine."

He parks outside my grandparents' Cape Cod–style house, then leans in. And for the fortieth time, I hope that he might kiss me. Hug me. Accidentally brush my arm. Give me *any* indication *at all* of wayward intent. But everything is disappointingly aboveboard as he climbs out of the car, then walks around to open my door. His chivalry[d] must just be a habit. "I hope that I didn't bore you too much today," he says as he lifts my bike out.

"It was all right," I reply, reaching for the handlebars.

As Avery passes me the bike, his right hand rests gently on top of mine. Firmly. It lingers there for a moment too long, as a shiver of warmth runs through me. I look up in confusion, hyperaware of every inch of contact. Then our eyes meet, and he steps away as if nothing happened.

"Good night, Billie," he says with a brusque nod, striding back around his car. I continue standing there, the warmth of his skin lingering against mine. My eyes focus on his right hand, noting how it grips the tan leather around the wooden steering wheel just a little too hard.

As I step inside, I'm greeted by the smoky aroma of shrimp creole and gossip from the harbor. Ben Kane caught a rare blue

---

[d] **Chivalry (n.):** *polite and kind behavior, especially by men toward women.* Derived from Old French *chevalerie*, "cavalry, the art of war," *chivalry* became a glorified term in medieval Europe for "a host of brave knights." Over the last 800 years, *chivalry* transitioned from the battleground to the bedroom, where the dashing white knight lives on as an ideal for all of us damsels in dating distress.

lobster today (a very lucky thing! It's the shellfish equivalent of winning the lottery), and it's all anyone can talk about. Upstairs, Grace cackles along with the laugh track to *Candid Camera*. And everything is so nice and normal that it makes the fog and Avery's speedboat seem even farther away.

## CHAPTER SIX

# SWIMMING DECORUM

*Don't wear a conspicuous bathing suit. And don't bathe with strange men; the etiquette of introduction is just as strict in the water as in the drawing room.*

Two rejection letters and four job applications today: the circle of life moves in fast-forward at the Eastport Post Office. As I mail out the letters of interest to various museums, I hold my breath and make a wish. Then I notice Mrs. Cobb tapping her foot behind me. My wishful thinking is taking too long.

"Happy third of July!" Mr. Townsend appears at my side with a jar of boysenberries and two boxes. I flush as I tuck the first package under my arm (a special order of frilly lace panties and bras from the Sears Catalog), then gaze warily at the second. "What could it be?" Mr. Townsend asks, eyes alight with curiosity. *Well, at least one of us has their dream job.*

I'm still smarting from the rejection letters as I weave through the crowds back to work. I'm going nowhere fast, but I'm still moving too quickly for the tide of foot traffic. As I collide with a slender, blond figure, the scent of pastry dough and fruity body lotion fills my nose. "Gosh, I'm sorry. What a dummy!" I bubble over with apologies.

My victim is your quintessential girl next door, with a simple blue sundress, bright white tennis shoes, and a pie carrier. She sways precariously under her precious cargo. Her long blond ponytail slices gracefully through the air as she almost–but doesn't quite–hit the pavement. Then she rights herself at the last moment with an adroit twist, raising to her full height. "Don't worry about it, hon," she says with a kind smile. "Thanks for keeping me on my toes!" She steadies the pie carrier against her chest with one hand, waves at a receding group of girls with the other, and rushes after them.

A cake carrier or pastry box must be a required fashion accessory today, because everyone seems to have one. Today is the July 3rd Bake Off–not to be confused with the Blueberry Pie Eating Contest, the Watermelon Eating Contest, or the Hot Dog Eating Contest. Other Independence Day highlights include: rubber duck racing, a dog beauty pageant, and balancing on a greasy pole over the harbor. The more pointless the activity, the greater we excel at it.

Back at Primp and Ribbon, Mrs. Pridmore is pure Americana, with a striped blue skirt and daring red blouse. She hums "America the Beautiful," as she opens a fresh shipment of high-waisted *Gidget*-style bikinis, then begins sewing loops of thread and attaching price tags. My sewing machine is unimpressed. The tension is all wonky, and the bottom layer of fabric keeps getting balls of thread stuck in it. The machine growls as Mrs. Pridmore swigs from her stars-and-stripes mug.

"It's your bobbin," she calls from behind the cash register. But I refuse to fix it, and the sound gets worse. Finally, Mrs. Pridmore sighs. "Get out of here. I can't take that racket." It's only 2 p.m., but I don't ask questions, just grab my things and flee before she changes her mind.

American flags litter the landscape like confetti, ornamenting every lawn, window box, and lobster boat. The air is perfumed by charcoal grills and coconut-scented sunblock. Wildflowers bob their heads as though participating in the festivities, and everyone is wearing red, white, and denim. Floats are lined up in preparation for tomorrow's parade, and trucks wear sashes like beauty queens. The baking contest is wrapping up in the Village Green, where the young woman I almost trampled holds a pie aloft, a second-place ribbon fluttering above her head. The red satin rosette catches the light, gleaming off her bright blond bangs. Her vanilla complexion is flushed with pride. Beside her, a poster proclaims, *Celebrate Our Heritage.* But it seems less our heritage, our nation, or even our pies that we're celebrating, so much as our love of American kitsch.

I make a quick detour on Key Street for my swimsuit. My shoes slap against the steps to my grandparents' house as I race upstairs. "Honey muffin!" Grace calls, but I'm already gone.

The pavement sizzles beneath my tires. The beige clapboard houses and white sand beaches sear themselves into my corneas as I try to out-pedal my impatience with living in a Wonder Bread commercial. It's a relief to reach the mainland and leave Eastport behind. The eastern white pines surrounding Boyden Lake rise up protectively above me, providing much-needed shade and blanketing my path with fragrant pine needles.

Trespassing is more difficult in high season, but I enjoy the challenge. I bike down one dirt road after another before I find a likely suspect. The little log cabin has weeds in the front yard and a general air of neglect. I stash my bike in a ditch and walk through a tangle of lupines and daisies in the backyard as dandelion heads burst under my feet. I approach a rickety dock and spread my towel across the uneven wooden planks. I put on my heart-shaped sunglasses and lie out in my new polka-dot bikini,[a] watching pontoon boats glide across the lake like obese swans. The sky is white with heat, glistening above me. I gaze out at the waves, and the waves gaze back expectantly. What am I waiting for?

Ice-cold water hits my skin. The cold is a welcome relief, pulling the heat from my pores as practiced strokes draw me past the cattails and lake weeds. I take a deep breath, then dive down to the bottom of the lake and shoot back up. Beads of water catch the sunlight as my arms break through the surface, then pull me back to shore. I climb out of the water and lie out across my towel as sunlight dries my swimsuit. I guess there are

---

[a] **Bikini (n.):** *a woman's two-piece bathing suit.* This summer wardrobe staple was designed by Louis Reard in 1946. Reard named his creation after the Bikini Atoll in the South Pacific, an atomic testing site. A truncation of *pikinni* from the Marshall Islands, composed of *pik,* "flat plane" and *ni,* "coconut." Reard wanted his bikinis to make an explosive fashion statement, although my bikini is less bombshell chic and more like a flat coconut.

a few perks to being trapped inside a Norman Rockwell painting after all.

Plus, it gives me something to rebel against.

My revolt is hidden in my straw bag. I rummage through it for Gertrude's diamond ring, a greeting card, and a ballpoint pen. The card has a watercolor of lilies of the valley (an odd choice for a blackmail letter, but I was hardly going to order new stationery for the occasion) and an envelope typed out with Teddy Brixton's address. Florence was right—he *is* in the phone book. I push my heart-shaped sunglasses up on my forehead, flip onto my stomach, and uncap my pen.

*My Poor Teddy Bear,*
  *Bad manners are never in style, and you've committed some serious fashion faux pas. I know what you did. And where, when, and with whom. And it would be a shame if everyone else knew, too.*
  *But I'm willing to keep your secret. For a price.*

I nibble my pen cap as a flock of ducks swims past. Obviously, I'm bluffing. I don't know Teddy's secret, but I know that he has one. I've never seen anyone so guilty in my life. He looked caught red-handed when the cops dragged him out of Webster Cottage, and I'd like to know why.

What would set the mood for a blackmail rendezvous? A cemetery in the middle of the night? A creepy island, like Jail Island or Hospital Island? The Wood Island Lighthouse, which everyone says is haunted? I bite my lip as I think of a mutually inconvenient place, then pick a date a month out to allow for postal irregularities.

> *If you want to keep your reputation intact, then meet me at 3 p.m. on August 3rd at Fish Camp in Friars Bay on Campobello. Come alone and bring $100. Or else.*

I'm not interested in a hundred dollars (although it would certainly enhance my personal library), but I *am* interested in Teddy. I'm also interested in the new bar on Campobello. Fish Camp opened last year to rave reviews. It's supposed to have stylish decor and an impressive cocktail menu.

> *Xo,*
> *Gertrude (just kidding)*

It's such a simple thing: a forgery. It's so easy to scrawl someone else's name across the bottom of a card. It makes me curious about the letter from Edgar that started all this. Why did he write to me, or was that a forgery, too? I put away the blackmail, pull on my *Lolita* sunglasses, then lie back across the thick navy stripes in my polka-dot bikini.

A loon cries out. The slippery song weaves into my heat-induced coma. I blink groggily at the low-hanging sun, the peach-fuzz sky, and the dock rotting beneath me. My back hurts, my lips are chapped, and I'm pink as undercooked salmon. My skin is already shivering with the promise of a sunburn. I pull off my sunglasses and riffle through my bag for my dress, then frown at the two boxes inside. My lingerie order and the mystery package. *What is it?* I shiver again. *I hope to God it's a sweater.*

The box doesn't have a return address, just my PO box number scrawled across the cardboard in blocky numbers. I grapple with the tape until the cardboard rips open, then gulp down a scream.

A knife is swaddled in a kitchen towel. The blade is about two inches wide and eight inches long, stained with rusty red drips. It looks thicker and sharper than your average kitchen knife. I press my pinkie finger against it, then wince as it slices my skin.

Blood glistens through the sherbet sunset as the blade clatters across the dock. I grit my teeth and apply pressure to my finger as I kneel down on the rotting wood. A prickly feeling of foreboding wells up as I glance from the ruddy stains to the diamond on my finger. I'd bet my whole (underwhelming) paycheck that the blood belongs to Gertrude. This is the blade that killed her. And now my fingerprints are all over it. *Perfect.*

A branch snaps, followed by the crunch of a shoe on dead leaves. *Shit.* I look around wildly. *The owners of the camp must have come home!* They're going to find me in a bikini, with a murder weapon, trespassing on their property. I suppress a hysterical giggle, because it's so awful that it's actually kind of funny.

I suck the blood off my finger as I pull on my sundress (inside out, but it hardly matters if I'm going straight to jail), then grab the knife and toss it in the box. I stash my sundries in the straw bag, then sling it over my shoulder. No time for shoes, so

I grab them and race forward barefoot, my pinkie still pressed to my lips.

But there aren't any lights in the cabin. No *oohs* or *aahs* from tourists getting all hot and bothered over the great outdoors. *So what did I hear?* I keep a cautious eye on the windows as I creep around the edge of the property. The dirt road is silky beneath my bare feet as I pull my bike out of the ditch and pause to slip on my saddle shoes. As I stow my things in the wicker basket, I finally notice the silence. The quiet announces itself so sharply. There's no wind in the trees or squirrels scurrying through the bushes, as if the forest is holding its breath. *Waldeinsamkeit* is the German word for "the intense feeling of being alone in the woods."

The fizzy orange sunset deepens to something more sinister as I hear crackles in the underbrush behind me. "I know you're out there," I call to the gathering darkness. I've felt eyes on my back for weeks. Heard footsteps trailing behind me. If someone is following me, I want to look them in the face and know why.

A dark shadow steps out of the gloomy forest and resolves itself into a man with an ugly hat. I frown. Did a stranger *really* follow me into the woods? Things like this don't really happen, do they? Not to nice young ladies in rural New England. Could this be a dream? But my sunburned skin and bloody finger assure me otherwise.

"Come out where I can see you." My voice quavers with false bravado as I hunt through my bike basket for the knife, then brandish it at my stalker.

Twigs cling to his creased trousers, and leaves are stuck in the rolled-up sleeves of his shirt. He's in his mid-forties, with broad shoulders, bristly hair, and a patchy five-o'clock shadow. His face might have been handsome once but has since fallen on hard times. He's the kind of ugly that some women find attractive. The kind of reprobate who they might coo over and say, *He's such a man!* as if it were a rare commendation and didn't apply to half of the population. His fedora was a poor choice.

"Ah, to be young and alive on a summer evening. You're going to look back on this someday with nostalgia." As he speaks, the hair prickles up on the back of my neck. Why does his voice sound so familiar?

"Who are you?" I point my knife at him again.

"It's rude to ask questions that you already know the answer to," the stranger retorts. His raspy laughter gives him away. *I know that laugh.* It's the same laugh that has been calling my house, disrupting my beauty sleep.

"You're Edgar," I murmur with wide eyes. So *this* is Gertrude's ex-boyfriend! He is Teddy's opposite in every way. Her taste in men was even more varied than I thought!

"Who else?" He shrugs as the crickets begin crooning softly around us.

"How long have you been following me?" I demand.

"For long enough to know your secrets," he replies, stepping forward.

As his shadow lengthens across the dirt road, I take a step back, shifting my weight as I look from him to the knife and then back again. The chirping insects echo my uncertainty. Should I tell him off? Threaten to call the cops once I get home? "Edgar, there must be some mistake," I finally say, erring on the side of politeness. "This is all some big misunderstanding. My name is Billie, not Gertrude. And I don't have any secrets, I'm just a nice, local girl–"

"One with a knife?" Edgar replies with one raised eyebrow, and my toasted skin burns a little hotter. "All you've got is secrets, you little fool. You're a thief and a liar, especially to yourself. I came here to warn you because Gertrude–"

"Gertrude and I have *nothing* in common," I snap, my terror quickly giving way to irritation. My ears perk up at the sound of tires crunching on the gravel road in the distance.

"Then why are you wearing her ring?" Edgar asks as the diamond catches the light from the oncoming headlights. "Gertrude, 'Billie,' whatever you want to call yourself–you're in danger. And I came here to warn you–"

Headlights illuminate the dirt road as a station wagon approaches. Edgar steps back to let it pass, while I hop onto my bike and make my getaway. My breath comes fast as I course down one road after another. An owl hoots softly from the branches overhead as I strain my eyes against the gloom, praying that I don't hit a pothole and go flying.

Amateur fireworks light my way back home. They flare across the antler curves of Moose Island as I coast past the dark beaches and slumbering boats. Another spark of electricity as I pass Webster Cottage, which is lit up like a Roman candle in the darkness. My left hand clutches the brake instinctively, but I relax my grip. *What am I thinking? I can't just show up uninvited. And why would I want to go there in the first place?*

The pyrotechnics exhaust themselves in one last brilliant fizzle as the mansion recedes behind me. Smoke settles across the landscape; it tastes sweet and metallic on my lips.

## CHAPTER SEVEN

# PARDON MY REACH

*Sometimes a couple dining in a restaurant wish to taste each other's food. This is informal but permissible, though only if a fresh fork or spoon is used. One must not reach across the table and eat from a companion's plate.*

A Sadie Hawkins date is when a girl asks a boy out, but what do you call it if she does so over blackmail?

In movies, the blackmailer is always a gangster with a briefcase in a revved-up Cadillac, never a girl in a sundress. And the rendezvous point is usually an alleyway or a warehouse under the cover of darkness, not a cute coastal bar in the mid-afternoon.

Fish Camp has several hundred buoys lining the exterior, an upside-down canoe suspended from the ceiling, and one pissed-off mustache. The tackle shop aesthetic is offset by copper light fixtures and lacquered wood. The porch looks out onto a row of circular salmon pens in Friars Bay, where several boats are out tending the fish.

Teddy is wearing a plain white V-neck, chinos, a simple black cardigan with the collar flipped up, and white sneakers. His chestnut hair catches the light as an oversize watch glistens on his wrist. His mustache twitches as he snaps his fingers at the bartender. "Is the chef sailing to France for my fries?" he barks, then turns back to his half-finished beer.

I climb up onto a stool at the far end of the bar and set down my straw purse on the counter. "One Bloody Mary, please," I ask, keeping my gaze trained straight ahead. My hair is wind-blown from sitting in the back of the postal boat, beside crates of mail bound for Campobello. I smooth it down as the bartender, with the cookie-cutter attractiveness of bartenders everywhere, serves my drink. I pour some Tabasco sauce in my cocktail, then bide my time.

It takes thirty seconds before Teddy scoots down the counter to join me. "Do you come here often?" he asks.

I glance up with a disinterested smile, then return my gaze to my tomato juice cocktail. *Thank God, he doesn't remember me!* "It's my first time," I reply primly, trying to contain my nervousness. "I'm just visiting."

"Me too. Where from?" Teddy's voice is just as nasal as I remember.

"Connecticut." I remove an olive from the tiny plastic sword garnishing my drink.

"Groovy. My girlfriend is from there," Teddy remarks, and I

nod imperceptibly. That's what Lieske said. My patchy, last-minute cover story was designed to prompt a few more details about the deceased. "Whereabouts?"

"Greenwich." I reply with one of the state's more affluent communities. "What a small world! I wonder if I know her family . . ." I trail off as the bartender approaches with Teddy's French fries. Steam curls off them appetizingly, and I eat the olive to content myself.

"Cool. She's from New Canaan, so right by you. Last name is Taylor." Teddy reaches for the ketchup and pours out half of the bottle in a single *glug*. It seeps across the wicker basket of fries, staining the newspaper they're wrapped in. "Oops. She *was* from there." He corrects himself. "God, I keep forgetting to use the past tense."

"Oh, she moved?" I ask innocently.

Teddy doesn't reply, just gestures toward his basket. "Help yourself."

"What brings you out here today?" I ask, eyes fixed on his fries. According to Miss Vanderbilt, the only polite way to eat someone else's fries is if a waiter plates a portion, then re-serves it to you. I would hate to cause offense by just digging in. "Did you read about it in *Down East* magazine, too?"

"I sail over here sometimes," Teddy explains through a mouthful of fries. The smell is mouthwatering. "I have a place down the coast, and one of my friends summers here. I like Campobello. There isn't too much riffraff." His sharp green eyes dart over to the embroidered lemons on my dress, as if trying to determine if I'm one of the "riffraff."

"How neat that you sailed here!" I bow to temptation and

dip a fry in ketchup. After all, Miss Vanderbilt probably wouldn't approve of blackmail, either.

"Yeah, it *is* pretty neat. I'm actually a pretty neat guy, I'm just a little thrown off today." He downs his beer, then signals the bartender. "Garçon!"

"Well, you don't show it. You seem very put together."

"I try my best." His mustache twitches with pleasure, there are a few salt crystals stuck in it. "I was supposed to meet someone here, but I don't think they're gonna show. Must have been a prank."

"How rude!"

Teddy heaves a sigh as the bartender refreshes his beer. "That's generally the theme around here."

"Could it be a friend playing a prank on you?" I glance around, then lean across the bar to steal a napkin.

Teddy takes a lingering sip of beer as his eyes darken with suspicion. "Where did you go to school? You look familiar."

I bite my lip, feeling caught. *Why didn't I research girls' schools in Connecticut?* I consider making one up, but decide against it. The only way to impress Teddy is by being even more ridiculous than he is. "The only education I need is at the debutante ball," I reply with a shrug. "School is so low class."

Teddy swigs from his fresh beer, nodding emphatically. "I couldn't agree with you more."

"Where did you go?"

"Harvard." He sighs, and it takes all my self-control not to laugh in his face.

"And what did you study?" I continue, perhaps a little too eagerly.

"Business administration. Wait, why are we playing twenty questions?"

I look around uncertainly, then relax when the bartender comes to my rescue. "Seventy cents, please," he says with generic charm,[a] wiping his hands on his half apron. "Anything else for the lady?"

"This was more than enough. Thank you." I withdraw the change from my wallet, then stand up. "I have to run to catch the ferry, but it sure was a pleasure, Teddy." I smile as I steal one last French fry. Gertrude's ex offers a dismal nod before returning glumly to his beer. As I walk away, I notice the top of a hundred-dollar bill sticking out of his back pocket.

My strappy yellow sandals carry me across the street and up a hillside overlooking Friars Bay. I sit down on a park bench and pull my father's binoculars out of my straw purse, training them on Fish Camp. It's nice that Campobello is deserted, so there is no one to comment on my field glasses. No one to impress with my bird-watching skills. I turn the focus wheel and squint through the eyepiece as Teddy emerges from the restaurant. He leans against the gray clapboard wall and lights a cigarette.

My eyes widen when Skip Ashcroft appears a minute later, his ginger hair flaring up in the August sun as he strides irritably down the sidewalk. I zoom in with my binoculars. Skip's

---

[a] **Charm (n.):** *the power of pleasing or attracting people.* In twelfth-century France, a *charme* was a "magic spell," derived from the Latin *carmen*, "enchantment, religious creed," and the PIE root *kan*, "to sing." The modern sense of "having a pleasing, attractive quality" didn't emerge until the seventeenth century, which led to the girlish *charm bracelet* (1941), *charm the pants off of* (1925), and *Lucky Charms* cereal (1964).

face is almost as red as the stripes on his boatneck shirt. I wish I could hear their conversation as Skip stomps around the corner of the building and throws up his hands. Teddy follows after him, trying to calm him down, but Skip isn't having it. He shakes his head, then looks both ways and kisses Teddy squarely on the mouth.

I set down the field glasses in my lap, feeling every bit the peeping Tom. So *that's* why Teddy got so upset when Gertrude mentioned Skip. Based on her tirade among the hothouse flowers, Gertrude was well aware of her fiancé's secret relationship. She was holding it over his head, using it against him. Could that be a motive?

I know it's rude to spy, but I can't help myself. I raise my binoculars to find their lips still locked firmly together. I bite my own lip. It's a pretty passionate kiss.

I heave a loaded, voyeuristic sigh, then glance at my watch. *It's 5 p.m. and I'm about to get stranded on Campobello!* I look toward the harbor but can't see the mail boat. Then my eyes pause on a man sitting at the far end of the empty park, wearing a sweater and a hat despite the August heat. *Wait, is that Edgar?*

But there's no time to dwell on that, because I'm already sprinting in the opposite direction. I race down the hillside, passing a motel overflowing with geraniums and a dilapidated church. My sandals start to pinch as I hurry down the ferry ramp. The driver of the mail boat shakes his head as I jump in with a minute to spare. I hand him fifty cents and show him my driver's license, then sit down at the stern beside the flagpole. A handful of tourists and a dozen crates of mail keep me company as we cruise into Friars Bay. The sun beats down as the waves crash against the sides of our little white boat. The ocean breeze ruffles my hair as the Maine state flag flaps behind me.

The Eastport breakwater is teeming with activity. As we pull up to the dock, I steady myself against the flagpole, then frown when my hand comes away greasy. I disembark, strolling past the tugboats and the mussel farmer's trawler. Maybe it's the post-not-blackmail glow, or the vodka in my bloodstream, or the balmy August afternoon—but I'm walking on air. Grinning foolishly. Not looking where I'm going as I barrel straight into—

"We've got to stop meeting like this." Avery steps back as I remove my hands from his chest in horror. I've left a gray smudge on his (formerly white) short-sleeved Riviera sweater.

"Oh, dear God." I've ruined his sweater.

But he doesn't seem to care. "Billie! What a pleasant surprise. What are you up to?"

"Accosting pedestrians. Trying to take down as many as possible." I wince. "I actually just came back from Campobello—"

"Human bowling? Canada has that effect on me, too." Avery falls into step beside me as we walk back to the breakwater. "I was just renewing my boat registration." He nods toward the Port Authority, a shack at the far side of the dock that's perpetually overrun with fishermen. As we reach Sullivan Street, I see his hunter-green Porsche on the opposite side of the road. It looks laughably out of place beside the rusty pickup trucks that line the harbor. "Can I offer you a ride?" he asks, chivalrous as ever.

I remind myself that I'm still mad at Avery. And if he wants to play hard to get, then I can, too. "Tempting, but I actually have a date."

"Oh, good, me too," he says, then grins at my frown. "With my mother. She's visiting for the weekend, and I'm taking her out for ice cream."

"And my date is with some library books," I reply, studying my straw purse intently.

"If you won't accept a ride, then will you at least accept an invitation to our end-of-season party?"

I stop in my tracks. "What's an 'end-of-season' party?"

He chuckles. "It does sound rather Victorian, doesn't it?"

"Excessively. I'm embarrassed for you. I can't wait."

"August twenty-second. Swing by anytime that afternoon. Hopefully, no one will die."

My bowling-ball energy carries down the stacks of the Peavey Memorial Library. I'm still buzzing as I dig through the Connecticut telephone books. After asking the librarian to xerox the page with all the Taylors living in southwest Connecticut, I wander into the reference section in search of further scandals. A baritone voice stops me. "Billie! So funny running into you—"

Luke Blackwood leans against a stack of leather-bound encyclopedias. Sunset falls through the stained-glass windows, highlighting his burnished tan beside the reference collection. My book slips through my fingers in surprise. Luke is off duty today, wearing blue jeans and an old T-shirt. Stylish with age, it has frayed sleeves and a few light tears along the bottom hem. I get the sense that once Luke finds something he likes, he holds on tight.

Case in point: he helped me when I dropped my tray in the high school cafeteria, and eight years later, he's still cleaning up after me. Luke grins as he picks up *A Practical Guide to Locksmithing* from the scuffed hardwood floor. "What a sensible hobby! I've been meaning to–"

But I won't allow myself to be distracted by his nervous smile or the faint suggestion of abs through his thin T-shirt. I was subjected to Chief Deputy Abbott's pit stains because Luke can't keep his mouth shut. "Apologize for telling on me?" I offer.

Luke straightens. "Come on, Billie. Don't be that way."

*I shouldn't be rude. I shouldn't be rude. I shouldn't–*"Be what way?"

"I only mentioned something to my boss because I was worried about you. You seemed a little too curious about the murder, and . . . this isn't a game. These are dangerous people. You and I go way back, and I'm looking out for you." Luke transfers his weight from one foot to the other, then straightens his T-shirt and squares his shoulders. "Would you want to see *The Moon-Spinners* at–"

"Luke. The second rule of dating is not to sell your love interest out to the police," I admonish, my voice flat.

He looks from me to the locksmithing manual, then back again. "Billie, did you read that somewhere? Because I don't think that's a real–"

"Luke, I was being facetious. But in the future, if you're trying to ask a girl out, you might want to think twice before siccing a sweaty cop on her." I remove the manual from his hands. "Now, if you'll excuse me, I have some important business to attend to."

## ETIQUETTE FOR LOVERS AND KILLERS

---

A warm breeze flutters through my curtains as I dream about Teddy. *That's the general theme around here*, he remarks with a saucy twitch of his mustache. Then the dream skips over to Gertrude, as she weighs the crystal ashtray in her hands. *You were such a lovely toy.*

I wake up with her words on my lips. As I nestle deeper into the pillows, I consider the tangle of Gertrude's death, which seems to grow more gnarled with every passing day. Teddy had two red-haired lovers—could the existence of one have driven him to murder the other? Everyone knows that love is worth fighting for, but is it also worth killing over? Would Teddy kill for love? What would I do in his place? And what might I turn a blind eye to?

My mind jumps from Avery's Riviera sweater to the fedora lurking in the park, then over to Luke and his genuine confusion when I told him that he'd broken one of the cardinal rules of dating. I smile into my pillow. That was *too funny*. As if there were some rule book for flirting and felonies. A book of etiquette for lovers and killers. I pull my covers tightly around myself, and I'm still grinning about how stupid it all is as I fall back asleep.


At 6 p.m. the discounted evening rates kick in on the telephone. I curl up with the *click, click, whirr* as I work my way through all thirty-one Taylors living in Fairfield County, Connecticut. Victor comes over to check on me in the gossip nook. He's wearing his favorite checkered shirt and pleated gray pants. His wire-framed glasses are smudged with flour. He mouths *Long-distance charges,* then turns away. I smell coffee cake. He generally only bakes if he's feeling anxious.

The Taylors are an unhelpful bunch. Mr. Hayden Taylor tells me where I can "stick" my phone book, and Mrs. Leona Taylor is hard of hearing. But Miss Paisley Taylor, owner of Beehive Beauty in Milford, Connecticut, is willing to talk.

"You're calling about Gertrude?" asks an animated voice on the other end of the phone. "Who are you?"

"Just a friend of hers from school," I reply vaguely. "I tried calling, but she won't pick up. It's kind of weird, so I just figured . . ." I trail off as I lose my nerve. This was a bad idea. Maybe I should hang up.

"You poor thing. What's your name, honey?" Paisley Taylor sounds concerned as she chews gum on the other end of the phone.

"Beth-Ann-Tina." Three different names converge on my tongue.

"Bettina. I think she mentioned you. You know, I closed early tonight to have some work done on the shop, so let's have a nice chat," Paisley murmurs with another smack of gum.

"Did Gertrude move? Did she go on vacation? Did she get a new—"

"Bettina. Honey. She's dead." Paisley Taylor swallows hard.

"Oh my," I murmur. Luckily my nervous gulp sounds more like a sob.

"You were close, then? My sister didn't have many female friends. You must have been really special to her."

"She was special to me." Another choked sound, as I drop my voice and cradle the phone closer to my ear. "What happened? When is the funeral? Should I send flowers or—"

"Bettina, sweetie, you missed it. It was small, just family. We're keeping this close. And quiet for now. There are some ... financial considerations that make this"—in the background, a male voice booms, *Paisley, do you want the new hair dryers over here?* and a muffled, *Yes! Perfect!*—"complicated," Paisley finishes with another snap of gum.

"That does sound complicated. So it was just family at the funeral? Not even Teddy—"

A humph across the phone. "That snob wouldn't dream of showin' his face 'round here. But he sent a note and"—she breaks off again as the voice asks, *What about the heat lamps?* Followed by a muted *Over there!*—"showed his support in other ways."

Clearly, with his checkbook. "Teddy is the pits," I murmur, hoping that she'll go on.

"Honestly, there were worse." Paisley smacks her gum, only too eager to gossip about her sister's love life. "That Edgar Gibbs was five miles of hard road."

"Edgar," I repeat the name warily. "Did he wear a hat?"

"A regular Dick Tracy, that one. They were engaged for a minute. Not my type, but then she always had a thing for the bad boys." Paisley blows a bubble, and it echoes through the receiver. "I think that my sister was mixed up with some real shady characters."

"But she ran in such an exclusive crowd. She was their poster girl," I protest, feeling strangely protective of Gertrude.

"More like the centerfold," Paisley replies with a thoughtful snap of her gum. "Bettina, baby, if you go looking for trouble, you're gonna find it. And my sister did. Don't make the same mistake." Her voice quavers, then she perks back up and chomps her gum loudly into the phone. "You're not wrapped up with that lot, are you?"

"What lot?" I ask in confusion.

"Gertrude's *friends*." She blows another bubble. "You sound like them. Kinda stuck-up."

I frown at the phone. I'm hardly in Gertrude's social circle, although I'm certainly preoccupied by it. Suffocatingly so. There's a commotion on the other end of the phone. A loud crash followed by *Miss Taylor, I'm so sorry*–and *Mitch, you big lug, that was expensive!* "Pumpkin, I gotta run." Paisley hangs up.

I continue holding the phone to my ear long after the dial tone has resumed. Given all the new equipment, it sounds like Paisley made a killing off her sister's death. Teddy definitely pitched in, but who else? Then I hear a *click*.

I check the kitchen, but Victor is mixing streusel topping. Upstairs, I find Grace watching *The Judy Garland Show* with the sound off. My grandmother's hands are idle, which is unusual. My eyes drift over to the pale green phone on her nightstand, and she raises a single purple eyebrow. I walk away, grinning. How long has my grandmother been eavesdropping on me?

**CHAPTER EIGHT**

# HOW TO RUIN A PARTY

*The guest no one invites a second time is the one who runs a horse to a lather; who leaves a borrowed tennis racquet out in the rain; who "dog ears" the books, leaves a cigarette on the edge of a table, who stands a wet glass on polished wood, who tracks muddy shoes into the house. Nor are men the only offenders. Young women have been known to commit every one of these offenses.*

Dusty Springfield spins on the record player as I lounge in bed with the pale pink phone receiver pressed to my ear. "Do you think he secretly likes me?" I ask Debbie. Once again, we've switched from the murder to the far more consuming mystery of Avery's affections.

"Well, he took you on that date—"

"But he specifically said that it *wasn't* a date. Although he might have been joking." I bite my lip as Dusty croons "Anyone Who Had a Heart."

"You said he has a rather dry sense of humor—" Debbie placates me.

"Everything is a joke with him! Nothing is serious!"

"Honestly, that's so obnoxious." She *tsks* her disapproval. "So what *is* the appeal? Besides him being pretentious and aloof?"

"Centuries of Cinderella[a] fantasies?"

"So you blame society for your crush?" Debbie seems unimpressed by my logic.

"Absolutely. I take zero responsibility," I concur as I nestle into my patched beige comforter.

"Okay, so *you* won't own up to your emotions, and *he* won't make the first move. Either take a chance or move on, because I'm getting bored," Debbie advises. "Get a hobby or come visit me at the Schoodic Institute. Everyone here is so painfully academic, they'll make you feel better about yourself."

"I assume that this invitation comes with a shopping list?"

"Well, I'd hate to impose, but since you asked—"

Following Debbie's advice, I channel my romantic frustration into something useful. There are certain skills that a young lady must hone for a rainy day—like learning to ice a layer cake, ride equestrian, or breaking and entering. *A Practical Guide to*

---

[a] **Cinderella:** *a story in which a lowly servant girl finds upward mobility through a romantic entanglement with a prince.* Derived from the Italian *ceneri*, "ashes," which inspired the iconic seventeenth-century fairy tale. Other cultures have a similar fable that dates back much further, among them the Chinese (850 CE), the Greeks (7 BCE), and the Egyptians (550 BCE), proving that sexy servant girls are a tale as old as time.

*Locksmithing* outlines the basic technique for "quick entry," which seems to involve mangling an entire drugstore's worth of bobby pins and destroying several dead bolts in the process. Victor finds me on the front step with a broken lock and the manual open before me.

"Wilhelmina Clementine McCadie, why are you trying to break into a house that's always unlocked?" My grandfather throws up his hands and sighs.

Eben Hollis swings by to install the new dead bolt. The locksmith's son has a devious smile and an Elvis T-shirt as he holds up the damaged copper cylinder. "You got this one good."

"I didn't—"

"You have to be gentle with it. Seduce it. Let me show you how it's done," Eben explains as he fits a replacement into the door.

On Monday morning, my training is put to the test. The door to Primp and Ribbon Alterations is locked, and my keys are sitting at home on my dresser. So I slip a bobby pin out of my hair and hope for the best. I remove the plastic bulbs, crimp one end with my fingers, and press both prongs into the keyhole. I push into the cylinder until one end fits against the grooves of the stator, then maneuver the second pin, gently raking it across the internal tumblers. I glance around furtively, but no one gives a damn what I'm doing, so I press harder, pushing until I hear the faintest, sweetest *click* from the latchwork. A breathless smile as the dead bolt retracts.

As I turn on the lights, the pastor's wife breezes in, making a beeline for my desk. Mrs. Coates drops off a small black bundle and murmurs, "Just fix it," without meeting my eyes. Then she turns on her heels and leaves without further explanation.

The problem becomes clear as I asses her revealing black lace corset. The seams are loose, and the long metal boning is poking out. It must be quite painful! But what is less clear is why the pastor's wife owns a sexy corset in the first place.

I bust open the bodice and tear out the seams, removing the gnarled boning. (*How often does Mrs. Coates wear this?*) I find some new boning in our haberdashery cabinet, then remove the casing. Mrs. Pridmore bustles in and provides a nagging commentary while I use an oversized needle to edgestitch the casing into the thick fabric. She shows me how to reinsert the new boning and pad the ends with cotton squares so the rods won't bother the pastor's wife.

A Maserati or a Bentley seems like a requirement for the Websters' "end-of-season" party. I wish my beach cruiser would magically transform into a Rolls-Royce, as I weave through the luxury cars to lean my bike against the Garage Mahal. I pull a bottle of sparkling wine out of my wicker basket, straighten my blouse, and approach the party.

The Beach Boys drifts across the gardens while the scent of fried clams and shish kebab wafts from the buffet table. Young people are strewn across the Websters' lawn. The partygoers are young and tragically hip, with the boys in plaid pants and mop-top haircuts and the girls in baby-doll dresses and beehives. They're all rich kids. Twentysomethings with trust funds and one-too-many degrees. The boys regard me with curiosity and the girls with suspicion, sizing up my pleated red skirt, sleeveless silk blouse, and Mary Janes, as if I were an imminent threat. My eyes are a little too wide and my cheeks too flushed, and it's written all over my face that I didn't arrive in a Jaguar.

I find Avery in the garden, toasting a pretty blonde. She has enormous blue eyes, a platinum bob, champagne-pink skin, and a black boatneck top. Her billowing gingham skirt is buoyed up by numerous petticoats. I stop dead in my tracks. It's the costume Brigitte Bardot wore in *Voulez-Vous Danser Avec Moi?* Bardot's film pulled gingham out of the picnic basket and into the limelight, investing the modest pattern with unexpected sex appeal. I was jealous of Bardot, with her casual bouffants and cute French accent, but now I'm even more envious of her real-life counterpart. The black gingham stands out in the sea of seersucker and khaki, as the young woman leans in toward Avery, playful and familiar.

"Billie goat's gruff!" Claude waves me over as the Bardot lookalike turns with a flutter of one jewel-studded hand. When Avery sees me, he steps away from her. "Miss Pearl Hamilton," Claude introduces her with a dissolute grin. "Pearl just returned from Paris, where she's been studying fashion at the Atelier Chardon—is that right?"

Pearl assents with a peroxide-white smile. "Isn't their place a gas? I've just been *dying* of boredom at my parents' cottage in Southwest Harbor so—" She speaks as if she's competing in the interview portion of the Miss America beauty pageant, over-enunciating every syllable as she nods and smiles along. Claude pinches her waist, and she swats his shoulder.

"And this is the famous Billie." Claude reaches for my waist, but I step out of his reach.

"Where do you summer?" Pearl asks, then her eyes, impossibly, grow even larger. "Oh my God, are you a townie?" She purrs as she lifts her champagne flute to her pale pink lips, then frowns when it comes away empty. "Be a dear and refresh my glass." She points airily at the bottle in my hands, and Claude takes it without asking. As he pops the cork, the Beach Boys sing "We'll Run Away," and I resist the urge to do just that.

"Should we offer some to the fuzz?" Claude swigs from the bottle, gesturing toward the bar, where Luke Blackwood stands at attention, looking daggers at me.

"Leave the security alone, Claude," Avery reprimands his brother, then signals a passing waiter to bring me a fresh glass of champagne.

Pearl's eyes seem to devour her face. "Oh, how *sweet*, another one of your little charity projects. Avery, you're such a *great* philanthropist." As Pearl pouts at me, I look down at my shoes, hunch my shoulders, and feel my self-esteem collapse in on itself.

But then I take a step back and evaluate the situation. The only reason for Pearl to tear me down is if she feels threatened in some way. It's bad form. Miss Vanderbilt wrote, "Good sportsmanship and courteous conduct are required by the rule book, [and] insults or abusive language should never be uttered audibly." Which I couldn't agree with more.

But why would this fashion plate feel threatened by me? I don't have anything she wants. Then I glance over at Avery, who is deeply fascinated by something on his shoes, and I feel

Pearl's eyes on me. A smile quirks up the corners of my lips. Maybe my hopeless infatuation isn't quite as hopeless as I thought.

Suddenly, it feels awfully important to take a chance. Why am I sitting on the sidelines hoping that someone will give me what I want? Maybe it's time to take it for myself. "Can I steal you for a moment?" I ask Avery.

"Absolutely not. No theft allowed, only murder." Claude chortles as Pearl giggles indulgently.

But Avery wants to be stolen. "Shall we?" He steps back and signals for me to follow, leading me around the house with impatience. Once we're out of sight, his shoulders noticeably relax, and he turns with a concerned grin. "I'm so sorry. They're barbarians."

I burst out laughing. "So that *wasn't* a joke? She's actually that rude?"

"How can I make it up to you?" he asks as he continues across the cobblestone drive.

"With a tour?" I suggest. A tour would accomplish two highly desirable objectives: 1. It would allow me to snoop around Webster Cottage. And 2. It would spare me from Pearl's prying eyes. "Show me the highlights of Murder Mansion."

"I hope you copyrighted that." He chuckles. "'Murder Mansion' has such a ring to it."

"You actually owe me a penny because you just said it," I inform him as we climb up the front steps. "Show me where the bodies are buried."

"Ah, that would be the gazebo–" Avery gestures toward the Victorian gazebo in the front yard, but I'm already reaching for the door. "Allow me." He hurries over to open the wrought-iron monstrosity, with sharp metal roses entwining around a curly *W*. "Where should we start? The wine cellar, the home theater, or the private chapel?"

"I want to be shocked, Avery. What about secret passageways or a panic room?" I ask as my Mary Janes track a fine film of dust across the shiny black-and-white marble floor.

"Oh, you mean Claude's bedroom."

I choke on my champagne. "You're terrible."

"You're worse," he replies, striding down the hallway to our left. Avery shows me a private library with carved walnut bookshelves stretching up to the vaulted ceiling, filled with leather-bound volumes with pristine uncreased spines. "We have the entire first edition of the Audubon set," Avery informs me with a wink as I sit down on the glossy chesterfield sofa and admire the silver *objets d'art* gleaming under a swathe of Moroccan lanterns.

Next comes the gallery. Sunlight streams across a wall of oil paintings of landscapes and seascapes—all objectively good, yet just as soulless as their surroundings. A wooden painter's easel lurks in the corner, supporting a single canvas. "My mother *had* to have an art room," Avery explains as I study the blank canvas, arguably the best piece in the house. "She tells people that she's a painter, but as far as I can tell, the only thing she's ever painted is her face."

"This is all too tame," I murmur, sipping my champagne. "What about a bowling alley or a fallout shelter?"

"How about the butler's pantry?" Avery offers.

I pause with my hand on the doorjamb. "Say that again."

"Butler's pantry."

"Show me."

The butler's pantry is a neat little room smelling of Pine-Sol with floor-to-ceiling shelves stacked with cut-glass pitchers and decanters filled with every possible shade of liquor. A rolling library ladder is pushed to one side, with a beige phone mounted behind it. A vase of rosemary and mint perfumes the air, as a crystal bowl of lemons glistens beside it.

"So by 'butler,' you mean 'bartender'?" I clarify.

"I believe that Hayes *did* study bartending at the academy."

I set down my champagne flute on the copper countertop. Everything here is so perfect that it makes me want to break it. My hands are dewy with August heat as I draw a finger across one of the glass curio cabinets. Avery's eyes widen as I reach for the next cabinet.

"Darling, don't be crass. That will upset Hayes." Avery reaches out to stall me, and I turn in his grip. His fingers clench around mine as our eyes meet.

"Or will it upset *you*?" I counter as I reach toward the crystal bowl. "Darling," I copy his upper-class mid-Atlantic drawl. "Don't make a scene. It will upset the help."

Avery frowns. "I don't sound like that."

"Darling, show a little decorum—"

"You're butchering my accent." He releases my hands with a scandalized grin.

And maybe it's the triumph of having defiled a surface in Webster Cottage, or maybe it's the faint aroma of Avery's aftershave—a tantalizing hint of sea moss, sand, and sage—but I finally succumb to temptation and step in.

His lips are warm and soft against mine. Gentle yet decisive. A supple contradiction. I close my eyes as I melt into his kiss.[b] I've thought about this for months. Waited, yearned, ordered skimpy lingerie, and–

Avery steps back, holding a hand up to his lips with an expression of... *Is it surprise? Astonishment? No–it's horror.* I flush with embarrassment as my mistake reveals itself. Avery's reticence wasn't due to chivalry or shyness, but glaring disinterest. I smudged a cabinet, then kissed a boy who isn't attracted to me. I'm every host's worst nightmare.

"Billie, I–"

My heart sinks so low that it must be with the dusty bottles of Château Margaux in the wine cellar. "I'msosorry." It comes out as a single, mortified syllable. A hush falls over us as "Hush-abye" drifts through the open window and I turn to escape. But the expression in Avery's eyes stops me. They're dark and gray, studying me with a steely intensity in contrast with the cheery yellow sunlight filtering between us. He's so close that I can feel his breath against my skin. I open my mouth to apologize.

"To hell with it," he says, then pushes me back against the wall and kisses me deeply. He presses his lips against mine in a way that I've always dreamed about. With desire, fervor, and an uncharacteristic lack of restraint. He kisses me as if he wants me, too.

---

[b] **Kiss (v.):** *to touch with the lips as a sign of love, desire, or greeting.* This onomatopoeia stems from the Sanskrit *cumbita*. Some languages distinguish between a casual kiss (the Latin *osculum*) and an erotic one (the Latin *saviari*). *Kiss* has inspired countless figures of speech, including the sixteenth-century *kiss and tell* (what I'm doing right now), the 1950s' *kissing cousins* (a close relation), and *kiss the dust* (but that's an idiom for a different chapter).

My lips respond before my brain can. My teeth run over his lips as he presses into me. The corded muscles in his biceps are strong under my fingertips as I grip his arm through his short-sleeved cashmere crewneck. The air feels charged and heavy between us—thick with expectation. I lean in, looping my arms over his shoulders as I relax into his embrace. His fingers trail over my skirt to rest on my waist, grasping me firmly and pulling me tightly against his hips. His tongue finds mine. One hand brushes over my flimsy silk blouse, fiddling with the top button. My pulse speeds up as my knees go weak, and my fingers itch to record every last detail in my diary.

Then he stops. "Goddamn it, Billie. This is insane. I'm sorry, but no." He steps back, his face growing distant.

Outrage prickles across my skin. "What's so insane about it?"

"This was a dreadful miscalculation." He shakes his head as he straightens his shirt, then strides resolutely down the marble hallway, while my Mary Janes scurry nervously behind him. We're halfway to the front door before he turns to me. "Billie, my sincere apologies if I've led you on, it was never my intent. I've genuinely enjoyed our time together, and I think you are a"—he pauses to search for the right word—"brilliant ... person."

"*Brilliant person?!*" I repeat, my words tight with disgust. "But—"

"But nothing. I have to leave." He resumes his march to the door.

"But Avery." I stifle a laugh. "This is *your* house! I should be the one to go—not you."

He grits his teeth with embarrassment. "I rest my case. You're absolutely brilliant, and I don't even know whose house

I'm in. Billie, you can do better than me." He opens that oversize rose-encrusted door, then motions for me to exit. "And so concludes our tour of Murder Mansion."

I grapple for words. Is there some way to salvage the friendship? Do I even *want* a friendship with Avery? I don't feel very friendly toward him, I mostly just feel like ripping his clothes off. "So you don't feel the same?" I ask bluntly.

"I also find butler pantries highly erotic."

My eyes narrow. Everything is a joke, nothing is serious with him, and it's *seriously* starting to piss me off. I turn on my heel and stride away to drown my sorrows at the bar. The butler stands at attention behind the counter, pouring champagne with muddled strawberries. "The Cherub's Cup, miss," Hayes says with quiet prestige, as a vase of baby's breath trembles softly beside him.

Over the rim of my Cherub's Cup, I watch Avery rejoin Pearl and Claude. He deserves someone like Pearl. Someone who can spend hundreds of dollars on French couture for a backyard barbeque. Avery returns to his world, so I return to mine, braving Luke's glacial stare to join him beside the ice chest.

"I told you not to come here," Luke says without looking at me. "These are bad people."

"Whatever gave you that idea?" I reply airily as I sip my champagne cocktail.

"All right." Luke shrugs. But from his expression I sense that it's not all right at all.

Another sip as I suppress a smile. Avery and Luke are polar opposites. Luke is so genuine that it hurts, and Avery considers sincerity the height of poor taste. Avery is too aloof, and Luke needs too much reassurance. It's funny that they exist in the same world, let alone the same garden party. "Luke, the third rule of dating is never tell a lady what to do."

"Are you a lady?" he asks indifferently.

"Yes, I am."

And because I'm a lady, I hand off my unfinished Cherub's Cup, then leave with my head held high. Keeping it together is a subtle act of defiance as I stride across the driveway. Pearl yips, "Townie!" behind me as Avery watches me bike away.

He doesn't like me (even though he kissed me like he did). He doesn't care (even though he motions for me to watch the road and narrowly saves me from crashing into a topiary dog). I'm not a love interest, just a miscalculation. I can't solve the mystery of his indifference. So I focus on the road ahead of me, a road that leads to real crimes and real mysteries. Ones that I might actually be able to solve.

The first breath of autumn sweeps in as I bike home. A smile for Victor, as he pulls a banana upside-down cake out of the oven, and a wave for Grace, whose hair is wrapped up in tinfoil. Then I lock myself in the bathroom and turn on the shower so they won't hear me sob. (The tub is another important item in the rule book of dating, it's the ideal place for a good cry.) My tears taste as cheap as my Lustre-Creme shampoo. I lather myself up with pink Dove soap as I gulp down a sob. What drew me to Webster Cottage? What pulled me into their shiny foyer under that gaudy chandelier? Why did I delude myself into thinking that I was bright and shiny, too? The suds burst over my skin as I sink down to the–

"Sweetie, if I don't rinse the bleach out of my hair soon,

you'll have something *real* to cry about." Grace bangs on the door.

The summer people migrate south with the honking Canada geese, and I wish that I could fly with them. The trees turn saffron and gold, a riot of colors against the cool gray sky. Bear-hunting season starts, and front yards are repurposed as pumpkin patches. As September breezes in, the evening news grows frigid as well. The Cold War deepens, like a chill you just can't shake, or a heartache that no amount of mint chocolate chip ice cream will heal. Special reports show East Germans streaming across the Berlin Wall as tensions mount in Western Europe. Radio specials cover the slow burn of nations *almost* at war, as I find an answering Cold War within myself.

Because I'm trapped in stalemate, too. Espionage is creeping at my doorstep. Tugging at my hand as I rip up unsent letters. Trailing behind me as I pull my carpetbag out of the closet and gaze at it longingly. Eavesdropping as I call the operator and ask for a number that I really shouldn't. "The younger son is in the South of France and will be away for the next month," a maid informs me. Of course he is, that *fils de pute*. He gets to *aller en* France. He gets to *prendre des cafés* in tiny bistros. To *errer sans but* in Saint-Tropez.

I shake my head and start packing. Because if he can leave, then I can, too. So I grab my things and get the hell out of here. *Dégage de lá,* is the French phrase for that.

## CHAPTER NINE

# LUGGAGE FOR THE SAVVY TRAVELER

*Whether you are going on a long journey or merely spending a weekend with a friend, your first concern is your luggage, which should look nice and give little trouble. Nothing makes a worse impression than broken-down bags and numerous carry-alls and bundles.*

Orange leaves flit across the empty train platform as autumn sun plates everything in gold. My carpetbag drags at my shoulder, heavy with Pond's cold cream, Cheez Doodles, and wine for Debbie. I poke my head into the railway office, where I find Joseph Adams relaxing behind a typewriter, his worn leather boots propped up on the battered desk. Opposite him is an oversize leather suitcase with gleaming brass hardware. It looks like something you would see on the Orient Express, luxurious, overpriced, and far too worldly for this humble space. It must be a lost item, but how could anyone misplace such an impressive piece of baggage?[a]

*Focus, Billie. No mysteries today.*

"One round-trip ticket for the Schoodic Peninsula, please."

Joseph Adams laughs with derision. "Why would you want to go there?"

*Why, indeed.* The Schoodic Peninsula is a scholarly secret tucked away along the Maine coast, an hour from the nearest town. I'd never heard of it before MIT sent Debbie there for the summer. She's been trapped there for months, cataloging their research library. The Schoodic Institute is old telegram money, built by John Moore, a pioneer of the telegraph industry. In the 1920s, it slipped into the hands of the Rockefellers, who were playing Monopoly with coastal Maine at the time. Now the National Park Service uses the facility for "the promotion of biological and other scientific research." But doesn't that sound like a cover for a mad scientists' laboratory?

The Schoodic Peninsula train station is a shack in the middle of the woods, with a single white van idling outside. "Ayuh, we got Rockefella Hall right here," my driver says in an indecipherable Down East accent as we emerge through dense pine forest before a French-eclectic-style château. I climb out, gazing in bewilderment at the elaborate collage of red and gray quarried stones and handwrought casement windows.

---

[a] **Baggage (n.):** *luggage used for travel.* Stemming from the Old Norse *baggi*, "pack, bundle," this noun inspired numerous idioms, including the eighteenth-century *let the cat out of the bag* (to confess a secret), the 1920s' *in the bag* (guaranteed), and the 1950s' *emotional baggage*, a bit of psychological slang from the psychiatrist's couch.

"It's weird, right?" Debbie grins as if she just told a clever joke. Her bob is neatly turned up at the ends, and her warm brown skin gleams in the autumn light as she waits for me out front. She's one of the more petite people I've encountered, with delicate features and an ice-pick-sharp wit. They called us a pair of scorpions back at college, although I'm still not sure why. Debbie loves a theme, and today she's playing the serious academic in a cable-knit sweater and pleated tweed skirt.

"You've been living in a period drama all summer and didn't bother to inform me!" I hug her as I take in the château. "I'm inconsolable."

Debbie shows me the facilities and her coworkers (she was right, they aren't much to look at), then leads me past the barracks-style research buildings to the fjord-encrusted coastline. She points out a ragged granite bluff overlooking Frenchman Bay, littered with radio towers and antennas. "That is Otter Cliff," she explains. "It was established by the navy during World War I as a strategic listening facility. They used it to triangulate the location of foreign warships."

"But that was decades ago, so why hasn't it been dismantled?" I peer at the eyesore in confusion. Some of the antennas look new. "What is Otter Cliff listening to now?"

"Otters?" Debbie replies with a shrug. "And just *look* at that lighthouse!"

Evening finds us in Rockefeller Hall, in an attic room overlooking a courtyard lit with flickering gas lanterns. An owl hoots as we sit on the floor between two single beds, sharing a bottle of wine.

It's like we're back in the dorms at the Ashburn Linguistics Institute. It feels like home. "What are they researching here?" I ask.

"Herons, sea cucumbers, snails–" Debbie lists animals as she pours herself a glass of rosé.

"And MIT sent you here because?"

"MIT is also in the otter business," Debbie replies flatly, reaching for a Cheez Doodle. In her pink pajamas and hair wound up in a silk scarf, she makes an unlikely code-breaker. But the copy of Turing's *Computing Machinery and Intelligence* on her nightstand tells a different story.

"So this is Cold War central, huh?" I assume she's messing with me, and Debbie's out here researching starfish and *not* Russian warships. But it's a nice dream. We're all waging a silent battle, although for some of us, it's more absurd than for others.

"It does get a little chilly at night," she murmurs, studying me in turn. "Bill, you seem a little blue. What happened with Mr. Dar–oops, I mean Webster?"

"Nothing." I glower at my rosé. Whoever said "time heals all wounds" clearly *wasn't* a twenty-six-year-old virgin.[b] Because the seasons may change, but my heart remains locked in that silly butler's pantry. "Let's face it, I'm not getting any younger–"

"Oh right, is your sixtieth birthday coming up?"

"–And I'm too old for this nonsense. Enough flings." I frown at the Cheez Doodle in my hand. "Enough mysteries. It's time to get serious. Time to focus on what's important."

---

[b] **Virgin (n.): 1.** *a person who has never had sexual intercourse.* **2.** *a chaste woman devoted to religion.* Virgin stems from the Latin *virga,* "young green shoot," and *virginem,* "new and unused." So essentially, a *virgin* is being compared to an unused blade of grass, which I can't say I find *terribly* flattering.

Debbie throws herself back against the bed and gazes up at the wood-paneled ceiling. "Oh la. So what do you propose? Should we join the convent together? Or is that too frivolous for you?"

I consider it as wind rustles through the woods. "Do you think they serve rosé?"

She smirks. "Holy wine only."

"Is that Cabernet? Merlot?" I wrinkle my nose with distaste.

"I doubt the convent has a sommelier—" Debbie sips her pale pink wine (a treat, as imported wine is hard to come by in Down East Maine), then tops it off with a Doodle. "By the way, thank you for these delicacies," she says with a wink.

"Don't mention it. Speaking of which—" I rummage through my carpetbag for my list of suspects. "I delivered your grocery list, so here is mine. When you're back in Boston, could you skim through your newspaper archives for these names? The microfilm in Eastport is a joke. I can't see a damn thing."

"I thought you would never ask." Debbie examines the list with pleasure, until her smile falls. "Billie, there is a name missing from this list."

"No, there isn't." I sound defensive, but I'm not sure why.

"Are you sure?"

"That name belongs to an individual so *timid* that he can't even kiss a girl. Such a *Boy Scout* that he was helping an elderly woman at the time in question. So *snobby* that he's currently eating croissants in France."

"I hate him *and* his pastries." Debbie pours more wine, then frowns at the empty bottle.

"It would be ideal if you wore a trench coat while you're

investigating." I return to the mystery at hand. "My detective agency adheres to a strict dress code."

We climb down the cliffs the next morning to have our *Persuasion* moment along the seashore. Banter and romantic conjecture carry us down the windswept coastline. The cove is covered in smooth round quartz stones in every shade of pink and gray. It's chilly out on the water, but we roll up our pant legs and wade out into the waves, gasping as they splash across us. The briny air mingles with the scent of crushed pine needles and sunbaked sea moss.

"Look, there's a puffin." Debbie points toward a black-and-white bird sunning itself on a rock. She reaches into her bag, then passes me a pair of binoculars.

"Maybe I should take up bird-watching." I rotate the dial to study the waterfowl. "Get a hobby that makes sense."

"And maybe I should stick to cataloging sea urchins and not deciphering Russian codes, but it's just so hard to stop," Debbie replies dryly, then takes the binoculars back and points at the water. "There, an otter."

I'm bored by the scenery on my way home. Yawning at the ragged coastline. I don't want grand vistas; I want lobster buoys and maple taps. Because it's the small, seemingly insignificant details that tell the real story.

Details, like the flames licking across a hayfield as a farmer burns his excess crops. Details, like the carved wooden bear outside the Pleasant Point General Store, holding up a sign that says *Fly Fishing Only*. Details, like the piece of yellow *caution* tape fluttering out of a trash bin at the Washington County train station.

Details, like the brown hair hiding Joseph Adams's face when I poke my head into the railway office. The astringent odor of bleach hits me like a slap. "I didn't do it," the station manager says to my confusion. His unruly hair quivers around his fingertips as I suppress a sneeze.

Details, like an unclaimed suitcase.

The newspapers are shocked, dismayed, and not-so-secretly delighted when the body of Clara K. Tabernathy is discovered in an oversize suitcase at the Washington County train station. Even at the best of times our train station doesn't get much action, so the suitcase gained a certain notoriety, even before its unsavory contents slid out across the floor. In this case, there is no lurking, omnipotent cabal to suppress news of this scandal, so the media digs in.

"It All Ended in a Suitcase," reports the *Presque Isle Star-Herald*.

"One-Way Ticket to Nowhere," the *Eastern Angus* quotes the popular Neil Sedaka song.

"Police on Vacation. No Leads in Luggage Murder," the *Penobscot Times* cuts to the quick.

"She was just accepted to the Bangor Ballet," Grace informs

me as she paints her nails Ballerina Pink. She seems to be confusing Bangor with Lincoln Center. "She was last seen leaving the Northern Lights Ballet Studio in Calais."

"The station manager was beside himself," Victor says as he trims salt pork for baked beans, somehow both pale with horror and flushed with excitement. "One of them real nice leather suitcases. Joseph watched it for four days, waiting to see if someone would come round to claim it. And then"–Victor lowers his voice for dramatic effect–"it started to smell."

"A sophomore at the University of Maine. She was supposed to help her aunt ice a layer cake, but she never showed," Marsha gossips as I measure the hem of her skirt. "Can you make it a little shorter? Florence says that we're only allowed to wear miniskirts."

"Cuts all over her hands and scrapes up her arms," Wendy Liu whispers as we stand in line at the Greene Deli counter. "That girl *fought*."

"And do you *know*–" Mrs. Pridmore gossips as I pin the gathers on one last puffed sleeve. It's homecoming season, and my fingers are cramping after eight hours of stitching frills and bows. "She was shot *in the neck*." My employer clutches her neck. "Can you believe it? The *neck*?! I can't imagine *anything* so depraved."

I remain silent because I certainly can.

"She was dead *before* she was stuffed in the suitcase," the seamstress announces.

"I should hope so," I reply as I line up the raw edges on the sleeve shoulder, then slide them under the presser foot of my sewing machine. "It would be odd if she climbed in willingly."

"But aren't you *scared*?" Mrs. Pridmore asks, bosom jiggling with fervor. "Don't you care *at all*?"

"It's just awful." I try to look outraged, but my heart isn't in it.

"You don't give a hoot about that poor girl." Mrs. Pridmore pouts as I knot my thread, then hang up the homecoming dress. "You act so above it all. So aloof. Well, I'll tell you what, missy— *you* are a cliché,"[c] she says, and I nod in agreement. I'm an amateur sleuth who lost interest in her investigation, and now someone else is dead. Nothing is more cliché than that.

"I just try not to get too emotionally involved in every murder I hear about. Have a good weekend." I nod as I step out into the crisp October evening.

Hickory woodsmoke perfumes the air as I make my way through town, pausing at the spot where I almost trampled Clara Tabernathy last summer. I remember the pie clutched to her chest, and her syrupy-sweet, fruity perfume, redolent of Jolly Ranchers. I can still hear her powdered-sugar voice as she said, *Thanks for keeping me on my toes!* If I'd acted differently in that moment, would she still be alive? Could I have warned her? Guessed that she would be the next target? The sky is as dark as my conscience as I climb up the steps to the post office.

"Billie, a surprise for you. Autumn olives." Mr. Townsend appears at my elbow with a plastic bag of bright red berries that couldn't look more poisonous if they tried. The "olives" are sweet and tart as I unlock my PO box. Three envelopes today

---

[c] **Cliché (n.):** *an overused phrase betraying a lack of original thought.* In eighteenth-century France, a *cliché* was "a copy of an original printing plate designed for mass-production." This onomatopoeia was inspired by the *clicking* sound that the printing press made when striking against the metal mold.

and a copy of *Vogue*. I stash the mail in my purse and wish the postman a good night, hoping that his berries won't kill me.

Autumn harvest is in full swing, with farmers rolling up bales of hay and lobstermen hoisting their boats out of the water for the winter. Screaming children race through apple orchards while housewives do their best *Bewitched* impressions. Homecoming season is rife with school dances, apple cider, and election campaigns (everyone knows that Lyndon Johnson will be reelected, but the Republicans still dare to dream).

The *Quoddy Current* News Bureau gleams like a jack-o'-lantern. The lights have been on at all hours since a local girl was found dead. Clara's face gazes up at me from the smudged newspaper box. The typical girl-next-door (not that there is any other kind of girl out here in the boondocks), Clara is everyone's daughter. Everyone's supermarket cashier. She's approachable, attractive, and deeply sympathetic. I study her snubbed nose, perky blond bangs, and innocent smile. Then I bend down until my reflection is superimposed on hers in the smudged plastic, my eyes blinking sadly up at me. How would it feel to be in her place?

As I walk back to my grandparents' house, I try to disregard the sound of footsteps behind me. Try to ignore the goose bumps rising across my skin. Try to will the hairs on the back of my neck to lie flat. *It's just residual guilt. No one is following me. I'm jumping at–*

"Bunny!" Florence's cheeks are flushed with cold and her blond hair is swept back with a headband. She's wearing a miniskirt, pearls, and her old varsity jacket. The retired homecoming queen is quivering like a frightened house cat.

"Are you following me?" I ask in astonishment.

"No. Why? Maybe?" Each word is shriller than the last.

"*Why* are you following me?" I rephrase my question.

Florence reaches out to steady herself against the lamppost. "Bunny, a policeman came to see me. He asked me about you! You're mixed up in something real bad, I just know it."

I narrow my eyes at Florence. "Was it Chief Deputy Abbott? Or Officer Black—"

"No, it was a *detective*. A *stranger*." Florence locks eyes with me as the last red wisp disappears from the sky and the streetlight flickers on above us. Standing there in her varsity jacket, with her blond bob glowing like a halo in the light, she looks like the patron saint of wayward cheerleaders.

"How do you know that he was a policeman?" *Could it have been Edgar?*

"He looked *professional*." Florence says the word as if it were an insult, then her face contorts. "Bunny, someone died!"

"Yes. In a suitcase." *She's just realizing that now?*

"No, at the party! At the cottage! We were *there*! He asked me not to talk about it, but I'm flipping out." Her lip quivers as she fixes me with a panicked stare, then we both jump when a distant cheer goes up from Shead High School on the hillside. "Darn it, I'm missing the football game because of you!" Florence fixes me with an accusatory glare, then wheels off in the direction of the distant fanfare. A cool breeze picks up a handful of dead leaves and sends them skittering behind her.

The Buick is gone; Victor must be at the football game as well. The lights are off and the Cape Cod–style house seems strangely empty. For once, I wish it were full of people. I take a wineglass from the kitchen and pour a glass of my grandmother's Paul Masson pinot blanc, wincing at how sweet it is. A faint glow emanates from Grace's door, and I hear the soft purr that she makes while sleeping. Then I open the door to my bedroom and stifle a scream.

A tangle of hosiery, prom gowns, dictionaries, scarves, graduation robes, and Greek translations is strewn across the whitewashed floor. My sun-bleached print of *Christina's World* has been pulled down from the wall. I sift through the debris with rising anxiety until I find Gertrude's engagement ring and slip it on. My heart pounds as I rush downstairs to lock the doors. I do a sweep of the house, but the wreckage seems isolated to my bedroom. I pause outside Grace's room. "I hear you out there, creeper," she says with a sleepy hiccup/laugh.

Well, at least she's alive. And, it appears, half drunk.

I survey the chaos of my bedroom, then pull my desk chair over to the closet. A cold sweat breaks out across my forehead as I reach for the dusty shoebox at the very top, then fight a wave of dizziness. *The knife is gone!* The knife covered in Gertrude's blood with a few drops of my own. My sweat drips across the dented cardboard.

As if on cue, the phone rings. Dread runs a cool finger through my hair as I jump down to grab it. "Gertrude—" Edgar's voice is gravelly on the other end.

*Of course it was him!* "How dare you break into my house."

"I didn't break in. The door was unlocked," comes his smart-aleck reply.

"If you come within a hundred feet of my family ever again,

I swear to God: I will kill you." My voice is almost as shrill as Florence's.

"And how do you propose to do that, now that I have your knife?"

I suppress another squeal, glaring at the empty shoebox on my pillow. *Why didn't I throw that knife in the bay when I had the chance? Now Edgar has it, and he has my fingerprints all over it, too!*

"How will you explain this to the police?" Edgar asks.

"Explain *what* to the police?" I retort. My heart booms as I peek past my curtain, as if the cops might already be on their way over. But Key Street is dark and deserted, with a scarecrow lurking in the Crimps' front yard, and the faint sound of a barking dog. In the distance, another cheer goes up from the high school football game.

"Explain that you killed her. I know you're guilty. I watched you wash the blood off your hands." Edgar grunts, and I roll my eyes. He's accusing me of something logistically impossible. I was eating a croissant at the time of Gertrude's death, and although I *did* wash my hands, it was because they were covered in butter. Not blood. "I took the knife in case they searched your room. They're coming for you, sweetie. Save yourself. Change your name. Leave while you–"

"Edgar, I am *not* your sweetie. And the only place I'm going is to the police," I retort through clenched teeth. "I'm going to tell them–"

"That a stranger has been calling you? That he broke into your house and stole a weapon that wasn't yours? That you received a ring that belongs to a dead woman? Or were there two rings?"

*It does sound a trifle far-fetched when you put it like that.* "Edgar, did you visit Florence? I'm warning you, stay away from my—"

"I've never been to Italy," he replies, avoiding my question. "I hate pasta."

"And what about Clara Tabernathy?" I drum my nails against the cold glass window.

"I don't mess around with little girls," Edgar replies. He hangs up in a huff, leaving me staring at the phone in confusion. *Did I just offend my stalker?*

I sit down on the bed and take a traumatized gulp of wine. I can't fix this mess, but I *can* clean my room. I fold my shirts, put away my slips, and line up my shoes, as if tidying my room might somehow civilize this situation. When everything is sorted out, I sit down on my bed and take another sip of wine, then frown at the mail sticking out of my purse. One rejection from the Walsh Family Library, another from the Spurlock Museum, and a third rejection from—

I note the tasteful stationery, wax seal, and second stamp, then turn away without a second glance. I hurry downstairs, refill my wineglass, and return to my room with trepidation. The envelope is eggshell white, made of fine cotton paper. I roll my eyes as I tear it open.

*You moronic, boorish bastard,*

Pinot blanc goes up my nose. Where the first letter was neatly composed, this one is a messy scribble. Whoever wrote it was not concerned with their penmanship.

## ETIQUETTE FOR LOVERS AND KILLERS

*I hate you with every bone in my body. You stifled me. Belittled me. Chastised me. You expected me to bend over backward for you but never raised a finger at my behest. You were shockingly bad in bed, always wanting to be coddled and reassured. Honey, I've had <u>desserts</u> with more sex appeal than you.*

*I hate your voice and your laugh. I loathe the blood vessel that bulges on your forehead. I despise your friends—all pretentious, self-absorbed pricks hiding behind their manners and cashmere sweaters. You taught me why people are driven to commit violent crimes—bloodlust, they call it. Well, the desire to rip the frown off of your face is the only kind of lust that you <u>ever</u> inspired in me.*

*But most of all, I hate your eyes. I hate how they watch my every move. I'm not a possession you can put on a shelf and admire. I'm a living, breathing human being. And right now, I'm one that is <u>extremely</u> pissed off.*

*Your private investigator is bullshit. But I found the challenge of losing him each day rather thrilling. I lost him any number of times, but I made sure he was tailing me when I met up with my ex to return his ring.*

*You were in rare form when you showed up at my apartment. I think that you wanted to hurt me, but you fell on your own face instead. Poor baby. Enclosed, please find your ring. You have terrible taste. Rose gold was <u>so</u> 1938.*

*With hate,*
*Gertrude*

When I turn the envelope upside down, a rose-gold engagement ring falls onto my beige comforter. I hold it up to the light. The diamond is multifaceted and brilliant, like the lantern of some tiny lighthouse. It's significantly larger than the first one.

I slip the new ring onto my right hand. Clutching my wineglass, I lean back in the little alcove beside my dormer window and gaze out at the sleeping fishing village. The high school marching band plays in the distance as questions flit past me like autumn leaves.

Why did Gertrude write to me from beyond the grave? Why do I have two last-season engagement rings? Who stuffed Clara Tabernathy in a suitcase? What did Edgar do with the incriminating evidence? And how did he know it was there in the first place?

Neither the wine nor the falling leaves offers any explanations. I think that they know more than they're letting on.

## CHAPTER TEN

# CALLS OF CONDOLENCE

*Letters of condolence need not be long. It is better to avoid the words "died," "death," and "killed." "Deepest sympathy" may be written on your visiting card [or] plain white paper. Mourning paper is much less used now and quite unnecessary.*

POLICE VOW TO "GET HIM," reads the *Quoddy Current*.

Down East Maine continues to reel from the discovery of Clara K. Tabernathy's body, as the hunt for the "luggage killer" intensifies. The 19-year-old was found in a large suitcase at the Washington County train station on September 24th. Miss Tabernathy was an aspiring dancer and the former cheer captain at Calais High. A candlelight vigil will be held in her honor on Friday, October 30th, at Salmon Falls Park.

I look up from the newspaper as my bus pauses at a railroad crossing. I'm heading to Calais for the vigil, although the timing leaves something to be desired. Why did they schedule a vigil for the night before Halloween? And will there be a séance afterward for the really exclusive mourners?

> "A bullet to the neck is an extremely messy way to kill someone," said Detective Winchester of the Machias Police Department. "The assailant possibly misfired. This points to inexperience. This was likely a first, or even, an accidental, killing."

*An accidental killing,* I muse as we pass a copse of pale birch trees, barren of leaves, lining the St. Croix River.

> "We found trace evidence of cotton fibers, likely from a sheet used to mop up excess blood," explained Nick Chamberlain, the State Medical Examiner. "The assailant wrapped the victim in trash bags and placed her in the suitcase. No blood was visible, as she bled excessively at the time of death."
>
> All the fingerprints found on the suitcase belong to railway employees. One witness saw a tall figure in a trench coat leaving the station in the early morning hours of September 24th. The Washington County Sheriff appeals to the public for help in identifying the person(s) responsible. Please call: 555-2368.

Calais is only twenty-seven miles away, but it seems like another world. Complete with a bookshop, a dance studio, and a JCPenney, this thriving border town is the height of Down East sophistication. Canada glints coquettishly across the river. Calais has outdone itself for Halloween, with gourds on every front porch and fake cobwebs dangling from every mailbox. The streets are crawling with mummies, witches, and ghouls who were just released from school.

I climb out of the bus, then ask for directions to 110 South Street. There is a lump in my throat as I approach the Tabernathys' dilapidated Queen Anne. My shoulders slump as I take in the empty driveway and the carpenter hammering away on the roof next door. I'd really hoped to see the Tabernathys on their way to the vigil, but, as usual, I'm running late.

I withdraw a sympathy card from my purse and drop the small tan envelope into the wall-mounted mailbox. It's the least I can do, and I'm sure my mother would approve. Then I pause. They've already left, but I suppose there's no harm in trying.

"Mrs. Tabernathy?" I knock on the door, then freeze when it nudges open under my hand. "Hello, Mrs. Tabernathy?" I repeat, poking my head around the corner. I squirm awkwardly on the front step. *I came here to offer my condolences, not to break in.* But when you're offered a present, it's rude not to accept, right? So I take a deep breath and step inside.

The Tabernathys' kitchen is shabby and cluttered. The lights are on and a coffeepot is sitting on their round scratched dining table. They must have just rushed out. A large plastic pumpkin sits on the lazy Susan, filled with Tootsie Rolls, Smarties, and Mary Janes (arguably the worst Halloween candy). My saddle shoes squeak as I stride across the blue-and-white vinyl floor to a board tacked against the far wall. It features photos of boys in cone-shaped party hats, listing Christmas trees smothered in tinsel, and a young girl with a guilty smile holding a fishing rod in one hand and a dead trout in the other. A newspaper clipping shows Clara holding up her award-winning pie last summer. Her blond hair looks white against the gray page. A program book for *The Nutcracker* is taped beside it.

Before I can consider or condemn my actions, I stride boldly up the stairs. The master bedroom is a dingy cave of unwashed laundry, and the boys' room is littered with sporting equipment, but the third bedroom is a prissy oasis. The canopy bed is made, and the shelves are neatly organized. The one imperfection is a pair of pointe shoes tossed in the corner. Battered and patched with brown spots staining the satin, they present a stark contrast to the rest of Clara's bedroom.

Frames ornament the walls. One has a senior portrait of Clara in her Calais Blue Devils cheerleading uniform. A second pictures Clara in a tutu and toe shoes with a man dressed as a giant rat, grinning cheesily at the camera. A third shows Clara with several girlfriends sharing a milkshake, one of the girls with whipped cream on her nose.

Clara existed in harmony with several other young women who were her nonbiological twins. She was the kind of girl who never did anything on her own—for whom walking down the street unchaperoned would have been social suicide. When I bumped into her, she was rushing after her friends, desperate to catch up. Which makes her murder all the more curious: How did the killer separate Clara from her squad?

Two vinyl cheerleading pom-poms bookend a black velvet jewelry box on her dresser. Inside, a tiny plastic ballerina spins round and round with a dazed smile. The box contains a strand of freshwater pearls and a cheap sterling silver friendship necklace. It's the kind of necklace favored by teenage girls, with the right side of a heart inscribed with the word *Me* (I assume one of the cheerleaders in the photos has the other half, which probably spells out *You &*). A charm bracelet features a flamingo, the Eiffel Tower, a ballet shoe, and a cherry.

My breath speeds up as my heart palpitates, and I reach out for one of the bedposts to steady myself. I *saw* Gertrude's body, but I *feel* Clara's death with an intensity that surprises me. When I stumbled into her last summer, she was so normal[a] and sweet. Which makes her murder even more awful. Someone treated Clara like an actual piece of baggage. They used her up, then cast her aside, without even bothering to bury her. Gertrude aroused my curiosity, but Clara ignites my indignation. *How dare someone treat her like that!* Gertrude was the main character, but Clara was the little sister. It's disgusting that she never got the chance to grow up.

I take a deep breath. I have to pull myself together.

Clara wasn't much of a scholar. Her desk contains a few stamps, some stickers, a Bible, and an unread copy of *Gone with the Wind*. I pick up the neglected paperback and leaf through it. As the pages slip through my fingers, a postcard falls to the floor. It features a bashful kitten surrounded by violets with the words *I Think You're Purr-fect* etched into the clouds. On

---

[a] **Normal (adj.):** *usual, typical.* In ancient Greece a *norma* was a carpenter's square with a ninety-degree angle. This tool inspired the Latin *normalis*, "properly following a rule or pattern."

the back is the message *Happy Birthday, twinkle toes. Until next week, Xx.*

I hold the card up to my nose. It even *smells* like a clue, reeking of Clara's syrupy, Jolly Rancher perfume. The *Xx* seems suggestive to me, but the newspapers didn't mention a boyfriend. Was Clara seeing creepy-kitten man in secret?

A car pulls up outside and my stomach lurches. I absentmindedly tuck the card in my purse as I gaze out the window. *Why aren't they at the vigil?!* I fight back a wave of guilt as I look around myself in horror. *I came here to drop off a sympathy note,* not *to break in!* But I can chastise myself later; right now, I have to move. I race downstairs and bolt though the kitchen, blood thrumming in my ears. I jump down the steps to cower behind the back wall as I catch my breath. The roofer stops hammering and tries to catch Mrs. Tabernathy's attention as she walks, unheeding, through the still-swinging door.

My heart is bouncing in my chest as I make my way to the vigil. Half an hour before my bus leaves, and I have to make it count. Salmon Falls Park is teeming with mourners. I survey the scene of cheerleaders, football players, and concerned old maids, noting a cluster of ballet-buns crying inconsolably beside the bandstand. But there aren't any familiar faces or luxury cars, so I move on.

Fifteen minutes before my bus leaves, and the stolen postcard is a deadweight in my purse. I feel it dragging me down as I stroll through JCPenney, while "Monster Mash" blasts through the speakers. I browse aimlessly through the department store until a slim tape recorder catches my eye. The Sanyo Micro-Pack 35 is an elegant piece of Japanese manufacturing. I walk past it, tell myself that I can't afford it, and then return a moment later.

The young salesman winks as he rings me up. "You're just like James Bond," he says, and I try to convince myself that it's a compliment.

Victor bakes a Spam quiche for lunch on Halloween. The aroma of cheese and processed pork wafts through the house while the CB radio chirps beside him. "Calling two units to High Street for a code ten-fifty-two," calls a voice over the radio. As Victor pulls the quiche out of the oven, someone knocks on the front door. The sound is precise and efficient, as if the person outside studied door-knocking professionally for several years.

"Trick-or-treaters comin' earlier and earlier each year," Victor grumbles to himself as he stomps down the hallway, still wearing his oven mitts.

"Mr. McCadie, is that right?" asks a voice as businesslike as the knock.

"The man of the hour," my grandfather responds dryly.

"Is your granddaughter home? Miss Wilhelmina McCadie?" the clipped male voice continues.

"Now look here, if you're tryin' to sell us something—"

I straighten the belt on my shirtdress, then step into the hallway, where Victor is giving his best impression of a watchdog. He's practically barking at the intruder on our doorstep.

"Hello, I'm Detective Wallace from the Maine State Police." With horn-rimmed glasses, a briefcase, pleated brown pants, and a lightweight tan car coat, Detective Wallace is the opposite of Chief Deputy Abbott in every way. Intelligence and professionalism waft from him like a sensible cologne.

"A detective!" Victor splutters. "Bless my heart."

"Could we have a moment?" I give Victor an apologetic smile, then steer the detective into our parlor. The plastic-wrapped couch squeaks as I sit down. Detective Wallace turns up his nose at my grandfather's La-Z-Boy, opting for a quilted wing chair instead.

"Thank you for speaking with me today, Miss McCadie," Detective Wallace says as he reaches into his briefcase, then sets a tape recorder down on the dusty coffee table. I gaze at it with envy, it's even smaller than the one I bought yesterday. "Do I have your consent to record this conversation?"

"Yes, of course," I reply, trying not to look too excited.

"Great," he says, then clicks *Record*. "This is Detective Randall Wallace from the Maine Major Crimes Unit. It is"–he pauses to consult his sensible leather watch–"ten o'clock on Saturday, October thirty-first, and I'm interviewing Miss Wilhelmina McCadie of Eastport. Now, Miss McCadie, you may be wondering why I'm here–"

"I assume it's about the body found at a party I attended last summer," I interrupt.

The detective furrows his brow. "That information has not been released to the public. Now, what brought you to Webster Cottage on the evening of June nineteenth?"

"A lobster bake," I reply curtly.

"And you were there because–"

"Avery Webster invited me. It is his summer home."

"You weren't there with"–the detective consults his papers–"Florence, Wendy, and–"

"No. I saw them at the party, of course, but I was there at Avery's invitation."

"*You* are friends with Avery Webster?" The detective doesn't bother to hide his skepticism.

"To a degree. And I know his brother, Claude, as well," I offer without enthusiasm.

"And your relationship with the Websters?" Mr. Wallace prompts me, his eyes beady behind his horn-rimmed glasses.

*Extremely frustrating.* "Friendly."

"I thought that the local girls only knew the Webster family in passing–because they're summer people." The investigator scribbles rapidly in his legal pad.

*Right. Avery belongs to the country-club set, and I don't even know how to play badminton.* "Maybe he just invited me for a bit of local flavor?" I offer, recrossing my legs.

"Did you know the deceased as well?" Detective Wallace withdraws a binder from his briefcase and opens it to a shot of Gertrude. Her hair is perfectly coiffed and her eyes glimmer against a cloudlike background. There is something confectionary about her portrait–as if Gertrude were a human cream puff, immortalized at her most perfect hour with a very short shelf life. I suppress a grin at the misleading photograph. She looks like just another beauty queen here, but she was so much more than that.

"I might have seen her at the bar." I muster an expression of forgetful concern. "Maybe there was a man with her?" I've read extensively about lying. The key to a good lie is to provide just enough information. We remember moments in brief bursts; if those bursts become overly elaborate, they trigger response signals in our listeners.

"Is this the man you saw her with?" The detective leafs through his binder for a photo of Teddy with his casino-owner mustache.

I affect a posture of uncertainty, cocking my head to the right. "Could be?"

"You know him?" The detective sounds surprised. "Did you see her with anyone else that evening?"

"I only saw her that once..." I trail off when I remember the *second* time I saw Gertrude, with her leg wrapped around Claude's thigh in the hallway. Then my eye twitches when I remember the *third* time, as she threatened her fiancé with an ashtray in the solarium.

"You mentioned Claude Webster. Was he at the party?" The detective flips to a photo of Claude in a collegiate cardigan with a winning smile. "And what about Avery Webster?" He turns to a photo of Avery looking far too attractive in a photography studio somewhere. "What was he doing?"

"Avery was busy." I avert my eyes. "He was schmoozing with the guests, showing people around, and helping old women. He was being a good host."

"The man of the year." Detective Wallace sounds equally unimpressed. "What about this fellow? What was he doing?" He shuffles through his booklet to reveal an image of a man in a jacket, scowling at the camera. A faint scar runs down his left cheek.

My eyes narrow at Edgar's poor fashion taste. I reach forward, unable to restrain myself. "Could I see that? Who is he? Maybe if I knew I could—"

"I'm afraid that I can't divulge that information." The detective withdraws the mug book from my hands.

"He's a walking stereotype, isn't he?" I ask, eyes fixed on Edgar's black-and-white photograph. "A fedora *and* a trench coat. All he's missing is a rough exterior hiding a heart of gold and a dueling caffeine and nicotine addiction." As I study Edgar's five-o'clock shadow, I remember our recent conversation. *I took the knife in case they searched your room.* Almost as if he *knew* that Detective Wallace would be coming to interview me. But how?

"You know him?" the detective asks with surprise.

"'Know' might be an overstatement."

Detective Wallace closes his binder with a snap. "Miss McCadie, in your own words, please describe what happened at Webster Cottage on the evening of June nineteenth. Tell me everything that you remember. Even the most trivial detail might prove invaluable to this case."

"Ummm . . ." I look from the detective to the tape recorder, and then down at the teal carpet, imagining Gertrude's body splayed out across the center of it. "The Websters threw a summer solstice party. There were fancy French chefs, a jazz band, and a table stacked with champagne coupes. I'd never seen anything like it before, it was such an opulent mess. Avery showed me his speedboat, then I went to the bar. While I was waiting for my drink, that woman in the photo walked over with her fiancé– I think they ordered whiskey? Then I went to the buffet and grabbed a croissant—which was *delicious,* by the way. Then I went—I mean—I screamed—I mean, I *heard* a maid scream." I scratch a hangnail until it bleeds, then watch a drop of blood soak into my skirt. I raise my eyes to find Detective Wallace grinning at me. I'm sure that it's possible to look guiltier than I do at this moment, although I can't imagine how. "Then everyone was asked to leave . . . but I didn't go. I went inside to find Avery and say goodbye. And *that's* when I realized that something was wrong. That something had happened. To Gertrude. Then I saw the police handcuff her fiancé, who seemed *quite* agitated by the way—maybe he realized that she was cheating on him?" The words slip out unheeded, and I raise a hand to my mouth, realizing my mistake. "Then I went home. And . . . that was it."

A long pause while I imagine other details I might add. Does the detective want to know about the diamonds hidden in my jewelry box? Or the knife stolen from my closet? Or the scent of Gertrude's perfume? Or the flavor of Teddy's French fries? Or the way that Claude's hands clenched my—I mean *her*—thigh?

The detective makes several scratches in his legal pad. "And how did you get home?"

"The butler drove me," I reply guiltily.

"So just to clarify: you *didn't* know the deceased, but you *did* know that she was cheating on her fiancé?" The detective smirks. "Why[b] do you think that someone would want to hurt Miss Taylor?"

---

[b] **Why (adv.): 1.** *for what cause, reason, or purpose.* **2. (n.)** *a baffling problem or enigma.* Unchanged by time, the modern *why* is a phonetic match for its archaic counterpart *kwi.* Our questions are as old as dirt, and the propensity

"Could it have been a mistake? A game that got slightly out of hand?"

"In my experience, people don't generally stab each other in the heart by accident." Detective Wallace narrows his bushy eyebrows at me. "That isn't a game I'm familiar with."

"Chief Deputy Abbott came to see me last summer," I murmur, scratching at a second hangnail. "Has he been taken off this case?"

"*Who* is interviewing *whom*, Miss McCadie?" Detective Wallace glares at his notebook. "The investigation proved too... taxing... for the local police force. Now if you remember anything else, please don't hesitate to call." Detective Wallace hands me his business card, then switches off the tape recorder. "And a word of advice, if I may: you might want to get your story straight before we speak again. It would be a shame if this blew up in your face."

Victor is beside himself. He was, unsurprisingly, lurking behind the doorway, listening to every word with bated breath. "I forbid you from returning to that house!" he shouts over his quiche.

"Oh, please," I reply as I poke a piece of Spam with my fork. "It's perfectly safe."

---

to doubt and have second thoughts is even older. I'm not the first person to ask *why*, and I'm not the first person to be consumed by it, either.

Grace was also eavesdropping. "Billie," she says under her breath when I swing by at happy hour with her Witch's Brew cocktail. "Next time, ask for a warrant."

"But why?" I reply as I place the wicker tray on her lap. "I have nothing to hide."

The rattle of her cocktail shaker keeps time with the distant shriek of trick-or-treaters. "Did you kill her because you were jealous?" Grace asks with a single raised eyebrow as she strains the cocktail into her glass. It's a sickly neon green and reeks of melon liqueur.

That night, over Hawaiian Death (a special treat of honey-baked ham, canned pineapples, and maraschino cherries that Victor only makes if something truly awful has occurred), my grandfather slips me a flyer for a law firm. "Billie, if you throw enough money at a problem, it will just go away," he murmurs, gazing despondently at his pineapple. Behind us, the doorbell rings.

"But I haven't done anything wrong!" I squeeze his hand as I get up and put on a polyester witch's hat. "There's nothing to worry about." As I hand out M&M's to a pair of black cats, my words echo falsely in my ears.

**CHAPTER ELEVEN**

# PRESS ~~RELATIONS~~ FLIRTATIONS

*The average individual patronizing newsworthy restaurants, charity benefits, and other places where society and gossip columnists gather will not find herself in print unless she makes news in some way... The debutante who, perhaps in sheer desperation because she has not been photographed as much as her sister debs, enters a night club with a gazelle on a leash, can be virtually sure to make at least a line of print somewhere.*

Gertrude is on the tip of everyone's tongue. She's a game of telephone that grows more salacious with every retelling. As Detective Wallace works his way through the Websters' guest list, her name gradually grows from a whisper to a shout. The town is abuzz[a] with gossip. Gertrude is the most interest-

---

[a] **Abuzz (adj.): 1.** *buzzing.* **2.** *full of activity.* Many attribute *abuzz* to Charles Dickens, who first used it in his novel *A Tale of Two Cities* (p. 1859). *Buzz* is an onomatopoeia from the fourteenth century, inspired by the sound of bees in flight.

ing thing to ever happen to Eastport, Maine, and I doubt we'll see her like again.

The news breaks on election day, as though Gertrude had been campaigning as well. Her photo dominates the front page, and President Lyndon Johnson is squished to the bottom. "Society Girl Slaying: Murder and Money on the Coast." The newspapers are almost as enamored with her as I am, gushing with details about Gertrude's love affair with high society. They don't give a hoot about the reelection, either.

At the Waco Diner I overhear: "Murder Mansion." "Who brought her?" "Lovely red hair."

Gertrude is the darling of checkout counters and special news reports. Her cream-puff eyes watch as Iris Swann rings me up for another bottle of Blue Nun wine. Her long eyelashes shiver on the television screen as Victor mutes the evening news during dinner.

Four different photos are in circulation. In one, Gertrude looks serious and dramatic, like the author of an acclaimed novel that no one actually enjoys reading. In the second, she's an artfully rendered Vermeer, with secrets hidden in the depths of her half smile. In the third, she's your classic Hollywood bombshell, making doe eyes at the photographer. And in the fourth, she's statuesque as a judge from the Westminster Kennel Club Dog Show—every inch the purebred.

"She's a stone-cold fox," Bobby Fernald volunteers as he leans across the soda fountain. The soda jerk tips his pressed white cap to her with a low whistle.

Why did Gertrude have these photos taken? Did she hire a photographer for no reason? Is that something women do?

Should I be doing it, too? Or was this a case of feminine intuition? Did she catch some whiff of trouble and have her portrait taken on the off-chance that she got murdered? It's almost as if she'd been preparing for her brush with fame. It's a shame that she isn't here to see her hard work pay off.

I study her petite nose and full lips, then lean in until my hair practically brushes across hers. If you look past the smoky eyeshadow and the screen-siren eyelashes, there *is* a slight resemblance between us. But no one would ever notice, because she's the leading lady while I'm the wardrobe assistant. She desperately wanted to be seen, while I desperately want to curl up on the couch with a cup of tea. She was a sex symbol while I'm an armchair romantic, buying frilly underwear that no one ever sees. But if you stripped away her TNT sparkle and my library frump to compare our actual features, you would find us very much the same.

Mrs. Pridmore spills her coffee when I breeze in. "Did you hear?" she splutters. "The detective! The estate! The murder!" She claps her hands and moans in ecstasy, as if she's been waiting her entire life for a murder spree in Eastport, Maine.

I look up with wide eyes, my fingers gently stroking the engagement ring in my pocket. "What murder?"


A discarded newspaper sticks to the bottom of my shoe outside the post office. I try to scrape it on the doorjamb, but it's stuck. I purse my lips and reach down to remove the soggy paper, then bite my lip when I find Gertrude's lightly soiled face gazing up at me.

Three pieces of mail are lurking in my PO box. I scoop them up, trade Mr. Townsend a smile for a tangelo, then return to the brisk November afternoon. Walking across the street to a picnic table overlooking the harbor, I climb up to rest my feet on the bench. Ashen leaves dart across a listless sky as I place the tangelo beside me. A seagull swoops down to perch on one of the adjacent canons as I slit open the first envelope.

*Be careful what you wish for. And come visit for the holidays? You know you want to. Xo* Debbie's pretty cursive is scrawled across an index card paper-clipped to a stack of printouts from the microfilm at MIT's Barker Library. The seagull provides a running commentary while I study her research.

The first article is from the Celebrations page of the *Greenwich Times*, a small Connecticut newspaper. My eyes widen as they take in Gertrude's boatneck sweater and classic Rococo features. Her stylish Hollywood flipped bob has a bold side part, with waves sweeping down to her shoulders.

> July 29, 1961: "Taylor–Gibbs. Mr. and Mrs. Calvin Taylor of New Haven, CT, are pleased to announce the engagement of their eldest daughter, Gertrude N. Taylor, to Edgar P. Gibbs of Bangor, ME. No date has been set for the wedding."

A snort, and the seagull looks over curiously. Edgar and Gertrude were really an item! But less shocking is the news that Gertrude *isn't* from heavenly New Canaan but abysmal New Haven. Gertrude must have lied to Teddy about her hometown. I wonder if Edgar was also a step up from where she came from.

## ETIQUETTE FOR LOVERS AND KILLERS

The second article is from the Engagements page of the Sunday edition of the *Boston Globe*. I swallow bile as I study a photo of Gertrude and Teddy standing together on a sand dune, clasping each other's hands in a truly sickening manner.

> Sept. 13, 1963: Boston, MA.: "Theodore J. Brixton proposes to Gertrude Taylor; student at Harvard and graduate from Wellesley become affianced. Wedding bells for the collegiate couple."

Another snort. Was Wellesley also a fib? How much of Gertrude's personality was a carefully constructed lie? The blurb is essentially a pedigree list of Teddy's blue blood and yacht club aspirations. I shake my head as I flip to the third article, then gape at Edgar's ugly face.

"Private Eye Caught Eavesdropping,"[b] reads the headline from the *Bangor Daily News*.

> Edgar P. Gibbs (40) of Stamford, Connecticut, pleaded not guilty yesterday to wiretapping. The Maine transplant trained at the police academy in Bangor before opening a detective agency in Connecticut. Gibbs's firm gained considerable repute until the PI was caught stalking a client

---

[b] **Eavesdrop (v.):** *to secretly listen to a private conversation.* In Old English, *yfesdrype* referred to the ground beneath the *eaves* of a building where the rain dripped down. This term gradually became associated with the unscrupulous individuals who lurked under the *eaves* of wealthy houses, trying to listen to the conversations taking place inside—entertainment being scarce in medieval Europe.

and bugging her phone line. The detective represented himself in court, arguing that covert surveillance was a cornerstone of his profession. The court found Gibbs guilty of violating the 4th Amendment protection from unlawful search and seizure. Gibbs was sentenced to two years at the Bridgeport Correctional Facility for a Class D Felony.

The seagull squawks as I study the date on the third article. *November 15, 1961.* So Edgar went to jail a mere *four months* after proposing to Gertrude. She must have been pissed! But she couldn't have lost too much sleep over it.

In two years, Gertrude climbed out of the middle class and into the upper crust. If she'd had another two years, what paper would she have been in next? Was she really content with a mustached lapdog, or would she have kept on climbing? The more I learn, the more convinced I become that everything about Gertrude was a lie. She was a case study in assumed elegance. A lesson plan on creating the illusion of old money. She must have studied the rules of etiquette at some point and used them as stepping stones into high society; until she grew bored, and decided they were beneath her. And what was her ultimate goal? Was she hoping to be the next queen of Andorra or one of the other small European monarchies? Or was her heart set on playing footsie in the Oval Office?

I notice my lips pinching together. Maybe Grace is right. Maybe I *am* jealous.

The next envelope is from my father's estate attorney in Boston. It's a dossier filled with legal forms, tax documents, and a bank application—all related to the execution of my parents' will. *Wilhelmina, I need you to sign these documents with a notary. You've postponed this for long enough*, Robert Liles, Esq. lectures me from afar. He's right, I've been procrastinating for two years, but I'd like to wait a little longer. As I study the papers, my head starts pounding. It feels like it's going to split open. The pages glare up at me, as if they know how angry I am. As if they know how unexpected and brutal my parents' deaths were. And to sign these forms, to acknowledge their loss, will make it even more final.

The third envelope is a form rejection from the Reddington Classics Library. The letter is a hackneyed photocopy with my name spelled wrong. I wonder if they bothered to read my submission, or if they just sent this out, sight unseen. I crumple it up, then reach for the tangelo.

I've tried to play by the rules. Tried to follow the steps and be a good little job applicant. But it's not working. My field is too competitive, and my résumé is too short. I'm desperate to escape my pink Singer Featherweight and my beige twin bed. There's so much of life that I long to experience, but I'm caught in this postcard of coastal New England and I can't get out. Short of kidnapping a museum curator and holding her hostage until she hires me (a hands-on approach to job "hunting" that gains appeal with every passing day), I'm not sure what else to do.

The exotic citrus scent unfurls around me. Whispering of far-off destinations and overpriced supermarkets. Fruit I yearn to pick off the tree for myself. The seagull raises its wings and swoops low over my head. I watch it fly off with a twinge of envy. I'd like a change of scenery, too.

That night the phone rings.

I struggle out of the deepest, darkest depths of sleep to blink at the phone on my nightstand. Moonlight cascades through the windows, falling across my pillows and bedsheets. I was dreaming about Gertrude again. She was teaching me how to use an ashtray as a weapon.

"Hello?" I murmur into the receiver, my voice thick with sleep.

"Let the dead rest in peace." Edgar's voice is gravelly on the other end of the phone.

"Mr. Fedora, how forward of you to call a young lady late at night," I murmur, my tongue heavy with sleep. I'm too tired to care. Too drowsy to be sure that this is anything but a dream. "Will you tell me about Gertrude?"

It must be a dream, because Edgar's voice softens on the other end. "She was beautiful and deranged."

"No, the *real* her." I pull the blankets over my head and burrow into my bed, taking the handset with me. "What did she smell like? What did her laugh sound like? Was she always loud and brash, or was there softness hiding there, too?"

My covers embrace me as Edgar's voice warms with recollection. "You know, she could actually be quite kind and silly, if she thought that no one was paying attention. And she smelled slightly peppery and sweet, like spiced vanilla–"

**CHAPTER TWELVE**

# THE RITUAL OF DRINKING

*Esoteric cocktails should be avoided. An Alexander, for example, would be a poor choice, especially with men present. Fancy mixed drinks are usually frowned on by men, though beloved of women who order them in restaurants. Standard cocktails are the wise choice.*

Tiny white flakes drift past my train window. The snow flutters down to disappear against the salt-and-pepper landscape. My reflection matches the view: pale, gloomy, with a few patches of dandruff.

I always feel uneasy when I leave Eastport, I guess because my family has lived here for so long. The McCadies are a product of these coastal waterways—salty as a tangle of seaweed, tenacious as a barnacle, and prickly as a cranberry bog. We've watched the changing tides and wind sweeping across fields of snow in winter. We've seen forests lit up like fireworks in the slow detonation of autumn and burned our hands on lobster pots. My father worked for a fishing company, my grandfather owned a boat repair shop, and my great-grandfather ran a sardine-canning factory, so I guess you could say that the smell of clam chowder is in my blood. If you go farther back in the McCadie lineage, I'm descended from a long line of fur traders, so perhaps Teddy was right, and I am part of the "riffraff."

I tried to cover my scent while I attended the Ashburn Linguistics Institute in Upstate New York. My female peers were all ladies of privilege. Desperate to blend in, I dusted off my mother's copy of Amy Vanderbilt's *Complete Book of Etiquette* and tried to read past the place-setting diagrams and picnic-outfit suggestions to the unwritten rules of sophistication. I wanted to wear refinement like a disguise, so that no one would guess where I came from.

Miss Vanderbilt wrote: "If each of us lived in a protective glass bubble, there would be no need for manners. We could simply do as we pleased. But since Homo sapiens is gregarious, rules of conduct are imperative. We must learn which ceremonies may be breached occasionally and which must never be if we are to live pleasantly with our fellow man."

I consider Amy's "Rules of Living Pleasantly" as we speed through Pleasant Point. Clara could have used one of those protective glass bubbles. As could Gertrude. I kind of wish that I had one now, as I venture into civilization.

The sky is dark by the time I disembark in Boston. The holiday season is in full swing at South Station, with light sconces dripping with tinsel and an aroma of exhaust, pretzels, and roasted chestnuts. Hot air bursts through the subway grates as

I connect for the train to Back Bay. I join the businessmen, students, panhandlers, bargain hunters, and matrons in their heavy fur coats, toting their holiday shopping like hunting trophies. Then I get off at Arlington station and lug my suitcase up to Commonwealth Avenue.

The College Club has lace doilies on every surface, and a pervasive scent of old lady perfumes the air. My room has abrasive floral wallpaper and a Pepto-Bismol carpet. The threadbare sheets are scratchy against my skin as I prop a book up against the lumpy pillows. *Midaregami* (*Tangled Hair*) is pretty in pink, with an art nouveau heart pierced by an arrow, bleeding rose petals across the page. Japanese writer Yosano Akiko is sensual, subversive, and Victorian. Her poetry collection was published in 1900, despite widespread criticism for her flowery metaphors for female desire. Her poetry was hailed as "obscenities fit for a whore," which obviously appeals to me.

I try to lose myself in *Tangled Hair* but keep getting distracted by thoughts of Clara's blond ponytail. Then my memory skips over to Gertrude's flipped Hollywood bob. *God, her hair looked good.* Then I catch myself dwelling on Avery's sandy hair flecked with silver, but I push those memories away because I hate him.

As I curl up with *Tangled Hair*, a telltale squeak issues through the paper-thin walls. As I listen to the mattress groan in the next room, I'm determined not to think about Avery's lips against mine. As I squint at the Japanese poetry, the squeaking continues. And I have to wonder: What is the point of having a body, if no one ever touches it?

The scents of frankincense and myrrh drift out of the gothic church on Boylston Street. The aroma of dirty martinis and lunch-break love affairs wafts from the lobby of the Copley-Plaza Hotel. What a treat it is, to stroll through a strange city. To eavesdrop on a conversation over a cup of coffee. To admire the parade of glossy mink coats on Newbury Street. To wander into the Boston Public Library and grin at the marble lions standing guard in the lobby. They both look horrified by the holiday garlands wrapped around their necks.

Privacy is such a novelty. I'm just one more stranger walking down Boylston Street. No one knows me here, so there is no one to report back to my grandfather on my every move. No one to tell him, for example, when I visit a store called Pandora's Jewelry Box.

The jeweler is as crisp and clean as his display cabinets. His black suit matches the black velvet tray he sets down before me. His skinny eyebrows knit together as I place the two engagement rings on it. He lifts a loupe to his eye, then measures, weighs, and catalogs each ring. "Is this for insurance?"

"Just personal curiosity. They're fake, right?"

"These are *not* synthetic diamonds." The jeweler frowns as if I've insulted his profession.

"They're real?" I ask with trepidation.

"The smaller *diamond*[a] is one carat. It's slightly included and

---

[a] **Diamond (n.):** *a precious stone composed of carbon. The hardest substance known to man.* The Old French *diamant* is a truncation of the Greek *adamas*, "an unbreakable stone," which stems from the PIE roots *a*, "not," and *deme*,

poorly cut. The subtle yellow tint hints at chemical impurities that some might consider charming," the jeweler says, looking less than charmed. "I would appraise its retail value at three hundred dollars."

"Well, I think it's lovely!" I protest, feeling oddly defensive over my cheap diamond.

"But the second diamond is a different story," he continues with grudging approval. "It's 3.1 carats with a meticulous old European cut. Virtually flawless, it's very slightly included and colorless to the human eye. The rose-gold setting is poorly considered, but objectively good quality. I would appraise its retail value at two thousand, and its resale value at twelve hundred." The jeweler pinches his thin lips as he takes off his gloves. "I will *not* ask how you acquired them."

A wry smile. "You wouldn't believe me if I told you."

I hail a cab, examining the rings as we inch through traffic on the way to my father's estate lawyer. I liked these much better when I thought they were fake. Gifts like this always come with a catch.

The taxi pulls up in the shadow of the recently built Prudential Center. An accordion gate makes an awful screeching sound as I climb inside a tiny elevator, then emerge on the top floor. Robert Liles's office is as chilly as his smile. Niceties and small talk. Shuffling papers. Frowning eyes behind Coke-bottle glasses. The dreaded dossier emerges as the notary (a secretary with the barest hint of a hickey) walks over. "Billie, you have to

---

"broken." I wonder what diamonds retailed for millennia ago, and if they still lost so much of their value in the resale market?

accept that your parents are gone," the attorney says. His secretary/notary(/lover?) nods in agreement.

"I accept it," I lie, then take off my white leather gloves and reach for his pen.

"Great. Then sign here and here." The lawyer's Montblanc pen is warm in my hand as I initial one page after another—confirming my parents' death. Attesting that I'm a lone ship, far from port, with just my grandparents as the lighthouse keepers, navigating me through the storm. "This will go into a trust, which you can access here in Boston—" My eyes glaze over as Mr. Liles explains the ins and outs of beneficiary law.

"We've helped other young ladies with similar trusts. Having your own bank account is very chic—it's *all* the rage nowadays." The secretary tries (and fails) to lighten the mood.

I window-shop and wipe away tears, trying to shake off the feeling of loss that trails behind me like a last-season perfume. I try on sunglasses and hats, as if selecting a disguise, because I'd like to pretend to be someone else for a moment. Someone who doesn't hurt quite so much. I pause outside a salon and gaze up through the big bay window at women reclining under giant hair dryers. The cones suspended over their heads look like tiny UFOs. On impulse, I step inside.

Sunset gleams off the cobblestones on Charles Street. The gas lanterns cast an amber glow across the holly and spruce in the window boxes ornamenting the brownstones. I feel like I'm walking through the pages of a Charles Dickens novel as I push through the doors of a British pub. The Sevens Ale House has worn leather banquettes and walls strung with Christmas lights. I survey the scene of paunchy old-timers and bookish young men before my eyes alight on Debbie. In her green velvet blazer and matching pencil skirt, she looks like she's dressed for a fox hunt. Her hair is curly today, falling around her head in a cloud of black coils.

"The flirty detective!" Debbie signals the bartender, and he brings over another whiskey sour. "Cheers to you and this do! Life is too short for boring hair." She raises a glass to my flipped Hollywood bob, curiosity flashing across her bourbon-brown eyes. She doesn't mention that it's the exact same haircut as Gertrude's.

"No, let's toast to your hair, which is always fabulous," I protest as the bouncy side part swoops down over my face, hiding one eye. "Was it really that boring before?"

Debbie kindly changes the subject, regaling me with stories about MIT's libraries and an overattentive mathematician. Debbie gets a lot of attention, but she never takes it too seriously, a trait I could stand to learn. "But enough about boys, let's talk murder. Dish," she says with a devilish grin.

How to say: *There are no leads and people keep dying* in a way that sounds fun and approachable? I glance at my whiskey sour, but it's even less articulate than I am. "I think it's time for a pivot," I reply vaguely.

"'Tis the season!" She nods in approval.

The Sevens grows increasingly British as the hours pass, with Christmas carols blasting through the jukebox and patrons yelling to be heard. I savor the silence of the ladies' room, then return to the fray. As I weave through the crowd, two large hands stop me.

"Billie goat." Claude digs his fingers into my shoulder. He towers over the other bar patrons, a colossus of male entitlement in a tartan shirt and red corduroy jacket.

"First off, a 'billy goat' is a male goat," I inform him. "If I *were* a goat—which I assure you, I am not—I would be a female goat. A nanny goat."

"My nanny goat!" Claude laughs and claps me on the back, then focuses on my hair. "What an *interesting* cut, Billie. Whatever inspired it?"

My shorn hair quivers in embarrassment. "You're smirking."

"Salivating," he corrects me.

"Gross!" I turn to escape, only to stumble straight into Pearl Hamilton. The fashion plate is dressed to the nines in black Chanel. *Klädd upp till tänderna* as they would say in Sweden, "dressed to the teeth." Her platinum hair is swept up in a twist and the pearls of her namesake gleam around her neck. The turquoise cocktail umbrella stuck in her updo adds a dash of Capote to her otherwise flawless visage. I wonder if she knows it's there. She looks like she got lost in the bar on her way home from *Breakfast at Tiffany's*.

"Is this man bothering you?" Pearl steps between us with a pout.

"I'm just teasing her." Claude chuckles with his deep, throaty laugh. "Teasing the tease."

"Pearl." She extends one black satin glove, as I suppress a laugh. What is the polite response if someone doesn't remember meeting you? Should I pretend that I don't remember her either? Fake amnesia? Assume an alias?

"Pearl, you've met Billie, before." Claude does the laughing for me. "At our end-of-season party. She's the one who—"

"Oh my God, what a *goose* I am!" Pearl squeals and batts Claude's arm away, her eyes wide as silver dollars. "And how unspeakably *rude* of me! Billie! How could I forget you? With your cute little face, and your cute little bike—"

"I'm surprised they let you escape," Claude interrupts, although he doesn't explain from who or what. "How long are you in town for?" he continues, removing the cocktail umbrella from Pearl's hair. I was right, she didn't know it was there.

"Two more nights," I reply, thankful for my return ticket. "Do you go to school here?"

"Harvard Law. Actual hell on earth." Claude heaves a long-suffering sigh, then reaches into his pocket. "We're having a holiday party on Friday. You should come." He runs two fingers along the inside of my wrist as he passes me a card, and I snatch my hand away. The invitation looks a little morose for the holidays, with gold lettering on black cardstock.

12 Old Orchard Road, Chestnut Hill
Midnight, December 18th
Have you been naughty or nice?

"Claude, do you really think—" The socialite grows as pale as the pearls around her neck.

"Pearl, don't be such a snob." Claude winks at me.

"Thank you for this." I incline my head toward the card.

"Now, I should probably get back before my partridge runs away with a pear tree," I murmur nonsensically. A surge of bar patrons pulls me away from them, back to Debbie.

"Who was that?" she asks as I slide onto the barstool beside her.

"Suspect number two."

"No!" she whips her head around to find Claude watching us. "He's atrocious. I'm smitten." She sips from her straw and locks eyes with him from across the bar. "And who's the broad? His accomplice?"

I signal the bartender. "No. I think she's just a cautionary tale about inbreeding."

My breath puffs up in tiny clouds as I hurry back to the College Club. The wind plucks at my jacket as I slip across the frozen walkways of the Boston Public Garden. I feel like I'm being followed, which is hardly exceptional. Is that an echo behind me? I stop, and the sound stops, too. Then I pick back up my pace, and the sound resumes. I roll my eyes as I duck around the corner of a large granite plinth and wedge myself into the base of a bronze statue of George Washington on horseback. I grow very still as a tall figure strides past. He's wearing a hat, but it is too dark to see if it's a fedora.

*I found the challenge of losing him each day rather thrilling,* Gertrude recites in my memory as I sneak around the monument and retrace my steps. Well, it seems like we have at least one—I reach up to touch my shorn hair—I mean, *two* things in common. How many more?

## ETIQUETTE FOR LOVERS AND KILLERS

---

That night I dream of quill pens. Of ink splattering across parchment paper. A steel nib dips into a glass bottle, then blots itself on a scrap of muslin. I wake up and dig through my suitcase for the love letters. Is that a smudge of pencil beneath one signature? I call down to reception and ask for the yellow pages.

FERNANDA PESTAÑA, EXPERT FORENSIC DOCUMENT EXAMINER, reads a brass nameplate on an eggplant-colored door. I suppress a smile. *Pestaña* is the Portuguese word for "eyelash" and a rather peculiar last name. Miss Pestaña's office is séance-chic, complete with dusty vases of peacock feathers and silk scarves draped over lampshades. The floor-to-ceiling bookshelves are overflowing with tarot cards, dried flowers, and antique books. Fernanda matches the interior. Her bun is coming lose at the nape of her neck, the buttons on her sweater are mismatched, and her lipstick runs outside the natural curvature of her lips. The room smells like decaying roses.

"Place your documents here," she says with a hint of a Brazilian accent, motioning toward a small table beside a cast-iron gas stove. "Can I have your name?"

"Bettina," I lie as I pull the two envelopes out of my brown leather handbag and set them down on the copper pedestal table between us. The first letter is penned in precise cursive, while the second is scrawled in a childish scribble. Fernanda examines the correspondence, then reaches for a magnifying glass on the bookcase behind her.

"These were written by two different people." She holds up Gertrude's letter, squinting at it through her Sherlock Holmes magnifier. "And both signatures are forgeries. They're terrible fakes." Fernanda brings Gertrude's letter up to her face, where it hovers dangerously close to her clumpy lipstick. "This one is a trace-over forgery. Whoever wrote it was nervous. The penmanship is jittery from attempting to disguise itself. And the tiny capital *I* indicates an inferiority complex. Do you see those *T*s? This guy has emotional constipation. He's an awful procrastinator with minimal forward momentum in his life."

"*His* life?" I clarify. "You think the letter from Gertrude was written by a man?"

"He wouldn't know femininity if it smacked him in the face. A woman would make a better fake." Miss Pestaña leans in to examine the first letter. "Do you see how every row is straight and lifted slightly above the line? And just *look* at the slant on those *T*s. This guy is a narcissist, but his vanity hides crippling self-esteem issues."

I frown, imagining what embarrassing traits Fernanda might read from my own writing.

"Could I analyze your penmanship? Just out of professional curiosity," she asks, then reaches for a pen and paper and places them on the pedestal table. I hunch over awkwardly on the cluttered surface while she observes me write.

> Penmanship *(n.): the art of writing by hand. Derived from the medieval* penman *(a scribe), which stems from the Old French* pene, *"quill pen," and the PIE root* pet, *"to fly."*

My curtain of hair swings down to cover my eyes as I jot down the definition, then hand Fernanda the paper. As she reads it, she raises one eyebrow. "Just *look* at the big loops on your *G*s. That indicates a powerful sex drive. I can tell that you yearn for something ... or is it some*one*?" she adds archly. "Is your real name Gertrude? It certainly isn't Bettina."

"I'm not Gertrude. I'm her opposite in every way," I reply flatly. Hoping it's true.

"I wouldn't be so sure of that," Fernanda murmurs with a knowing grin, then leans back to scrutinize the letters again. "How did you acquire these? Were they sent to you?"

"No. They have nothing to do with me."

"That's good. To be honest, I sense something threatening here—not in the tone, so much as the penmanship. There is a feeling of suppressed violence. Of manipulation and restraint. I'm glad that you weren't the intended recipient. Because if you were, I might say that you're in trouble."

I rise unsteadily to my feet, suddenly desperate to get away from Fernanda and her sharp eyes. "Thank you for your help. How much do I owe you?"

Miss Pestaña laughs. "I don't charge people to tell them things they already know."

I start to argue, but stop myself. Fernanda's right. She simply confirmed a couple of half-formed hypotheses: that a dead woman *hadn't* written to me from beyond the grave, and that more than one person was in on this hoax.

As I step outside, I notice a man in a trench coat loitering in a nearby doorway. He lifts up a newspaper and retreats into the shadows. I roll my eyes and hurry in the opposite direction.

Unease follows me through Back Bay, nipping at my heels as I browse through a used bookstore. My Spanish is almost as dusty as their foreign language section, so I pick up a few books to practice. I continue to the Public Garden and sit down on a bench, watching two swans cower together on Duck Island, a patch of earth in the center of the man-made lake. The naked boughs of a willow tree hang down above them, swishing back and forth laconically. I heave a sigh. I'd like to go back to Maine now; I've had enough of city life. *Dépaysement* is the French word for that, "the unsteady feeling of being far away from home."

It would be nice to have someone to go on holiday with. A beau to snap my photo beside the swans, then suggest we grab some coffee to warm up. He might order us cappuccinos, then over cups of espresso and frothed milk, I would confess my story. My lover might reach across the table while he offered some benign insight. *What incredible research, Billie! Have you considered joining the FBI?*

For our last dinner, Debbie and I slurp lobster bisque and laugh as we try (and fail) to extract escargot from their shells. Tomorrow, Debbie is off to Killington, Vermont, to celebrate the holiday on the slopes, and I'm headed home to Murderville, Maine. We've always wanted to try Locke-Ober, a former gentlemen's club from the nineteenth century. With painted ceilings, dusty gas lanterns, and carved mahogany cherubs, eating here feels like dining with Dorian Gray.

The classic French fare is paired with a prolific menu of

dated cocktails, like the Montauk Riding Club and the Ping-Pong Special. I order a Death at Dusk, which seems apropos. The crème de violette is sweet on my lips, the absinthe bitter, and the champagne, impossibly, ties it all together. The cocktail tastes and looks like poison. But a bourgeois sort of poison—if you have to die, you might as well do so in style. Debbie and I toast each other with etched crystal glasses as the scent of foie gras wafts over us.

"I heard about this new place where you should apply," Debbie murmurs as a waiter in coattails approaches with our Baked Alaska. He sets it down, then backs away warily, as if it might explode. "It's a private collection. Some rich guy on the beach with an artifact problem. He's on a shopping spree and hasn't even *started* looking for archival linguists."

"Which beach?" I frown at the blue flames licking across the meringue topping.

"Montecito." She shrugs. "It's somewhere in California."

I glance at the bulky sweaters, pale faces, rattling windows, and aging pianist playing an insipid rendition of "Autumn Leaves." Then I imagine a warm breeze gently ruffling the fronds of a palm tree, while "Surfin' U.S.A." drifts out of the windows of a passing Chevy Malibu. "Well, if you insist."

After dinner, we say our goodbyes, then hail our respective taxis. "Where you headed?" asks my cabbie, a scruffy young man with a double chin, a Boston Red Sox baseball cap, and a gruff Southie accent.

"Can you take me to Comm—" I stop when I find the invitation from Claude in my jacket pocket. "Actually, let's go to Chestnut Hill." I regret the words before they've even left my mouth.

Twenty minutes later, we pull up outside a twenty-foot wall with cornices and spires peeking out from behind it. Twelve Old Orchard Road is an English Baroque manor that somehow got lost in the suburbs. A square turret frames a central portico flanked by Corinthian columns and two pavilion wings. "You're joking, right?" The cabbie eyes me with skepticism.

"And the joke is on me," I reply with misgivings. "Could you come back in an hour to pick me up?" I climb out of the cab to stand in the dark, hugging my arms around myself as the massive gates part before me. My kitten heels clatter across the salted cobblestones, then up a black carpet leading to a pair of oversize doors. Two men stand on either side. They both look ridiculous in black trench coats and fake white beards.

"Who invited you?" asks one, his voice slightly muffled by his fluffy beard.

"Claude?" I offer, and the doors open.

Guttering candelabras flicker through a gloomy interior with a vaulted ceiling lost in shadow. A black Christmas tree dominates the center of the room and poinsettias cast eerie shadows across the walls. "Santa Baby" lisps through the speakers. A woman in a French maid uniform and white reindeer antlers attends to the cloakroom, her back turned to me. Her petticoat rustles as she turns, then the blood drains from my face.

"*You*," Lieske exclaims in her clipped Dutch accent, antlers shaking furiously.

## CHAPTER THIRTEEN

# UNMENTIONABLES

*Be over-scrupulous about your undergarments. The edge of a soiled petticoat, or the glimpse of a rent stocking, is singularly disenchanting.*

"I've read your stupid paper every week," she exclaims with another indignant shake of her antlers. "You didn't share a *single one* of my cleaning tips!"

My eyes widen in astonishment. *She still thinks I'm a reporter!* "I'm sorry, my editor decided to go in a different–"

Lieske glares as she puts her hands on her hips. "Ms. Bean, what are you doing here?"

I remove my black wool coat, hoping that the more comfortable I get, the less likely she'll be to throw me out. I try to affect an air of brisk professionalism as Eartha Kitt recites her holiday wish list through the speakers. "That's classified information."

"Did the newspaper send you," she asks, then adds sotto voce, "to investigate undercover?"

I suppress a smile at the idea of the smallest newspaper in America heading up a sting operation, then give her a meaningful look and tap my nose. Lieske's eyes widen as she considers me for a long moment, then breaks into a wide grin. She turns and hurries into the cloakroom, emerging a moment later with two glasses of champagne and a pair of black antlers. "Then take off your dress," she instructs in her curt Dutch accent.

"Wait, what?"

"Look, if you're bringing these people down, then you need to fit in. So strip."

"What kind of party is this?" I ask, my jaw dropping.

"It's a naughty-or-nice party," Lieske says as she helps me with my zipper. She steps back to consider my black satin slip and kitten heels, frowning until I put the antlers on. "Now *proost*!" She hands me one of the champagne flutes, then clinks her glass against mine.

The naughty-or-nice party is a tacky mix of fine art, designer lingerie, and ugly Christmas sweaters, all canoodling together under the mistletoe. A long, dark hallway leads me into a circular vestibule with a white grand piano and a Picasso nude with a Santa hat perched jauntily on the frame. The painting is from his cubist period, of a nude woman with a square head and triangular legs reclining across a sofa. I stroll past three wise men in silky red boxers and crowns, bent over a silver platter. Three church mice saunter over to join them, all young women in plunging silver teddys with mouse ears and sleeping masks pushed up on their foreheads. The Christmas lingerie party is a kitschy subset of the genre, but the yuletide camp somehow makes it more accessible for me.

## ETIQUETTE FOR LOVERS AND KILLERS

Glib falsetto voices lead me past a row of closed doors. Murmurs drift out of some, and bursts of laughter issue from others. The farther I go, the louder the music becomes, until I identify it as "I Only Have Eyes For You" by the Flamingos. I pass a woman in a sheer red baby-doll negligee with feather trim reclining across a velvet chaise. She has a tiny Mrs. Claus hat perched on her head and a crystal telephone pressed to one ear. One foot is raised in the air, absently swishing back and forth in time with the dreamy doo-wop.

The satiny male vocals draw me into a trophy room. The walls are mounted with the heads of leopards, stags, and impalas, with Christmas ornaments dangling from their antlers. A fire crackles in the hearth, and the mantel is draped in pine and tinsel. A leather chesterfield gleams in the firelight occupied by several young men in bathrobes, Santa hats, and gold-toe socks. The room smells of cigars, whiskey, and something acrid and sour that I can't identify.

Claude has taken a liberal approach to holiday costumes. He's sprawled across a wing chair in a brocade dressing gown with a pair of devil horns perched on his head. "Like a lamb to the slaughter." His lips twist into a rakish grin when he sees me. "Billie, you're a vision of modesty. Can I interest you in some marching powder? Or perhaps you would prefer something more bohemian?"

"No, thank you," I reply politely as the Flamingos build to a saccharine climax. I sip my champagne as I look around for Avery, but of course he isn't here. I assume he wouldn't be caught dead in a scene like this. (Not that I care or anything.) I take another sip of champagne, then frown at it. It tastes expensive. Top-shelf liquor must be a requirement—no one wants to attend a budget sex party.

"Don't pretend with me." Claude chuckles. "You're not as square as you look."

*You have no idea.* I grin into my almond-scented champagne. Because, mortified though I am by the couple getting hot and heavy in the corner, I'm also intrigued by it. I've always dreamed about attending a sordid affair like this, I just never imagined that it would also involve Christmas sweaters. "Is this your house?" I change the subject.

"It's my mother's." Claude shrugs. "Sometimes I borrow it. It's a bit gothic for me."

The amorous couple retreats into the hallway, and I follow their lead. "Something's Got a Hold on Me" plays as I climb up a sweeping staircase. I pause on the mezzanine, where I find Pearl balanced precariously on a black velvet chaise with tall white go-go boots thrust in the air, holding a Polaroid camera at arm's length. Crystals sparkle from every surface, white resin earrings dangle from her earlobes, and a white lace "merry widow" corset cinches her waist. I gaze at it longingly, having recently circled the trendy lingerie when Mrs. Pridmore was ordering merchandise. But of course she didn't order it—because we don't have any "merry" widows in Eastport, just bitter ones.

"My little country mouse!" Pearl beams. "I'm *so relieved* that they let you in."

My steps falter as Etta James sings her heart out, her raspy voice reverberating through the stairwell. "Excuse me?"

"I'm *so glad* that the doormen didn't turn you away," Pearl says with a flutter of her shimmery pink fingernails. Her nail polish shines under the tiered waterfall chandelier.

Another sip of almond-flavored champagne as I look from the Vegas-casino chandelier to the diamond print carpet, then over at the socialite falling across it. As Pearl gushes about the elegant surroundings, I'm struck by how tasteless it all is. Amy Vanderbilt was also disenchanted by the nouveau riche and urged against gilding the lily: *"'Rich' seems more vulgar than 'wealthy,' but the dictionary has nothing against either."* As my eyes rove across the gaudy interior, I can't help wondering what she would have to say about Mrs. Webster's suburban château.

*Isn't it hideous? We could start by burning that one down.* Avery chuckles into my memory. And I grin into my champagne flute as I imagine doing just that. Etta James trills a cheerful revolt, as if she might join us.

"–don't know an *amuse bouche* from an amusement park. And *that* is why I do so much charity work," Pearl concludes with a pageant-queen smile and extremely dilated pupils. "Won't you be a dear and take my photo. I look *too good* not to document it." Pearl pushes her Polaroid into my hands, and I'm only too happy to retreat behind the lens. The *click, whirr, buzz,* of the Polaroid camera fills the lull in conversation, then the wet film drops into my hand.

The rhythm and blues keep time with my kitten heels, pulling me upstairs. Skip pushes past, wearing an ugly Christmas sweater and an even uglier expression. "Never again," he mutters to himself as he strides down the diamond-print stairs.

A pair of double doors opens onto a palatial bathroom. The

ceiling is strung with mistletoe and the floor is tiled with gold-veined marble. A large tub occupies one corner of the room. Two girls are soaking in it, blowing bubbles into the air, then laughing as they burst. A Bettie Page look-alike in a plaid teddy and matching pumps leans in to refresh their champagne.

Speaking of teddies—my steps falter as I spy a mobster mustache. Teddy is silky tonight in pajamas and an ascot, with a black satin handkerchief embroidered with the word *Naughty* tucked into his chest pocket. His chestnut hair is slicked back and his mustache is carefully styled. He leans in toward the vanity mirror and curls up the ends with a tiny brush.

"*You,*" Teddy whispers through clenched teeth. He grabs his martini with one hand and my elbow with the other, all but dragging me into an adjacent dressing room. His mauve pajamas swish as he flings himself down across a tufted linen couch. A Siamese cat had been napping on a dressing table. It meows indignantly at the interruption.

"What a surprise!" I feign delight as I sit down gingerly on a pouf.

"You're the one who ate my French fries! What in hell are you doing here?" Teddy demands as the cat glares at me.

"One of my girlfriends invited me. Do you know Pearl? So funny running into you!"

"You're friends with Pearl?" Teddy eyes me doubtfully.

"What a small world! I've just been *dying* to get out of Greenwich. By the way, is your girlfriend here? You said that she's from Connecticut, too, right? I wonder if she knows–"

"*How* embarrassing." Teddy interrupts with a sip of his martini. "My fiancé is actually dead. I should have mentioned that last time. Yes, it's shocking and unspeakably sad"—he holds up a hand to silence me—"but I think she might have been cheating on me."

"You poor thing," I murmur as the Siamese cat daintily licks its paws.

Teddy runs a hand over the woven upholstery in Mrs. Webster's boudoir.[a] "Don't get me wrong, I'm not *glad* that she's dead. But I'm just a little . . . *relieved*? She hadn't touched me in weeks. Said she was depressed—I *tried* to be understanding." His mustache twitches again. "Have you ever wanted someone, and both hated them and wanted them more because they didn't reciprocate?"

"Never." I certainly didn't spend an hour today searching for a dress the color of Avery's eyes. As I shake my head, I spill champagne on my lap. "Oh shoot, what a klutz."

Teddy reaches into his pants pocket and passes me a cloth. "Fix yourself," he advises. As I mop the champagne off my slip, I examine his ivory handkerchief. It's embroidered with the initials *t u b* in curly lowercase script. *tub*! I suppress a laugh at the stupidest monogram in history. Teddy's middle name is probably Ulysses or something equally pretentious.

"Here you go—" I try to return the soiled handkerchief, but he waves it away with unexpected passion.

"Kitten, you take it. Get it *out* of my sight!" Teddy exclaims. I tuck the handkerchief in my purse as he takes another sip of

---

[a] **Boudoir (n.):** *a woman's private dressing room.* "Pouting rooms" were all the rage in eighteenth-century France, stemming from the French *bouder,* "to sulk or pout." Although ladies' private dressing rooms are no longer *en vogue,* having a "place to sulk" never goes out of style.

his martini and resumes his sob story. "Gertrude was out of my league. She was so vivid. So self-absorbed. The world spun a little faster around her. I was *completely* obsessed. But then I walked in on them and—" He haltingly lowers his martini to the floor as his green eyes darken. "You must think I'm a fool. Clearly, she did, too. The rest of the evening is just one lamentable blur." His lip trembles as he lets out a sad little laugh.

"Sorry, Pearl is probably looking for me. I should go find—" I exit the dressing room without further ceremony, desperate for some fresh air. As I stride across the slick bathroom floor, I collide with one of the bathing beauties. She yelps as we tumble across the marble tiles. "I'm so sorry." I reach out to steady myself against a heated towel rack.

"Don't be. At least *someone* touched me tonight." The young woman laughs. She's wrapped in a bath sheet with a towel twisted around her head like a turban. As she walks down the hallway, she leaves a trail of soapy footprints behind her. "I saw you talking with our resident *enfant terrible* in there. Glad you made it out alive."

"Barely," I reply shyly as we begin descending the stairs.

"Hate to be crass, but Gertrude is better off dead than tethered to him," she says with a jaunty, possibly British, lilt to her voice.

"What do you mean?" I ask as we reach the empty mezzanine.

The young woman sits down on the black velvet chaise and begins toweling off her strawberry-blond hair. Her citrine skin is flushed from soaking in the tub. "Teddy Brixton has a mean streak, and everyone knows it. He was awfully jealous and possessive of her."

"Even though he's—" I wait to see if the kiss that I witnessed is public knowledge.

"In love with himself?" my companions supplies, and I smile into my champagne. *So Teddy has one secret, but how many more?* "She tried to end it, but he's like a chihuahua–kick him away, and he'll just come back. I'm sure that his money didn't help matters–it's hard to content yourself with scraps once you've tasted the finer things. It's a shame, though. I liked Gertrude, she was such a"–she brushes off a soap bubble as she searches for the right words–"petty bitch."

I choke on my champagne. "That's a terrible thing to say!"

She glances over with a fiendish grin. "Gertrude was the type of girl who everyone knew, but no one *really knew*. Like deep down, no one had *any idea* what was going on with her. She was like a Jell-O mold. All you see is the glossy exterior, you have no idea what's hiding in the layers underneath." My companion trails off as "Carol of the Bells" rings out through the sound system. "But I heard that she wasn't always that way."

"What way?" I frown at the speaker. It seems like an odd choice.

"Once she had a soul," my companion replies gaily, shaking out her layered shag cut. "Upward mobility requires a certain degree of degradation."

"How so?" I cock my head in confusion.

"Gertrude was a social climber. Ascending the ladder of high society one man at a time. She thought they were just tools–just rungs you clung to. But in the end, she'd climbed so high that she was completely trapped. And then . . . she must have slipped." My companion shrugs as the chorus soars above the treble clef, then she pauses to study the towel in her lap. "Which is hardly unusual—voluntary entrapment is so trendy nowadays."

"Is it?" I frown at my empty champagne glass.

She grins. "No need to be coy. Claude is very particular about his guest list. He invited you here for a reason. Honey, you're one of us." She gazes at me with wide amber eyes that look dead inside, then rises unsteadily to her feet. "Groovy hair, by the way. You look just like her."

The Siamese cat bolts down the stairs, hissing at us as it darts into the underbelly of the château. The girl follows after it with a final mirthless giggle as "Carol of the Bells" exhausts itself.

I seek asylum in the asexual haven of the kitchen, cluttered with pizza boxes, crates of wine, and a half-eaten tray of oysters. A brunette in a fox fur coat nibbles a slice of pizza while a man in an advent calendar sweater drinks a beer. The scent of pepperoni and decaying shellfish makes my stomach churn as Claude strolls in. He's still wearing his devil horns, with his brocade bathrobe open to the waist.

"My little lamb." He drapes an arm across my shoulders, overpowering me with his gasoline-and-pine-trees musk.

"Do you know what time it is?" I ask, trying not to breathe through my nose.

Claude admires his watch with an indulgent smile. "Billie, do you have any idea how much my Cartier cost?"

"The time?" I repeat.

"The stroke of midnight," he replies archly. "The witching hour."

## ETIQUETTE FOR LOVERS AND KILLERS

"Oh great, my taxi is here," I murmur. I've never wanted to leave a party so badly in my life. As I turn to go, I'm suddenly struck by a wave of compassion for Avery. These people are awful, and he's trapped with them *all the time*. I get to leave, but he never does.

Claude steps in, pressing me up against the doorway, as I'm hit by another whiff of his lumberjack-on-drugs cologne. Suddenly, the image of him pushing another woman up against a wall consumes my vision. "Are there any leads in Gertrude's murder?" I ask recklessly.

The kitchen goes quiet, and someone audibly gulps. "Billie, you're even stupider than I thought." Claude snickers. His laughter trails behind me as I rush away.

I hurry down one dark hallway after another, hunting for the room with the white grand piano. I steady myself against a wall as I fight another wave of nausea. I'm lost and my stomach is roiling. What made me sick? Was it the Baked Alaska, the escargot, or the bad manners?

I glimpse the grand piano at the end of the hallway and pick up my pace, only to clatter to a halt when I notice Teddy seated before it, performing an off-tempo rendition of "Chopsticks." He looks up with a glassy smile and a sinister[b] twitch of his mustache. "Just the person I wanted to see."

---

[b] **Sinister (adj.):** *ominous, threatening, evil.* Virtually unchanged from the twelfth-century Latin *sinister*, "on the left-hand side," which gradually became associated with "unlucky, unfavorable." The right hand is generally the dominant one, with only about 10 percent of people being left-handed. The etymology of *sinister* offers an unexpected glimpse into our deeply rooted fear of that which is other (including, apparently, everything on the left-hand side).

"So nice running into you!" I exclaim brightly. "Happy holidays!"

Another twitch. "I knew that I'd seen you before. Now I remember."

*Shit.* "Right! At the Fish Shack on Campobello."

"No. At the Webster's party. You were there the night she died."

*Shit. Shit.* "The night who died?" *He was too drunk to remember me. I can play this off.*

Teddy stands up and advances toward me. He's unsteady on his feet, and his voice is slurring. "I never forget a face. You were there on the porch while we were fighting."

*Shit. Shit. Shit.* "I'm sorry, I don't know what you're—"

Teddy steps in. "So you *definitely* blackmailed me," he says, tracing the left strap of my slip with one sticky finger. "But did you *also* kill my girlfriend?"

I try to push past him, but Teddy blocks my path. "You were there the night she died, and now you're back. Asking questions. Stirring up trouble. Why are you obsessed with her? You even have the same haircut." He's so close that I can smell his breath. He ate the oysters *and* the pizza—I've never smelled anything so repugnant before in my life. "You lied to me. What should your punishment be?"

"You're jumping to conclusions. Let's talk this out in a rational . . ." I trail off, suddenly exhausted. My stomach is churning. All I want is to go back to my hotel room and lie down. "I'm so sorry, but I really need to—"

"Shhh." Teddy reaches out to stroke my hair, and I freeze in shock. Then he winds his fingers through the bouncy layers and pulls. Tears spring up in my eyes. *It really hurts!* No one has ever intentionally hurt me before. As our eyes meet, my breath catches, and Teddy's lips quirk up in a cool smile. He's enjoying himself.

"I really need to–" As I step back, Teddy's fingers close in tighter, and the pain intensifies. I try to pull his hand out of my hair, but he holds tight. Another wave of nausea hits as "Baby, It's Cold Outside" plays through the speakers. A few strands of hair snap as Teddy yanks harder, then–

I push him away as I vomit champagne and Baked Alaska across his velvet loafers. Bile burns the roof of my mouth as tears streak down my cheeks. I steady myself against the piano, gulping down air as I see stars and the world spins around me. Teddy looks on with undisguised disgust. I murmur something about dry cleaners, then bolt into the foyer.

Lieske is waiting for me. She takes one look at my face and gives me a hug. "Oh, my *schat*." She whispers comforting Dutch words as she helps me into my dress and jacket. "Good luck with your article, Ms. Bean! Don't use my name!" Her antlers bob as she waves goodbye.

My kitten heels clatter across the icy cobblestones to my waiting cab. I open the window regardless of the cold and gulp down fresh air as we drive away. I take off the antlers and stow them in my purse, then bite my lip when I discover Teddy's handkerchief. I'd forgotten about it. I dry my tears on his stupid monogram as we race back to Commonwealth Ave. "Baby, It's Cold Outside" is stuck in my head. I can still feel Teddy's hand, pressing in on me. It makes me want to rip my skin off.

## CHAPTER FOURTEEN

# JUST DESSERTS

*Sticky cake is eaten with a fork. Dry cake, such as pound cake or fruit cake, is broken and eaten in small pieces. Tiny confection cakes (served at wedding receptions, etc.) are eaten in the fingers. Cream puffs, Napoleons, and éclairs, all treacherous as to filling, are eaten with a fork.*

He's as complacent as a lapdog, but I suppose that even poodles go rabid, Avery's voice echoes through my ears as Massachusetts's slush gives way to New Hampshire's forests. I take a deep breath as my train passes the paper mills in Southern Maine, their tall brick chimneys sending dusty plumes into the sky, and the Penobscot River, as loggers push fallen trees down the rapids. The farther north we go, the whiter the landscape becomes, until I find an answering stillness within myself.

A visit to the café car yields a box of Cracker Jacks and a

newspaper. My eyes widen at Gertrude's screen-siren portrait on the front page of the *Portland Gazette*. I crunch on a mouthful of caramel-coated popcorn as I study the public interest piece. My fingers leave caramel smudges as I flip to page six to continue reading the article by Conrad Marshall. I don't want to share her with Conrad—I want her all to myself. I want to blackmail her boyfriend, wear her diamonds, and dig to the bottom of the Jell-O mold. The article seems half-assed at best. Conrad doesn't know Gertrude. He hasn't taken a walk in her shoes. And he certainly hasn't thrown up on her fiancé's loafers. I just don't think he has what it takes to solve this murder.

Munching on Cracker Jacks, I reach out to touch my Hollywood bob. I wish there were some way to go back in time. I want to stand in the parlor beside Gertrude. To look into the face that killed her. Someone so besotted, obsessed, or threatened that it drove them to murder. And I'd like to hold her hand, so she doesn't have to face them alone.

The train hurtles into the oblivion of Down East Maine, with extended periods of darkness broken by short intervals of blinking lights. Moose Island is tucked into bed by the time we approach Eastport, with dark windows lit by flickering Christmas candles. As we pass Webster Cottage, the train begins to slow, and I squint up in surprise. Have I gone completely bonkers, or is there a light in the attic?

I shake my head. That's impossible. The Websters left for Rhode Island months ago. It would cost a fortune to heat that drafty old house in the middle of winter.

But, then again, nothing screams "understated luxury" quite like excess utility bills.

Nice: Maine at Christmas. The crackling fire, high-fat content of the lobster Newburg, and my grandmother's raspy laughter as we watch the stop-motion *Rudolph the Red-Nosed Reindeer* are all undeniably wholesome. Everything about the holiday season here is so nice that it makes Claude's party seem even farther away. Even the blizzard on Christmas Eve strikes me as rather festive, with the congregation bundled up in winter coats, shivering together in the pews. The power goes out midway through mass, and the priest conducts the remainder of the service by candlelight. And that strikes me as rather cozy, too.

Naughty: Christmas Eve dinner. The menu consists of clam fritters topped with white clam sauce, and "holiday salad." Holiday salad is a rare treat of ginger ale, pineapple, celery, marshmallows, pimentos, and cream cheese, all frozen to perfection in a Jell-O mold. Victor makes it each year with a dreamy look in his eyes. Along with Edgar's fedora and the misuse of *their*, *there*, and *they're*, "holiday salad" is one of my greatest fears.

"How many dead bodies do you figure?" Victor asks as he spears a clam fritter, then tops it with the "salad."

"Victor! This is hardly appropriate for Christmas—" I push the food around on my plate.

"Ayuh."[a] He nods thoughtfully. "I think there are more, too."

"Silent Night" wafts through the windows, sparing me from further conjecture. We set down our napkins and hurry over to

---

[a] **Ayuh (interj.):** *I acknowledge what you've said.* Peculiar to New England's coastal communities, *ayuh* is best spoken with a thick Maine accent. Etymology unknown.

the window. Our breath fogs up the glass as a fire truck plods up Key Street with Christmas carols blasting from its speakers. A fireman stands on the back of the truck, dressed like Father Christmas. He's lit by the red glow of the taillights, with the blizzard swirling around him. "Ho, ho, ho," he shouts into a megaphone. The scene is straight out of a Norman Rockwell painting: wholesome, nostalgic, and bile-inducing.

After dinner, I cuddle up with my diary under the blankets. The Christmas light flickers on my windowsill as I add a few notes to my ever-developing list of suspects. But the phone interrupts me. Only one person ever calls this late. I consider letting it ring, but then set down my pen and reach for the handset. Christmas must be a lonely time of year for stalkers. "Hi, Edgar, did you miss me?"

"Billie—" Avery's voice sounds concerned on the other end of the phone.

And just like that, the Cold War ends.

"Oh dear," I murmur.

"Yes! Deer! I heard that you were seen, dressed as a reindeer at a rather unsavory event."

I bite my lip and twine the phone cord around my fingertips. I'd forgotten how deep his voice is. "Who told you?"

"I ran into Pearl tonight at church in Newport, and she—"

"Pearl—" I repeat her name warily as I watch the snow pile up on my windowsill.

"Yes. The most obnoxious person on earth. You might remember her," Avery replies impatiently.

"And you were at church?" I study the notes in my diary. "Like a real Protestant church?"

"I know, it's cutting-edge at this time of year. I think it might catch on."

"Was Claude with you? In this 'church'?"

"Unfortunately. He does tend to show up for these things. What are you getting at?" Avery asks with a mixture of amusement and confusion.

"Interesting."

"Billie, are you all right?"

"In what sense?" I murmur, pulling the blankets tighter around myself. That seems like a rather forward question.

"Was everything... okay at the party? Did anyone try to... steal your reindeer antlers?" Avery's anxiety radiates across the phone as the snow pelts down outside. "Is there anyone I need to beat up? Any duels I need to pencil into my planner?"

I burst out laughing at the idea of proper Avery engaged in a scuffle. Wouldn't it mess up his hair? "Well, you might want to sign Pearl up for finishing school," I reply after a moment of deliberation. "She was rather rude to me, then asked me to take her photo. And ... you might also want to have Teddy's loafers dry-cleaned."

"And why would I do that?" Avery's voice warms on the other end of the phone.

"Because I vomited on them," I whisper, biting my lip.

"What! Why?"

"Why not?" I retort, and his laughter is warm, too.

"Well, I'm sure he deserved it," Avery replies diplomatically.

"Billie, why did you attend the party in the first place? Were you there investigating?"

I haven't mentioned my query into Gertrude's murder, but it seems like, unfortunately, Avery is smart enough to put two and two together. "Investigating what?" I play dumb.

"Just promise me that you'll be careful. Don't do anything foolish. And you might want to avoid Claude's get-togethers in the future. 'Nice' isn't one of his ongoing themes, and 'naughty' is a regrettable understatement." Avery takes a deep breath. "Speaking of which, I'd like to apologize for—"

"For what?" I study the phone cord as the snow drifts down in feathery tufts.

"For handling a situation poorly. And for being a bit more reserved than I probably ought to have been," Avery murmurs, and I look up in surprise. I didn't realize he could be so serious. "And for being a fool. To be honest, I'm used to dealing with nitwits like Pearl. And I *do* think you're brilliant. And... I would like to make amends," he says persuasively. I hold the phone away from my ear and consider it. *Is* he trying to persuade me? And to what end? "Anyway, could I call you sometime?"

"You *do* realize that we're speaking on the phone right now?" I tease.

I hear him grin from Rhode Island. "Maybe Pearl isn't the only nitwit. Will you take my photo, too?" he asks, then hangs up.

"Is it nature or nurture?" Gertrude asks. She's wearing a tulle robe with cascading feather trim that swishes back and forth as we lounge outside of Webster Cottage. The wicker table between us is set for high tea, strewn with petits fours, a rainbow of French macarons, and a vase of lilacs. The sun glints on the glass dome at the top of the Deer Island Point Lighthouse and flickers off the diamond on Gertrude's ring finger.

"Huh?" I shade my eyes to look at her.

"Are you naturally a pushover, or did society make you that way?" Gertrude replies as she spears a cannoli with her fork. Creamy goo oozes out of the pastry as she carries it to her plate. "If Teddy got aggressive with me, I'd make him pay for it. He was rude to you because you're weak." She smiles as she reaches for her knife and cuts the cannoli cleanly in half.

I resist the urge to correct her table manners. According to Miss Vanderbilt, creamy pastries may be sliced with the side of a fork, but never a knife. But I keep this observation to myself and reach for my lemonade instead. Condensation drips down the glass as perspiration beads up on my forehead. "But isn't that a little hypocritical?" I ask.

"How so?" Gertrude's laughter is as sharp as her knife.

"You think less of me because I didn't fight. Because I didn't punch Teddy and raise hell." I wait for her to contradict me, but she remains silent. "But when someone threatened *you*, you didn't struggle. Your clothing was perfect. Your hair was done. Your nails weren't even chipped!"

"I thought it was a *game*. A sexual *aperitif* to whet my appetite." Gertrude pauses to take another bite. "By the time that I realized I was the main course, it was too late." She blots her lips on a napkin, then stands up. The wind ruffles the tulle train of her dressing gown as she approaches me, hair fluttering prettily around her shoulders.

As I rise to my feet, I note with surprise that we're the same height. Gertrude's robe tickles my skin as her orchids-soaked-in-whiskey perfume wafts over me. "Who did this?" I ask softly.

"Who didn't?" she replies, then leans in, brushing her lips against mine. They are soft, cool, and sweet with pastry cream. She gently trails her teeth across my bottom lip. Then she bites down, and I wake up with a start.

I start the new year off with a dozen cannolis from Mingo's Bakery. Terry Mingo gives me a sympathetic grin as I pick them up. "Best hangover cure in town," he says with a wince. "Better than the hair of the dog."

"I'm sharing them! And I'm not hungover," I protest.

"Sure," Terry says. He doesn't believe me.

But the truth is that I *am* a little hungover from that dream. I can still hear Gertrude's laughter ringing in my ears. Can still feel her teeth biting my lip. I can't get her out of my head. I want to eat her pastries, wear her perfume, and kiss her again.

"What if I moved to Connecticut for the winter?" I ask Grace when I bring up her happy hour cocktail with a cannoli. I'd love to delve into Gertrude's background. To see her childhood home, her school, and her sister's beauty salon.

"Nope." Grace strains the cocktail shaker into a martini glass.

"But—"

"Sugarplum, I don't know *what* your crisis is, but Connecticut is *not* the answer," my grandmother says, lips mint green from her grasshopper.

"Sugarplum," I repeat, thinking of the photos of Clara dressed as the sugarplum fairy on her bedroom wall.

"Ballet?" Mrs. Pridmore repeats incredulously.

"Yes! I just thought, new year, new me! So if I could get off work early on Wednesdays, that would be swell." I've signed up for the adult ballet class at Clara's home dance studio. Gertrude might be out of my reach, but Clara is just a drive away.

A dozen ballerinas are draped across the lacquered floor at the Northern Lights Ballet Studio in Calais. I feel ridiculous in a flimsy pink dance skirt, black leotard, and pink tights. I turn to leave, but an ancient pair of leg warmers blocks my path.

"Good evening, *mes petites colombes.* Do we have any new faces?" The dance teacher has an affected French accent, a decade's worth of porcelain foundation, and a long stick. As she clicks across the floor in her character shoes, the other young women slink over to the barre mounted to the wall.

I raise my hand as I scramble over to find an empty spot at the barre. "I'm new, ma'am. Ballet class is my new year's resolution."

"Call me Mistress Brandt. If you can't keep up, you *may* return for the children's class on Friday," the ballet instructor says as she walks over to the record player and lowers the needle. "*Pliés* and *port de bras* in first." She taps her stick against the ground, and the girls bend their knees and move their arms in unison. "And second." Another tap as their feet slide out. "And third." There is a military-style precision to their bends, slides, and curtsies. *Tendus* lead to *dégagés* then *frappés* and *grands battements*–but my French is of little use here, because everyone else is fluent in a physical language that I've never spoken before. "*Centre! Bras en seconde!*" As I step my feet out, giggles resound across the room.

"Your *arms*, silly," whispers one of the more perfect dancers. Her black hair is wound in a bun, and her olive skin gleams in the lamplight. I recognize her from Clara's photos. I look to see if she's wearing the second half of the friendship necklace, but her neck is hidden by a scarf.

The ballet mistress taps my knee with her stick. "Control your legs! Now, alone!"

Some part of me always knew this was coming. Cavorting across the floor like a dying goose, being mocked by an old woman with a fake French accent. As I sink through the various stages of hell, Mistress Brandt smacks the wall.

"Look at that *tombé*." One of the dancers smirks as I tumble to the floor.

Mistress Brandt is queen here. Her rule is law, and all of the dancers are her ladies-in-waiting. At the end of class, they curtsy and bow to the old woman, showering her with applause. And it's just one more etiquette lesson. The only way to investigate Clara's death is by studying the rules she lived by. Maybe if I learn to curtsy, nod, and point my toes the way that she did, then I'll understand the real her. The secret her. The hidden heart of a ballerina that led to the lost-luggage rack at the Washington County train station.

"... missing her so much." "I watched *The Nutcracker* and cried." "Remember when she made us eggnog pie?" The changing room hushes and darkens after class, as the girls reminisce about their fallen soloist. Clara is like first position—every step begins and ends with her at the Northern Lights Ballet Studio.

The streetlights cast orange shadows across the snowdrifts as I hurry across the frozen parking lot to Victor's car. As a devout patron of the arts, Victor has given me grudging approval to use it on Wednesdays for dance class. As I unlock the Buick, the Good Samaritan from ballet class approaches. "Hi, I'm Vicki," she says as I toss my bag in the front seat.

"Nice to meet you! I'm Diane. Thank you for the pointers today."

"Don't mention it. And don't let Miss Brandt get you down. You know what they say: Sticks and stones may break your bones, but only pointe shoes can hurt you!" Vicki says, then does a dorky pirouette in her boots, glossy black hair fluttering around her in the amber light. And despite my smarting pride and aching calves, I know that I'll be back next week.

On my way home to Eastport, I slow down as I pass Webster Cottage. I made headway tonight with Clara, but what about Gertrude? My eyes narrow at the sleeping monolith, then widen with surprise. There *is* a light in the attic! Shining through one of the dormer windows in the roof. I *wasn't* hallucinating the other night. Someone *is* squatting in Webster

Cottage! Who are they? And what do they know about Gertrude's murder?

My questions won't let me rest the next day. They nag at me as I replace a zipper on a winter jacket. Distract me as I ring Marsha up for a Bond-girl bikini (an odd choice for the depths of winter, but that's a mystery for another day). Trail behind me as I wander into Fernald's Pharmacy to pick up a home-perm kit for Grace.

Clara and Gertrude sit center stage on the newspaper rack, watching intently as I riffle past them for this month's issue of *Master Detective.* I narrow my eyes at the pulp-art cover and garish font, then flip through the magazine, pausing on an advertisement for a reel-to-reel, the crème de la crème of home recording devices. It features a woman in pearls and a cocktail gown, cuddled up beside a robust tape recorder. The reel-to-reel makes my Sanyo Micro-Pack 35 look pretty paltry in comparison, but its four-hundred-dollar price tag puts it solidly out of my reach. As I sigh at the magazine, a postcard flutters down to my feet. It shows a vintage candlestick telephone and the tagline: "PHONE TAPPING: ANYONE CAN DO IT."

*But can they?*

I steal Victor's car keys after work to find out. My hope: to bug Webster Cottage. My fear: that I'll get murdered in the process.

A Bach violin concerto adds a dreary elegance to the

abandoned mobile homes and decaying fishing boats on my way to the nearest electronics store in Machias. It's pitch-black by the time I park outside RadioShack. Slush splatters my pantyhose as I hurry inside, gazing in wonder at the push-button phones, hi-fi stereo consoles, radios, calculators, and extension cords stacked high to the ceiling.

"Record players are that way," mutters a young man between bites of a Pop-Tart. He has the coarse hair of a Jack Russell terrier, and his shoulders are stooped. His skin is the same tired beige as the portable television behind him. His striped sweater vest is scattered with crumbs.

"What about me screams 'record player'?" I pause before the counter.

Beady eyes regard me from behind black-rimmed glasses. The sales clerk brushes pink crumbs off his lips as he considers my black wool coat, burgundy scarf, and matching beret (which I'd really thought was rather chic). "All of it," he says with impatience.

"I'm actually looking for—" I fidget with my beret as I outline my request and finish with, "It's for a school project, and I'm *soooo* confused."

The sales clerk shoves the remainder of the Pop-Tart in his mouth, then stands up. He leads me down one aisle after another, as pink crumbs fall in his wake. He grabs various items without bothering to look at them. "People charge a lot of money for this setup, but it's a total scam. You just need a few household items and a brain big enough to put them together."

The sales clerk gives me rapid-fire instructions, and I pull my diary out of my purse, struggling to jot them all down. He returns to the counter and picks up a pair of wire cutters. He cuts off the end of an electrical cable, then uses an X-Acto knife to scrape off the enamel coating around the copper filaments. He pauses to unwrap a second Pop-Tart as he twists the exposed metals together and cuts off the end of a phone cord. I feel a little starstruck, watching him work. Never underestimate a bored, small-town nerd.[b]

"Ten ninety-five, please. And good luck with your 'assignment.'" Mr. Pop-Tart smirks as he takes another bite.

Steam swirls up from my grandfather's Waco Diner mug as I sit behind the wheel of the Buick. The hot coffee fogs up my sunglasses as I flip through a book and glance at Murder Mansion. It's Saturday morning, and the cottage appears deserted. But I know what I saw. Someone is squatting in Webster Cottage, and I'm going to find out who.

I'm brushing up on my Spanish with *Dos Mujeres* by Gertrudis Gómez de Avellaneda, following a love triangle in aristocratic nineteenth-century Spain. Eighteen-forty-two was a big year for female novelists. While mousy Charlotte Brontë was putting her finishing touches on *Jane Eyre* in Northern England, Avellaneda was idolizing slutty widows in Madrid. Her intelligent portrayal of a steamy love affair was a sensation in hot-blooded Spain but was received less warmly in less

---

[b] **Nerd (n.):** *a person with great technical knowledge and poor social skills.* This 1950s American slang derived from the obsolete *nert*, "someone stupid or strange," which stemmed from the Victorian colloquialism *nut*. In Dr. Seuss's *If I Ran the Zoo* (p. 1950), the *nerd* was one of the odd creatures on exhibit.

temperate regions of Europe. Case in point: her novel has never even been *translated* into English. Not because it lacks literary merit, but because it oozes sensuality. Critics hated *Dos Mujeres* for romanticizing hedonism, promoting women's liberation, and subverting the status quo. It seems like appropriate reading material for staking out the local aristocracy.

My eyes light up as a car drives across the Websters' driveway. I sink down behind the steering wheel, taking my coffee with me. The two halves of the double gate swing inward, admitting one black Ford truck. I watch the receding shape of the Ford F-100 with suspicion. Who is Mr. Black Ford Truck and why doesn't he drive a tiny sports car? Is he a worker? A robber? If so, very sharp of him to steal the gate key.

My tote bag swings from my shoulder as I squeeze between the two halves of the gilt *W* and walk up the frozen driveway. Weak winter sunlight brushes timidly across my cheek. *Lux brumalis* is the Latin phrase for that, "the light of winter."

The front door is hidden behind a snowbank, but a shoveled path leads to a service entrance. The door is locked and bolted, but I've brought reinforcements from the dress shop. I pull two glover's leather needles out of my purse. They're both longer and more durable than bobby pins, one bent at a ninety-degree angle at the end. I hold them in my right hand between my thumb and index finger, then slip the crimped needle into the keyhole. I push until the bent piece catches, applying tension to the cylinder. Then I insert the second needle into the lock, gently coaxing the tumblers. An infinitesimal *click* as the spring falls into place and the dead bolt pulls back. I hold my breath as I slide my library card down the doorframe. A moment of hesitation and pressure as it catches under the lock, then the door swings open.

Just because I'm breaking and entering doesn't mean it's okay to track snow through the house, so I pull a pair of pink slippers out of my tote bag and set them on the doorstep. *Rule #4: Always be a good houseguest, whether or not you're invited.* While this is more of a general etiquette tip than a dating rule, it certainly applies when visiting a love interest's home. I leave my dirty boots under the eaves, put on my slippers, and step inside.

It's even colder indoors than it is outside. The shutters are drawn, and sheets are thrown over the furniture. It feels as if the deserted mansion is watching me. Gauging me. Seeing how much it can get away with. As I tiptoe through the frozen corridors, goose bumps prickle at the back of my neck. I square my shoulders and step inside the butler's pantry.

I've spent many hours trailing my fingers over the texture of my summer memories. Remembering the smell of Avery's aftershave. Listening to the chorus of the Beach Boys wafting through the open window. Reliving that shiver of anticipation as he pressed me up against the wall and grazed his fingers across my waist. Fantasizing about his deep laughter echoing off the spotless cabinets and the phone mounted to the wall. I thought it was ridiculous at the time, because what self-respecting butler makes phone calls when he's busy mixing Manhattans? I imagine the likelihood of anyone actually *using* the beige phone tucked between the shelves is marginal to nonexistent.

I unplug both ends of the curly cord from the butler's pantry phone (Cord A) and coil it up. Then I pop two D batteries into a black plastic transmitter and snap a connecting wire into the bottom. The wire is spliced, with electrical tape holding a capacitor into place, connecting it to the exposed copper filaments from a clear phone cord with a pair of alligator clamps. The transparent cord is from RadioShack, which Mr. Pop-Tart so kindly spliced open for me. One end of Cord B is sealed off with electrical tape, connecting it to the bootleg transmitter. The other end has a standard wall jack. I unravel Cord B and snap the wall jack into the dial pad of the butler's phone, then switch on the transmitter at the other end. A green button lights up. It works!

I grab the rolling library ladder and unspool Cord B behind me as I climb. When I reach the top, I stash the tangle of wires in a crevice behind the crown molding, then slide the bugged phone line over so it hangs down from the top of the cabinet, leading to the beige phone. It disappears against the taupe wall.

Cord C looks like the Websters' original phone cord, but it has only one phone jack. I cut off the second one last night, then superglued both ends together. I plug Cord C into the handset and watch it dangle down to hide Cord B. You would have to pick up the handset to realize that it isn't connected to anything. And I'm willing to bet money (I've bet $10.95, really), that no one will try that anytime soon.

Whoever is squatting in Webster Cottage has dirt. They're bound to gossip about it at some point. And when they do, I'll be listening (work schedule and weather conditions, permitting).

I sling my tote bag over my shoulder then push the ladder back into place. As I step into the hallway, my eyes rove around greedily. I'm desperate to snoop. To see what's hidden in the fridge. (Are there tins of caviar? Half-eaten jars of jam? Or once you cross a certain wealth threshold, do you start throwing away preserves after every serving?) To inspect the prescriptions tucked away in Mrs. Webster's medicine cabinet, and to see what type-A insanity lurks in Avery's sock drawer. But Mr. Black Ford Truck could return at any moment, so I resist the urge and promise myself that I'll snoop around another day.

My cold, wet boots are waiting for me. I lock the door, then wade through the slush back to the front gate. As I squeeze between the two halves of the W, the black Ford truck barrels down the road. I swear as I scramble behind the gatepost.

The next few days are a study in impatience as the coast is slammed with winter storms. Business slows to a halt at Primp and Ribbon Alterations as tensions mount behind our idle Singer Featherweights. On the third day, the freezing rain lets up, residents emerge from hibernation, and I test out my handiwork. Mud puddles splatter my jacket as I bike away from the dress shop after work. Mr. Black Ford Truck might have noticed the Buick on Saturday, so sadly, it's a wet winter bike ride for me.

I stash my bike behind a tree and shimmy through the front gate. My boots break through the icy crust of frozen flower beds as I approach the creepy Victorian gazebo. My transmitter only has a range of four hundred feet, and this is the only shelter within spying distance. I really hope that Avery was joking about this being where the bodies are buried.

Sweeping some snow off the bench, I pull out my walkie-talkie. I switch it on, but it's painfully quiet. I bite my lip, silently cursing the RadioShack clerk for selling me faulty equipment. Then the gate groans as headlights reflect across the icy cobblestones, and I crouch down behind the latticework. My eyes follow the black truck as it makes its way toward the Garage Mahal. A dark figure emerges and walks over to the service entrance. Five minutes later, a light flickers on in the attic.

I stare at the walkie-talkie. *Please work. Please work. Please work.* Then a scratchy sound emerges from the two-way radio. It's impossible to tell if this is an incoming or outgoing call. But that becomes obvious when a voice answers.

"Hello?" my grandmother rasps through the speaker.

## CHAPTER FIFTEEN

# TELEPHONE P'S & Q'S

*Invitations by telephone should not be administered except to the most intimate friends ... For most social matters the use of the telephone is questionable at best.*

"Hello?" Grace McCadie's voice quavers through the walkie-talkie. "Son of a bitch, I'll tar and feather you, then hang you out to dry. I'll beat the living daylights out of–" My grandmother's voice rises with each idle threat until she exhausts herself. A chuckle from the other end of the phone, then the connection goes dead.

I narrow my eyes at the handheld radio. *Why did Webster Cottage just call my house?* Then the walkie-talkie vibrates again and my heart sinks a little lower as another familiar voice broadcasts through the walkie-talkie. "Hello, Maine Major Crimes. Detective Wallace speaking."

"Wallace, did you catch that Bruins game last night?" Edgar's gravelly chuckle grates through the transceiver as I struggle to pick my jaw up from the icy gazebo floor. *Edgar* drives the black Ford truck! *Edgar* has been squatting in Webster Cottage! *Edgar* is calling Detective Wallace to joke about hockey! *What the hell?!*

"Don't get me started," Detective Wallace retorts. "The Waterville Bruins are on their deathbed. Newfoundland will take you down."

"What do the Newfoundland Growlers and the *Titanic* have in common?" Edgar asks.

"I don't know, what?"

"They both looked pretty good until they hit the ice!" Edgar wheezes.

"Look, I'm hanging up now to investigate a *crime*." Wallace is unimpressed.

"Yeah, that's why I called." Edgar struggles to keep him on the line. "Did you see the newspaper yesterday? They're really looking into her past. What if they find out about—"

"Don't worry. I'm doing what I can to keep you out of this," Detective Wallace reassures him. "No one has picked up on you yet, so we should be able to—"

My palms are sweating through my leather gloves. *How do Edgar and Detective Wallace know each other? Is Wallace in on it, too? No wonder this investigation is taking so long, if the detective is friends with one of the suspects!*

"Thanks, Wallace. You're a good man."

"Don't worry about it. Focus on what's important, like mopping up your tears when the Bruins lose. And send my regards to your mother," Detective Wallace says, then hangs up.

I study the two-way radio as the wind blows across the frozen flower beds and the moon rises over Deer Island. It reflects off the miniature icebergs lolling in the bay and gleams across the white mirror of untouched snow. As the minutes pass, my stomach growls, but I can't bear to tear myself away from the little radio pressed between my gloves. It buzzes again and Edgar's grainy chuckle grates across the phone line. "Hello, princess."

"Don't," replies a nonplussed voice. "You know I hate it when you call me that."

"My apologies, Your Highness," Edgar continues dutifully. "I planted more tulip bulbs in the side garden today, so those should flower consistently in the spring. And the mice are back in the basement, fucking nuisance, so I set up more traps. Then your mother wanted those rattan pendant lights replaced in the solarium—"

"A mercy killing," Avery interjects.

My eyes light up. The wiretap was 99 percent to investigate Gertrude's murder, but spying on Avery may have also been a slight incentive. I'd hoped that the squatter would call him eventually, but I never guessed that it would be Edgar, or that they would speak on the first night.

"And Newport?" Edgar asks.

"The DMV waiting room would be an improvement," Avery responds dryly, and I grin at the phone. "There's the tedious background music, the soul-crushing overhead lighting, and the feeling of being in trouble, although you aren't sure, entirely, for what."

"You always get this way during the winter," Edgar replies without interest. "Go down to the house in Palm Beach. Get some sun. It'll brighten up your disposition."

"Honestly, I'd rather be up in Maine. If everything is going to be dark and dismal, then I might as well embrace–" Avery pauses. "Did you hear that? I thought I just heard a click."

"You're paranoid." Edgar laughs, and I gaze at the walkie-talkie in astonishment. Is Edgar *teasing* Avery? Are they *friends*? "You know the phone lines up here are a joke."

"You're right. So tell me all the gory details about those pendant lights–"

After five minutes of property-management reports, the two hang up and I reluctantly switch off my walkie-talkie. I'm surprised by Edgar's skills as a groundskeeper. He seems to genuinely care about the property. But as I trudge back to my own DMV waiting room, I'm left with more questions than answers. Among them: Why are the police in cahoots with a handyman? Why is my grandmother so aggressive on the phone? And why is Avery so witty?

I'm lost in thought as I slip across the icy cobblestones, glancing up briefly at the shadow in the attic window. Edgar is standing there. Motionless. Gazing into the darkness as I stumble away.

The weeks are measured not in hours or minutes, but by the click of the walkie-talkie. It becomes the second hand that my days revolve around. There are headlines. Blizzards. Pineapple upside-down cakes. Brontë novels. Blazers to be mended. Fishing bibs to be patched. Outbursts from Victor. ("This is Eastport! People don't die here!" he bellows at the news, and I don't have the heart to tell him otherwise.) Rejection letters. Run-ins with Florence. ("Does this bring out my eyes?" She pouts as she tries on a purple peacoat.) The beat of Mistress Brandt's stick against the dance floor. A nor'easter. A papaya from the mailman.

But mostly ... there's just the walkie-talkie.

I wonder if I'm the first girl to ever wiretap her crush? I can't help thinking that Jane Austen would approve. With the advent of technology, use of surveillance in dating seems like the obvious next step. Espionage adds a little extra spark to our flirtation. I suppose that I *could* just pick up the phone and call Avery like a normal girl, but that seems overdone. And what if I called and a girlfriend picked up? At least this way I can't be rejected.

Between the stakeout, the dress shop, and ballet class, my schedule is packed. I forget about the rejections piling up in my PO box and my empty social calendar. Who needs a life when you're busy investigating a murder? The long twilight hours in the gazebo don't yield anything useful. Edgar's just as stumped as the rest of us—as he tells his mother on multiple occasions. But the wiretapping offers an unexpected glimpse at an unlikely friendship. I watch January spill into February as I listen to Avery's sarcastic jokes and Edgar's smart-aleck responses.

I come home later and later to find leftovers congealing on the hot plate. I eat alone, face flushed with cold, while Victor's CB radio beeps beside me. On Wednesdays I commit a code ten-thirty-seven and drive to Calais in the Buick. I slowly learn the steps, cut the feet off my tights, and pull on short-shorts to adhere to the unofficial dress code. "*Développé devant!* Lift in *cou-de-pied*. You should be able to balance a *teacup* on your heel!" Mistress Brandt taps my triceps with her stick. "Your arms jiggle like a *poulet*."

"If you want to hurt my feelings, you're going to have to try harder than that." I grin.

The girls slowly warm to me. "You're feisty," says one. "You remind me of a girl who used to dance here. She was a fighter, too." She blinks away tears as the changing room goes silent.

But as I leave class that night, Luke blows my cover. "Billie!" the young police officer exclaims as I hurry down from the second-floor dance studio. He's leaning under a streetlight, wearing a bulky jacket over his police uniform. "What are you doing here?"

"Dancing?" I reply with a smile. I'm shocked that the police ever got here. After four months of tepid investigations, they're *finally* delving into Clara's social calendar.

Luke frowns in annoyance. "Billie, please don't tamper with my witnesses. I came here to interview the ballerinas. Whatever you're doing has to stop. I don't want you to get in–"

Vicki barrels down the steps and tumbles straight into me. "Looking good today!" she calls as she regains her balance, black ponytail swooping in the amber streetlight.

The young cop watches her stroll away with a confused half smile. "She's nice,[a] Luke. You should try introducing yourself," I tell him. Because I won't.

---

[a] **Nice (adj.):** *pleasant, agreeable.* Another word that has transformed over time, *nice* stemmed from the Latin *nescius*, "ignorant," which later shifted to the twelfth-century "clumsy, foolish." In the fourteenth century, *nice* became

## ETIQUETTE FOR LOVERS AND KILLERS

Romance is in the air as Valentine's Day approaches.

The February sky is murky with unfallen snow and unsent love letters. Mrs. Pridmore fills the shop with plastic roses and blasts love songs on the radio to mask the howling wind. A dusting of snow breezes in as she bustles over to the butcher's shop to give her husband a Valentine's Day card. Tony Bennett croons "I Left My Heart in San Francisco" as the door jingles open. I look up to find Detective Wallace standing in the entrance, wearing one of those tall, furry Russian hats. *Ushanka* is the Russian word for that.

"Miss McCadie." Wallace eyes the pastel interior with distaste. "Is now a good time?"

"Not really." I disentangle myself from the tweed sheath dress I've been taking in, then hurry over to the front door to turn the *Open* sign to *Closed*. I motion toward one of the chairs we reserve for bored husbands. "My boss just stepped out for a moment."

"This won't take long," Detective Wallace says as he tracks snow across the floor. "I find myself in need of a better understanding of the Websters' social life. What does a party at their estate look like? Please keep in mind that I'm focused on murder, not misdemeanors." He sits down, then takes off his furry hat.

"Extravagant," I reply succinctly. "Everything at the solstice

---

associated with "dainty," but it wasn't until 1769 that it was first associated with "agreeable."

party was top-shelf. There was gourmet food, expensive wine, and a jazz band. It was tasteful but fun."

"What about gatherings where the parents aren't in attendance? Claude mentioned that you attended a recent social function in Boston."

"I... umm... maybe?" I blush. What could Claude have told the detective?

"Can I quote you on that?" The detective looks unamused.

"Things get a bit wilder when the parents are away. Claude is the instigator."

"Are there drugs?" The detective makes a note in his legal pad.

"I believe so," I reply, remembering the acrid, chemical scent in the trophy room.

"And sex?"

"That's generally the eventual goal of a party, don't you think?" There's no need to mention the shadows on the wall in Chestnut Hill.

"And what about the deceased?" Detective Wallace frowns as Tony Bennett builds to a lusty climax.

"I don't want to speak ill of the dead, but Gertrude *may* have had a reputation," I reply judiciously. "She normally had a boyfriend but... she was rather uninhibited when left to her own devices."

"So I've gathered." Detective Wallace suppresses a laugh. "You met the fiancé?"

"I saw her with–" I start to say Teddy, but my fedora-obsessed brain says, "Edgar."

"Edgar?" Detective Wallace looks startled.

"Teddy," I correct myself.

"But how do you know Edgar?" the detective presses.

Edgar's name hangs between us like a riddle. The question isn't so much *who* Edgar is—as *what*. Is he a handyman? A stalker? The detective's hockey buddy? Avery's friend? A hired gun? I open my lips, then close them again, at a loss for words.

The average American has about thirty-two thousand words in their vocabulary, while more advanced English speakers have approximately forty-five thousand words at their disposal. As a trained linguist, I know at least fifty-two thousand words, yet none of them could sufficiently describe this situation to Detective Wallace. Although I'm pretty sure that a few of them could get me arrested.

And even if I were to "come clean," then what? Nothing is "clean" about Gertrude's death. How to explain the engagement rings in my jewelry box, the bloody knife stolen from my closet, or the walkie-talkie in my purse? There are 414,800 words in the *Oxford English Dictionary*, yet none of them are absurd enough to solve this riddle. Like a word from a lost language, my own experience is untranslatable.

"I don't understand what links you to this crime." The detective glares at his legal pad, while the piano music fades in the background.

"But you think there is something, don't you?" I ask, curious to hear his take.

"Yes, of course. Why else would you be one of my top suspects?"

"I'm a top suspect?" My breath catches. "But I barely know Gertrude!"

"Know?" The detective raises one eyebrow as the studio audience applauds.

"Knew," I correct myself. "I only saw her that once."

"And *that* is why you're so suspicious. You're a terrible liar! It's written all over your face that you had some sort of *relationship* with the deceased." The detective spits out his words.

An icy gust slams against the side of the building; the Alka-Seltzer jingle plays on the radio. "Relationship," I repeat as I raise a hand to my mouth, remembering the sensation of Gertrude's teeth softly digging into my lower lip.

"Withholding information from the police is a prosecutable offense, Miss McCadie." Detective Wallace taps one of his galoshes impatiently against the hardwood floor. "Gertrude seemed *unbothered* by society's expectations of her. Perhaps her romantic inclinations were even less conventional than we initially thought. Sexual deviancy plays an important role in this case. This could be a fantasy homicide, where the offender is influenced by his—or *her*—sexual fantasies. I've heard that *you* have quite the active imagination."

"Why are you so preoccupied with her love life, detective? Are you jealous? Were you seeing her, too?" I ask, then bite back a grin at his expression of horror. "Don't worry, I'm joking. After all, love isn't a crime."

"There are certainly times when love *is* a crime, Miss McCadie," Wallace replies flatly.

"Gertrude was attracted to *men*, Detective," I protest. "How many guys was she seeing?"

"You realize that you're digging your own grave right now? Why would you care if you weren't romantically involved with the deceased?" The detective looks down at his legal pad to hide his blush.

"I saw her kissing Claude in the hallway," I blurt out.

"What a revelation."

My mouth drops open, as the opening strains to "In the Still of the Night," trills through the speakers. "You knew about them?"

"Who didn't?" Wallace's high-pitched, squirrel-like laughter fills the room, as the Five Satins croon out their *doo wop, doo wah* refrain. "Miss McCadie, I've found considerable inconsistencies in your testimony. Would you consent to an interview conducted with a polygraph machine? It could help rule you out as a suspect." Detective Wallace waits for a response, then makes a note in his legal pad. "Is your silence a refusal? That won't look good for you in court."

"I'm not refusing. I'm just scared." I try to look pathetic.

"There you go, lying again," Wallace smirks.

"No, I'm not," I lie.

"And again!"

I study the detective. "How do you know that I'm lying?" I ask, curious despite myself.

"Most people look over to the left when they're trying to remember something, and then up to the right when they're creating something new. You always look right." The detective puts on his *ushanka* and walks over to the entrance, pausing with one hand on the door to deliver a parting shot. "One last question: Are you in love with Avery Webster?"

My pulse quickens as my cheeks burn. I think about Avery standing on the top of the lighthouse with the sunset in his eyes.

I remember the concern in his voice when he called over Christmas. And I think back to that first afternoon, when I just about died laughing on the sidewalk. *Am I in love with Avery? Could I be? I really hope that I get the chance to find out.* "Absolutely not," I reply coolly. *Rule #5: Don't kiss and tell; plead the fifth.*

"You're looking right again, Miss McCadie. Watch out or you'll strain your neck," the detective replies.

Mrs. Pridmore returns with a box of chocolates and an aroma of roast beef. She works her way through the chocolates as I resume my fight with the tweed dress. As I pinch the raw edge of the fabric into the fold and flip the dress over, my thoughts return to Detective Wallace. "Damn it." I wince as my finger gets caught under the presser foot.

"Valentine's Day has *someone's* panties in a twist," Mrs. Pridmore observes. She asks if I want to take my lunch break, but I decline. *Who can think about food at a time like this?* When I prick my finger on my sewing needle for the third time, she asks me to leave. "Go bleed on someone else's clothing," Mrs. Pridmore says between bites of a chocolate truffle.

Wallace's insinuations keep time with my wheels as I pedal up Washington Street. I'm so heated up that I barely notice the dusting of snow on my handlebars or the dark tracks my tires leave through the powder. Everyone is hurrying home with red roses and cheap red wine, but I'm racing away in the opposite direction. Because right now, I could really use a friend. (Even if that friend is unaware that I'm spying on him with military-grade equipment.)

## ETIQUETTE FOR LOVERS AND KILLERS

I stash my bike behind a shrub, then stride down the Websters' driveway. The snow erases my footprints as I climb into the gazebo and glance at my watch. It's 5 p.m. At 6 p.m., I'll leave, no matter what. I remove my gloves to bite my nails while I wait. I've only bitten one when the walkie-talkie beeps to life.

"Is there a storm tonight?" Avery asks.

"You have a gift for understatement," Edgar grumbles on the other end.

"I read about it in the newspaper. By the way, did you see that headline?" Today's headline was "Romance, Murder, and Maine's Last Gilded-Age Mansion," which seemed suitable for the holiday.

"The newspapers are obnoxious." Edgar's voice sounds even gruffer than usual. "I think that a reporter tried to sneak onto the property. The pests are making her out to be some saint—"

"When she was actually the devil incarnate. Yes, I know. Well, that's the media[b] for you," Avery replies with a short laugh. "At first, I thought it was a joke. I thought that she'd staged her death as some appalling party trick. I still feel sick when I think about it."

"Because you would have stopped it or joined in?" Edgar chuckles.

"Edgar, your sense of humor is rather off-putting." Static ripples across the walkie-talkie as I wrap my arms around

---

[b] **Media (n.):** *the main means of mass communication (broadcasting, publishing, etc.). Media derived from the Latin medius, "in the middle," and the PIE root medhyo, "middle." Which is fitting, because the media is the original middleman, straddling the gap between knowledge and the consumer.*

myself to keep warm. "*Obviously*, I feel guilty. I could have saved her. I could have stopped whoever–"

"Well, I'd buy him a beer," Edgar interrupts, and I choke on a laugh. But my smile falls when I glance out at the yard. The snow is really coming down now. I should go, but I can't bear to leave. I've been waiting for them to talk about the murder for a month.

"Why are you acting so cavalier about this whole thing?" Avery reprimands his groundskeeper. "Don't get me wrong, I didn't like her, and I *hated* her relationship with my brother. Even *bad people* like them can find each other, so why am I always alone?" Avery asks, and I glance sharply at the phone. So he *is* alone. Maybe there's hope after all. "I try to be nice. To be courteous and attentive. But every time that I really open up to someone, they go sprinting off in the opposite direction. It gnaws at me."

*It gnaws at me, too!* I want to shout. Who was I kidding? I can't leave now.

"Do you ever feel that way?" Avery continues. "Like you would gladly trade places with someone else? Or anyone else, for that matter?"

"Yeah, someone without a criminal record." Edgar laughs. "What about that other one?"

"Other criminal record?"

"No, the other *girl*, stupid–the one you were–" Static swells across the two-way radio as my heart drops. I glare at the walkie-talkie and knock it against the side of the gazebo. Switch it on and off again as my teeth chatter.

"Honestly, I don't think she's worth the effort." The walkie-talkie crackles back to life, with what sounds disturbingly like Edgar offering dating advice. "The storm is picking up. I'm going to grab some beer before everything shuts down," he says, then hangs up abruptly.

*Were they talking about me? Am I the other girl?* I gaze at the walkie-talkie in shock, then at the yard in dismay. The rose garden is hidden behind a moving wall of white. My head feels fuzzy and my brain is sluggish. My heart is thudding in my chest. Maybe I waited too long. Maybe I should have eaten something today. Maybe I should have worn long underwear. *Shoulda-woulda-coulda,* Victor quips in my brain.

I can barely see ten feet ahead as I stumble back to the street. I grope around blindly until the gate emerges through the whiteout. The wrought-iron bars are cold through my gloves as I steady myself, watching the blizzard swirl around me. Another gust of wind as the full weight of my stupidity reveals itself. *I can't bike home through this. Hell, I can't even walk in it!* Case in point: I take one step and fall flat on my face. The slush has frozen and the road is covered in black ice. *Perfect.*

I scramble to my feet, only to stumble a second time. As my knees smack against the pavement, my bag falls, and I hear something clatter across the ice. *Goddamn it. The walkie-talkie!*

As I grope around blindly for the two-way radio, something growls in the distance. Is that a bear or a snow plow? I strain my ears until I decipher the faint whirr of an approaching engine. As I strain my eyes against the whiteout, I consider my objectives. What do I want? To retrieve my walkie-talkie? To survive the next ten minutes? To warm up in the tub with a cup of tea? But more than anything, I'd *love* to write about this in my diary.

This would make such a nice departure from the usual content. A bit of Jack London thrown into my Down East gothic romance. *I was in the middle of a blizzard, fighting for a life that had always underwhelmed me.* I compose the opening sentence as I rush across the icy street. There is a certain safety in narration. In writing rather than living. Being a protagonist is such a risky occupation, it's far safer to be the narrator and observe the situation from afar. To find the poetry in a blizzard, the irony in an icy road, and the suspense in a car barreling forward with zero visibility.

When life gets too daunting, I retreat behind my words, thinking, *Well, at least this will make one hell of a diary entry.* And somehow, that makes me feel less alone.

I reach the telephone pole a millisecond before the car hits me. A moment of equilibrium. Of squealing breaks, screaming lips, and swirling snow as I throw my arms around the wooden post. My breath catches as my knees buckle, and a bottle of Liquid Paper tips over, smearing across the page in white. Then the awful blankness of winter sweeps in to erase my unwritten words as whiteness swallows everything up.

## CHAPTER SIXTEEN

# THE CLOTHES OF A BACHELOR

*It is not correct–no matter what you occasionally see–for a man to wear a dinner jacket or tail coat in the daytime unless, perhaps, he's being buried! (And to follow this lugubrious aside, if the family does decide to attire the deceased in formal clothes, give him a morning coat. A tuxedo doesn't seem quite right.)*

"You fool."

Calloused hands dig into my shoulders. The fingers are strong and rough, with dark hair growing out of the knuckles. I blink at them in confusion. Why are they so ugly? Then the past few hours come rushing back, and I realize that ugly fingers are the least of my concerns.

"Get your paws off of me!" I thrash in Edgar's grip as he helps me into his truck. Snow billows around the telephone pole behind us.

"Would it kill you to be polite?" Edgar asks as I sit back in the passenger seat. He slams the door, then walks around to climb into the driver's seat.

"How?" I gape at his woolen hat. I've never seen Edgar without a fedora before. He looks strangely naked without it.

"I was heading out to grab some beer. When I pulled onto the road, I saw this dark shape skidding past. I thought it was a wild turkey." Edgar turns the key, and the engine hiccups to life. "What the hell are you doing here?"

I pull on my seat belt as my teeth chatter. I've lost my walkie-talkie and been caught leaving Webster Cottage. My wiretapping days are officially over. "Just being stupid," I say with resignation.

"Well, at least you're honest." Edgar whistles as he pulls onto Route 190. The wind pushes the truck across the road while I dig my fingers into the worn leather seat. The windshield wipers struggle against the onslaught of snow. My parents crashed in a storm like this, and I've tried to avoid poor driving conditions ever since. As we approach the outskirts of town and the first houses appear through the snow, I try to relax.

"Listen, kid." Edgar makes a right and turns into the IGA parking lot, where the supermarket gleams like a lighthouse through the storm. "Whatever you're playing at has to stop. I warned you to be careful. I told you to leave well enough alone, but no one ever listens to me. You're just like Gertrude, and if you aren't careful, you'll end up the same way."

"Gertrude and I have nothing in common," I retort numbly.

"That's exactly what she would have said." Edgar smirks as

he pulls into a parking spot. "The hair is a nice touch, by the way. Maybe try dyeing it red?"

I reach out to touch the ends of my bob, peeking out beneath my beret. I suppose that Gertrude and I have both acted out. She played with fire in her romantic relationships, while I'm playing with fire now, on my hunt for her killer. She lived out her fantasies while I live inside mine. But is there something else that binds us?

"I'm running in to grab a six-pack. Don't steal my truck." Edgar eyes me warily but leaves the engine running.

And I *would* steal his truck if I weren't quite so lazy, but the sad fact is that I prefer being driven, so the Ford and I are still here when he returns. Edgar climbs in, sets his bag in the back, then pulls onto the road. I don't bother giving directions, because he clearly knows the way.

"Madame, we've arrived," he says as my grandparents' house glows warmly through the whiteout.

I unbuckle my seat belt, then turn to Edgar at a loss. "What am I missing?"

"Everything?" he replies with a gruff laugh.

The blizzard swirling around me, I look back at the groundskeeper / stalker / disgraced detective as I open the door. "Thank you for the ride. And . . . for saving my life." I hesitate to consider what would have happened if Edgar hadn't roared up in his F-100 tonight. "And . . . I'm sorry," I add lamely, although I'm not really sure what I'm apologizing for. That Edgar is stuck in this mess? That I'm trapped in it, too? That he has mice in his cellar and a bug in his phone?

The nor'easter swirls around me as I hurry up to my grandparents' house. Inside, Victor is bustling about in the kitchen. He fusses over me as the smell of meat loaf and popovers envelops us. "Happy Valentine's Day, love." He squeezes my shoulder.

And I laugh, because I'd forgotten what day it was.

I'm not the only one whose Valentine's Day wasn't all candy hearts and roses. While I stormed the gates of Webster Cottage, Marines laid siege to the beaches of Da Nang, Vietnam, the first U.S. troops to enter Vietnam after a decade of political foreplay. Whispers of a coming draft. Cries of impending doom. The Vietnam War drowns everything else out, until a corpse in a tuxedo[a] usurps the headlines.

"Black Tie Horror in Down East Maine," reports the *Ellsworth American*.

> EASTPORT (AP)—A black tuxedo, a cigarette tax stamp, 50 cents in his pocket, and a tattoo with the initials *tub*. Those were the only clues, on Valentine's Day, as police tried to identify another corpse in Eastport, Maine.
>
> Armed with a bouquet of red roses, Doris Cobb (78) entered her family crypt at the Hillside Cemetery. Each year on their anniversary, Mrs. Cobb left a bouquet on her husband's casket. But this time, she had company.

---

[a] **Tuxedo (n.):** *a suit, usually black, worn for formal social occasions.* Originating in 1889 in *Tuxedo* Park, NY, this men's evening wear quickly became a wardrobe staple. *Tuxedo* is an anglicization of the Algonquian word *p'tucksepo*, meaning "curving river."

## ETIQUETTE FOR LOVERS AND KILLERS

The man was of East Asian descent, between 30 and 35 years old, 5 feet 10 inches tall, and an estimated 150 pounds. The John Doe wore a polyester tuxedo and black button shoes, but no hat or coat. Nick Chamberlain, Maine State Medical Examiner, reported that two of his left ribs were broken, which points to foul play.

He died almost a year ago, but thanks to unique environmental conditions, the body is remarkably well-preserved. "The Hillside Cemetery is situated on an old cranberry bog. The ground is covered in sphagnum moss, which soaks up minerals and drastically slows decomposition," Chamberlain informed reporters.

When viewing the body under black light, the forensic pathologist noted the lowercase *tub* tattoo. "This guy was a huge fan of home appliances," theorized Detective Winchester. "His interest in interior decor is one lead we're following up."

The remains were moved to the undertaking rooms of the Leonard-McGhee furniture store / funeral home. Then the John Doe (nicknamed "John Tux," thanks to his memorable attire) returned to the Hillside Cemetery to be buried at the county's expense. Exhaustive efforts are being made to uncover his identity. Officials ask anyone with information to step forward.

I find Victor hunched over the kitchen table with a pair of scissors and a glue stick. I glimpse a salacious "John Tux" headline over his shoulder. "I told you there were more bodies!" he exclaims as he glues the newspaper clipping into his scrapbook.

"Why are you saving that?" I ask, pouring myself a glass of lemonade.

"Oh, I just think it's kind of neat. I love bathtubs, too."

I take my glass and exit the kitchen. *Neat! My grandfather has* lost *his mind.* Upstairs, I open the top drawer of my dresser and pull out the handkerchief that Teddy gave me at the holiday party. I sip my lemonade as I consider the curly lowercase initials: *tub*.

John Tux died almost a year ago, then a few months later, Teddy's fiancée passed away as well. I consider Teddy's searching green eyes, used-car-salesman mustache, and mauve pajamas. This tuxedo murder has Teddy written *all over* it. Literally. The John Doe even has his *initials* tattooed on his wrist. I frown at the ill-advised monogram on the handkerchief. Is John Tux another lover? A faux pas that followed him home from a black-tie event? Do all of Teddy's love interests end up six feet underground? And what about Clara? Was she seeing Teddy, too?

I hold the *tub* handkerchief up to my nose and inhale deeply. But it doesn't offer any insights, just the slightly salty scent of dry tears.

Victor isn't the only one with "John Tux Fever," as the newspapers are calling it, a highly contagious disease that has infected the local population. We sell out of men's formal wear at Primp and Ribbon, and the Saints and Sailors Ink Shop is crammed with local youths who want their own *tub* tattoos in solidarity. John Tux has become a local celebrity and a style icon.

I puzzle over the growing body count as I stroll over to Doris Cobb's house after work. With its steeply pitched roof and carved gables, the granite building is an architectural advertisement for the Cobb Granite Quarry. A black-and-white cat licks its paws on the front steps as a handful of busybodies loiters on the sidewalk. A bony hand draws back a black lace curtain to peek at the onlookers. As the widow glares at me, I remember how Gertrude insulted her during the party.

Mrs. Cobb has been in close proximity to two murders now. She was inside Webster Cottage when Gertrude died, and now there's a John Doe hidden in her crypt. Was John Tux's final resting place a mistake, a coincidence, or a message? And were Gertrude's insults whiskey-induced rudeness, or something more? Is this slight old woman an innocent bystander or a suspect?

The door opens and Mrs. Cobb tosses a glass of water at the stray. As the cat hisses and darts away, the widow straightens. She fixes the crowd with a withering glance and we depart as well. As I walk to the post office, I feel her eyes following me.

One rejection and three job applications today. One to the Wadsworth Atheneum, another to the Frick Collection, and a third to the Oldbury Ranch House (that's the "rich guy on the beach with an artifact problem," as Debbie so poignantly referred to him). As I mail out my letters of interest, Mr. Townsend appears with a pomegranate. And I can't help but smile. Because I'm still submitting and still getting rejected, but mostly, I just notice the fruit.

At ballet class, the girls are stuck on John Tux, too. "I just love a bad boy with tattoos." Vicki giggles. I stop mid pique-turn as she tumbles into me. *Of course, the tattoo!*

The Saints and Sailors Ink Shop is empty. I've taken an early lunch break in hopes of catching the tattoo[b] artist before his first customer of the day. The island melts around me as I approach the redbrick building. I keep an eye out for falling icicles as I step inside.

Zack Piervicente is tattooing himself, with the tattoo gun pressed to his forearm. He clenches his jaw as veins rise up on his wrist. "One sec." He glances up for an instant before returning to the tattoo needle. Above him, the walls are lined with illustrations of skulls, bulldogs, snakes, and boxing gloves. The Standells spin on the record player—a hip rock band that has no business in square little Eastport.

The Brooklyn transplant caused quite a stir when he roared into town three years ago on his Harley-Davidson to corner the market on mermaid tattoos. Florence was smitten, but Zack was spoken for. His girlfriend has come to visit a few times—a petite Cuban bombshell with tattoos of her own and a black

---

[b] **Tattoo (n.):** *a design inlaid with pigment in the skin.* Derived from the Tahitian onomatopoeia *tatau*, this practice was introduced to the west in 1644, when sailors traveled around the world with Captain Cook. The sailors loved Tahitian *tattoos* and brought the custom back home with them. Centuries later, the *tattoo* remains the mark of a well-traveled life.

leather jacket to match. The tattoo artist has never so much as looked in my direction.

But going unnoticed has a few advantages, namely, that Zack has never noticed me before. So when I place her business card on the steel trolley littered with ink jars and sterilizing equipment, he has no idea I'm *not* Diane Bean of the *Quoddy Current*. Zack wears a cologne of leather, ink, and black coffee. A faint film of sweat moistens his temple as the waspy buzz of the tattoo gun echoes between us.

Zack finishes inking a line into his café au lait skin, following a stencil mapped across his left arm. Then he transfers the gun to his left hand and swivels his rolling chair around to reach for a black box on the floor with a glowing red light bulb. As he switches it off, the buzzing stops. He sets the machine down on the streel trolley and turns toward me.

"Heart, cat, or rose?" he asks with a cocky grin.

"Huh?" I respond with confusion.

"This is clearly your first tattoo." He smirks at my tan blazer and matching pencil skirt (both "on loan" from the dress shop). "And I'm guessing that you want a heart, a cat, or a rose. You don't strike me as the butterfly type."

"I'm actually here following up a lead on a crime that I thought you might have some insights on." I nod to the business card.

Zack rolls his eyes as he reaches for a pale blue rag and wipes down the fresh ink on his arm, then takes off his latex gloves. "You think I'm a criminal because I have tattoos?"

"And you think I'm a prude because I'm wearing a khaki blazer?" I rebut as I reach for the handkerchief in my purse. I set it down on the trolley, so the tattoo artist can see the *tub* monogram in the corner. "Have you ever given a tattoo like this?"

"More than I can count." The tattoo artist laughs as he flexes, then unflexes his left hand, the wet ink glistening on his forearm. I squint at the tattoo. Is that a sardine?

"*Before* the whole craze started," I explain, my words crisp and professional. "Maybe a year or two ago? In the late spring or summer. A kind of fancy guy?"

Zack's eyes widen. "You think that I tattooed the John Doe while he was still alive?"

"It would be weird if you tattooed him when he was dead. To be honest, this might not lead to anything. It's just something I'm curious about. Do you remember anything?"

"You're from the local paper? I didn't realize that you do investigative reporting. That's pretty hip." Zack walks over to a black tanker desk against the wall and sips from a mug of coffee as he reaches for a large ledger book. This surprises me, as Zack doesn't strike me as the recordkeeping type. He starts flipping through it with a frown. "Give me a sec," he murmurs as the Standells finish one song, then begin the next. "Hell yes!" he exclaims, making a fist. "July tenth, 1963. 'Weird guy with a classy broad. *tub* tattoo!'" He pumps his fist with each word.

"You're sure it was the word and *not* some bubbles or a clawfoot?" I ask.

"I remember now. It was a weird font. Almost cursive. Fancy, like the lady with him."

"And it was *definitely* a lady? Not this fellow?" I reach into my purse and withdraw the engagement photo from the sand dunes. I've folded it down the middle, so only Teddy is visible.

The tattoo artist laughs. "He has too much facial hair for a lady, even this far north."

Zack offers me a cat tattoo on the house, but I politely decline. As I step outside, I see the retired cheerleaders across the street, exchanging words.

"I could kill you! That was *personal,* and you told *everyone.* Our friendship is *over,*" Florence squeals at Wendy as an icicle almost skewers them. "You're a total dead end."

I do a double take. *Could* Florence kill Wendy? Is there anyone in Eastport who *isn't* capable of murder? Then I turn to find Zack watching from his window with a faint smile.

It gives me an idea. A big, expensive, wildly illegal idea. I keep circling around the same characters and the same locations. Hitting the same dead ends.

Maybe it's time to try a different dead end. One that's a bit more final.

## CHAPTER SEVENTEEN

# IN DEFENSE OF THE LITTLE WHITE LIE

*Politeness is just as much about what you don't say as what you do.*

First comes the phone call, to see if my idea is even possible (which it probably isn't). Eastport's one phone booth is positioned directly outside the police station. I keep a cautious eye on the grim gray building as I wrestle open the smudged metal door. I pop a stick of Wrigley's Big Red in my mouth, raise the oily phone to my ear, and drop a dime in the coin slot. I'd rather be at home on the gossip bench, but this phone call requires privacy, of which there is precious little at 80 Key Street.

"Long distance!" squeaks the operator. "Deposit fifteen cents for the first three minutes." I do as I'm told, then hear more buzzing and clicking. "Bell Atlantic of Eastern Maine connecting you now."

The phone rings three times before a harried voice picks up. "Office of the Chief Medical Examiner. Dale speaking."

I chew my gum and try to get into character. "Hi. I'm calling about personal effects."

"Name, please," Dale replies coolly.

"Paisley." I snap my gum for reassurance. "But the effects belonged to my sister. Her name was Gertrude Taylor. She passed away last summer." There is a 99 percent chance that the Taylors have already picked up Gertrude's property. But given the lack of organization or genuine grief that I heard on the phone with Paisley, I think there's a chance that they haven't followed through yet.

"Paisley Taylor." Dale's voice warms on the other end of the phone. "I've been trying to get ahold of your parents about your sister's belongings. But they won't call me back."

"I know, they're the *worst*." More snapping gum as I curl a lock of hair around my fingertips. "They're just *so* busy, blah, blah, blah, but who isn't? This year is just *flying* by! But I'm putting my foot down and coming up to Maine next week. If you still have her belongings, I would love to swing by and pick them up."

"This is highly irregular. We're supposed to confiscate property after sixty days. But . . . you're in luck." Dale pauses, clearly waiting for an apology.

"Oh, you poor thing, I'm so sorry for putting you out, and how *sharp* of you to hang on to her things," I coo as I tap my nails against the side of the greasy booth. Chief Deputy Abbott pauses outside the police station to scowl at me, and I turn in the opposite direction.

"It's no trouble." I can almost hear Dale smile across the receiver.

Next comes the bar, to obtain information. I "borrow" a trench coat from Primp and Ribbon, wrap my hair in a green scarf, put on a pair of oversize sunglasses, and try to channel Audrey Hepburn in *Charade*.

"What is wrong with you?" Victor stands at the foot of the stairs, barring my path.

"What isn't?" I stifle a laugh as I squeeze past him.

The sky is moody and overdramatic, as if it's also pretending to be in a spy film. The moon transforms the harbor into a world of harsh lines and shadows. As I make my way to the dock, I receive several stares. The fashion police are everywhere.

The Thirsty Whale isn't the sort of place where young ladies go unchaperoned. The day I spoke with Teddy on the sidewalk was the closest I've ever come. Tonight, I push through the swinging saloon doors, taking in the tugboat-inspired decor, complete with anchors fixed to the walls, lobster-trap coffee tables, and fishing nets dangling from the ceiling. A swordfish is mounted to a plaque, with its saber nose pointed up snobbishly at the aquarium of oysters underneath it. The slimy mollusks look like a case of food poisoning waiting to happen.

The clientele looks a bit feral as well. Mr. Swann plays cards, while the coast guard and harbormaster spar off beside the jukebox. Eben Hollis waves at me from behind the counter with a basket of fried clams. Edgar glowers at me from the far end of the bar.

During my wiretapping sessions, I learned that Edgar is a

regular here, and when he's not gardening or gossiping with Detective Wallace, he's at the bar. His fedora slips down his forehead as I slide onto the stool beside him. "Can I have a glass of white wine?" I ask Eben. I'm surprised to see him, I didn't realize that the locksmith's son moonlights as a bartender.

"Don't. She's not staying," Edgar growls, then fixes me with a scowl. "To what do I owe this honor?"

I try to look worldly and nefarious, like someone who can pull off wearing sunglasses at night. "I need your help." I square my shoulders, bracing myself for derision.

But instead, Edgar grins. "You decided to take my advice!" he exclaims. "Hollis. A pen and paper!" I hold my breath as Edgar snaps his fingers at the bartender, then writes *Of Moose and Men* on a scrap of paper. "Bangor. Any night. Ask for Mick. Now *go*."


Mrs. Pridmore is only too happy to give me time off work to go "on a spa trip to Quebec," but it offends my grandmother's delicate sensibilities. She sets down her hand mirror and points her tweezers at me. "Honey muffin, have I taught you nothing? If you're going to lie, come up with something halfway convincing. 'Quebec' isn't fooling anyone." Grace shakes her head in resignation, then resumes plucking her eyebrows.


With a carpetbag full of disguises and a brain full of reservations, I plod into the soggy purgatory of central Maine. I got off the train in Bangor. Featured in the song "King of the Road" as a premier destination for hobos and freighthoppers, Bangor is the sort of place that people describe as "past its prime," although it's unclear if it ever had a prime to begin with. I lug my carpetbag to a nearby motel, complete with a taxidermy bobcat on the check-in desk and a bear in the lobby. Then I spritz on perfume and put on my borrowed trench coat.

My third stop is a seedy dive bar to acquire the necessary credentials for my trip to the coroner's office. I adjust my scarf and push my sunglasses up on my forehead as I step inside the Of Moose and Men Saloon. Big Red tingles on my tongue as I wade into a dense cloud of cigarette smoke. Posters of snowmobiles and scantily clad women ornament the walls, and the requisite moose head lolls drunkenly over the counter, its antlers regal and immense. A few dissolute husbands atone for their sins at the bar, while a pair of men in mechanic's caps shoot pool at the billiard table. The bartender is sleaze personified, with a striped T-shirt straining across his chest, a fringed vest, and a patchy five-o'clock shadow.

"Is your name Mick?" I resist the urge to turn on my heel.

"Who wants to know?" Mick tosses his oily shoulder-length hair as he places a cigarette between the grooves of an ashtray.

"I was told to ask for you." I pass him an envelope labeled *Items for Fake ID*, containing a photo, name, and address. "I need a Connecticut driver's license with this information."

"How do I know you ain't the heat? Who sent you?"

"Edgar." I try to contain my outrage. *Do I look like a police officer?!*

Mick grunts, then picks up his cigarette. "It's gonna cost you."

"And I need it by tomorrow."

## ETIQUETTE FOR LOVERS AND KILLERS

"That'll be double," he says, then whispers an exorbitant sum in my ear. While I don't enjoy being swindled, I can hardly call the cops on him, so I reach for my wallet. All eyes are on me as I count out twenty dollars and place them in a second envelope labeled *Forgery Money*.

Of Moose and Men is even more depressing by the light of day. The sun highlights the peeling vinyl stools and greasy Formica countertops. The moose looks hungover and Mick does, too, nursing a beer while *General Hospital* plays on the television behind him.

"Some of my finest work." He places a card on the sticky countertop. "Can you dig it?"

The freshly laminated license is still warm in my hands. The black-and-white ID wouldn't hold up in court, but it *does* have an expiration date, a state seal, and a signature. My photo is on the bottom left, with the name "Paisley Marie-Antoinette Taylor" in the upper right.

"Marie-Antoinette." My voice is tight with distaste.

"Pardon my French." Mick shrugs, then returns to his soap opera.

My next stop is the Maine State Police Complex in Augusta. I slip on my white leather gloves as I step beneath a crumbling brick facade inlaid with the words *Integrity, Compassion, Fairness,* and *Excellence*. I squint through my oversize sunglasses at the directory, then hurry down the hallway in my slingback heels. I'm on high alert. The coroner's office is housed in the same building as the Major Crimes Unit, and I imagine that if Detective Wallace caught me on-site with a fake ID, I'd skyrocket from suspect to convict in seconds flat. I knock briskly on a door labeled OFFICE OF THE CHIEF MEDICAL EXAMINER and am duly admitted.

The coroner's office has plastic seats, a sickly-looking fern, a few battered copies of *Reader's Digest*, and a distinct aroma of black licorice. I look around myself in disappointment. Where are the cobwebs dangling from the ceiling? Or the gramophone playing a scratched copy of Mozart's "Requiem"? Dale is also a letdown—he doesn't have a hunched back, a monocle, or a tattered lab coat, just a black turtleneck, an insincere smile, and skin the color of cauliflower left in the refrigerator a little too long. "Love the glasses," the young man calls, his slicked-back hair gleaming under the fluorescent lights. "How can I help you?"

"We spoke a few days ago." I chew my gum as I push my sunglasses up on my forehead. "I've come for my sister's—"

Dale's eyes light up. "Of *course*, you look *just* like her!" Which seems like a rather forward thing to say, seeing as Dale has seen Gertrude without her knickers on. "If I could just see your driver's license, then sign *here* and *here*." He passes me a release form and a blank sign-in sheet. "Sorry, sometimes we get freaks in here."

"How appalling," I reply as I slide my freshly minted ID across the counter.

There is a certain decorum to dishonesty. Rules of etiquette that govern even our most devious instincts. Emily Post condemned the malicious falsehood: "To tell a lie in cowardice, to tell a lie for gain, or to avoid deserved punishment—are all the blackest of black lies." But her contemporary Mary Wilson Little applauded the tactful fib: "Politeness is half good manners and half good lying."

I wonder which category I would fall under as I write *Paisley Taylor* on the sign-in sheet. It's certainly in poor taste. But Paisley doesn't want Gertrude's personal effects, neither do her parents, and the cops seem to have hit a dead end. Am I really hurting anything if I take a peek? Is a lie really that bad if it helps solve a murder?

Dale gives the ID a cursory glance. "Far out. I'll xerox this while you're—" He slips off his seat, then reappears a moment later at the door. "I'll just be gone for a minute while I'm grabbing the—"

"Are you sure you don't want some company?" I ask with a coy half smile. "I could help you carry things. I'm very strong."

Dale laughs, his eyes trailing from my scrawny arms to the sweetheart neckline of my dress. "Why not? Normally, I bring up the personal effects, but it's slow today, so if you're curious...."

"Only slightly." I try not to look curious as hell.

Dale leads me down the hallway as the aroma of licorice soaked in chemicals trails behind him. "I'm the pathology technician, so I assist the coroner with his autopsies, then eviscerate and reconstruct." He chatters blithely while he flicks on a light switch and pulls a set of keys out of his pocket. "Are you staying here? Want someone to show you around?" Dale asks as he leads me down a staircase into the basement.

"That sounds swell," I reply absently as he ushers me through a wire gate at the bottom. The security door clangs behind us as fluorescent lights flicker on overhead. The damp basement is filled with row upon row of steel shelves, supporting an army of banker's boxes. I gaze at them in wonder. There are so many secrets here! So many stories! My fingers itch to open every single box.

Dale leads me to the last row on the back wall. "These are the unclaimed personal effects. Some are from people without next of kin. Others are from cold cases."

I nod, having spent the last week reading up on cold cases. If a murder isn't solved within a year, it's reclassified as a cold case. Gertrude's one-year anniversary is rapidly approaching, so Detective Wallace better get a move on, or she'll slip away from him entirely.

Which is embarrassing, to say the least. Over the last twenty years, U.S. detectives have gotten progressively better at their jobs, culminating in a record-breaking high of 93 percent of "cleared" murders in 1962. Which means that the cops got their bad guy, the homicide was solved (to the best of everyone's knowledge), and there was a doughnut free-for-all in the break room. The remaining 7 percent became cold cases and ended up in storage lockers just like this—the ultimate dead end. As one of the least populated states, Maine's percent of violent "index" crimes is notably lower than the national average.

Or it was, until last year.

But Gertrude, Clara, and John Tux are ruining our shining record, and with it, the FBI's bragging rights. The unsolved murders must be a monumental thorn in their side.

Dale pulls a banker's box off the top shelf, then sets it down on a wire rack at waist height. "Take your time," he says.

I gape at the meager collection of odds and ends. Gertrude's personal effects are even more of a letdown than the coroner's office. "But what about her dress? And her ring?"

"Those are in evidence. Major Crimes keeps their stuff down here, too," Dale replies with an unhelpful sweep of his hand that somehow indicates everywhere and nowhere simultaneously. I frown at the box as he inches forward, brushing his hand against my skirt.

"Could I have a moment to mourn?" I try not to jerk away. "In private."

"Of course. Swing by on your way out." Dale strides away and the door clangs after him.

I frown at the remnants from Gertrude's final hours. A pale pink scarf bears a lingering trace of her perfume. Her lipstick has the name *Shocking Revelation* printed at the bottom. The color is a deep red that would completely wash me out. Her elegant satin stilettos have been stained beyond repair. I rummage through the box to discover two red bobby pins. *How depressing. This is all that remains of that feral society girl.*

Something flashes at the bottom of the box and I fish out a small plastic bag, with one rose-gold garnet earring and a platinum cuff link engraved with *T.B.* Why isn't this in evidence? I narrow my eyes at the all-too-familiar initials. Why did Gertrude have Teddy's cuff link? Was she struggling against him? Ripping at his shirt while he choked the life out of her?

I try to restrain myself. Try to convince myself that it's morbid, profane, and inexcusably rude, but impulse control has never been my strong suit. Against my better judgment, I slip on one of Gertrude's heels, then gasp when it fits. My slingback heels are off within seconds, and I'm wobbling around the basement in her pumps. I totter up to the first row of shelves, faltering when I see a box titled *John Doe–Eastport*. Another marked *Tabernathy, Clara*. And several boxes labeled *Taylor, Gertrude*. I could have cried, it felt so nice to see them all stacked together like that. I frown up at the dark stairway. *How long before creepy Dale returns?*

Gertrude's bin is overflowing with evidence: papers, notebooks, mini-cassettes, interview transcripts, and forensic reports. I catch my breath when I find a plastic bag with a diamond ring and hold it up to the flickering fluorescent light. *Is this diamond* smaller *than the second one I received? It is! What the hell?!* I riffle through the box until I find a crumpled bit of something in a clear plastic sleeve. My eyes widen as they take in a single typed page stained with dark spots.

> Dearest Gertrude,
> 
> Darling, destroy me. Tease me, taunt me, and make me your slave. Let me worship at the altar of your beauty, then burn it to the ground.
> 
> I dreamt about you again last night. I was tearing off your clothes, ravenous to taste you. I lifted you up so your legs curled around my waist, then I pressed your back against the wall. Your nails dug into my shoulders. They were scorching hot, branding me, as flames flickered in the depths of your eyes. The temperature rose as steam curled off of your body. It ate away at your

skin as if it might undress you for me. And honestly? Medium-rare has never looked so good.

I tried to save you. Sort of. I grabbed a fire extinguisher and hosed you down, but the flames consumed you from the inside out. As you died in my arms, I stared at your charred hands. At your burnt little heart behind your charcoal ribs. And I thought to myself–what a waste of a half-decent shag.

Then the dream shifted, and *I* was the one on fire. Gertrude, you've burned me one too many times. I hate you. I love you. I want you six feet underground.

And yet, I lust for your soft skin. For your red hair gleaming in the sun.

Xx,
Claude

I don't read the letter, so much as devour it. Once finished, I read it again and again. My gloves leave greedy impressions in the sheet protector as I study the brown spots splattered across it. Maybe it's wine, but more likely, it's blood. Is this the paper that I saw sticking out of her pocket at the crime scene?

Claude's signature is scrawled across the bottom in bold, masculine strokes. I hold it up to the light, but there aren't any pencil marks or pen lifts, just Claude's arrogant scrawl and a watermark of the Webster family seal. I drop it in the box and press my hand to my cheek. I'm burning up, blushing so hard that I might also catch fire.

This letter is a death threat. Here is Claude's motive: he'd said too much to Gertrude and exposed himself as a self-obsessed psycho, so he killed her. Given his sadistic tendencies, it can't have been an entirely unpleasant chore. But the letter is *also* an admission of some viscerally real feelings. Claude has the exterior of a brute but the heart of a pathetic poet.

A high-pitched squeal rings out at the top of the stairs.

Detective Wallace's unmistakable squirrel-like laughter drifts into the basement, as I dart behind the nearest rack. "... And that surprises you?" Detective Wallace calls from the top of the stairs, followed by a muffled response from someone in the hallway. The fluorescent light spasms as if it's also hyperventilating.

Detective Wallace's footsteps grow louder as I cower behind the shelf. My vision blurs and my knees wobble. Is this breaking and entering? Tampering with evidence? Obstruction of justice? I'm committing so many crimes at this moment that it makes me dizzy.

The mesh door clangs open as Detective Wallace steps inside the evidence locker. He's so close that I can smell him, meatballs and marinara sauce. As he stops before me, the banker's box in front of my face begins to move. My life flashes before my eyes. But I square my shoulders and try to be brave. Or, at least, try to fake it. I resist the urge to gasp or fidget, but stand very still as I pray to whatever god might have mercy on stupid, stupid girls, and then–

My prayers are answered.

The door squeaks open at the top of the stairs. "Hey buddy, got a call on your tip line," shouts a voice. "You're gonna wanna hear this. It's about that girl–"

The box slides back into place as the detective's meatball-sub breath retreats. I thank the patron saint of stupid, stupid girls as I grab my shoes and count to fifty. Then I teeter out of the basement into the miraculously empty hallway, Gertrude's stilettos ringing out across the linoleum floor.

I don't start running until I reach the sidewalk.

I don't twist my ankle until I'm a block away.

Despite my sprained ankle, I leave Augusta on a high. The radio plays "Ring of Fire" as the state capital recedes in the rearview mirror of my bus. An hour and a half later, I'm back in Bangor, limping into a downtown café. I massage my ankle as I order a bowl of French onion soup. I inhale deeply, savoring the aroma of caramelized onions and Gruyère, trying to dispel the lingering fragrance of formaldehyde.

I'm too keyed up to eat, so I order a glass of Pouilly-Fuissé. A literary move, as the French white was recently featured in Hemingway's *A Moveable Feast* (which I actually enjoyed). When the waiter asks for my ID, I reach for my wallet, then my heart skips a beat. *I left the fake ID with Dale! The ID for Paisley Marie-Antoinette Taylor.* As I hand the waiter my real driver's license, something prickles at the back of my neck. I hope the guillotine isn't waiting to drop.

I take a sip of chilled wine and pull my little black book out of my purse.

*Dear Diary,*
    *Today I broke into the Maine State Police Headquarters.*

My pen hovers over the confession. I surprised myself in that evidence locker today. I didn't stammer or stumble, but performed my role admirably. I'm starting to think that the only way to solve Gertrude's murder is by solving the mystery of myself. We're all wound up in this together, and as I uncover details about her, I discover new facets of myself in the process. I want to investigate, to trespass, and to take chances. And if that means committing multiple felonies to steal a pair of stained satin pumps, then so be it.

I glance at the next table, where a couple is having a *Lady and the Tramp* moment over a bowl of spaghetti and meatballs. I smile, because I wouldn't trade places with them for the world.

Sure, it would be nice to have someone to share this with. But even alone, it's one of the best moments of my life.

The final stop on my journey into the heart of Gertrude's murder is a bookshelf on cardiothoracic surgery at the University of Maine in Machias. The university has the only medical reference section within driving distance of Eastport. Seeing the blood on that letter made me curious about the stab wound that killed Gertrude. Her death was "by the book," so I'm headed to the library.

I climb down from the train in Machias and limp past a tiny, ugly river toward the university. The sidewalk is coated in a layer of salt, and I leave a salty trail behind me as I hobble through the college library to the medical reference section in the very back.

I sit on the faded blue carpet to examine a few creased pages in a dated surgical textbook. My eyes widen as they study the lending pocket in the back, the sign-out card tucked inside, and the red OVERDUE notice stamped across it. *Got you.*

There, for anyone to see, is the name and the date of the last person to borrow this book. A person who should have known better. A person whose only reason for borrowing such a book would be premeditated manslaughter. I squint at the loops of blue ink across the manila card. How could such a messy fellow have such a precise signature? I pull out my diary and trace the handwriting sample for later analysis.

A librarian comes over to find me sitting on the ground with my carpetbag, swollen ankle, textbook, and scandalized grin. "Can I help you?" she asks with concern.

"Oh, a boy broke my heart, so I'm just trying to fix it." I shrug, holding up the book on cardiac surgery.

## CHAPTER EIGHTEEN

# IN DEFENSE OF THE LITTLE BLACK DRESS

*Black has lost its meaning as the badge of bereavement ever since Chanel launched the "little black dress," which has since become an essential of the wardrobe during World War I. Prior to that, women seldom, if ever, wore black except for mourning.*

It's as if Paisley's returned to Eastport in my place, because everything feels different. My soap smells weird. My Folgers coffee tastes stale. The texture of my bedding is all wrong. Even the phone rings out at a strange new decibel. I jump when it chimes during dinner.

"Don't," Victor says as he ladles "hot dog surprise" into a soup tureen. The "surprise" consists of a package of pink hot dogs, a can of Campbell's tomato soup, cheddar cheese, mustard, and horseradish.

"Don't do what?" I gaze at the "surprise" in trepidation.

"Don't *answer it*," my grandfather advises, garnishing his

bowl with cocktail crackers. "It's a prank caller. We've been getting them all week. I pick up, say 'Hello,' and the line goes dead. Don't give them the satisfaction. Hooligans."

After dinner I pull the sun-bleached print of *Christina's World* off my bedroom wall and grab a marker. I scrawl my list of clues[a] across the faded floral wallpaper. They've outgrown my diary. I want them out where I can see them. Where they're the first thing I look at in the morning, and the last thing I see at night.

*The Clues:*

- *A bloody knife*
- *Two engagement rings*
- *One letter from a confirmed narcissist*
- *Another from a man with "emotional constipation"*
- *A kitten postcard alluding to a secret relationship*
- *An embroidered handkerchief*
- *A pair of stained satin pumps*
- *An overdue library book*

I bite my nails as I consider them. What thread weaves through these items and binds them together? *Is* there any link? Because as far as I can tell, the only link is me.

---

[a] **Clue (n.):** *a piece of evidence that helps unravel a mystery.* The Middle English *clewe*, "a ball of thread," is borrowed from Greek mythology. In the myth of the labyrinth, Ariadne gives Theseus a large ball of thread to help him navigate his way out of the maze.

## ANNA FITZGERALD HEALY

---

Spring is in the air. The birds are gossiping, and the dandelions are losing their heads on the sidewalk. The April sun kisses my skin as I walk to the post office, then blink at my empty PO box. Mr. Thompson appears with a bag of cream-colored berries, and I blink at those as well. They look like strawberries with the life sucked out of them.

"What are those?" I ask.

"White strawberries," Mr. Townsend replies enigmatically.

"And where did you get them?" I ask, suddenly realizing that the mailman and I have spent years nodding and smiling at each other but never engaged in a real conversation.

The mailman shuffles his feet, gazing at them with a bashful grin. "They're special, like you," he says after a moment of hesitation, expertly avoiding my question. "From far away."

"But Mr. Townsend, I'm from here!" I reply, hoping I don't embarrass him. The mailman is almost as shy as I am. Or as I *was*? Funny, I haven't tripped over my words for a while now.

"But you'll leave," the elderly postman replies with a certainty that surprises me. "You've sent out more mail to more zip codes than anyone I've seen, in all my years here. And one of them will take you away," Mr. Townsend says with a wistful smile, then retreats into the mailroom.

I snack on the mysterious berries between fittings that afternoon—they're tart and juicy, vaguely reminiscent of pineapple. It's Friday, and Primp and Ribbon is buzzing in preparation for the Spring Fling. All the high school girls seem intent on looking like a cross between Twiggy and an Easter egg. As I add one last bow to a canary-yellow gown, I check my watch. It's 4:45 p.m. Ballet class has switched to Friday nights, and I'm going to be late.

As I run out of the shop with my dance bag slung over my shoulder, Mrs. Pridmore stops me at the door. "Billie, you seem—" She looks me up and down.

"Preoccupied? Exhausted? Covered in bruises? Anxious?"

She laughs. "I was going to say 'happy.'"

I'm still grinning about the unexpected compliment as I race up the steps to the Northern Lights Ballet Studio. The dancers are already in position as I hurry over to my spot behind Vicki, tugging on my ballet shoes. While I'm doing a series of *grand battements*, Mistress Brandt approaches. I eye her stick warily, but she pats my shoulder. "This is slightly less awful," she says with something resembling warmth.

The ballerinas are extra chatty after class, sitting before the vanity mirror, caking on mascara, as if preparing for their solo in *Swan Lake*. One says, "He called!" and they all giggle in unison.

"Who called?" I ask as I pull pants on over my tights.

"Clara's lover boy!" one says, then they erupt with all of the juicy details.

"He called to ask what day the advanced class is."

"Not too many handsome men call here."

I bite my lip. "Does he have a mustache?"

"We've never seen his face."

"Then how do you know that he's handsome?"

"You can just *tell*. Sexy voice."

"And a sexy car. We used to see it parked outside."

"What kind of car?"

"It's orange."

"No, it's gold!"

"It's blue."

"Ferrari."

"Mustang!"

The ballerinas are the worst witnesses in history. Given the precision of their *pliés*, I'm shocked by how unobservant they are, but a warning bell is still going off in my head.

"He always called to check the class schedule. Then we would see his car waiting to pick her up. *Such* a gentleman," Vicki gushes as she pouts her lips and applies a thick sheen of bright red lipstick. I think she has a date tonight.

"What did his voice sound like?" I ask.

"Like a *man*," one dancer says, and they all twitter in unison.

Back at home, I shower and stress, running through the conversation for the hundredth time. This rules out Edgar, as his gruff voice is unlikely to incite passion from even the most boy-crazed ballerina. As I dry off, the phone rings. I wrap myself in a towel, then grab a second one for my hair. Edgar is still on my mind as I hurry into my bedroom to answer it. "Mr. Fedora," I say, picking up the phone. "You're a man who wears many–"

"Hats?" Avery offers on the other end.

"Oh no, not you," I reply in surprise. "You should remain hat-free, if possible."

"I'll try my best." Avery laughs. "So, red, white, or bubbles?"

"But what are we celebrating?" I parry as I sit down on my

bed and resume drying my hair. "I can hardly pick the wine if I don't know the occasion."

"You, and what a 'brilliant person' you are," Avery replies dryly. "And my ability to give the worst compliment in history."

"That sounds like white wine to me. Contrite and acidic. When are we drinking it?"

My heart flutters in time with my bike wheels. *Kinikilig* is the Tagalog word for that: "a mix of butterflies in the stomach and goose bumps caused by the thrill of romantic expectation." As I bike to Webster Cottage, fog seeps in to cover the sleeping homes and fishing boats. It mutes the sound of my footsteps across the cobblestones and spangles my pleated black skirt. I'm wearing a dress with a fitted bodice that buttons up the front and a skirt that hits just above the knee. Underneath it is the matching black lace set that I finally got to cut the price tags off of.

Webster Cottage is dark, but the gas lanterns are on in the garden. Flickering amber lights lead past rows of daffodils and tulips down to the dock. The mist is thicker here. It muffles the patter of my saddle shoes as I hurry across the wooden planks, and it deadens the clunk of Avery's boat shoes as he walks over to join me. He's wearing jeans and a knit white jacket over his signature cashmere crewneck, his sandy hair in languid disarray. I stop in my tracks, feeling vaguely baffled. I'd forgotten how attractive he was. "Hi," I say softly.

"It's nice to see you," he replies with a reserved smile. An electric current races up my arm as he helps me up to the prow of his boat, and I scramble into the hull.

A few blankets are folded up on the bench at the back, along with a bottle of wine, two glasses, and a bouquet of yellow buttercups. The water swishes softly as Avery uncorks the bottle. Standing there in his nice white jacket with his shy smile, Avery looks *so* nervous, far more anxious than I am. And it gives me such a hopeful feeling. Because it means that he cares, too.

He hands me a glass and we cheers. The white wine is bitter and sweet, and it makes me feel a little bittersweet as well. In one moment, Avery has single-handedly ruined wine for me. He's given me something far better than I deserve, and nothing else will ever compare. I bite my lip, wondering what else he might be able to offer me.

"Do you like it?" Avery asks, watching me curiously. "It's a Bâtard-Montrachet."

"It's palatable," I reply, studying him over the rim of my glass.

"The description is rather droll." He pushes the hair out of his face, then pulls a scrap of paper out of his pocket. "'Polite[b] yet racy with a smooth taffeta texture. Its youthful austerity hides great inner strength. The bouquet takes time to emerge, but then shows hints of oak with fresh apple notes to finish.'"

I burst out laughing. "Oh my God, what poetry! Who *wrote* that?"

---

[b] **Polite (adj.):** *marked by consideration, tact, or courtesy.* This genteel term derives from the Latin *politus,* an obsolete term for a "smooth and glossy" interior. At the turn of the century, the dictionary defined *politeness* as: "a deeper, more delicate, and more genuine thing than civility."

"It's the stupidest thing I've ever read. I wanted to share it with you."

"So what entices you most?" I look up with bright eyes. "Is it my 'youthful austerity' or my 'taffeta texture'?"

"Definitely the 'hints of oak,'" he replies with a slight eyebrow raise. "To be honest, my palate isn't very refined, I've always been rather self-conscious about it."

"How embarrassing for you," I murmur as I walk over to lean against the side of the boat. I glance at him, then look away, trying not to stare. I hadn't realized how much I missed Avery until this moment.

"I came across a word the other day that you might enjoy." He clears his throat as he walks over to join me, and I grin at my wineglass. How much homework did Avery do for this evening? Will he hand me a term paper next? "It's French: *trouvaille*."

"A lovely chance encounter," I supply automatically.

"Of course, you already know it. Well, it's how I feel about you. I wasn't expecting to meet someone like you here. And from the very first moment, you've been charming and unexpected, and . . . can I tell you a secret?"

"Please don't. I hate secrets." I gaze up at him with wide eyes.

He grins. "Your inability to lie is one of your most redeeming qualities."

"So, there are more?" I ask, hoping that he'll go on. I would gladly listen to Avery compliment me all night.

"Just one or two," he replies quietly. He studies me as if I were a painting in a museum, with appreciation, as if all of my imperfections were beautiful. As his eyes gently brush across my skin, my breath catches. Because no one has ever looked at me like that before. We share a long silence that isn't silent at all, then break it in unison.

"I'm sorry—"

"I'm angry—"

We overlap with a laugh.

"You first," he murmurs.

"You are the most frustrating person that I've ever met." I take a sip of wine as I force myself to voice my hurt and confusion. "We hit it off last summer, but then you took me on a date and said it wasn't a date. And you kissed me, but said it was 'insane.' And . . . I'd just like to know why. Why did you let me in so close, but no closer?" I bite my lip and look up into his eyes. Force myself not to shy away. "Why aren't I good enough for you?"

"Forgive me if I'm mistaken, but I seem to remember *you* kissing *me*." He chuckles.

"Semantics," I reply curtly. "I want answers, and I want them now."

"Isn't one mystery enough for you?" Avery asks, and I laugh, because, obviously, it isn't. "Billie, my reticence wasn't a commentary on you. I try to be courteous and respectful, but sometimes it comes off as stuffy and withdrawn. If anything, I think that you're too good for me. You're smart, silly, and resourceful, and . . . it terrifies me a little bit."

"Witty banter terrifies me, too. You're wise to keep your distance," I reply, and he laughs lightly in response. As our eyes meet, I feel my resolve start to crumble under the warmth of his gaze. A soft breath of mist fills the space between us. "I think that it gets lonely for you, always being the smartest person in the room. But it's also safe. And actually connecting with someone frightens you. So *that's* why you pushed me away last summer, not out of courtesy or respect."

Avery turns to gaze out at the water, as the waves tremble softly around us. "A trait we certainly don't have in common."

I open my mouth to tell him off, but pause. He's right. I've spent years on the outside looking in. A wallflower and a page-turner. An observer, watching life from a safe distance. Occasionally highlighting a passage and furrowing my brow. Grinning when I find a typo that the publisher should have caught. There was security in living vicariously through my characters rather than living for myself. But something changed this past year, and now I'm the romantic lead faced with one fleeting moment to give away her heart. I'm the detective, following strange clues, evading villains. I'm the protagonist.

"I *was* aloof"—I grin—"until I fell flat on my face in ballet class."

"Ballet!" Avery yelps.

"Does that scare you?" I bite my lip, studying him intently.

"Absolutely. Those girls are so hyperfeminine, I'm intimidated just thinking about it. What do you even talk about?" He looks genuinely anxious at the thought. Then he gathers himself, squaring his shoulders. "Billie, I've missed you, but I'm just not sure if I'm the kind of guy who you want to get involved—"

"Oh, I'm sorry. I thought it was *my* decision who I got involved with—not yours," I counter with a wry smile. The mist seems to draw in closer around us, painting his features in a soft, monochromatic haze. As I study him, I realize that he's studying me, too. Taking in my black dress. The tousled coils of my hair. And the confidence that I seem to have stumbled across without realizing it.

"How *unspeakably* rude of me," he murmurs, voice dry. We lock eyes again, his glinting with a smoky intensity, as myriad emotions pass across them. I feel my anger start to dissolve, to be replaced by quite the opposite. "To be honest, I'm finding it rather difficult to act completely civilized with you right now."

"Really? Then how would you like to act, instead?" I study his reflection in my wineglass as the mist seeps in around us, until it fogs up my glass and erases him entirely.

He takes my glass and sets it on the console. "I'm sure you can infer . . ."

"Putting two and two together has always been a struggle." I drop my voice as I step in, my lips just barely grazing his earlobe. "You might have to spell it out for me."

And he does. Through one page and then another. The story unfolds around us as his hand comes to the small of my back, drawing me to him. His lips brush against mine as his fingers clench my hips. I rest my arms over his shoulders and relax into his embrace. His lips taste like salt water and desire—I get drunk in one sip, and yet I want more and more.

Mist draws around us like flimsy curtains as he leads me to the bench at the stern of the boat. We sit down and he pulls me onto his lap. His hands press against my waist as he kisses me deeply. So fiercely that it makes my breath catch. Then he pauses. "We should stop."

"Oh my God, why?!?!" I protest with an abundance of exclamation points.

"I don't want to make you uncomfortable."

"Avery, I'm comfortable." I lean back against the cushions to glare at him.

"But . . . have you . . . had a boyfriend before? Do you–"

"Will you *stop* making decisions for me!"

"It does sound a trifle–"

"Condescending?" I supply.

"So I've offended you?" he asks, then resumes unbuttoning the tiny buttons on my bodice.

"Terribly," I murmur. "Avery, this is my decision. Being good sounds awfully boring, I'd much rather be experienced instead. And surely the idea of a woman owning her sexuality can't be *that* groundbreaking. I'd like to engage in–"

"Revolt?" he offers, eyes widening as he glimpses the black lace underneath.

"Exactly," I reply, pulling off his white knit jacket and tossing it to the ground.

"Rebellion looks good on you." He chuckles.

"Please stop. Don't give me any more sincere compliments. I can't bear it."

He curls a lock of my hair around his fingers. "Do you have an embargo on sincerity?"

"It's tolerated but frowned upon. There's a steep import tax," I murmur. He finally succeeds with the buttons as my dress tumbles to the floor and another page turns.

The pages are turning so quickly now, and either I turn with them, or I'll never catch up. Sentences slip past us as the night slips into something more comfortable. Clothing and confidences are strewn across the hull of the boat like flower petals after a spring rainstorm. Avery pulls me to him as I dig my hands into the tops of his thighs. His muscles are taut under my fingertips as his body tenses against mine. He trembles lightly as I kiss the soft skin at the top of his neck. I glance at him. Is he shivering with cold, desire, or—

*Goddamn it. With restraint.* As always, he's holding back. Being the perfect gentleman.

"Will you stop being polite?" I ask softly. But my eyes beg.

Fog drifts over the water as he pushes me back against the cushions. I bury my fingers in his silky hair as he runs a hand over my bra, then his fingers tighten around me. I gasp, but the pain isn't entirely painful. The mist envelops us as he rips off my stockings and tosses them on top of my black dress. And in the midst of my wordy life, conversation ends, and silence takes over.

Desire smolders in the depths of his eyes and lingers on the edge of his fingertips, as I find an answering ache within myself. The mist plates his face in shadows as his hands run down to clench my hips. The ocean stifles a gasp. It's freezing out on the water, but cozy under the blankets. We hold each other tightly and drift in and out of sleep until the first rays of dawn penetrate the fog over the Western Passage.

My whole life, I've wanted to be like the heroines in my books. To lead a life worth writing about. And to find the kind of romance that people write stories about. Something intoxicating, compelling, and maybe even a bit strange. As I look into his eyes, words tremble on my lips.

"I think I'm falling in love with you." My voice is soft in his ears.

And I guess that I've finally found it.

And another page turns.

## CHAPTER NINETEEN

# THE GENTLEMAN'S SOCIAL PROBLEMS

*A gentleman does not lose control. In his self-control, lies his chief ascendancy over others. Exhibitions of anger, fear, hatred, embarrassment, ardor, or hilarity, are all bad form.*

The sun rises over Campobello. It peeks out over the cliffs that line the Canadian border and laps against the distant shore. I pull on my dress and wrap myself in a blanket, then step out onto the dock. The wooden planks are cool beneath my bare feet. Webster Cove extends before me, a thin sheet of water stretching across seaweed and tide pools to mirror the apricot-colored sky. It takes my breath away.

Or it would, if I had any breath left to take.

I'm half expecting Avery to climb out of his boat and ask me to leave. None of my daydreams have prepared me for the morning after, and none of my reading has offered adequate instruction on the complexities of the human heart. The rules of affection can't be broken down with stems and roots, studied back to their origin, and traced to the Bronze Age. I might have said a few words last night that I really wish I'd kept to myself.

"It isn't as beautiful as you are, you know," Avery says as he walks up beside me. His eyes are warm in the rising sun.

And just like that—my fear evaporates. "Avery, I thought we went over this last night. Rule number six is to never be overly sincere. It makes me very uncomfortable."

"But what about rule number seven?" he asks, a wry glimmer in his eyes.

"What is rule number seven?" I ask, then yelp as he scoops me up and carries me to the house.

"Where are you getting these rules from?" he asks as the scent of Italian espresso wafts around us. I don't respond, just watch him scoop the ground coffee into a small tin, then set it in a stovetop espresso maker. The kitchen is honey colored in the early morning sunlight, with a pitcher of tulips on a farmhouse table under a wall of windows. There is warmth and normalcy here, in contrast to the frigid elegance of the rest of the house.

The percolator burbles as Avery pours us two cups, and I pull myself up to sit on the counter. "It's nice that there isn't a team of chefs and maids right now. I'd hate to scandalize them," I murmur, blowing on my coffee to cool it. The thick porcelain mug has an elaborate crest for *Le Royal Monceau*.

"Only when my parents are here. I can't stand the pageantry of it." Avery leans against the counter. "But the staff have a high tolerance for scandal. For instance, that mug is stolen."

"Stolen!" I examine my cup with newfound appreciation.

He grins. "My mother steals things everywhere she goes."

"But why? She has all the money in the world!"

"It's not about the money," he says as he stacks a tray with pastries, then leads me upstairs. Avery's bedroom is as spotless, classic, and devoid of personality as I would have guessed. As I survey the high-pile carpet, elegant furnishings, and framed blueprints carefully hung across inoffensive blue wallpaper, I glance over at him. Who would Avery be if he didn't have to appease his parents? I hope that someday I get the chance to find out.

Big bay windows look out over Deer Island, Marble Island, and Cherry Island. The islands are small, plump, and prickly with pine needles. Giant coils of water billow between them, marking the massive currents that traverse Passamaquoddy Bay. About a mile out, the water spins in an understated spiral. From here, even the whirlpool looks tasteful.

I sit down in a blue velvet wing chair and peruse the breakfast offerings. Another cup of coffee. A torn croissant. I brush off pastry flakes as Avery tells me about his architecture firm in Rhode Island, and I terrify him with a few stories from ballet class. He absently rests a hand on my knee as the smell of coffee curls around us. I wasn't expecting to feel so comfortable with him.

"Why architecture?" I ask as I sink back into the plush armchair.

"Well, it might sound stupid, but I love designing things," he replies with a self-conscious grin. "I enjoy drafting a blueprint, then watching everything come together in real life. Nothing is more satisfying than the seamless execution of a detailed plan. I love walking into a building, knowing that every line and angle came directly from my brain."

"Your God complex looks great on you," I tease as I tear off a bite of cheese Danish. The mascarpone is sweet and tangy on my tongue as I finally ask my burning question. "So, who do you think did it?"

Avery raises one eyebrow. "Was this all just a ploy to get into the house?"

"You see through me," I reply as I wipe my lips on a linen napkin.

"I do. And I saw through that lacy black underwear you were wearing last night."

"Am still wearing," I correct him. "But we have to stay on topic, we can't get distracted from murder by lingerie."

"Can't we?" Avery asks, then sets down his coffee. "Is that another one of your rules?"

The next few hours are suspiciously lovely. I don't even bother putting *suspicious* in quotation marks, because the feeling of perfection is so surreal that I actively distrust it. We take the boat out to Popes Island, a little barnacle rising out of the surf, ringed with cliffs and windswept trees. We skip rocks, cloud watch, and speculate about the investigation. And it turns out that murder really is the best pillow talk.

"I mean, your brother is—"

"Insane," Avery interjects as we kayak back to the speedboat. "And Teddy is reckless—"

"But homosexual."

"Billie!" Avery stops rowing to scold me. "You can't spread rumors like that!"

"Who said it was a rumor?" I grin.

"I don't care what it is. It's not your story to tell, so you should keep it to yourself." He resumes paddling, then grabs the ladder on the side of the boat and motions for me to climb up.

"What about the black magic angle?" I ask as I pass him my paddle and reach for the ladder, shading my eyes against the low-hanging sun.

Avery's eyes light up. "Don't tease me. Go on."

How to say, *I lied to your maid and found out that she's cursing people,* without bringing down the mood? As I kneel on the wobbling surface and consider it, the kayak flips over.

The icy shock of the North Atlantic. I choke on a mouthful of salt water as I hit my head against the side of the kayak and the current takes over. The water runs its hands down my ankles, then yanks hard as I thrash against it. *Perfect. I've spent my whole life praying not to die a virgin, only to drown immediately thereafter.* I shake my head at the cruel irony of it all as the wave clutches at my feet.

But Avery clutches harder. A hand grips my shoulder as he hauls me out of the water.

"Got you," he says with a triumphant grin. He pulls me to safety, then gently places my hands on the ladder of the speedboat. As the kayak bobs away, Avery helps me into the boat, then turns to gaze out at the bay. Anger temporarily transforms his features. He looks furious at the ocean for attempting to steal me away. Passion puts a swoon-worthy pout on his lips. And I find myself oddly attracted to this assertive, hidden version of Avery. Then his outrage dissipates and the doting man-servant takes over. He clasps me against his cashmere sweater. I'm soaking and dripping with seaweed, but he doesn't care.

"My lifeguard," I murmur, eyes bright.

He trails a finger along my jaw to lift up my chin. "Billie, if anything happened to you—" He blinks away tears as I reach up hesitantly to touch his cheek. Then I lock eyes with him as I lift my finger to my lips. His tears taste like the ocean. His lips meet mine as his lean, sinewy arms wrap around my waist. The cold eddies around us, chilling my wet skin. Then he pulls away to study my soaked dress. "Darling, you're shivering," he murmurs, opening a cabinet to grab a towel.

"Pool boy, help me out of these wet clothes. I'm going to catch my death of cold."

"So, I've already been demoted from the lifeguard to the pool boy?" He laughs as he wraps the towel around my shoulders, then hands me a sweater.

Night isn't black out here on the water—it's every shade of blue. *Poppy* slices through the deep indigo waves as the chill of night splashes against the hull. I'm leaning against Avery's shoulder, dreaming about a hot shower, when he nudges me awake. I squint up at the shoreline, where Webster Cottage is lit up like a bonfire.

"It must be Claude." Avery grimaces as he pulls up to the dock, then throws down the rubber fenders. "Billie, I'm taking you straight home. You shouldn't have to put up with him after all you've been through."

My heart sinks so far down that it must be somewhere with the sunken ships at the bottom of the bay. I'd conveniently *forgotten* about Claude. Forgotten that I *really should* have called the cops on him by now. "I should stay," I reply with a heavy sigh. "I'd rather deal with your insane brother than explain to my grandparents why I look like a drowned rat."

"But a cute one." Avery squeezes my arm.

"A cute, dead rat?" I burst out laughing.

"Yes, I'm sure that one exists."

Clanging drums, an eerie transistor organ, and a voice like breaking glass echoes through Webster Cottage. Claude has left his red Aston Martin out front and a large Louis Vuitton suitcase just inside the door. I trip over the remnants of a vase as I step inside the foyer. Cobalt-blue porcelain is smashed across the black-and-white interior.

"What did I tell you? He just loves breaking things," Avery says with a rueful grin.

"It's because he's sensitive," I reply automatically.

"Sensitive!" Avery exclaims as he ushers me upstairs. "Darling, how hard did you hit your head?" Then he shuts the door to his bedroom and the psychedelic rock vanishes. "Take a shower and warm up. I'll see if my mother has anything that will fit you."

Hot water strips the seaweed out of my hair and pulls the salt from my skin. The soap smells of lavender, but I can't get the scent of old library books out of my nose. I've spent hours studying the tracing from that library card, trying to imagine Claude's expression when he checked out that surgical textbook. But harder still is imagining Claude visiting a library in the first place.

I suppose I could call the cops, but what would I say? And what if I'm wrong? The John Doe *does* have Teddy's initials, after all. It seems unlikely that two boys in the same friend group would both be killers. And I can't imagine anything worse than accusing the *wrong person* of murder. I wish Miss Vanderbilt had covered detective work in her etiquette manuals, because I could use some of her social grace right now.

Egyptian cotton is soft and fluffy against my skin as I towel off, then find my purse and dab on some makeup. I emerge to find a pale blue dress and a pair of blue rabbit fur slippers laid out for me on Avery's bed. The dress is an old-fashioned button-down that must have been hanging in Mrs. Webster's closet for decades. I slip it on and pull on the slippers (unworn and curiously my size).

A frantic guitar solo leads me into the hallway. I lean against the banister and gaze downstairs as Simon & Garfunkel croon out the opening verse of "You Can Tell the World." In the distance, I hear shouting. "You set me up." "Genuinely worried." "Jealous prick."

Enticing as that sounds, I turn in the opposite direction. Goose bumps tremble across my skin as I finally take my exclusive tour of Murder Mansion. Dark doors lead down darker corridors as I snoop through forgotten rooms with antique fixtures draped in cotton sheets. Webster Cottage is where colonial American furniture goes to die. A light pulls me toward the end of the hallway. Would that be the home theater or the private chapel?

I push open the heavy, oak-paneled door to find a four-poster bed with a burgundy velvet comforter and a Rococo fireplace with sporting trophies displayed on the mantelpiece. An acrid scent of patchouli, bergamot, pine needles, and gasoline identifies this as Claude's bedroom. I inspect a bottle of cologne on the dresser. It's Brut[a] by Fabergé. *Oh, you great, big beautiful brut* is the tagline, which Claude may have taken a little too seriously. *Eau de wounded masculinity.*

Claude has only been home for a few hours, but he's already trashed his room. I tiptoe between piles of clothing to his desk, then root through the drawers, hunting for anything with his signature. It *must* be Claude. The library book has his name, but I have to be sure.

But there's nothing. Just an unused pink eraser, a slide ruler, some flyers, a card for the Glass Slipper Gentlemen's Club, and a few documents with the crest for Harvard Law School. As Simon & Garfunkel build to an overzealous climax, a drum sounds, and I drop a flyer.

The trifold is a glossy advertisement for the Mermaid Dance Center in Jonesport, Maine. The front features a ballerina in a tutu and toe shoes on a rugged stone beach. The inside contains the class schedule from last summer. The Tuesday *Pointe III* class is circled.

I tear Claude's desk apart. My lips form a silent *no* when I find a schedule for Tanski Dance Arts in Ellsworth, where *Contemporary Jazz* is circled. Next comes a flyer for Mainely Dance

---

[a] **Brute (n.):** *a rude or violent person.* From the Latin *brutus,* describing someone "stupid or unreasonable," which later expanded to include, "violent animals." *Brute* is not to be confused with *brut,* "an unsweetened, dry sparkling wine." It's funny that this homonym describes my most and least favorite things.

in Cherryfield, then I break out in a full-body sweat when I find a trifold for the Northern Lights Ballet Studio where *Advanced Ballet* is circled. I lean against the desk as I remember the giggles and gossip about Clara's "lover boy" in his orange-gold Mustang-Ferrari.

My feet move on autopilot, pulling me into his closet. I glance around wildly. What am I looking for? Men's canvas ballet shoes? A pair of footed black tights? But there's nothing. Just a deeper stench of Brut, a tie organizer, and a letterman jacket from Phillips Exeter Academy. I pause before a display case containing watches, cuff links, and a wolf lapel pin. My eyes widen when I discover the left half of a cheap sterling silver heart. Engraved on the front is the word *Bite*, and scratched into the back are the letters *xo- C*.

This is the second half of Clara's cheap heart pendant: *Bite Me*. Clara probably thought she was being cute when she gave it to Claude, never imagining that he would take the inscription quite so literally.

The cool metal pendant digs into my fingers. I drop it then back away. My limbs seem to move of their own accord, as if some invisible current were carrying me through the hallway, washing me down the stairs. As I rush through the foyer to the Louis Vuitton suitcase, a piece of porcelain lodges in the bottom of one rabbit fur slipper, but I hardly notice.

It's a large brown trunk, durable and deluxe, with gold-toned hardware and the iconic *LV* monogram. My fingers tremble as I struggle with the zipper, until the top opens to reveal the pristine beige lining. It's empty.

## ETIQUETTE FOR LOVERS AND KILLERS

Blood rushes through my ears as I wrestle with the huge front door. Tears drip down my cheeks as I pull at the wrought-iron monstrosity. I can't stop thinking about Vicki and the other girls from the ballet studio with their silly *Swan Lake* dreams. My head feels fuzzy, I'm breathing too fast, and everything is falling out of focus. I grab onto the doorframe to steady myself as I step outside.

But a hand yanks me back inside as another slams the door behind me. I blink up at Claude, gagging on the testosterone-fueled aroma of Brut. My chest feels empty where my heartbeat should be, and I'm actually frozen with fear (which I'd always thought was just a trope of gothic fiction). "My goat," Claude gloats as his lips twist into a sneer. His eyelids are heavy and lidded from alcohol. "Didn't your mother tell you that it's rude to leave without saying goodbye?" He wraps an arm around my shoulders. "We *must* teach you some manners."

Webster Cottage is the most sophisticated and dangerous place I know. Home to priceless antiques: Tiffany lamps, Lalique sculptures, and the complete first edition of Audubon's *Birds of America*—but nothing is quite as precious as its secrets. I should be running away from the house where Gertrude and Clara died, but instead, I allow myself to be escorted down the hallway as the striped pearl wallpaper encloses me like prison bars.

Claude steers me into the kitchen, then leans back against the marble counter and reaches for a rocks glass. "The Sounds of Silence" booms in my ears as a hush settles over the kitchen. Branches scratch across the dark windows as the acoustic guitar keens a warning. I plant both hands on the countertop and will them to stop shaking. I look around in confusion. Where is Avery? I hope he's not trapped in a suitcase, too.

My captor is dressed to impress, in a short-sleeved shirt with the top four buttons undone, exposing his unruly swath of chest hair. The shirt is tucked into flared brown corduroys, accented by a belt buckle featuring a stag's head supporting a suit of armor. The silver crest looks spiky and sharp. I hesitantly raise my eyes to his face, which bears a crooked grin.

I should have read more Raymond Chandler, because I have *no idea* how to proceed. Should I threaten Claude? Bargain with him? Pound my fist against the kitchen island and question his motives?

"Why did you kill Gertrude?" I ask, cringing inwardly. It's hardly an inspired opening.

"I didn't," Claude growls, and I nod impatiently. *Right. It always starts with the denial.* He leans back against the marble countertop as he lifts the glass to his lips. "Because I *wouldn't* have fucked it up this badly. That's the *injustice* of it all. Avery says that they're bringing me in for questioning—which is pretty *fucking* inconvenient. I have an invite to the Silver Factory next weekend."

"Ooh," I murmur, momentarily distracted from murder by parties. "Why is it silver?"

"Because Warhol wrapped the entire loft in tinfoil. It's exclusive as hell, and I really want to go. Why would I set myself up like that when I have such groovy shit going on? And why would I murder *some bitch*—who wasn't even that great in the sack, mind you—in the *middle* of a *lobster bake*? I go to Harvard

Law; I'm not a complete idiot," Claude says with a ditzy lilt to his voice. He seems genuinely offended by the implied incompetence of the murder accusation.

"That *is* a shame. It's also a shame about Clara; I'm sure that she would have liked to attend the party as well." The words are out before I can take them back, as "Wednesday Morning, 3 A.M." reverberates softly through the speakers.

"Clara," Claude repeats her name with a languid sip of whiskey. It's the first time I've seen anything resembling warmth from him and it chills my blood. "I thought she was special. I liked how small she was and how hungry she looked. And I *loved* how fucked up her feet were. She was such a pretty girl, but she had the ugliest feet I'd ever seen. They were covered in scars and calluses. Gnarled like claws. I loved how badly she was willing to hurt herself." Claude shakes his head as his expression hardens.

"But she was just like all the others. She wanted to get tossed so I brought her over here. She was tolerable when she was sober, but her voice was so high-pitched when she drank. Gave me the most awful headache. Then she started laughing. I gave her some weed–anything to shut her up, but that just made her laugh more." Claude's sneer turns into a laugh. As I watch his lips move in their jerky, slobbering way, I think about the letter in the evidence locker. I try to remind myself of how sensitive he is.

"Then she started stripping," he continues. "She took off her sweater and her skirt, but I couldn't stop staring at her feet–I wanted the rest of her to match. Then I hit her, and my headache lightened up, so I hit her again. Hit her until my headache was entirely gone. Then I just. . . ." He trails off with a dreamy expression.

"Shot her to put her out of her misery?" I supply as the wind picks up outside and silence blasts through the downstairs. The whirr of the needle skipping across the final groove of the album.

"It wasn't personal. I still remember how she felt in my arms. Barely weighed more than my suitcase," he murmurs. As Claude sips his whiskey, I consider the flyers upstairs and the Louis Vuitton suitcase in the foyer. What did he mean by "all the others"?

He throws his drink and crystal shatters against the hardwood floor as whiskey splatters across the wallpaper. He turns to gaze at me as if he would also like to stuff me in a suitcase. Claude's pupils are as vacant and dilated as the windows behind him. "Listen to me: if I kill someone, I don't get fucking caught."

"Excuse me, but I really must be—" I bolt down the hallway.

Claude barrels into me. His hair tickles my cheek as he presses me against the wall. A dispossessed corner of my brain notes with surprise that we're in the same spot where I saw him with Gertrude that first night. I envision Gertrude's red hair. Her fury. Her condescension. She was Claude's match, while in my bunny slippers, I feel like an easy victim. I gaze longingly at the front door, but it might as well be miles away. I can't reach it.

Claude bangs my head against the wall and I see stars. My whole body seizes up as he grapples with my dress and rips the collar apart. As he pushes me down against the black-and-white marble floor, I hear my spine pop. I watch him bring a knee to my torso as though viewing a suspenseful film, then gag on my own bile.

I try to imagine what Austen or the Brontës might recommend, but their heroines would have been saved by some gallant suitor long ago. I look around hopefully for my own white knight, but he's nowhere in sight.

But it's 1965, and women's lib is all the rage, so I should probably save myself. I take a deep breath and curl my fingers into a fist. I've never punched anyone before, but my hand instinctively knows what to do. A jolt of pain as my knuckles connect with his cheekbone.

"Can't you hit any harder than that?" Claude laughs. "Harder," he whispers. "Harder, please." As he pummels me, I watch a plume of blood splatter across the white marble. Then he smacks me against the floor and a second plume follows. Red across black. I'm too stunned to feel any pain as his fingers wrap around my neck. He smiles faintly. Then the unspeakable occurs, and his lips extend toward mine.

Claude's touch ignites a rage hidden deep inside me. I'm outraged by the indecency of polite society. Furious with Claude and the fragility of the male ego. Angry at Detective Wallace for letting a murderer be on the loose. And livid at Avery for leaving me alone with his brother.

"No,"[b] I yell as my nails scrape down his cheek. They break

---

[b] **No (adv.):** *not so, not one, not at all, not in any degree, none, zero, nothing, never.* No is one of the twenty-three words upon which language was built, with its cognates present across 700 modern languages. *No* existed for the last 15,000 years and survived the last ice age. In Sanskrit (6,000 years ago) it was pronounced *na*, in Old Avestan (4,000 years ago) also *na*, in ancient Greek (3,500 years ago) *ne*. Perhaps the oldest word in English, *no* is not a

through the skin to rip the smug grin off his lips. I claw his face and gouge at his eyes. Claude's jagged belt buckle slices through my dress to cut into my ribs, but the pain barely registers. His hands encircle my neck, squeezing tighter and tighter until my eyeballs feel like they might pop out of my skull.

All the while, a detached corner of my brain continues to wonder: *How could Claude have written the letter in the police lockup?* It was vulnerable and oddly lyrical, but where is his poetry now? As Claude presses in on my throat, it finally dawns on me: *What if he didn't?*

"Darling, destroy me." My voice is a choked whisper as I quote the opening line.

But there is no light of recognition in Claude's eyes. No embarrassment or shock. He just grunts in his boorish way and squeezes harder, until I feel like my neck might snap apart. The blood rushes through my ears. Is that a shout and pounding footsteps in the distance, or is it just my ragged breathing? I choke on the scent of Brut as my world goes black.

---

delicate sound, it's as guttural as a punch. So even if Claude were a caveman, he would *still* understand the word *no*. Honestly, he might have better manners if he were.

## CHAPTER TWENTY

# THE DEBUTANTE AND THE LAW

*If you are picked up for flouting the law, treat the officer as the representative of the public that he is, not as an enemy. Answer his questions quietly. Above all, never threaten or try to bribe a policeman. Trying may land you in even hotter water.*

My nails are broken and my fingers are sticky with blood. Pompous American-dynasty-asshole blood. From the next room, I hear a thud, a crash, and shattered glass. A voice growls, "Never touch her again," followed by the sound of receding footsteps.

I look down at myself in confusion. Mrs. Webster's dress is ruined. The bodice is torn and the skirt is stained with whiskey and blood. Red droplets lead across the checkerboard floor to the room beyond it. I glance at an overturned entry table and a discarded silver candlestick. The sconce is caked with hair and gore. Beside it is a bloody crystal ashtray. The whole scene looks ridiculously macabre, like the setting from some melodramatic high school play.

I follow the sound of ragged breathing across the hallway, clutching a Corinthian column to steady myself. My legs shake as I stagger into the next room. And slumped there in the center of the mint-green parlor, right where Gertrude's body had been, is Claude.

Or, at least, I assume it's Claude. He isn't terribly recognizable.

One of his eyes is black and blue, and his lips are scratched and swollen. Blood drips down his forehead as a purple welt rises across his temple. A chunk of hair is missing from his scalp. His shirt is pulled up to reveal several ragged marks across his abdomen. He's comatose, lying in state before the emerald-green couch.

Warm arms wrap around me. Avery's hair is mussed, and the sleeves of his sweater are rolled up. A trickle of blood trails artistically down one cheek. He embraces me so fiercely that if Claude hadn't broken me, this hug surely would. "Billie, I'm so sorry. I'll never forgive myself for–"

"Shhh." I place a finger on his lips and look up into his eyes, glistening with tears. I don't want his apologies or clever words right now, I just want to feel his arms circling around me, reminding me that I'm not alone. That I'm cared for and protected. The parlor blurs as I blink away tears, and his arms tighten around me. I rest my head against his shoulder and take a deep breath, feeling his chest rise and fall in time with my own. And it feels so incredibly nice, to know that we're in this together.

I suppress a shiver as Claude's head lolls to one side. I glance at Avery, my eyes flicking from the sweater I've been crying on to the supplies in his hands. He has a coil of rope, a roll of duct tape, and a pair of handcuffs. *Why does Avery have handcuffs?* "Pool boy, let's restrain the Big Bad Wolf before he wakes up. A second fight to the death would be redundant."

Avery chokes on a laugh as he puts an arm around my shoulders. "Well, at least he hasn't broken your spirit."

As we carry Claude to a crushed velvet wing chair, a detached part of my brain notes that the green rug has been replaced by a navy blue one. My feet sink into it as I clamp the handcuffs around Claude's wrists and Avery binds his ankles together.

"I was upstairs on the phone with Detective Wallace when I heard a commotion in the kitchen," Avery brings me up to speed. "I thought the cops might want to hear what was going on, so I ran to grab my tape recorder, and I–"

I pause with my hands around Claude's forearms. "You recorded our conversation?"

"Yes, of course, with my reel-to-reel," Avery responds impatiently, and I wrinkle my nose. *Of course he has a reel-to-reel.* It's the Rolls-Royce of home recording devices. I've been lusting over it for months in issues of *Master Detective*. "Detective Wallace is on his way over now to listen to it."

"Goddamn it," I mutter. The police are coming and Avery has a recording to share with them. They're going to sweep the house and find my wiretap in the butler's pantry.

"What's wrong?" Avery studies me with concern.

"Nothing, I just need to take another shower," I reply tersely, handing him the rope. A poor excuse, but it's the only exit strategy that presents itself, and I need to take care of this *now*.

"Of course. Would you like some tea to calm your nerves? Or perhaps a shot of—"

But I'm already backing away. I hurry up to Avery's bedroom and turn on the shower, then creep back downstairs. I hear him on the phone in the kitchen as I pad down the hallway. It sounds like he's talking to Edgar, who is working at their home in Rhode Island right now.

The butler's pantry is a site of devastation, littered with half-drunk decanters of amber liquid. *Poor Hayes, Claude made such a mess.* I shake my head for the absent butler, then pull the sliding ladder away from the wall and start climbing. Everything hurts. My ribs ache as I reach the top rung and strain for the wiretap equipment hidden in a crevice beneath the crown molding. The cut from Claude's belt buckle opens up, and I wince but keep going. A dust bunny floats past my cheek as my fingers connect with plastic and wires. I clutch at them blindly, sucking in a sharp breath as the phone cord, transmitter, wires, and alligator clamps all crash to the floor.

I hold my breath and freeze. There's nowhere to hide. No lie will fix this.

But there's nothing. Just Avery in the kitchen, being a Chatty Cathy on the phone.

I find a wastepaper bin lined with an empty plastic bag beneath the sink. My hands shake as I retrieve the items and stash them in the bag, then turn my attention to the phone. After restoring the phone to its original setup, I clutch the bag of surveillance equipment to my chest and walk briskly to the stairs, pausing beside a massive oriental floor vase with an arrangement of pussy willows and cattails. I push the fluffy stems to one side and drop my parcel into the depths of the vase. It thuds hollowly at the bottom, then I rearrange the dry catkins to cover it. The cops won't find it here, then I can return to deal with this properly later.

Avery's bathroom is billowing with steam. I close the door behind me, then sink to the floor in exhaustion. My hand unconsciously reaches for the lock, but I stop myself. The villain is tied up, the surveillance equipment is dismantled, the detective is on his way over, and my doting lover is probably trimming candlewicks, or whatever he does to calm himself. Everything is fine.

*But is it?*

The shiver of apprehension creeping up my spine isn't so sure. I try to wash away my misgivings, but the soap keeps slipping out of my hands. I emerge from the shower to find another one of Mrs. Webster's dresses laid out for me. This one a buttercup yellow that clashes horribly with the green welts rising across my skin. I shrug it on, then put on some makeup. Leaning into the mirror, I examine the discoloration around my neck where each of Claude's fingers pressed in and the red thumbprint in the hollow of my throat. I've never looked so broken before.

I find Avery sitting on the stairs with a bottle of wine. I sit down beside him and we both gaze straight ahead, wordlessly passing the bottle between us. When the police arrive, Avery and I look guilty and deranged, smelling of fear and white Burgundy.

Detective Wallace raises an eyebrow when I open the door but just beelines toward the parlor. Chief Deputy Abbott stops in his tracks when he sees me and presses a finger to his lips, perspiration dripping down his bulbous features. Luke bursts into the foyer, then stops midstep. No one has ever looked quite so disappointed in me before.

Police swarm through the interior, documenting every smashed glass, blood spatter, and broken Imari vase. Luke takes photos of me along with the other evidence, as if I were a damaged Fabergé egg to be submitted to insurance.

Detective Wallace had his sights set on Claude from the beginning, then spent months building a criminal profile, corroborating evidence, and validating testimony against him. Given the Websters' prominence within the community, Wallace had to prepare an iron-clad argument before he could bring the young law student in for questioning. Tonight's slipup provided Wallace with the opportunity he'd been waiting for. Claude's confession to a similar killing, paired with his attempt on my life in the hallway, constituted probable cause to detain him for Gertrude's death. Wallace had never guessed that Claude was involved in Clara's murder, but he's gratified by it all the same. "Fits the profile," he murmurs, examining the Louis Vuitton suitcase.

*But does it?* An annoying corner of my brain isn't so sure. I take a long sip of white wine as I try to find a few hard truths to hold on to.

Fact: Claude killed Clara.

Fact: That's why he's been coming to Eastern Maine. To satisfy a craving in an area without the resources to catch him.

Fact: A delicate incision sliced between two of Gertrude's ribs to pierce her heart.

Question: Is Claude capable of that? *Delicate* isn't the first word I would use to describe him, and I imagine that Clara would agree with me.

Fact: Gertrude's murder was contrived and audacious. She commanded attention, even as a corpse. Her death presents a stark contrast to Claude and his shrill ballerina. Why would Claude be so brutally efficient with one murder and so theatrical with the next?

Fact: Our quaint coastal village is an unlikely criminal hotspot. The turbulent waters offer a bounty of fish and lobsters, but hunting on land has always been subpar. Until now. Of the sixteen homicides that occurred last year in Maine, three happened in Washington County. Logically, they *must* have all been committed by the same person–but how? Clara and Gertrude could have both been crimes of passion, but what about the guy in the tuxedo?

"What about John Tux?" I ask Detective Wallace as he approaches me on the staircase.

"What about him?" The detective shrugs as he sits down beside me on the beige carpet. "He doesn't fit the profile. I try to focus on one killer at a time."

"And what about your buddy Edgar?" Edgar is another clue in this crossword puzzle that doesn't fit. "Is he still a suspect?"

"How do you know that we're friends?" The detective looks startled. "We did our training together. It's a shame how things worked out for him. Edgar had such promise at the academy, but then he went private, and–" Wallace trails off, eyeing me curiously. "Edgar had nothing to do with this. He was working the door the entire night. He didn't get a single break."

I'm baffled into silence, as I tie together the various pieces one by one. So Edgar worked as a private investigator until he was convicted of stalking a client. After his release, he got a job working for the Websters and started tailing me instead. But doesn't Wallace think it's a *kind of big coincidence* that a convicted felon with a personal vendetta against his fiancée was present at the time of Gertrude's death? What is the Maine Police Academy teaching these would-be detectives? Because I'm not sure if Detective Wallace could investigate his way out of a paper bag.

"What about Teddy?" I swallow the white Burgundy along with some choice words.

"You think *Teddy* is capable of this?" The detective chokes on a laugh.

"He acts soft, but it's a lie. And he has a motive–" Teddy is destructive, belligerent, *and* he has a secret. A secret that Gertrude held over his head. Personally, I think that everyone should live and let live, but mine isn't the prevailing opinion. And the thing about explosive secrets is that they tend to blow up. Paisley Taylor said he made a donation to her shop. Teddy was aggressive with me, he offered Gertrude's family money, and there just happens to be a corpse sporting his initials. Teddy is sweet, destructive, and fragile, but is he a killer? I just don't know.

"That poor sod doesn't like getting his hands dirty," Wallace says as his gaze travels up my arms to my bruised neck. "Why do you ask? You're living proof that Claude is our man. He kissed you, then he tried to kill you. Just like Gertrude and Clara. This was a thrill kill, in which he acted out his most sadistic fantasies. Everything points to Claude. We have mountains of evidence against him."

"Mountains?" I try to raise an eyebrow, but it hurts too much.

"We just found a knife under his bed."

The knife stolen from my closet! The knife with *my* fingerprints and a few drops of *my* blood! I take a big gulp of wine.

"We'll test it, of course, but I already know that his prints will be a match. Pretty damning testimony, if you ask me. That's the kind of evidence I like. Not sexy or pretentious, just cold, hard facts." The detective beams with self-satisfaction.

"But isn't that all circumstantial?"

"The best evidence always is, Marie-Antoinette."

"No." I look around wildly for a means of escape.

"The coroner's assistant gave me the driver's license." Detective Wallace smirks. "Said some girl came in posing as Gertrude's sister. I knew it was you before I even saw the photo."

"Are you going to arrest me?" My eyes widen as I gaze at the handcuffs dangling from his belt buckle. They swish back and forth maniacally.

Detective Wallace reaches for them without taking his eyes off me. "You got off easy this time, but don't make a habit of it. You're kind of cute when you're scared. I'm beginning to understand what Avery sees in you after all." Wallace winks, then ambles down the stairs.

Avery approaches me on the steps. "Well, that was fun, wasn't it?"

"Fun!"[a] I laugh. "You have no idea what that word means, do you?"

"You know, I've actually been told that before." Avery chuckles as he helps me up. "Come on, let's go look it up together."

---

[a] **Fun (n.):** *lighthearted pleasure.* The eighteenth-century *fun,* "enjoyment," was preceded by the seventeenth-century *funn,* "trick, hoax," and the thirteenth-century *fonnen,* "befool." The obsolete verb *fon* described someone who had the wool pulled over their eyes (much like my eyes, at this precise moment).

## CHAPTER TWENTY-ONE

# A FEW DON'TS

*Don't think that because you have a pretty face, you need neither brains nor manners. Don't think that you can be rude to anyone and escape being disliked for it. Never put your hand on a man, except in dancing. Don't allow anyone to paw you.*

There's something funny I've noticed. When everything falls apart, one thing randomly goes right. What is that? Is it fate? Is the universe playing tricks on me? Is this all just one big joke?

Two days after Claude tore my world apart, I braved the stares and whispers downtown to check my PO box. Then burst into tears when I found a large manila envelope from California.

Dear Miss McCadie,
    We reviewed your application with much interest. Mr. Oldbury was impressed by your résumé and references (which are glowing, by the way). Your sample

translation was impeccable. We would be honored to engage your translation services at our antiquities archive. This would be a contractual, mail-in position to start, but could easily grow to a permanent role at the Oldbury Ranch House. Enclosed, please find the initial retainer and documentation of the first text requiring your expertise.

Mr. Oldbury is adding to his library at an unprecedented rate. If this initial project goes well, we will send more compositions for your review. While a considerable undertaking, we believe that you are up to the challenge this Hellenistic text represents.

As an aside, I've tried calling you on multiple occasions, but there seems to be some interference. Please reach out at your earliest convenience to discuss the terms of your contract. If you are available for a visit, we would love to introduce you to the rest of the classics team. Welcome aboard.

Yours truly,
Elias Landers
*Classics Curator*

Tears gather at the corners of my eyes as I hold the offer letter up to the fluorescent lights. My relief is so acute that it's actually uncomfortable. I study the stationery for watermarks or signs of tampering, then turn over the manila envelope, half expecting a diamond ring to clatter across the floor, or for Teddy to breeze in and yell, "Got you!"

But there's nothing. Just Mr. Townsend watching me with polite concern, a kiwi perched on the counter beside him.

"It's okay." I blink away tears. "I got a job."

But I guess that's how life works, right? It changes very quickly or not at all.

I walk home from the post office, still waiting for the punch line. When I hear footsteps behind me, I grin. *I knew it. This was just a hoax.*[a] *Gertrude's murder has taken one last turn of insanity.* The steps are gaining on me. I turn, expecting to find Edgar lurking in the shadows or Chief Deputy Abbott looming. Then my jaw drops when I see Diane Bean from the *Quoddy Current*.

"Miss McCadie!" She waves me down. As I take in her tan pencil skirt, matching blazer, and pageboy cap, I feel like I'm having an out-of-body experience.

"I beg your pardon?" I ask. *Who told her that I've been impersonating her?*

"You *are* Miss Wilhelmina McCadie?" the reporter asks. "The one who–"

"It wasn't me!" I protest, and the reporter cocks her head in confusion.

"Here is my card." The reporter reaches into her purse for one of the ivory business cards with the lobster-boat logo. "I write for the *Quoddy Current* newspaper. You're the local girl,

---

[a] **Hoax (n.):** *a humorous or malicious deception. Hoax* is an abridged version of the English *hocus,* "cheat," which stems from *hocus-pocus,* a magical formula from the seventeenth century. This spell is a perversion of the Latin blessing *Hoc est corpus meum,* meaning "This is my body."

right? The one who was at Webster Cottage when the elder son was arrested?" As she speaks, my jaw drops. *She has no idea that I've been impersonating her! And she doesn't remember meeting me in the first place!* "The deputy said you were on-site when he arrived. My readers are awfully curious about the goings-on of the well-to-do, and would be absolutely thrilled to hear—"

I allow myself a bored smile as I accept her card. "Sorry, I'm not taking any interviews right now. I need to consult with my publicist first," I reply with a cordial nod. Then I continue up Key Street, under the sheltering arms of the crab apple trees.

Mrs. Pridmore is overjoyed when I give my notice. The log cabin where I trespassed last summer is available for rent. And my grandparents are strangely relieved to see me go.

"Cupcake, I think we could all use a little space. You need peace and quiet for your work, and I need more real estate in the bathroom." Grace's long violet nails flash as she pours herself a Pink Squirrel martini. "Plus, I don't want to get murdered."

Spring blossoms and so does my telephone bill, racking up long-distance charges with Mr. Landers in Montecito. Life swells and deflates with the tides. President Johnson increases the personnel in Vietnam, and the monthly draft doubles. *My Fair Lady* breaks box-office records, and birth control becomes mass-produced. Civil rights marches in Alabama, the space race continues, and the Cold War does, too. And as the world changes, the rules of etiquette struggle to keep up with it. But some customs never change: like house-warming presents and tearful goodbyes. Victor bakes a ginger ale Bundt cake, and Grace slips me a pamphlet titled *Sex Manual: For Those Married or About to Be*. I find out why Avery had the handcuffs. Those aren't included in the sex manual.

I pinch myself as I move into the vacation rental. The furniture is cheap, but the feeling of privacy is pure luxury. What a dream, to sweep out the kitchen and stock the shelves (shelves that *aren't* crammed with strawberry syrup or Jell-O packets) with white wine and tea. My Hellenistic anthologies look at home on the bookshelf, and my box of clues and detective supplies fits nicely under the kitchen sink. Murder and blackmail were just a strange little nightmare that I had last summer, that's all over now.

But as I lie on the couch with Avery, I can't quite shake the feeling that I'm dreaming. He reads aloud from the Arts section while I do the Sunday crossword as rain pours down on the roof. And I remind myself, for the fortieth time, that this is everything I ever wanted. But the presiding sentiment isn't so much joy at a dream come true, as it is terror that I might wake up.

### "NOW I PROBABLY CAN'T RUN FOR PRESIDENT"
### Charges Pile Up in Webster Scandal

MACHIAS, ME (AP)—Claude Webster "adamant" in his denial of wrongdoing. The law student was found guilty on two counts of involuntary manslaughter and sentenced to ten years in prison. The trial concludes a series of tragedies that rocked the Maine coast.

Webster's arraignment and deposition took place over one week in the first-floor courtroom of the Washington County Superior Courthouse. The redbrick building was crowded with concerned citizens. The trial began at 9:02 a.m., when the county clerk called Webster to the stand. "How do you plead, guilty or not guilty?"

"Not guilty." Webster's voice was soft but it held steady.

Judge Seldom asked to hear the charges against Webster, including a colorful testimony from Detective Wallace of the Maine State Police Department. The alleged murder weapon was brought forward, bearing two blood types and two sets of fingerprints. The forensics lab found Ms. Taylor's blood type on the blade, and Mr. Webster's prints on the handle. The second party was not identified.

Maine Attorney General Steven Bueller vouched for the defendant. "Claude is a young man of impeccable character. He is a figurehead in the community with unfailing..."

I pour out the dregs from the teapot and set it down on the offensive news article. In a shocking turn of events, Claude got off easy. Dark rings blur the photo of his winning smile outside the courthouse. Avery and I both saw the article, but neither of us mention it. Instead, we talk about pleasant things. About spring rainstorms and dinner plans ("Should we make lobster *stew* or lobster *bisque* tonight?"). About the crackling fire and the five-letter word for "Run with a hon."

"Elope," Avery says without raising his eyes from the newspaper.

I fill in the five little boxes, then pick up the tea service and retreat to the kitchen. As I boil water on the cabin stove, I pull down my mother's tea chest. My hand hesitates over packets of vanilla chai and Earl Grey crème. Today has already been sweet enough.

My one complaint about Avery is that he's a little *too* vanilla. Even when he tries to play tough, he's so endearingly sweet. I keep thinking back to my call with Debbie when everything started. While Avery certainly meets the four requirements for dating—he's smart, funny, polite, and sexy as all hell—I can't help wondering if he has an edge. Perhaps there is a fifth criteria for desirability: if their darkness matches yours. And I'm just not sure if he's got it.

"Would you like something stronger in your tea?" I call, reaching for the decanter of whiskey. It's only midafternoon, but I'm already craving something with more bite.

"Darling, destroy me."

I gasp and drop my teacup. Painted china splinters into a thousand tiny pieces across the cabin floor, as a hundred fragmented details resolve themselves into a single cohesive unit inside my head. *I fucking knew it.*

Avery is instantly by my side. "Stay where you are. Don't move. Glass is everywhere."

I stand stock-still while my charming, chivalrous, and

psychotic (?) lover sweeps up the broken teacup around my feet. My eyes narrow as I consider him. Consider the extent of his depravity, as he gives me a worried smile, then returns to the living room. My hands shake as I pull the box of detective supplies out from under the sink. They're trembling so hard that I drop the handkerchief from Teddy and some papers across the floor. I bend down to pick them up, frowning at the stupidest monogram in history. Then my eyes dart from an article that Debbie sent me to the handkerchief and back again. "Oh, that's so funny." I laugh with a mixture of surprise and relief.

"Darling, are you—"

"Nothing. It's nothing," I reply distractedly. I put the photocopies back in the box, stuff the handkerchief in my pocket, then open and close the bread box. I pour a shot of bourbon in two bone china teacups and carry the tea service out to the living room. I find Avery kneeling before the fireplace, the uneven stones stained a deep gray from decades of smoke. Logs smolder in the hearth as he tends to the fire. I sit down on the creased leather sofa and watch the shadows flit across his face.

"One lump or two?" I ask as I reach for the teapot. My tone is brisk and impersonal, but my hand gives me away. The sound of rattling china reverberates through the room.

"One." Avery sits down on a braided rug before the fire, studying me with concern. "Are you all right?"

"I could murder you," I say as I drop in a sugar cube, then top it with a splash of cream.

"Really? How?" His slightly raised eyebrow speaks volumes. I pass him his tea, then lean back against the couch, as Earl

Grey crème sloshes dangerously close to the edge of my teacup. "You've broken every rule, Avery. How do you plead?"

"Obviously, I would like to hear the charges leveled against me first," he replies with mild boredom, as if discussing the weather.

## CHAPTER TWENTY-TWO

# A GUIDE TO TACTFUL CONVERSATIONS

*Listen, refrain from expressing an opinion, and stay objective, though vaguely sympathetic. Personal questions can be unsettling unless you develop enough sophistication to cope with them gracefully. A naturally witty person knows well enough how to reply.*

I give you a nine out of ten for execution, seven out of ten for creativity, and ten out of ten for general weirdness," I babble in a cool, detached stream. "I know that you killed Gertrude, and I think I know how and why, but what I can't quite work out is why you had to drag *me* into it." Bergamot, vanilla, and bourbon swirl across my tongue as I study him over the rim of my teacup. "Everything else makes sense, but not that."

"Billie, I can't handle it when you do this." Avery tries to look somber and apologetic, but I see amusement in the depths of his eyes. He's been waiting for this. "It makes me absolutely dizzy when your mind darts around to a hundred ideas at once.

If we're going to do this—which I think we should—then I would suggest that we proceed with some degree of decorum. Perhaps try starting from the beginning?"

"Oh, I would *hate* to make you uncomfortable." I take another sip and glare at him through the rising steam. "First and foremost, this was a game. Chess was too stuffy, cribbage too dated, and Charades too undignified, so you created something more suitable. Something a bit more . . . *immersive*. The game begins with a kiss. A sidelong glance. A surprised smile. You weren't expecting her to be clever. You thought she would be boring like everyone else, but you couldn't have been more wrong."

He takes another sip. "Go on."

"The flush of new romance. The excitement of a secret. It was the first time you had sex with someone you cared about, and it must have been intoxicating." I look down at my teacup in embarrassment as rain lashes across the windows. "You lost your head. She was already engaged to Teddy, so you ordered an identical ring, but the diamond was twice the size because she deserved twice the man. Am I right?"

He smiles in his careless way. "You aren't wrong."

"But before you could propose, you discovered Gertrude and Claude. And you, who barely ever feel anything, suddenly experienced the complex mess of heartbreak. And it was all very tawdry and lowbrow and you didn't care for it at all. So you decided to take control."

"Billie, have you ever considered radio dramas?" Avery asks with appreciation. "I had *no idea* that you had this gift for narration."

I frown as an onslaught of rain pummels the walls of the log cabin. "On April thirtieth, 1964, your life of crime began with an overdue library book." The storm is speeding up, just like my heartbeat. I'm not sure if my elevated pulse is from caffeine, whiskey, or the excitement of finally figuring it all out. "Having swiped Claude's ID, you checked out a copy of *Techniques in Cardiac Surgery* from the University of Maine in Machias. Stabbing someone in the heart is harder than Agatha Christie would have you believe, and even trained surgeons have difficulty with it. You have to slice directly between two ribs in an exact location. But you longed for the poetic justice of trading one broken heart for another, so you did your homework."

Avery gets to his feet and heads to the kitchen. He reappears a moment later with the decanter of bourbon and pours a splash for each of us. "You think the poetic details are disgusting," he says without meeting my gaze. "But I wanted to do it right. She was punctured directly in the right ventricle. The whole thing was over within thirty seconds. It wasn't painful, it was impeccable."

"On the contrary. That's why I gave you a nine out of ten for execution. I admire the dedication to your craft." I take another sip as rain drips down the windowsill. It seeps inside to puddle across the floor. "Always the overachiever, you selected five suspects in total. Personally, I think it was overkill, but what do I know? Suspect number one was the most obvious with the clearest motive: Teddy Brixton." I rub my scalp where he pulled my hair. "Gertrude's jilted fiancé *couldn't* have been more suspicious. His already deplorable temperament was heightened when he discovered Gertrude and Claude at your party and threw a fit. He performed his role admirably, but everyone knows that the first rule of a murder game is to discount your top suspect, because he's just *too* obvious.

"Which brings us to suspect number two: Claude Webster." I shiver and massage my neck. "Claude didn't require much coaching, he just needed to act like his usual, charming self. One day you requested his signature, and he didn't bother to ask why. I assume it was the same with the murder weapon—you just waited for him to use it in the kitchen. On the night of, you put him and Gertrude in the same room and watched the sparks fly," I murmur as the fire crackles in the hearth. I take another sip of tea, but my tastebuds aren't working.

"Some people believe that killers are born, and others that they are raised. Either way, you and Claude share the same nature and nurture, so it's hardly surprising that you share some of the same vices. Although he's not as adept at hiding them." Thunder echoes through the silence as I wait for Avery to contradict me. "But what about Clara? That's the part that really bugs me. Did you know that he did it? Did you just allow him to continue? I'm friends with those girls."

"Billie, I had *no idea*." Avery shakes his head in chagrin. "I'm terrified of him and try to keep my distance. I think it's disgusting that he was targeting defenseless young women. And please don't think that this was all some ruse to screw Claude over. I had a change of heart, and he was the likeliest suspect to pin it on. When I invited him up to the cottage that night, I thought that I might coax him into letting something slip, but I never guessed that he would be in a cold-blooded rage, or that you would decide to play the lady detective and goad him into—"

"I didn't goad," I interrupt, crossing my legs.

"Oh please, you goaded the hell out of him," Avery retorts. "I'm just glad that I got there in time. Billie, if he hurt you, I'd never forgive myself. I hate him so much–"

"That's it." I shake my head at my teacup.

"Pardon?" He looks at me quizzically, then stands up to put a fresh log on the fire.

"All of this hate inside of you. Can you let it go, or are you just too damaged?"

Avery's dappled gray eyes flicker in the reflected firelight. "It has actually been rather difficult."

"What has?"

"Focusing on hate, when I'm rather preoccupied with the opposite," he says, and the expression in his eyes warms and deepens, while my chest tightens in response. "It's hard to remember how I felt when I set all this up. The pervasive gloom–"

"Like being trapped in the DMV waiting room." I roll my eyes.

"You *were* listening!" His face lights up as he sits back down. "I *knew* that phone was clicking too much!"

I look down at my hands to hide my grin. "You thought that I was spying on you?"

"*Hoped* you were," he corrects me. "If so, I thought it was very cool of you."

"Cold, actually." I bite my lip. "So all of the whining about your hopes and fears–"

"I was really whining at you," Avery replies. "It was such a great way to let you in, and to see if it sent you running off in the opposite direction. And what better way to seduce someone, than when they're spying on you?"

"Rule number seven: surveillance is the ultimate flirtation." I offer him a reluctant smile. "So chocolates and drive-in movies never occurred to you?"

"Darling, please. What do you take me for?"

I mull over our year of romance and lies while thunder rumbles in the distance. "Which brings us to suspect number three, Gertrude's estranged ex, who just happens to have a criminal record, surveillance training, and a flair for drama. Edgar Gibbs was just curious, desperate, and pissed-off enough to play the magician's assistant in your game of smoke and mirrors. Gertrude bragged about her ex being a detective, so you reached out to him. You needed help, he needed a job, and he wasn't entirely unamenable to the nature of his employment. He was instrumental during the murder, and for keeping the other suspects in line, particularly me. You promised that he wouldn't go down for it and he believed you. And you had dirt on him, too, right?" I look to Avery for confirmation.

"No dirt, just finances. Is that the same thing?" Avery offers with a mild shrug. "Edgar lived beyond his means with Gertrude and was already drowning in debt *before* prison. And after—well, it's virtually impossible to get a well-paying job after incarceration. The criminal justice system did the dirty work for me."

"He got lucky when Detective Wallace was assigned to the case."

"Yes, I was happy about that. I really care for Edgar."

"He's *such* a people person," I reply, then we both chuckle lightly and sip our tea. "Moving along to suspect number four and your alibi for the evening: Mrs. Doris Cobb. Okay, I have to know: Why the widow? And how did you know about her cat allergy?"

Avery shakes his head with a wry grin. "It's funny. Gertrude always hated her–"

"Of course she did." I burst out laughing. "But why?"

"She never said. But every time the widow attended an event, Gertrude would go *out of her way* to be rude to her. Maybe it's because of what Mrs. Cobb symbolized? She's old. She's at peace with herself. She's content being alone. She's from a well-established family. The nouveau riche were Gertrude's lifeblood, and anything else struck her as singularly distasteful. I asked around about the widow and discovered her cat allergy. It's strange about that corpse found in her–"

"On the night of the party," I interrupt because I'm not ready for that part of the conversation yet, "you gave Mrs. Cobb some concentrated form of dander–"

"Edgar has a Maine coon." Avery shrugs. "I asked him for some saliva."

"Yuck." I wrinkle my nose in distaste. "So you slipped it in her drink, then offered her your handkerchief when her allergies took off. The handkerchief was soaked in–"

"Diluted chloroform," Avery supplies helpfully.

"Which was enough to make her pass out, but not enough to kill her. Then you rushed to her side and played your signature role as the dashing white knight. While the widow was out cold, you led Gertrude into the parlor. She thought it was a marvelous joke when you produced a knife and gloves but, too late, discovered the joke was on her. You planted Teddy's cuff link in her hand, put the fake Claude letter in her pocket, and changed into a clean suit. Edgar disposed of the tainted clothing and the murder weapon while you woke up Mrs. Cobb with smelling salts. She said that you never left her side, and who would dare contradict her? I expect that no one was sober enough to clock your vanishing act. The widow's proximity to the crime scene, paired with the discovery of a corpse in her crypt made her a suspect, albeit, an unlikely one. But don't you think that widows are a little played out?" I ask, and Avery grins.

A brief lull in the rain as I lean back against the worn leather sofa and consider the reserved young man before me. And I'm suddenly struck by how lonely he is. By how isolating it must be to always be ten steps ahead. "How does it feel to create something so perfect, knowing that you'll never be able to share it with anyone?"

The fire crackles as Avery glances at me sharply, a series of conflicting emotions passing across his pewter eyes. "Well, darling, that's where you come in. You are my audience."

The storm builds to a climax as I reach the end of my litany. Avery is pale now, and I'm even paler. I pick up the whiskey, contemplate it for a moment, then set it back down. Avery reaches forward and our fingers brush. I jerk away with a start.

"You already had four suspects, but something was missing. Some bizarre detail that would transform Gertrude's murder into a masterpiece. You needed someone naive and open to suggestion. A pawn you could manipulate to your advantage. And every great story needs a love interest, right?" Lightning flashes through the window as I swallow the lump in my throat. "Suspect number five had no connection to your social circle, which made her the perfect scapegoat. You dispatched an engagement ring and love letter to pique her curiosity, then engineered a chance meeting. She was fascinated by the mystery and flattered by your attentions. On the night of the murder, she was just as nosy as you hoped, and seamlessly inserted herself into the proceedings. You sent her the murder weapon two weeks later, and she obligingly incriminated herself."

"Billie, how long are you going to talk about yourself in the third person?" Avery asks.

"Suspect number five was gaslit,[a] stalked, and driven half mad. When Detective Wallace came to see her, what he assumed would be just another interview presented him with a fifth suspect. As time passed, she gradually inched her way up the list. The detective wanted it to be her, if only because it told a better story." Thunder echoes overhead as I lean back against the sofa and study the shame painting Avery's features. "But in the end, after all that work, it was Claude, regardless of all your pretty words about it being a 'change of heart.'" I bite my lip and fight off a wave of embarrassment. "Here's what I don't under-

---

[a] **Gaslight (v.):** *to make a person question their sanity.* Coined in 1938 by the British playwright Patrick Hamilton in his play *Angel Street* and also used in its ensuing movie adaptation, *Gaslight.* The story followed a husband who manipulated his wife into thinking that she'd lost her mind by dimming the gas lights around their home whenever he did something shifty. Although gas lights have largely been replaced by electric light bulbs, psychological manipulation remains as trendy as ever.

stand: you planned to seduce and frame me, right? But then why didn't you ever touch me? Ever kiss me?"

"Well, in all of those books you read–"

"How did you know about my books?" I pull a crocheted blanket over my lap defensively.

He chuckles, taking a thoughtful sip from the decanter. "That's hardly classified information. The librarian was more than happy to–"

My jaw drops. "What a violation of privacy!"

Avery shrugs. "Your favorite books are all about tortured love affairs. The more drawn out and convoluted, the sexier. So I figured that the more reserved I was, the more you would like me. I wanted to be like that incredibly dull, droll fellow from–"

"The audacity!" I glare at Avery. "Get out," I say through gritted teeth. My lover has just confessed to murder, but all *I* care about is that he played hard to get. I'm sillier than Kitty and Lydia Bennet combined.

"But–"

"Out." I point to the door.

"But darling, there is *no reason* to–"

I pick up the whiskey bottle and hold it out, ready to hurl it against the wall. "Avery, it's you or the decanter. One of you has to go." I fix him with a heavy stare, then he hurries over to the door and slips on his shoes. He steals a worried glance at the decanter as he puts on his tan canvas barn coat. I set it down and turn away, keeping my eyes trained on the shadows flickering across the hearth. "One last question: Why are we still dating? You won. The woman who wronged you is dead. Your abusive brother is in jail. I was just a pawn in your game. So why am I still on the playing board?"

Avery's shoes squeak across the old plank floor. "Because the game isn't finished—"

"Oh?" I raise one eyebrow as rain lashes against the cabin walls.

"It has simply entered a new phase. All of the other players are gone, so there is no one to prevent you from advancing." Avery reaches into his jacket pocket and withdraws a small heart-shaped box. "And when a pawn reaches the far end of the chessboard—"

"Oh no."

He gets down on one knee.

"Avery, I see where you're going with this, and you have to stop," I protest, the color draining from my face. "It's *too* cheesy. I'm embarrassed for you."

"She becomes a queen." He opens the top to reveal a rose-gold engagement ring nestled in navy blue velvet. It's very slightly included with an old European cut, and the biggest diamond yet. "From the very first moment, something drew me to you. You were such a romantic figure, walking alone along the seashore. Then we spoke, and you were witty and strange and—you're just about the only person I've ever met who I haven't hated on sight."

I try not to smile. "*Mulkvisti.*"

"What is that?" he asks.

"It's Finnish. It means 'One I hate less than the others.' It's how they say 'I love you.'"

He laughs. "Forgive me if my feelings aren't quite so understated. They're actually rather over-the-top." He studies the ring with a mixture of fear, hope, and longing, and I really hope that I always remember how he looks at this moment. This is the first time I've seen him look anything less than perfect, and it's how I like him best. "And you're right. I *did* pick you as an easy mark, but then I developed feelings for you, and . . . I felt too awful. I felt too guilty. So I called the whole thing off. I hoped that eventually I would stop wanting you, but I never did. I *wanted* you to be a part of this. I *wanted* you to play the game. And then you started trying to beat me at it, and I *wanted* you to succeed. But more than anything, I just wanted you."

I wonder how many times Avery has rehearsed this speech. Has he had the engagement ring in his coat pocket for months, waiting for me to piece it all together? "And the second ring?" I ask, reaching for the decanter.

"Oh, I sent that because I loved you," Avery says, and I choke on a mouthful of whiskey. "Billie, the last year has been one endless inside joke, and I don't want it to end. I have no reason to hope, but I still have to try. I can't offer you much." He pauses, and I suspect that he's being facetious—because we both know that he's offering one of the largest fortunes in America. "But I *can* promise you that our life together would never be boring. Everything you've ever wanted could be yours."

"But what about my heart?" I gaze sadly at the heart-shaped box in his hands.

"Well, it's no secret that we're madly in love[b] with each other—"

---

[b] **Love (n.): 1.** *intense affection.* **2.** *a deep interest in something.* **3.** (in tennis, squash, and badminton) *a score of zero; nil.* Derived from the Old English *lufu*,

"'Mad' does seem to be the operative word in that sentence," I reply as thunder growls in the distance. I've always dreamed about chivalry and wild passion, I just never imagined that it would also involve murder. I look down at my fingers, remembering the moment when Avery and I first touched. When he shocked me with his boldness in taking my hand. Do I want his hand in mine when I'm old and gray? And what kind of woman would I be to accept a proposal from a murderer?

I look from him to the diamond ring, my mind whirling. "Why is this all about you? Don't you want to know about the skeletons in *my* closet? The lies, the spying, the—"

"Billie, I love a mess, and I would gladly spend the rest of my life uncovering yours," he says with a surety that surprises me.

"Darling, if you hop in your Porsche right now, you *might* make it to the Canadian border before the authorities catch you," I lie coolly. I need a moment.

"And then you'll go down to the soda fountain to commiserate with Wendy and Florence?" he replies in turn.

"Of course. My real friends."

"Billie, will you just admit that you've had the time of your life this past year?"

"It was mediocre at best."

He shakes his head and rises to his feet as a fresh leak drips through the ceiling. "I know it's no excuse, but Gertrude *was* a monster," he adds quietly. "She was as sadistic as Claude is, in

---

the Latin *lubet,* and the Sanskrit *lubhyati, love* is little altered from its PIE root *leubh,* "to care for, desire," which dates back to over 15,000 years ago.

her own way. Nothing gave her more pleasure than inflicting pain."

"Yes, I'm well aware." I reach for the whiskey.

"But how?"

"Well, she killed John Tux."

"*No!*" Avery bursts out laughing, then sits back down. "Tell me everything."

"What was Gertrude's middle name?" I reply cryptically, leaning back against the worn leather sofa.

"Naples," he supplies with the faintest hint of a smirk. "I know, how tacky, right?"

I pull the handkerchief out of my pocket and pass it over to him. "What does this say?"

Avery's eyes narrow. "*t u b* in curly lowercase script. Just like the tattoo that poor sod–"

"Your valet," I reply, then grin when his jaw drops. "There was a Malaysian man on your staff, right? And he left suddenly last spring?"

"But how could you possibly–"

"It doesn't matter. Now flip the handkerchief over. What does it say?"

Avery turns the handkerchief upside down, then reads aloud with a growing smile, "*g n t* for Gertrude Naples Taylor."

"Did you know that she was sleeping with your valet?"

"I had *no idea.*" Avery beams. "How droll."

"The *t u b* stumped me for a while, because I thought it implicated Teddy. He gave me this handkerchief at the Christmas party. I assumed it was his monogram, but Teddy's initials are actually *t j b,* and this was a keepsake from Gertrude. When

John Tux was discovered, the coroner *also* read the initials upside down, and it was *Gertrude's* initials on the corpse. They were involved and she went with him to get a tattoo. When the fling ran its course, she disposed of the problem in her classically haphazard fashion."

"You're a genius!" Avery exclaims. "But how do you know?"

"I have enough information to make a calculated guess. Also... it's just so wrong that it has to be right. For about thirty seconds, I thought John Tux might have been you."

"Sorry to disappoint you, darling." Avery grins wryly as the fire crackles and smokes.

"You strike me as the kind of boy who does his homework. And I assume that even the posh prep schools teach 'practice makes perfect.' The John Doe's left ribs were broken, so he *could* have been stabbed in the heart. I thought you might have practicing for Gertrude. But his murder was—"

"Sloppy." Avery is ready with his critique. "With the tattoo, the weird moss, and the memorable clothing. Very poorly done."

"If you *did* practice for Gertrude, I assume it didn't hit the papers—"

"Sorry to disappoint you there as well, darling," he replies with a self-deprecating shrug.

I wash my misgivings down with a sip of whiskey, then direct my glare to the rain dripping in the corner. "Why didn't you just kill Claude? That seems like a much more direct approach to the situation," I murmur, frustrated by Avery's logic.

"Don't you think the whole Cain and Abel thing is a trifle overdone?" he parries, but his sarcasm falls flat. "To be honest,

I didn't think I would survive the encounter. Claude nearly killed me for a look, and he's just been waiting for an opportunity to finish what he started." Avery's voice cracks, and I look up, shocked by the sadness, shame, and pain hewn into his features. "For a long time, I tried to not care. Tried to distract myself and play by his rules. But then I met you, and everything changed. You've given me something to fight for. To live for. To love. I'm not the man who devised this game. I can't go back to who I was, and what's more, I don't want to. Would it be terribly cliché if I asked you to love me as I am?"

A blush wells up as my cheeks burn. And despite my best intentions, I feel my breath catch, arrested by the passion of his words. "That would be a direct violation of rule number six, Avery." I glance down at my hands, surprised to find that they're still holding the whiskey bottle. "Why are you still here? I thought that I asked you to leave. Go now or the decanter gets it. Ten."

"But–"

"Nine." He stands up. "Eight." He hurries to the door. "Seven." He pauses with a hand on the doorknob.

"One question, it was that phrase from Claude's letter that gave me away, right? I had *no idea* that you'd read it. I thought it was locked up in police evidence. How did you get it?"

I jump ahead in my count. "Three. Two."

He steps out into the rain, then pokes his head back around the doorjamb. "I'll come by in two days," he says, then closes the door quietly behind himself.

"One." I set down the decanter and walk over to the kitchen. Then I pull the Sanyo Micro-Pack 35 out of the bread box and hit *Stop* on the tape recorder.

# CHAPTER TWENTY-THREE

# THE CIVILIZED PROPOSAL

*The number of men today who ask, in so many words, that a girl marry them is very limited, despite the testimony of the movies and fiction. Any girl with common sense knows when a man is trying to propose and either helps him commit himself or discourages him. An obstinate coyness often deters a man.*

The pastor's wife watches as I lock up my Schwinn on Water Street. Her eyes trail behind me, marking my progress as I stop by the library and the post office. It's funny, a year ago you couldn't have paid anyone to notice me, and now I'm front-page news.

I pop into Fernald's Pharmacy and stroll down the hair-care aisle, weighing a box of dye in my hands. Should I dye my hair black, move to New York City, and start a new life? Or should I bleach my hair blond, buy a cowboy hat, and head out West? I can't decide, so I opt for a root beer float instead. Florence and

Wendy are conspiring together at the soda fountain. As I climb onto a barstool beside them, I suppress the urge to ask if they've been paid to wait there for me.

"Florence, if someone gave you two options, and one was the right thing to do and the other was the wrong thing, which would you pick?" I stir my straw around in my float.

Florence leans in to steal my sundae glass. "Well, which one is better dressed?" she asks, locking eyes with me as she takes a lingering sip.

It's a relief to leave town. To feel the wind in my hair as the seagrass rustles beside me on the sand dunes. I slow down as I bike past Webster Cottage. Lieske is out front. She's casual today in jeans and a T-shirt, taking out some aggression on an Oriental rug, suspended from a tree branch in the front yard. She pummels it with a rattan carpet beater, then stops and turns. And—is it my imagination?—or does she bite her lip and wink?

The sun hangs low as I return to the cabin on Boyden Lake. I pull out my suitcase and throw in some lingerie, a peach Pucci slip dress that Avery gave me, and an old raincoat. I toss in my ballet shoes, Gertrude's stilettos, my diary, and my mother's copy of *Etiquette*. Next up is *Northanger Abbey,* an etymology book, and my jewelry box. I fish out the two engagement rings and study the diamonds, watching how they flicker in the tawny late afternoon sun.

This year really *did* follow the formula of a Jane Austen novel. It began with a flirtation, which led to rumors, a romantic setback, and a half-hearted investigation. Then the truth was handed to me on a silver platter along with an engagement ring. Now I'm working myself into a tizzy, faced with the classic dilemma: Do I marry the man of my dreams, or do I send him to jail?

I suppose I *could* do nothing. Or I *could* call the cops, then see how long it takes Avery's lawyers to point out the second set of prints on the murder weapon. Even if I *wanted* to turn him in, it would ruin my life. I *should* do the right thing.

But doesn't that sound boring?

It's hard to imagine any of my favorite heroines accepting such an egregious proposal. Elizabeth Bennet and Catherine Earnshaw would both send him packing. Jane Eyre might consider it, but she always had a bit of that self-destructive-madwoman-in-the-attic energy herself. Madame Bovary might accept his offer, and we all know how that works out.

I grew up reading stories with great heroines. Women who lead vibrant, intellectual lives. Who love recklessly. Who make beautiful mistakes in the name of the plot. How would they recommend that I end this story?

If Avery left, then everything would go back to normal. I'd just be an average girl with an above-average secret. And this would be a story I wrote that no one would ever read. That consumed my life for a year. That took me to great heights, awful depths, and almost destroyed me. Gradually, that book would become dusty, mildewed, and eaten by moths until it was entirely forgotten. But I don't want to go back to being the girl who read other people's stories rather than living for herself. So what if I've ended up in a Highsmith rather than an Austen? I'm the main character, and I need to start acting like it.

*There are certainly times when love is a crime.* Detective Wallace raises an eyebrow in my memory.

## ETIQUETTE FOR LOVERS AND KILLERS

Well, this is certainly one of them.

I sit down on the floor beside my half-packed suitcase with a brain full of half-baked ideas. Can Avery be a good husband, even though he's a murderer? Is there some rule that says he can't? I consider my beau. The most civilized and uncivilized person I know. The doting manservant and the calculated killer. The pool boy, assassin, and best friend. And I'm not sure which version of him I love more.

But I suppose that we all play different parts. I might be a shrew at work, a trollop at happy hour, and a sloth at bedtime. Within each of us is a great wellspring of roles we're designed to perform. The lover. The sinner. The saint. The kindergarten teacher. Why can't Avery be a charming gentleman *and* a killer? And why can't I be the levelheaded skeptic *and* the blushing fiancée?[a]

*Yes or no?* As the sun fades, it hangs low through the window to gleam off Amy Vanderbilt's *Complete Book of Etiquette* in my suitcase. I burst out laughing, because the answer was always here, staring straight at me.

Diamonds flash on my fingers as I leaf through Miss Vanderbilt's opus. There it is, in black and off-white: "Hardly romantic, but necessary to mention, is the prenuptial agreement.... It must be handled with delicacy and diplomacy. If a young couple thinks a prenuptial agreement makes sense, which it does in certain cases, it should be discussed before the engagement

---

[a] **Fiancé(e) (n.):** *a person formally promised to marry another.* Borrowed from the French *fiancer,* "to betroth," and the Vulgar Latin *fidare,* "faith," *fiancé(e)* is one of the prettiest words I know. Even the shape it makes on your lips feels like a kiss.

is officially announced. All the particulars need to be worked out."

*Yes* to prenups.

Avery finds me in the kitchen mixing a pitcher of Sherry Cobbler. *Whipped Cream & Other Delights*, by Herb Alpert's Tijuana Brass plays on the record player while I sway my hips in time with the beat. I'm wearing Gertrude's stilettos and my slip dress, and my hair is flipped up at the ends. He puts an arm around my waist, and I smile up at him. This might be the last time we ever see each other, so I want to make it count.

It's one of those lovely spring days when everything smells of lilacs. A warm wind ruffles through the wildflowers as we sit on the porch and sip our drinks, discussing a new beach house Avery is designing. We don't mention murder, marriage, or handkerchiefs. The sun puddles across Boyden Lake, painting the gentle waves in shades of blush. Twilight settles across the landscape as jazz filters out of the living room and crickets sing their lazy lullaby. And I start to doubt myself. Do I really want to ruin all this?

"The suspense is killing me." Avery places the velvet box between us. "Yes or no?"

"A tentative yes," I reply with the faintest hint of a smile. "But if you aren't terribly offended, could we forgo the whole ring situation? It just feels a bit barbaric to me."

"Should we get matching tattoos instead?" Avery raises an ironic eyebrow, then offers his hand.

"I know a guy," I reply brightly, accepting his proffered grip.

As we walk down to the dock, Avery slips the ring between my fingers. "How far can you throw it?"

I'm about to toss the ring in when Gertrude's reflection swims up through the shallows beneath us. Her voluminous curls billow across the still water. Her eyes are amused behind their long lashes. Her lips twist into a sardonic smile. Then I realize: I'm gazing at my own reflection.

I've learned so much from Gertrude over the past year. She taught me how to talk, to walk, to kiss, and kill. Gertrude was an exceptional tutor, offering invaluable lessons in sex appeal and bad behavior. But she can spare her lessons, because charm school is over and I'm not going back.

Her reflection dissolves as I toss in the very slightly included diamond and ripples ring out across the lake. Then the ring is gone, sinking to the bottom of the lake where the sun never reaches. Where its secrets will be covered by countless gallons of water, and no one will ever see it glitter. I trip and reach out to Avery to steady myself, only to succeed in dragging him down with me. Gertrude's heels slip off my feet as we topple into the shallows. He runs his hands through my wet hair and draws me close, and my skin shivers in response. I wonder if this is how it will always be? I sure hope so.

I try to memorize every detail of this moment. How the lake laps in time with his breath. How he draws me to him as a loon cries out in the distance. How the last ribbon of sunset gleams across the water, gently rising and falling with the waves. Because it's perfect. And nothing is as easy to destroy as perfection.

# EPILOGUE

# THE LOST ART OF LETTER WRITING

*Love letters are sometimes bombshells. It has often been said that nothing should go into a letter that couldn't be read in court. Letters are often opened by mistake, or by prying hands. A gentleman should never write anything in a letter which might damage a lady's reputation.*

Sunlight melts over the bedsheets to get tangled in Avery's hair. He looks for me, but I'm gone. Then his eyes widen as he takes in the pen and paper on the pillow beside him. The stationery is off-white, made of cheap carbon paper. No wax seals or watermarks, just my loopy handwriting and a few words that I don't have the guts to say out loud.

*My favorite nemesis,*
*It's criminal, the things you do to me. I should have you put away for life without parole, but instead, you've proposed a different life sentence. One involving a frilly white gown, a*

*tuxedo, and a tiered layer cake. Murder is just the cherry on top.*

*Given your impolite behavior, an etiquette lesson is in order. Your first lesson will be in economy of language. One must always be scrupulous with one's secrets, because one never knows who might be listening. Or recording, for that matter. You might be interested to learn that I recorded your recent confession, then sent it to my lawyer. I included explicit instructions: he's only to play the recording if something were to happen to me, which includes being arrested, dying, or disappearing mysteriously.*

*Your second lesson is in humility. When sitting on a high horse, it's easy to forget how the other half lives, and impossible to imagine life in the gutter. But sometimes people fall from grace and hit rock bottom. There are no wine cellars or towel warmers in prison, and the thread count also leaves something to be desired.*

*But luckily, we have etiquette to cushion us when we fall. Because what is legality, if not the height of good manners? Rule #8 is the prenuptial agreement. Because in a battle of wits, the only difference between love and war is careful planning. Given the series of faux pas that led to our betrothal, the only reasonable answer is a strongly worded prenuptial agreement. "I'll ruin your life if you ruin mine," and vice versa. A truce, with us each bound by the other's civility.*

*How does it feel to be blackmailed rather than the blackmailer? If you don't care for it, then I suggest we go our separate ways. It would be a pity, though, because our life together could be quite thrilling, but only if we're on equal* terms. I won't be your hostage, but I will be your fiancée, provided you agree to a rather unusual provision. The signature line is on page ten. It's your call.

They say the art of letter writing is dead, and I'm inclined to agree. Or it was, until you first wrote to me. My life started when I opened that first envelope, and I would gladly continue reading your twisted love letters until my dying day.

Maybe that's why I'm at such a loss for a closing. "Xo" seems too juvenile, "Xx" too adult, and "With all my heart" too on the nose considering your surgical expertise. "Sincerely" is too generic, and "Best regards" too formal—as my regards for you are wildly inappropriate. "Always" could work, although I'd hate to jinx it. And "Goodbye" is too final, because I really hope this isn't the end.

Your old ball and chain,
Billie

P.S. Pink champagne cake with a side of collusion might be nice.

## AUTHOR'S NOTE

In all the hustle and bustle of modern life, we often forget to stop and say thank you. Rarer still is the thank-you note, which has largely become a thing of the past. I'd like to offer my sincere appreciation to the women who wrote the cumulative book on etiquette. I'm eternally grateful to Amy Vanderbilt for her wit, wisdom, social grace, and instruction on the proper method of eating an avocado (with a spoon, halved, in its shell). I'm also indebted to Emily Post, whose promotion of civility and kindness is just as relevant today as it was a century ago. Other manners mavens who have found a place in my heart and bookshelf include the inimitable Mary Wilson Little, Cecil Hartley, Florence Hartley, and an anonymous butler from the nineteenth century.

I'm equally indebted to, though no less charmed by, the linguists, lexicographers, and etymologists who write dictionaries, breathe life into dead languages, and deftly navigate the changing landscape of the written word. In particular, I would

## AUTHOR'S NOTE

like to thank Douglas A. Harper, whose love of archaic slang eclipses my own; Phil Cousineau, for his ongoing linguistic investigations; and my forever crush: the *Merriam-Webster Dictionary*. Any playfulness or liberties taken with these words is mine alone, although I like to imagine that the flirtation isn't entirely one-sided.

# ACKNOWLEDGMENTS

## Bread and Butter Letters

*The thank-you is obligatory. A little more human, something that indicates a little more thoughtfulness, is a note, handwritten if your handwriting is legible, typed if it is not, but in any case, graceful and friendly.*

Recently, a boy asked if he could come over to "write together." It was 7 a.m. I looked from my computer to my pajamas to my third cup of coffee in horror, and texted back, "Sorry, writing is a solitary activity for me."

Which is, undoubtedly, the biggest lie of all.

Writing this story has been a labor of love from start to finish, and I've made such lovely friends along the way. I hope you will forgive me for breaking Rule #6.

To the Healy, McCurdy, Ingalls, and Willard clans of Down East Maine, thank you for my childhood running wild in the woods. Thank you for your cabins, boats, and lobster Newburg.

## ACKNOWLEDGMENTS

Special thanks to my father and sister, for helping me stay connected to coastal Maine, even when I wander far away.

To my agent, Daisy Chandley, my profound gratitude for your ongoing lessons in deportment. Thank you for staying up all night reading that insane first draft, and my apologies for any other sleepless nights I may have caused you since then. Thank you for navigating these literary international waters with such creativity, drive, and passion. It's such a lovely thing to meet a kindred spirit, and I'll never be able to thank you enough for seeing the hidden potential in this book (and me!). Also at Peters Fraser + Dunlop, many thanks to the *queen* of International Rights, Rebecca Wearmouth. Your savvy and professionalism are an inspiration. I feel so lucky to have you on my team.

To my conspirators, my editors, thank you for RSVPing to the sordid affair at Webster Cottage. Please pick up a gift bag on your way out, and text me when you get home. I wish your names were on the cover beside mine, because you've left an indelible mark on these pages. At Putnam, Kate Dresser was late to the party, but she crashed it with style, seeing Billie with a clarity that surprised me. Thank you for civilizing the writing, turning up the heat on the romance, and sweeping this story off its feet. At Fleet in the UK, Rhiannon Smith has been a VIP since day one—reshaping the novel with her love for mysteries, passion for puzzles, and fabulous structural eye. But most important, Rhiannon helped to make these characters into people worth fighting for. I'd also like to thank Gabriella Mongelli for initially falling for Eastport, offering her develop-

## ACKNOWLEDGMENTS

mental expertise, and getting this party started. Your enthusiasm for this story was humbling and inspiring.

Many thanks to everyone at Putnam who attended. Tarini Sipahimalani was an important figure at the VIP table, with her hard work, flawless social grace, and endless patience. I'd also like to thank my copyeditors for making my writing sound far better than it deserves and bringing grammar and punctuation to the table. My sincere gratitude also goes to the production, design, and sales teams at Putnam and Fleet for bringing my dreams of sexy murder to life. I'm honored that my strange little love story found a home on your shelves.

My real-life conspirators also made a splash at Webster Cottage. My sincere thanks to my mother, for sharing her love of fiction, which has been my saving grace in life. To early readers: Hannah, who asked if I'd ever heard of a cliffhanger, and Carissa, who was so upset by the first (long deleted) ending that she didn't talk to me for a week. To Francesca, whose motivational talks over champagne on the beach have been nothing short of iconic. To Naomi, who responded to hectic early-morning texts with flawless French. To Khoe, for her sleepy FaceTime dates. To Kelly, for loaning her copy of *Wuthering Heights* on day one, and Evie, who received frantic requests for "names that sound rich" on day one thousand. Representing the male demographic, many thanks to my father for scoping out the Maine State Police Headquarters with me. To Cava, for suggesting that we open a detective agency, long ago. And to Chris, for rescuing a damsel in design distress.

I've cried too many times during this process. Books have

## ACKNOWLEDGMENTS

my heart and soul, and getting the chance to meet the people who make them, who build them into tiny paper worlds, has been the defining experience of my life. To those I've missed, to those I haven't even met yet, thank you for being a part of this.

But most important, thank you to the book lovers (but hopefully *not* killers) who make it all worth it.

# SOURCES

Vanderbilt, Amy. *Amy Vanderbilt's Complete Book of Etiquette* (Doubleday & Company, Inc., 1952, 1954), 117, 137, 159, 175, 199, 215, 218, 232, 236, 287, 411, 414, 481, 599, 663.

Tuckerman, Nancy, and Nancy Dunnan. *The Amy Vanderbilt Complete Book of Etiquette* (Doubleday & Company, Inc., 1995), xi, 2, 248, 629.

Austen, Jane. *Pride and Prejudice*, edited by Sicha, Frank, Jr. (Ginn and Company, 1917), 113.

Hartley, Cecil B. *The Gentlemen's Book of Etiquette and Manual of Politeness* (G. W. Cottrell, 1860), 210.

Hartley, Florence. *The Ladies' Book of Etiquette, and Manual of Politeness* (G. W. Cottrell, 1860), 37, 159.

"An Island Playground off the Coast of Maine," *The New York Times*, July 7, 1964.

"For the Surf Girl," *The Philadelphia Times*, May 14, 1896.

Post, Emily. *Children Are People: How to Understand and Guide Your Child* (Funk & Wagnalls Company, 1959), 215.

Post, Emily. *Emily Post's Etiquette: The Blue Book of Social Usage* (Funk & Wagnalls Company, 1922), 112.

Post, Emily. *Etiquette in Society, in Business, in Politics, and at Home* (Funk & Wagnalls Company, 1922), 48, 177, 258, 410.

Little, Mary Wilson. *A Paragrapher's Reveries* (Broadway Publishing Company, 1904), 215.

*The Duties of Servants* (Frederick Warne & Co., 1890), 52.

## SOURCES

A Woman of Fashion, *Etiquette for Americans* (Duffield & Co., 1909), 187.

Harper, Douglas A. *Online Etymology Dictionary*, 2021, retrieved May 7, 2024.

*Oxford English Dictionary* (OED), Oxford University Press, Oxford, retrieved May 7, 2024.

Cousineau, Phil. *The Painted Word* (Viva Editions, 2012).

Beek, Lucien van, and Robert Beekes. *Etymological Dictionary of Greek* (Brill, 2010).

Simpson, J. A., and E. S. C. Weiner. *The Oxford English Dictionary* (Oxford and New York, Clarendon Press and Oxford University Press, 1989).

Whitney, William Dwight. *The Century Dictionary and Cyclopedia* (The Century Co., 1902).

Tucker, T. G. *Etymological Dictionary of Latin* (Ares Publishers, 1976).

*The Concise Oxford Dictionary of English Etymology* (Oxford University Press, 2011).

Partridge, Eric. *Slang To-day and Yesterday*, 3rd ed. (Routledge and Kegan Paul, 1960).

*Merriam-Webster's Collegiate Dictionary*, 10th ed. (Merriam-Webster Incorporated, 1999).

Onions, C. T. *Oxford Dictionary of English Etymology* (Oxford University Press, 1966).

*Copyright © Christopher Doody*

**Anna Fitzgerald Healy** grew up on the Maine coast. She studied at Emerson College. Now she works in Los Angeles, living in a (possibly haunted) miniature castle in the Hollywood Hills. Her writing has been featured in several literary magazines and short story anthologies. *Etiquette for Lovers and Killers* is her debut novel, best paired with a cheese plate and a spritz.

⌾ AnnaLovesWords
𝕏 AnnaLovesWords